SILK AND STONE

SILK AND STONE

Dinah Dean

Barrie & Jenkins
London

ISBN: 0 7126 3453 3

British Library Cataloguing in Publication Data
Dean, Dinah
Silk and stone.
I. Title
823'.914 [F]

ISBN 0–7126–3453–3

Printed and bound in Great Britain by
Mackays of Chatham PLC, Chatham, Kent

For Barbara, Daphne, Hu and Peter

AUTHOR'S NOTE

Many of the characters in this book were real people, and many of the incidents described actually happened. They are taken from a chronicle written some forty years later by the lad called here 'the seventh thurifer', whose real name we do not know. Two copies of the chronicle survive in the British Museum's Harleian collection of manuscripts under the title *Tractatus de inventione Sancte Crucis nostre*.

Being no Latinist, I am indebted to Dr K N Bascombe, Mr F Baker and Dr L Watkiss for the use of their translations of the manuscripts, and apologize to them and the chronicler for the liberties I have taken with the time-scale and with the account of Matthew's miracle.

The 'real' people include, beside the seventh thurifer, Lady Mabilia, Sir Richard (who later became the Master of the English Templars), Matthew, Crispin (who had two unnamed sisters), all the named canons, Lukin Dulpain, Matilda Mayngod, Robert of St Albans, Alvin Bisemare, Humphrey de Barenton, and, of course, those better-known characters, Henry of Blois, Robert of Gloucester, the Empress Matilda, Geoffrey de Mandeville and Gilbert de Montfichet.

The nave of Waltham minster still stands, a very fine and active parish church, and masons like William of Norwich and his lodge are working on the fabric even now, restoring the wear and tear of eight and a half centuries, at a cost which would have frightened Bishop Henry's Chancellor out of his wits!

ANTESCRIPTUM

The bridge of the Holy Angel was crowded with people, a human river flowing across the Tiber towards the basilica of St Peter. There were pilgrims, dusty-clothed and shabby after weeks of travelling from far countries to visit the shrine of the Apostle, mingling with citizens of all levels of Roman society, from wealthy merchants with their plump wives and children to ragged beggars from the poorest back streets, all perforce afoot where no horses or carts were allowed.

Most of the pilgrims stared about them, agog at the ruined splendours of the second most holy city of their faith, and the citizens eyed the pilgrims speculatively, wondering whence they had come, what news or diseases they brought, and, most importantly, what money they carried. Those pilgrims who were not staring at the great castle before them, or at the roof of the basilica, just visible to their left over the crumbling city wall, were praying, their eyes on the ground or the heels of the person before them, while the citizens gossiped among themselves, the wealthy covertly inspecting the Sunday finery of the other wealthy, and the poor, shuffling among them, thrust aside by their betters, wondering if they would even be allowed inside the basilica to hear the Holy Father celebrate Mass.

Amidst this varied throng, one group stood out particularly and attracted much interest, not all of it friendly or approving. There were twelve men-at-arms wearing faded black cloaks over their mailcoats, looking much alike with the nasals of their round helmets obscuring their faces, marching along two by two, led by a tall knight in a white cloak whose stride was so purposeful and unhesitating that he seemed to cut through the slow-moving crowd like the prow of a ship. Between him and his followers were three women, plainly dressed and veiled, but in cloth of excellent quality, who had to hurry to keep up with him.

'Templars!' said a bad-tempered-looking priest to his

8

companion. 'Disgraceful! Armed men pretending to be monks, carrying arms and shedding blood under the excuse that they fight for Our Lord, and all with the Holy Father's blessing. It's not right, I tell you, whether the Holy Father and Bernard of Clairvaux favour them or not.'

'But surely they only fight the heathen in the Holy Land and protect the pilgrims?' his companion protested gently. 'Someone has to protect the Christian kingdoms in Outremer, or the heathen will overrun them and degrade the Holy Places.'

'Then let laymen do it!' the first priest snapped. 'Fighting men are evil, whoever they fight. In any case, look at them – they boast that they keep their threefold vows better than monks, yet here they are, flaunting their women in public. Disgraceful, I call it, and I don't care who hears me!'

Elys de Wix heard him as she hurried along in the wake of her uncle, sandwiched between her mother, Lady Mabilia and Maud, her mother's gentlewoman. The latter had flinched away from the crowd so much that she was pressed against Elys' side and had already tripped them both twice in crossing the bridge. Elys gathered from the priest's glare when she glanced back at him that he disapproved, but she had not sufficient command of Italian to understand what he said.

The bridge debouched through a gateway into an open space within the walls of the castle, and the road then turned to the left and passed through another gate into the piazza before the facade of St Peter's. The crowd, like wine released from a bottle, flowed out across the wide area and slowed its pace, no longer pressed on by those behind, but the Templar knight, Sir Richard de Hastings, strode on more swiftly, and his followers quickened their pace to keep up. Almost before Elys had time to look at the basilica, they were climbing the steps and slowing down again as the flood of people entered another bottleneck, the great triple-arched entrance, which was high but not wide enough for all those who wished to pass through.

Sir Richard seemed to have no difficulty in forging through the press, spear-heading the way for his followers, and Elys soon found herself entering, not the basilica, as she had expected, but a garden, paved and set about with tubs of small trees and flowers and made cool and pleasant by the tinkling of several little fountains. Five paths crossed this atrium, and Sir Richard headed unhesitatingly along the widest, the middle one, towards the central of the five doors of the basilica beyond.

The doors were guarded discreetly by dark-clad men, not visibly armed, who directed most would-be worshippers to the smaller doors into the double aisles, but they bowed slightly as Sir Richard approached, and waved him and his companions on into the nave.

The interior was surprisingly quiet after the hubbub outside, for people seemed to fall silent as they entered, and very dark after the bright sunlight, but as she advanced up the centre of the long nave, Elys was gradually able to see that the building was long in proportion to its width, and the nave rose to a considerable height. Eleven small windows were set in each wall, right up under the roof, so that most of the light they admitted fell on the roof timbers, and little reached ground level. The side aisles were very dark indeed, and did not appear to have any windows, but it was just possible to see that they were crowded with people, pushing their way further in and spilling out into the nave, only to be waved back again into the aisles by more of the dark-clad guards, who were preserving the rather less-crowded central area for important folk.

Her eyes drawn back to the light, Elys looked up again, and saw that the walls around and below the windows were painted with worn and faded pictures, presumably of saints and biblical scenes, and she glanced quickly along one side, trying to catch a glimpse of something clear enough for her to make out its subject. This led her eyes westwards, to the great arch at the far end of the nave, and she caught her breath. Here was a picture she could see clearly, for the whole area of the wall above the arch was filled by a vivid mosaic, sparkling as the light from the windows caught the golden *tesserae* in its background. In the centre was the figure of Christ enthroned, many times greater than life-sized, and on either side and a little below, two figures stood in attitudes of worship. One, who carried two keys, was clearly St Peter, and the other, who was robed and crowned and carried a model of the basilica, must be the Emperor Constantine.

Sir Richard stopped and turned suddenly, impatiently beckoning the three women forward, and Elys was able to see what had been hidden until now by his broad back. Beyond the great arch with its mosaic was a blaze of light, coming from the top of a golden canopy, which rose to a peak to support a gilded crown, and was surrounded by a mass of golden lamps, each shaped like a dolphin and burning much more brightly than a candle. The canopy was supported by six white stone columns, the shaft of each inlaid with gold in spirals, wave-patterns or diamonds. Within the shelter of the canopy was the altar, raised high on a dais and approached by a double flight of steps, between which was an opening, as if more steps went down to a level below the altar.

'Stay close at hand,' Sir Richard said quietly, gesturing the three women towards the north side of the narrow central path of dark marble. Elys hesitated, thinking that he was sending them the wrong way, then recollected that this was one of the very old churches they had found where the altar was at the west end. Lady Mabilia took her stance near to the central path and Elys steered Maud past her to stand close alongside, while the Templars formed themselves up two deep on the men's side of the path, beside Sir Richard, who fixed his eyes firmly on the altar and ignored everything else.

Elys had visited so many churches in the past few years that she knew something of the layout of a basilican church, and craned her neck a little to see if there was an apse behind the altar. She saw that there was, and it contained a seat for the celebrant, though only a low one, not a bishop's throne, for this was not a cathedral. At that point, her mother's elbow in her ribs reminded her to concentrate on her prayers, and she closed her eyes obediently, feeling a surge of excitement that at last they had reached the goal of their pilgrimage, the longest and most difficult that they had undertaken, and, please God, the final, successful one.

Silence fell in the crowded church, broken only by the

quickly-hushed cry of a child, the rustle of the silk gown of a rich woman nearby, and the scuff of leather shoes on the marble floor as people shifted their weight or edged to a better position for a view of the altar.

Presently, a murmur ran through the crowd – a whisper that the Holy Father had arrived from his palace in the Lateran – and died again into silence. A brief pause, and then the sound of chanting voices, seeming disembodied, which re-echoed in the stone vault of the transept as the choirs entered from either end of it and moved to their positions on each side of the railed sanctuary.

Elys did not see the Holy Father enter, but suddenly he was there, a tall, lean figure, glowing in a robe of cloth of gold and wearing a white cap set within a golden crown, quite unlike any mitre she had ever seen.

The magnificence of the setting, the brilliant light of the dozens of lamps, the gleaming gold, the stiff hieratic movements of the priests and acolytes, made the Mass seem strangely remote and unfamiliar to Elys, who found herself wishing that they were back home in England, hearing Mass in some ordinary little church with a few candles and a priest in a simple alb. This was too magnificent, too over-powering, and a swift glance about her showed that the nave was filled with prosperous, well-dressed people. Where were the poor ragged folk she had seen outside? Relegated to the dark aisles, to the back of the church, perhaps even still outside . . .

After Mass, Sir Richard dismissed his men to wait outside in the atrium, and joined his womenfolk as the basilica slowly emptied. Presently, a priest came to engage him in a whispered conversation, and Elys guessed, from the few words she caught and the gestures of the priest, that he was establishing Sir Richard's identity, and enquiring why he had brought females with him. They were speaking French.

'My sister and niece,' she heard Sir Richard reply, ignor-ing the poor gentlewoman, as most people did, then a fur-ther exchange which she could not hear, followed by an indignant 'Certainly not! I consulted our Chapter, and they approved unanimously. Is it not among our duties to protect pilgrims?'

The priest raised his hands in a placating gesture, bowed slightly, and said, 'Perfectly in order, my lord. You will wish to pray at the shrine, and then I will conduct you to His Holiness. Please take as long as you need. I will wait here.'

'A chaplain to the Holy Father,' Sir Richard whispered to his sister. 'Speaks good French, but with a Provençal accent. Come along now, don't dawdle. I can't keep the Holy Father waiting.'

He led the way into the sanctuary, where an acolyte sprang to open the gate in the railing for them to pass, and they descended the steps to a small space below the front of the altar. There was barely room for four people, so Maud drew back without waiting to be told, and waited humbly, peering between the others to catch a glimpse of the shrine.

'Is the Holy Apostle in there?' asked Lady Mabilia nervously.

'Yes,' Sir Richard replied crisply, stepping forward to lay both his hands flat against the marble wall which was set back a foot or two under the dais on which the altar stood, and was framed between the two columns that supported the heavy stone structure above.

Elys, feeling awed and ashamed of her own lack of saintly qualities, went to stand beside her uncle, placing her hands as he had done. The wall was white marble, veined with blue, and narrow bands of purple porphyry were set into it for ornament. It was cool, like any marble, and she felt a slight disappointment. This was the tomb of St Peter, the Apostle, a man who had known Our Lord, had spoken with Him, touched Him, lived and worked with Him, day by day, through many months. Of all the shrines she had visited, this was the most important, the only one of a saint who had actually seen Our Lord in the flesh, but it felt like any other shrine.

'Don't be stupid,' she told herself. 'How else would it feel? It's only marble. The relics are behind it, and St Peter himself is in Heaven.' She closed her eyes and concentrated on her prayers, asking the Apostle's intercession for poor, dear Matthew, for her mother and uncle, for her other brother and her sister, far away in England, and, with a prick of guilt, for Maud, the gentlewoman. Then she quietly moved back and let the poor woman take her place.

'Well, then,' said Sir Richard briskly when they had finished praying and left the sanctuary, 'I have an audience with the Holy Father now, and you may go back to our lodging. My sergeant and two others will escort you.'

'You won't forget to ask him to pray for Matthew . . .' Lady Mabilia said, catching his arm as he turned away.

'Of course not, but my audience with him concerns the affairs of the Temple, not personal matters. I'll endeavour to find an opportunity to mention Matthew – I think it would be justifiable, as he means to join the Order when he's healed.'

'I shall go to the Cathedral before we return to our lodging,' Lady Mabilia said pensively. 'St Paul is there, and St Peter's head . . .'

'As you please, but you've prayed at St John's three times, and climbed the Holy Stair on your knees twice. There seems little point in doing the same thing repeatedly,' Sir Richard said practically. 'You'd do better to pack your boxes and rest. We start for home tomorrow.'

'So soon?' Elys protested. 'But we've hardly seen anything of the city!'

'You've done what you came to do, and there's no other reason for your being here,' Sir Richard snapped. 'I shall finish my business today, and I must return home. I'll remind you that England is in a state of civil war and near anarchy, and Heaven knows what may be happening there.' He marched away to join the waiting priest.

'Yes, Heaven only knows,' Lady Mabilia echoed softly. 'Oh, surely this time it will happen, Elys. Surely St Peter and St Paul will prevail.'

'I hope and pray that they will,' Elys replied, her heart sinking a little as she thought of all the other times they had returned home full of hope, only to be disappointed. If this pilgrimage failed in its object, the next would surely have to be to Jerusalem . . .

CHAPTER ONE

'Why have you stopped?' demanded her uncle irritably, reining in his palfrey beside Elys's mount. She was gazing at the prospect before her, lips slightly parted and her soft brown eyes searching the view as if she feared to miss some detail of it. All morning, the party had been travelling along the Via Bononia as it wound between the descending foothills of the Apennines, and suddenly, turning between two steep cliffs, it had emerged onto the broad Lombardy plain.

The old road ran on to a walled town at the edge of the plain, then continued, a straight paved line between low green banks, until it disappeared in the haze on the horizon. On either side of it, the rich golden-brown earth lay freshly ploughed, stretching away, quite flat, into the infinite distance. It was intersected by rows of the tall, feather-shaped poplars peculiar to the region, and scattered here and there were small farmhouses, their brick walls and red-tiled roofs glowing in the declining sun. To Elys it was beautiful, and yet depressing, for she had expected to see the Alps rising in the distance, but the flat plain seemed to continue, ahead and on either hand, to the very edge of the world.

'Elys! I spoke to you!' Sir Richard exclaimed, his dark, straight brows drawn together in a scowl and his lips taut with annoyance.

She started, causing her horse to toss its head, and she took a surreptitious grip of a handful of its mane, feeling insecure on the side-saddle, so high above the ground.

'I'm sorry,' she said. 'I was surprised to see . . . the country has changed so suddenly, and the road runs so straight . . .'

'What do you expect of a Roman road on flat country?' Sir Richard said impatiently. 'By the Holy Face of Lucca, girl, we'll never reach London if you will stop to look at every novelty that catches your eye! Mabilia, why cannot you and your foolish daughter travel in a litter? It's not

15

suitable for females to ride horseback, flaunting themselves before the eyes of strangers.'

Lady Mabilia, who had come up and stopped on Elys's other side, twisted in her saddle to look at her brother. A small, determined woman with sharp, almost black eyes, she was one of the few people of Sir Richard's acquaintance who was not in awe of him, the Seneschal of the English bailiwick of the Poor Knights of the Temple of Solomon, already renowned throughout Christendom as the Knights Templars.

'Have you ever travelled in a litter?' she asked drily. 'If you had, you'd not ask why I prefer to ride! No doubt Elys agrees with me – she's not a complete fool!'

'She behaves like one!' Sir Richard snapped. 'For Heaven's sake, can we not proceed, or does the Lady Elys intend to spend the rest of the day staring at Northern Italy?'

The two sergeants and half-dozen men-at-arms of the vanguard of their escort stared blank-faced in front of them, the discipline of the Order holding firm; only Sir Richard's squire, but recently come into his service, allowed himself a sly grin, which he concealed by bending down to look at the great feathered feet of his principal charge, the destrier he was leading.

'Interesting country, from the military point of view,' observed Baldwin, the more experienced of the two sergeants, with professional intent. 'See how the road-ditches are set back on either side, and no hedge or spinney near enough the highway to cover an ambush. Not good country for horses, though – too many dykes and drains, and the soil looks wet and heavy. Unhealthy, I should think – too much water about. Ague country, I'll . . .' He hesitated, having been about to say 'wager', but, knowing that the word would bring a crushing censure from his commander to the effect that Templars did not gamble, '. . . be bound,' he finished a fraction too late.

'Your opinion was not requested,' Sir Richard said coldly. 'Are we to reach Bologna today, or to spend the night here, contemplating the countryside?'

With that, the seneschal set off down the hill at a brisk

trot, his white cloak billowing around him and his back stiff with military pride and irritation. His soldiers followed, two by two, and the ladies had to hurry to keep up with them and regain their places behind the vanguard, and ahead of the baggage wagon, in which rode Lady Mabilia's gentle-woman. Behind that came the grooms with the spare horses, followed by another six men-at-arms for rearguard.

'Do you annoy your uncle by design or accident?' Lady Mabilia enquired as they recovered their proper order in the cavalcade.

'Accident,' Elys replied. 'I do try to please him, but if I say anything, he treats my remarks or questions with scorn, and if I'm silent, he says I'm sulking. I don't know why he dislikes me so much.'

'You're female,' her mother replied.

'But so are you, yet he takes notice of what you say!'

'Because I'm his elder, and habits acquired in childhood tend to persist throughout life. No doubt he still remembers the times I saved him from a beating, or dried his tears after one. You realize that we could hardly have made this pilgrimage to Rome without his help? With the war in England, the Templars are the only knights who can leave the country without breaking their oaths of allegiance to the – to Count Stephen or the Lady – I mean the Empress Matilda . . .' It was symptomatic of the problems of English people concerning the rights and wrongs of the succession to the throne that Lady Mabilia tried to be non-committal, even to her own daughter, and betrayed an uncharacteristic confusion in the attempt.

'But which, Mother? Every man has had to choose one or the other, and risk the consequences of a wrong choice! I wonder they haven't all found excuses to travel abroad.'

'At least dear Matthew is safe from the choice!' her mother said evasively, her sharp features softening at the thought of her beloved elder son. 'That's the one good thing about his lameness, and I'm sure that when he's healed, as he may well be by now, he'll choose to enter religion. Indeed, we shall all do so, in thanksgiving for God's mercy to him!'

'All?' Elys exclaimed. 'What do you mean?'

'You and I will join Judith in the nunnery at Wix. Your uncle, of course, is already a Templar, and Matthew is promised to join him, or else take orders, as your brother Crispin has already done. The whole family will be dedicated to His service! A very satisfactory conclusion to the whole business!' Lady Mabilia smiled and nodded her head with pleasure at the thought.

'But I have no vocation to be a nun,' Elys protested, horrified. 'I could never be shut up in a nunnery! You know how ill it made me when we spent those awful weeks in Wix priory the year before last.'

'Had you been concentrating your attention properly on your prayers for poor dear Matthew, you'd not even have noticed the walls,' her mother replied tartly. 'No doubt it was your preoccupation with your own minor discomfort that rendered the retreat ineffective! Well, you may please yourself, as you always do! I shall go to Wix and take my vows as soon as Matthew is healed, and you must either come with me, or fend for yourself. What could you possibly do in the world? Your dowry has already been paid to the nuns.'

'I want to be married, and have children,' Elys replied, desperate to make her mother understand. She had felt herself near to madness with claustrophobia during a month's retreat in Wix priory, yet her mother understood so little that she could refer to it as 'discomfort'. 'That is my vocation, to be a wife and a mother, not a nun, shut up within four walls!'

'You make the poorer choice,' her mother pointed out.

'I think not, truly, Mother. It's important for the world that men should have good wives, and children good mothers.'

'For the world, indeed, but Heaven is more important than this imperfect place! Chastity is infinitely more pleasing to God than marrying and child-bearing.'

Elys could not agree, but she prudently decided to leave the matter for the time being. After all, there was still a long journey before them, and no guarantee that they would find Matthew cured at the end of it! How many times now they had returned, full of hope, from one or other of the

18

many shrines in England or Normandy, Anjou, Burgundy, Paris . . . , only to find her brother a little worse, not cured after all, despite their efforts and prayers. Pray God it might be different this time, after such a long and trying journey to Rome and back!

The party reached Bologna before nightfall, and set out again early next morning, after hearing Mass in the cathedral. They headed northwestwards across the plain, jogging along on a paved road which had not been repaired for centuries, yet it was still perfectly usable. It was a day like so many others before it, passed by Elys in a series of stages.

At first, she was interested in the novelty of crossing flat country after long days in the mountains, and she looked with interest at the pleasant farmsteads, each with its small vineyard beside it, the small villages, the people at work on the land, the occasional town; but long before noon, she was stiff and cramped, with a nagging ache in her back from riding in the twisted position necessitated by her side-saddle, and the country no longer held her attention, being but the same view repeated over and over again, with only minor variations.

They stopped from time to time to bait the horses, but Sir Richard, used to long journeys on the business of his Order, had less consideration for their riders, and permitted only a brief time to stretch stiff limbs and walk about. As soon as their mounts were ready, they must go on again.

At noon, he allowed a scanty half-hour's stop at a wayside inn for a meal of bread and cheese, and half of that time was taken up by the recitation of the sixty Paternosters which every member of the Order was required to make before eating. No wine or water was allowed at table, and there was barely time after eating for a cup of the rough local vintage before they must mount and ride.

No conversation was tolerated during meals, and the sergeants and men-at-arms were forbidden to look directly at any woman, let alone speak to them, on the road. Elys talked to her mother from time to time, but the only speech she had with her uncle was an occasional irritable comment from him on the unsuitability of her insistence on riding

19

instead of travelling discreetly hidden in a litter, on the overbright colours of her gown and cloak which were, respectively, dull blue and russet, and, today's particular dislike, her temerity in allowing her hair to show from beneath her veil on her brow and hang in a long thick plait, visible to anyone who cared to look, down her back to below her waist.

'Shameful,' Sir Richard insisted. 'Your mother keeps her hair decently covered, and you should do the same!'

'But the fashion has changed since Mother was a girl,' Elys protested. 'Even the Empress wears her hair as I do.'

'And what if she does? Is that woman any example for a decent female to follow? Full of overweening pride, with insufficient sense to hold London when it was handed to her. She's stolen Church property, alienated good men who were willing to keep their oaths to her father, King Henry, and make her Sovereign of England, despite the obvious fact that no woman is fit to rule a kingdom. Don't cite the Empress Matilda in your defence, girl! You might as well cite the Devil.'

Elys, who found her uncle's fulminations amusing almost as often as they were irritating, was moved to comment slyly, 'So you favour Stephen of Blois for king of England, then?'

'I said nothing of the matter,' Sir Richard replied curtly. 'The Temple takes no part in the petty squabbles of kings. Stephen would do well to follow the example of his father and go to the Holy Land. What military ability he has would be better employed there than in devastating the kingdom he's tried to usurp.'

'Has he any military ability?' Elys enquired with a carefully-cultivated air of one seeking enlightenment. 'He was taken prisoner at the battle of Lincoln, surely?'

'He fought very well – it was hardly his fault that half his men deserted him and the other half behaved like imbeciles and let the Empress's brother Robert fool them.'

'If Robert of Gloucester is the Empress's brother, why is he not king?' Elys asked, for this point had puzzled her, although she could guess a likely reason.

'Because he's a bastard,' Sir Richard snapped, 'if you

know what that is, although, Heaven knows, a girl about to enter a convent should know nothing of such matters.'

'I am not about to enter a convent,' Elys said clearly and distinctly. 'God doesn't call me to be a nun, but a wife and mother.'

Sir Richard grunted. 'I've always said you're a fool. How do you expect to find this husband you claim God means you to wed? Marriage is a matter for careful negotiation and arrangement, and an orphan girl in all but name with no dowry'll find it well-nigh impossible to bring about. You'll get no help from me. No one should marry – it's displeasing to God, who desires all men and women to remain chaste.'

'But if no one married, the world would come to an end in a generation,' Elys protested.

'Precisely, and why should this world continue when there's a better one to be attained?'

'If no sons were born, you'd have no soldiers to fight for your Order and defend the pilgrims on the road to Jerusalem.'

'Neither would the Saracens have men to attack them,' Sir Richard replied sneeringly. 'Make up your mind to it, girl. You must go to the nuns at Wix, once my nephew is healed, or go your own way and starve – or worse.'

'Worse?' she enquired. 'What could be worse than starving?'

'How do you imagine a female can live in the world, without land to support her or a man to protect her?'

'Matthew will . . .'

'Matthew will join our Order as soon as he's healed. His place awaits him, and he'll return to Jerusalem to complete his training. There's no place for a female in a Templar's life, be she sister, mother or – or anything else! Our Rule bids us have no truck with the female sex.'

'Yet you agreed to take Mother and me to Rome.'

'I did no such thing. It suited me to visit the City at this time, and my Order's principal duty is the defence of pilgrims. It was . . . convenient . . . to carry out that duty while I sought privileges from Pope Innocent for our Order's properties in England.'

21

'How can the Pope grant privileges to property in England? Surely only the King can do that?'

'England has no king, only a soft-hearted fool on the one hand, and a scheming, arrogant female with an ambitious, devil-born husband on the other.'

Sir Richard gave a grunt of displeasure, and turned his attention to criticizing the appearance of one of the sergeants, who had a small streak of yellowish dirt on his black cloak.

Late in the afternoon, as dusk was falling, they reached the great Benedictine abbey at Polirone. Sir Richard complained that they should have travelled as far as Mantova in a day, although both sergeants, who had been this way before and knew the capabilities of palfreys very well, raised their eyebrows at such an ambitious statement. The hospitaller made them welcome, and Sir Richard shepherded his party into the abbey church, to pray for the soul of its former protectress, Matilda of Canossa, Countess of Tuscany, before they even washed off the dust and mire of their journey.

Elys wondered, as they quietly entered the dark building, lit only by the altar candles, why Sir Richard should wish to pray for a woman's soul enough to give it priority over everything else, but her uncle's fervent catalogue of the Countess's Christian virtues enlightened her.

The stone floor of the church was extremely hard and cold to her knees, although she had bunched her long skirts under them as best she could. Her eyes tended to wander, once she had ascertained that Sir Richard's were closed, to take in what little she could see of the building. The flickering shadows concealed most of the detail, but she caught a glimpse of a carved capital here or a marble column there, and reflected that there seemed to be a deal more carved work in Italian churches than in the many she had visited in England in the course of a dozen or more pilgrimages on poor Matthew's behalf.

Eventually the prayers ended and the group rose stiffly from their knees and went with the hospitaller, who had courteously waited in the shadows for them, to the guesthouse, where a little tepid water was provided for the ladies to wash themselves – the men must make do with cold, as the monks did – and then they were served supper in the guesthouse refectory, where their fellow-guests had already eaten and departed.

The meal consisted of a good thick pottage in generous quantity, followed by bunches of grapes, some apples, and a good, strongly-flavoured cheese, which the hospitaller said came from Parma. Sir Richard was heard (but not by their host) to murmur that the Benedictines were much declined from the former purity of their lives if they actually bought cheese instead of making it for themselves, but he subsided when the hospitaller added that it was specially obtained for their guests, and the monks ate only their own produce.

Lady Mabilia, Elys and the gentlewoman were allocated a small cell with two narrow plank beds, a truckle and a crucifix for its furnishings, and slept well on hay palliasses with a thick blanket apiece, but the men slept in the guest-house dormitory on straw, wrapped in their own cloaks, and considered themselves fortunate, for the straw was spread as thick as it was in the stables for their horses.

The major event of the following day was the crossing of the River Po. It was the widest river, apart from estuaries, which Elys had ever seen, for the outward journey to Rome had been made overland to Marseilles and thence by sea. She had expected a difficult and perhaps dangerous crossing on a ferry – probably only a raft – but, to her surprise, there was a bridge. It was obviously very old, and not precisely in an excellent state of repair, but it served its purpose well enough, and they were across it in a few minutes, the river running dark and shrunken beneath it after a long, dry summer. She felt a little disappointed.

They had started out late from Polirone, as Sir Richard had decreed that everyone should take the opportunity of making confession, it having been several days since they had last had a chance to do so, and it was perhaps this that made Elys expect the river-crossing to be dangerous. Her own confession had taken very little time, as she had few sins to admit, the chief being a rebellious spirit and an ungrateful resentment of her uncle's contemptuous attitude towards her. She was instructed to practise the virtue of patience, and set the slight penance of darning a small tear in one of the abbey's altar-cloths, which she quite enjoyed, being an excellent needlewoman, as the cloth was made of the finest and fairest linen she had ever handled. The embroidery, however, was a little coarse and uneven by her own standards. When she returned the mended cloth to the Sacristan she asked in her careful Latin who had embroidered it.

'Some nuns in Parma,' he replied. 'Do you admire the work?'

'To be honest, no,' she replied. 'My mother and sister could do better.'

'And you?' he asked quizzically.

She hesitated, then said, 'Well, yes, I think so.'

'You should turn professional broiderer, then! The nuns do their best, for their prioress would not allow otherwise, but they have no love for the work, and I believe that a lack of love in the doing will always show in the result! Your darning is quite beautiful, my daughter. Thank you.'

Elys left him with a half-formed thought in her mind that there might be a means for her to earn some money, if she ever needed it, if he was right.

Sir Richard seemed to take a remarkably long time over his confession, and she wondered what burdens his conscience carried which required so long to unload, but she was not to know that his confessor had been to Jerusalem and took the opportunity to reminisce and enquire for news of people and places in the Holy Land.

Because of the delay, they did not approach Mantova until the afternoon.

The guards at the gates of Mantova were more watchful and efficient than those at Bologna had been, but Sir Richard had passports for his party from the Grand Master of the Templars and from Pope Innocent, so they were admitted without difficulty, and directed to an inn in the heart of the town, at one end of the old forum. It faced the cathedral, which had one of the tallest bell-towers which Elys had ever seen, and she wondered how it had been persuaded to stand on such marshy ground.

The inn was a rambling building, rather low and dark,

but very clean, and the innkeeper seemed a cheerful and welcoming fellow, who greeted them with a beaming smile, wildly-gesturing hands and a flow of staccato Italian, which all seemed hospitable and encouraging. He showed them a room for the ladies with a large bed which sported clean sheets and a feather-stuffed mattress, and a small dormitory for the men, which he said they could have to themselves as there was another for his other guests, and, being religious, they would probably prefer to be apart from the laity. Even Sir Richard seemed to be a little impressed by this thoughtfulness, and the two sergeants returned from the stables with words of praise for the warmth and dryness of the building, the thickness of the straw, and the quality of the oats and hay.

There was, of course, a drawback, but it was one from which most inns suffered – there was only one common-room for guests, but at least it was apart from the room where the townsfolk gathered to drink their wine, and there were only two other guests to share it. They were both in the room when Sir Richard's party entered it for supper, and they looked towards the newcomers with lively interest, and rose to their feet to bow to the ladies with a proper show of courtesy.

The taller of the two caught Elys's attention so that she hardly noticed the other, for he was strikingly handsome, with crisp, curly dark hair and beard, a straight, well-cut nose, long-lashed dark eyes and shapely red lips, which framed a set of gleaming white teeth when he smiled, which he did frequently. He introduced himself as Fulk Fitz-michel, a knight in the service of Henry of Blois, Papal Legate of England and Lord Bishop of Winchester, speaking in the clearly accented Norman-French of the governing class of England.

'An Englishman, then!' Sir Richard exclaimed.

'Norman-English,' Sir Fulk corrected gently, with unruffled charm and his attractive smile.

Sir Richard introduced himself and those of his companions whose rank merited introduction. As they sat down on the stools and benches about the table, he enquired,

'Are you recently come out from England? Have you any news of affairs there?'

'I've been in Rome since June, and am now on my way home, but I was requested by my master to find my companion here and bring him back as he's been in Italy near two years, and the Bishop has need of him,' Sir Fulk replied, with a gesture towards the other man, who had resumed his seat by the open hearth and was writing or drawing in a large notebook with a silverpoint. 'Aylwin of Winchester,' he added by way of introduction.

The second man looked up, rose sufficiently to make a bow, then sank back on his stool, closed his notebook, and looked at the newcomers, his eyes moving from one to another, noting the set of an ear, the angle of a nose or jaw, the fall of a draped sleeve or tunic, but he said nothing.

'Another of Bishop Henry's knights?' asked Sir Richard in a slightly condescending tone, for, to judge by his name, the man was English, and, in any case, a religious knight, like any religious, thought poorly of secular knights.

'His master-mason,' Aylwin replied in French, but with an English accent. 'He sent me here to see the great churches in Rome and elsewhere, and gather ideas for his own buildings. My chief interest is sculpture.'

Sir Richard, his sister and his niece, looked at Aylwin in silence for a moment, all three being slightly nonplussed. A fellow-countryman, in the service of one of the greatest men in England – indeed, the greatest as far as strength of position and power were concerned – and travelling in the company of one of their own class – yet – a master-mason? An artisan? Where, precisely, did such a man stand in rank?

Sir Richard, who had some experience of church- and castle-building, slotted him in neatly on a par with his own squire. Not equal to a knight, but worthy of respect, and likely, if his skill were great, to attain sufficient wealth and standing for his sons or grandsons to aspire to knighthood. Lady Mabilia thought he looked a sensible, capable man – more so than Sir Fulk – and decided to treat him on the same terms as she would her steward, to whom he bore some resemblance. Elys did not know what to make of his rank, but saw him as a man who created things, and therefore interesting, for the few men of her acquaintance were knights, soldiers, servants or religious, and consequently destroyed, did humdrum work, or prayed.

'Do you carve in wood or stone?' she asked.

'Either. I prefer stone,' he replied briefly, giving her one hard, searching look before turning his attention to Sir Richard, who was exchanging news with Sir Fulk, all of it, as far as English matters were concerned, at least four months out of date. Elys was left to study him with mild curiosity, comparing him with the handsome knight, not entirely to his detriment.

Aylwin had a thick thatch of straight fair hair, cut rather short below the tips of his ears, and tending to flop forward over his brow, deep-set grey or blue eyes, and a firm mouth, set in a lean-jawed face. He was clean-shaven, and plainly dressed in a short dark blue tunic with long sleeves and a plain leather belt, with no more than a narrow band of embroidery at the neck and wrists, hose to match, and leather boots ornamented with a band of punched work between rows of steel rings at the top and ankle.

Sir Fulk, by contrast, was arrayed in the height of fashion. His dark curls fell to his shoulders, where they were carefully combed into ringlets. His beard was waxed and parted in the middle, and his heavily embroidered over-tunic fell almost to his ankles, gleaming with gold threadwork and glass stones. He was girded with a metal belt which had the look of gold, set with gemstones. Although he was conversing with Sir Richard, his eyes slid towards Elys from time to time, and she was glad that she had put on one of her more fashionable gowns. Her mother would not allow her to corset her waist, but she was slender enough for her fitted gown to sit well without it, and the gown was covered with her own embroidery of odd little birds and flowers, with a long girdle to match. She had brushed and replaited her hair, and put her best gold circlet over her head-veil, and was conscious that she looked her best, although she did not consider herself anything of a beauty.

Presently there were indications that supper was soon to be served, and Sir Richard broke off the conversation in order to embark on his religious exercises. He and his companions withdrew from the table to kneel in a circle on an area of clean boarded floor by the window. Lady Mabilia and Elys, as had become their custom, and Sir Richard's expectation, joined them. Sir Fulk hesitated, then, with a resigned shrug, plumped down on his knees beside Elys, but Master Aylwin merely shifted on his stool, opened his notebook, and inspected the tip of his silverpoint.

'Will you not join us?' Sir Richard invited him.

'I've already made my devotions, thank you,' Aylwin replied with no particular expression in his voice, and bent his head over a fresh page in his book. He glanced up briefly from time to time as the sixty Paternosters droned on, and, if anyone had been watching, they might have noticed that his eyes fell on Elys every time.

Prayers over, Sir Richard called for supper to be served, and they all took their seats at the table. Sir Richard took the central seat at the high table which formed the cross of the T, with Lady Mabilia on his right and Elys on his left, and invited Sir Fulk to the next seat to his right. Sir Richard's squire sat next to Elys, with Maud next to him. The men-at-arms and grooms had already sorted themselves into their proper order down both sides of the long table, with the sergeants at the top, and there remained only Sir Fulk's squire and Master Aylwin to be seated. The latter, without putting anyone to the trouble of allocating him a place, sat down at the short end of the high table on Elys's side, putting his silverpoint carefully into his purse and his book on the floor under his stool. The squire stationed himself behind his master, but Sir Richard suggested that, as the inn-servants were about to serve the meal, he might be allowed to have his supper while it was hot, and Sir Fulk graciously indicated that he might sit at the other short end of the high table, opposite Aylwin.

There was a deal of to-ing and fro-ing of servants for a while, with platters and trencher-bread, bowls of slippery-looking pasta and vegetables, dishes of meat, horn cups for the commonalty and goblets for the gentry, and the inn-keeper himself brought in leather bottles of wine.

'The Rule of our Order does not allow the serving of

drink with our food,' Sir Richard informed him primly in bad Italian.

'Ah, but not all of us are governed by your Rule!' put in Sir Fulk, managing to intercept the bottles before they were removed. 'I'm sure you'll not grudge the rest of us a cup of drink, for I, for one, am very thirsty!'

Sir Richard gave a surly nod of acquiescence, and Sir Fulk invited Lady Mabilia to take wine, and poured for her, himself and his squire. Master Aylwin silently reached out a long arm to take a bottle from the innkeeper's tray as he passed, and filled the goblets of Elys and Maud without a word, but when Elys looked at him to thank him, he flicked her the merest suspicion of a wink, which seemed to convey that he found Sir Richard more than a trifle pompous, then closed his eyes while Sir Richard said Grace.

Normally the Templars ate in silence, but it was difficult for Sir Richard to prevent Sir Fulk from talking if he had a mind to do so, which he had. Fortunately, he confined his conversational addresses to Lady Mabilia and his squire, respecting the Rule as far as Sir Richard was concerned. Master Aylwin ate in silence for the most part, and a great deal more neatly and quietly than Sir Fulk, who tended to gobble and speak with his mouth full, but he did make an occasional remark to Elys, and she was presently emboldened to ask him a question.

'I noticed that the cathedral here has a very tall belltower,' she said. 'Do you know how they've managed to make it stand on such marshy ground?'

Aylwin looked at her with interest, a spoonful of thick soup halfway to his lips, put the spoon down in the bowl, and replied, 'The town itself stands on an island in the marshes, so the ground's firmer than you'd think, but such a tall tower requires a deep foundation. Provided it goes down far enough into firm ground, you may build your tower high, but the taller the tower, the deeper the foundation. There's a question of balance, as well.'

He took a few manchets of bread, broke them swiftly and neatly into blocks, and built a tower of them, then showed how it would stand as long as its centre of balance was contained within its base, but fall if it leaned too far. Everyone at the high table, and the sergeants, watched the demonstration with either interest or surprise, Sir Richard scowling and compressing his lips, no doubt longing to make some scathing comment, but being prevented by the discipline of the Order.

'How strange!' said Sir Fulk. 'Do you mean you could actually build a tower that leaned like that in stone?'

Aylwin nodded. 'If anyone was foolish enough to wish for one! It would never be entirely safe, for a slight shift in the foundations could bring it down, but a short tower could stand like that for centuries!'

He collected up his building blocks and used them to mop up the remaining soup in his bowl, then helped Elys and the gentlewoman to some of the meat which formed the next course. When Sir Richard's attention was distracted for a moment, he refilled their wine-goblets, and asked Elys if she had noticed any of the buildings in Rome. As she was an observant person, she had, in fact, noticed a great many, and the rest of the meal passed in pleasant discussion of them, to which Sir Richard listened with reluctant interest, surprised to hear his niece talking quite sensibly about things which he had not noticed at all, and being listened to with apparent attention by an expert on the subject of her remarks.

After a final Grace, he cleared his throat and said to Aylwin, 'Have you been long in Mantova?'

'A few days.'

'Have you by any chance seen ... I believe there is a Church of the Holy Sepulchre here. Have you seen anything of it?'

'You mean a round church?' Aylwin asked.

'Yes.' The 'of course' was implicit.

'It is, in fact, dedicated to San Lorenzo. I'll take you there in the morning, if you wish.'

CHAPTER TWO

'Your uncle is a Templar, then?' remarked Sir Fulk as they walked down the street to San Lorenzo's the next morning. 'I don't believe I've met one before. The Order's much talked about these days, since Pope Innocent's Bull last year gave them so much in the way of privilege. I'm puzzled about the other two men walking behind him at the moment – they appear to have authority over the common men-at-arms, but they wear black cloaks. I thought all Templars had to wear white ones.'

'Only the Knights,' replied Elys. She was walking with Sir Fulk and her mother, but Lady Mabilia was praying silently, preparing herself for Mass, and ignoring the young man. 'The sergeants wear black or brown.'

'They have a choice?'

'Not really. Black wool becomes brown as the dye fades.'

'Ah, yes, I see. I never wear either colour myself.'

Elys was not surprised by this statement, for he obviously favoured bright colours. This morning he was clad in a long crimson tunic, with a bright yellow supertunic falling to his knees, and a green cloak decorated with diagonal bands of embroidery in bright silks. His black curls were topped by a conical cap of the same fabric as his tunic. Elys felt her own dress to be quite subdued in contrast, for her gown and cloak were a dull steel-blue, albeit with fashionable bell-shaped sleeves and some gold and silver embroidery at neck and cuffs.

It was a fine, sunny morning, and the citizens of Mantova, hurrying about their daily affairs, looked curiously at the little procession crossing their vegetable market. It was led by Sir Richard and Master Aylwin, who was pointing out features of the buildings they were passing, which did not seem to interest the Templar at all. Behind them came Sir Richard's squire and the two sergeants, then Lady Mabilia, Elys and Sir Fulk, with his squire at his heels, and the men-at-arms plodded along behind, staring about them, but maintaining their usual glum silence.

'You're returning from Rome, I gather?' Sir Fulk asked rather than stated. 'I thought Templars didn't usually travel in the company of ladies.'

'We're on pilgrimage,' Elys replied. 'My uncle had business in Rome and allowed us to travel under his escort, as his Order's chief duty is to protect pilgrims.'

Aylwin and Sir Richard had come to a halt before a small, circular dark red church standing at the corner of a narrow street. Elys, as she came up with them, looked at it with great interest, wondering if it really resembled the Church of the Holy Sepulchre in Jerusalem at all closely.

'I thought it would be a Templar church,' Sir Richard was saying.

'Not all round churches were built by your Order, or even by the other one,' Aylwin replied. (He meant the Knights Hospitallers, but refrained from naming them, as there was no great affection between the two orders). 'In fact, this church is older than your Order by at least thirty years. It was built by a group of townsfolk who'd made their pilgrimage to Jerusalem. Shall we go in?'

A few people were entering the church, obviously going to Mass, so Sir Richard's party followed them, and found themselves in semi-darkness, for there were only a few small windows in the outer wall. An aisle running all round the interior, with two orders of narrow arches, supported a gallery and a small central dome. The wall immediately below the curve of the dome was pierced by more small windows, which barely illumined the frescoes painted in it. The walls above and between the arches were also frescoed, with saints and Biblical scenes, which seemed to move in the flickering light of the altar candles.

'Up there,' said Sir Richard brusquely, directing the ladies to a flight of steps in the thickness of the outer wall. 'Your place is in the gallery.'

Lady Mabilia obediently led her daughter and her gentlewoman up the stairs, which were narrow and steep, and they emerged in the gallery, where a few other women were standing along the parapet, waiting for the service to begin.

The newcomers found places where they could look down on the altar, and see their menfolk, who were grouped to one side, near the front, as befitted the rank of the two knights.

The service was beautifully chanted by a priest, a deacon and a small choir, and Elys felt inspired and satisfied by it, and by the thought that this church had been built by people who had actually seen the Holy Places, and, presumably, had been moved to build their own replica of one of them. She was bold enough afterwards to mention this feeling to her uncle, but he gave a snort of dismissal, and replied, 'Nothing like! The only thing it has in common with the Holy Sepulchre is its roundness! It's as like the real thing as a child's mud copy of a castle!'

'Well built, though,' said Aylwin, looking up at its tiled roof, for they were standing outside, waiting for Lady Mabilia, who had lingered to light a candle for Matthew.

'What kind of stone is it?' asked Elys, looking at the walls. 'I've seen several buildings made of this red sort, and it puzzles me.'

Sir Richard muttered something about everything puzzling a fool and walked away, but Master Aylwin smiled down at her and said, 'What is it that puzzles you?'

'The stones are always small and very regular in size and shape, and they don't show any tooling marks.'

'They're bricks.'

'Bricks? What are they?'

'They're man-made blocks, fashioned out of clay mixed with straw and other things, and baked in a hot oven.'

'Like tiles and pots?'

'A little, but it's a more complicated process than tile-making. The old Romans knew how to do it, and the Italians must have learned from them. We've lost the art in England, but I expect we'll learn it again one day. Bricks would be cheaper than stone in many places a long way from the quarries.'

Aylwin's interest was obviously more on the building than on Elys, for his eyes had returned to the curving roofs of the aisle and the dome above it, and his hand was fishing in the purse on his belt for his silverpoint. He found it, produced his book from under his cloak, and began to sketch some detail of the roof with quick, sure lines.

Elys ventured to crane her neck to look at his work, and saw that the page facing the one he was using was filled by a beautiful drawing of a Madonna, her head bent and eyes closed in prayer. The line of her profile was regular, clear-cut, and her hair framed the line of her jaw, then fell forward over her shoulder.

'What a lovely face!' she exclaimed.

Aylwin gave her a startled look, then smiled as if she had said something amusing.

'I thought so,' he said. 'Don't you recognize her? I believe I've caught a good likeness.'

He turned the book so that she could see better, but, after looking carefully, she shook her head and replied, 'No, I'm sorry. I've never seen her, I'm sure.'

'I suppose it's difficult to see your own profile, unless you have a couple of good mirrors,' Aylwin said, adding two or three lines to the hair in his drawing, then surveying it critically. 'It's very like. What do you think, my lady?'

This was addressed to Lady Mabilia, who had just come hurrying out of the church. She looked at the drawing, then at Master Aylwin, her sharp eyes searching his face.

'You should ask permission before you do that, young man,' she said. 'I'll forgive you, though, for it's a beautiful picture. What do you mean to do with it?'

Aylwin produced a small knife from his wallet, cut the page out and presented it to her with a courteous bow. 'I meant no offence, my lady. I draw anything that may be of use to me.' The words were apologetic, but the tone was one of explanation, not excuse.

'But it's not you, Mother,' Elys said, looking over her mother's shoulder at the drawing.

Lady Mabilia laughed and rolled up the piece of parchment with great care. 'Bless the girl! She doesn't recognize herself. Come along – by now my brother's halfway to wherever we're bound for next, and no doubt fuming that we're lagging behind.'

As they were hurrying along the street, Elys said shyly to Aylwin, 'You must think me foolish not to realize . . .'

'Have you never seen your own profile?' he asked.

'No.' She had only seen her full face reflected in water, or, occasionally, her mother's polished bronze mirror, but those glimpses had been surreptitious, for Lady Mabilia condemned mirror-gazing as unseemly vanity in a young lady, and kept her mirror locked in her great clothes-chest.

'Then you've discovered something today.'

Elys gave him a questioning look.

'That you're beautiful,' he clarified.

She hardly knew what to say to that, for it was not the kind of remark she was used to hearing addressed to anyone, least of all herself. She was both embarrassed and excited by it, but her natural confusion was modified, because it had not sounded like a compliment, but simply a statement, similar to his earlier comment that the church was well-built. She could think of no suitable reply, so said nothing, and hoped that he would not notice how warm her cheeks had become. A sidelong glance show her that he was not even looking at her, but at the cathedral, which had just come into sight at the end of the street. Her embarrassment gave way to a touch of indignation as she recalled that he had presumed to record her face without asking her permission, and had intended to use it in his work. After all, he was only an artisan, and English at that!

On the other hand, it was pleasant to know that someone – a man *and* an artist – considered her beautiful. Being beautiful might help her to find a husband, although it could never really compensate for lack of a dowry. She sighed and felt a qualm of fear for the unknown future, but she was all the more determined not to submit to being incarcerated in a nunnery.

Instead of starting immediately on the next stage of their journey, Sir Richard gave his men leave after dinner to spend the rest of the day as they chose, adding that he expected them first to carry out any desirable repairs or maintenance work on their gear, look to the welfare of the horses, and attend to the wagon, which needed to have its axles greased. He told his squire, who made the mistake of looking pleased at the idea of a half-holiday, to go over his ringmail hauberk and grease it, as the damp countryside hereabouts was likely to cause it to rust, and to take his destrier and two palfreys to be reshod.

Having cleared the commonroom of the inn of all but the gentlefolk and Master Aylwin, Sir Richard then fell into discussion with Sir Fulk about the best route onwards.

'Of course, my brothers in the Order would have been glad to provide a guide and reliable information,' he said. 'I've not made this journey overland before, as I've always travelled by sea between Rome and Marseilles on earlier journeys. Unfortunately, the weaker members of my party were unwell on the outward voyage, and decline to endure the hardship a second time.'

'If by "weaker members" you mean Elys and myself,' interrupted Lady Mabilia sharply, 'I can confirm that nothing will persuade me to take ship again, save the lack of any alternative!'

She and Elys had, of course, not been sitting idle meanwhile. As soon as it became apparent that there would be no travelling today, they had sent Maud for their embroidery, and were sitting by the window which looked out on the main square to get a good light on their work. For the same reason Aylwin was with them, drawing in his book.

'This is my third journey back from Rome,' said Sir Fulk modestly. 'I think I may fairly claim to know the way by now, and I'll be pleased to act as your guide, while taking advantage of your escort. The road is reasonably safe nowadays, but there are other dangers besides brigands in the mountains.'

'I was planning to stop in Milano for a few days,' said Aylwin firmly.

Sir Fulk looked a little annoyed, but, to Elys's surprise, instead of telling him that it was out of the question, said in a conciliatory fashion, 'It would be as well to stop there for a day, at least, to make sure that the horses are well shod and to buy supplies for the mountain crossing.'

'Which pass do you suggest we take?' asked Sir Richard.

'That which rises above Aosta, the St Nicholas pass. There's a hospice at the top of it, where we may shelter for a night, whereas there's little in the way of lodging by any other route. It's maintained and staffed by one of the regular orders.'

'Which one?' asked Sir Richard, frowning. 'Not the Hospitallers?'

'No – no!' Sir Fulk replied hastily and reassuringly. 'They're canons – Augustinians.'

Sir Richard snorted, having a poor opinion of canons, whether regular or secular, and produced a rolled parchment from his wallet, which he carefully unrolled and spread out on the table at which he and Sir Fulk were sitting.

'This is a drawing of the route suggested to me in Rome,' he said. 'Is it the one of which you speak? It appears to go to Aosta, and then turn into the mountains, eventually descending to the valley of the Rhône.'

Aylwin silently got up from his stool, tucking his book under his arm, and went to the table, where he leaned over between the two knights to look at the map. 'Quite good,' he said. 'The hospice is marked in the wrong place, and they've left out the other pass. That goes off to the left from Aosta, and the Roman road follows it, but it's the more difficult of the two further on. There's a hospice there, as well.'

'You know the route?' asked Sir Richard.

'I've passed that way.' Aylwin appeared to have lost interest, now he had seen the map, such as it was, for it was little more than a few lines, with the names of villages written in here and there, and some little triangles to indicate mountains. 'I dare say Fulk and I can guide you between us. In any case, you may hire a guide in St Rhémy.' He went back to his stool, leaving the knights to discuss more details of the journey, and said to Elys, 'Are you making an altar cloth?'

It was a reasonable guess, for she was working on a long piece of white linen, the area she was stitching stretched across a small tambour, and the rest rolled up in another cloth to keep it clean.

'Yes,' she replied, 'and my mother is making the other cloths to go with it. It's for the church of the nuns at Wix, in Essex, where my mother intends to take her vows when my brother is healed.'

Lady Mabilia looked up with a frown, but saw that the man's attention was on the embroidery, not the girl, so she said nothing.

'Your brother is ill?'

'Not exactly.' Elys hesitated, then, thinking that Aylwin might be moved to pray for Matthew if he knew his history, and another source of prayers was not to be underestimated, she went on, 'Matthew – my brother – went to the Holy Land with my uncle, Sir Richard, to begin his training, in hopes of joining the Templars. He was involved in a fight with some Saracens . . . Have you heard of Greek fire?'

'Yes. It's some sort of secret mixture which burns.'

She nodded. 'The Saracens use it in many ways, throwing it into towns and at ships by catapult, in jars. When the jar breaks, the – the stuff flies out and sets everything it touches on fire. Sometimes they throw a small amount at a person . . . That happened to Matthew. A tiny piece of it touched his right foot and burned through his shoe and into the flesh. That was five years ago. It still won't heal.'

Elys glanced at Aylwin's face, and saw that he understood the horror of what she was telling him.

'It gets worse, little by little,' she went on. 'At first, it was a small hole, no bigger than my little finger nail, but it slowly spreads and gets bigger, and deeper. When we left home this time, it covered half his foot and was beginning to spread to his ankle, and in the middle of the wound, it was eating into the bone . . .'

'And what remedies have you tried?' Aylwin asked.

'Every remedy for burns, for ulcers, for cankers, that we can discover. My mother and I have been on pilgrimage on his behalf to Holywell, St Cuthbert at Durham, St Edmundsbury, Canterbury, Winchester, Lindisfarne, Glaston, St Denis, St Rhémy, Cologne . . . oh, a score of places! Each time, we return home hoping, only to find it's a little worse . . .'

'And now you've been to Rome.' It was a statement rather than a question. 'That leaves only the Holy Places.'

'Surely, this time he'll be better . . .' Elys faltered, seeking reassurance, for she had almost lost hope, and felt guilty about her lack of faith.

'I pray that he may be healed,' Aylwin replied gravely. 'I'll pray for him every day, if you'll permit.' He looked at Lady Mabilia as he spoke.

'Permit?' she replied bluntly. 'We'll be deeply grateful to you for it. No need to ask permission for that, bless you. My son needs every prayer anyone can be moved to say for him! I'm sure Our Lord and Our Lady will grant him a cure this time. All these weary weeks of travelling – surely they count for something?'

Master Aylwin silently drew a little squirming devil in one corner of his page, looking grave and thoughtful, and said, 'I hope so. I don't think one can make bargains with God, but only ask for His mercy.' He said nothing more for some time, and then raised a totally different subject.

'The days begin to grow shorter,' he said. 'Would you care to take a stroll about the market with me while it's still light?'

Lady Mabilia brightened considerably at the suggestion, saying that she had noticed good fruit for sale there, and other things which might be useful. She retired briefly to the room which she shared with Elys and Maud, and returned with cloaks for herself and Elys, and a leather purse on a stout belt about her waist. They set out, leaving Sir Richard and Sir Fulk deep in a blow-by-blow discussion of the taking of Jerusalem, despite the fact that neither had been born when it happened.

The sun was still shining, but with the brassy dullness of late afternoon. It gleamed on Aylwin's bright hair, for he went capless, and gilded the grapes on the market stalls. Lady Mabilia bought several bunches, passing them to the long-suffering Maud to carry, and then she entered into a lengthy session of bargaining at another stall for two steel needles, chattering enthusiastically in a mixture of French and Latin, with her few odd words of Italian thrown in where they seemed to fit. The stallholder waved his arms, clapped his hands to his head, and called on half the saints in the calendar to witness his ruination, and finally agreed to part with the precious articles for half the price he had first asked.

'And two reels of thread,' Aylwin added in Italian, pointing to some large wooden bobbins wound with fine linen thread.

The stallholder informed St Ambrosius of Milano, who apparently hovered invisibly just above his head, that this man was a tyrant, a veritable leech, a grinder of the faces of poor men, to which Aylwin replied cheerfully by telling St Edmund of England that this stallholder set too high a price on his goods, thereby depriving a poor widow of the means of making fair linen cloths for the adornment of the altar of her parish church, and he would no doubt pay the penalty in the next life.

'Is she really a widow?' asked the stallholder, struck by a horrible doubt. Aylwin nodded solemnly, and swore by St Edmund that she was, and the stallholder immediately became apologetic and added three bobbins of thread to the two precious needles, together with a small piece of pumice-stone for cleaning and sharpening them. Elys discovered, many months later, when all the thread on one bobbin was used up, that they were most beautifully made of turned olive-wood, with very pretty markings.

Lady Mabilia observed the conversation and its results with a lively interest, her eyes sparkling with amusement, and thanked Aylwin for his intervention as soon as they were out of earshot of the stallholder, telling him he was a man after her own heart. Elys found it all rather surprising, but did not pay a great deal of attention, for there were more interesting things to see in the market than a piece of bargaining.

Aylwin puzzled her. He was, after all, only an Englishman and an artisan, yet he behaved as if he were the equal of Sir Fulk, and even, to some extent, of Sir Richard. Besides, she had noticed that his notebook contained something other than drawings – there were written notes by some of the pictures, so he must be able to read and write, which even her uncle could not do.

This supposition was confirmed a couple of days later in Milano, where they visited several churches. In one, a tiny baptistry by the ancient cathedral of St Maria, Aylwin read out an inscription which stated that here St Ambrose had baptized St Augustine of Hippo.

Milano was the last large city the party would enter before the long crossing of the mountains, so there was much to do in preparation for the hazards ahead. The sergeants could safely be left to supervise the necessary attentions to the horses and the wagon and the buying of food supplies, but it would be cold in the mountains, so more clothing must be obtained, and the ladies wished to buy a few personal items, before they faced the rigours of the mountain crossing. The only member of the group who seemed unconcerned about the preparations was Aylwin, who left his horse for Sir Fulk's squire to take to the farrier, and went off to St Lorenzo Maggiore, which was being rebuilt, to spend a few hours with his fellow-masons. He returned to the inn where they were staying in time for supper, looking very dusty and with a cut on his cheek, caused by a flying chip of stone from a careless axe – someone else's, not his, he assured them with a grin. Apparently he had been doing a little stone-cutting with his temporary friends, and it seemed to have given him a deal of pleasure.

Sir Fulk looked a little put out by his companion's dishevelled appearance, but Aylwin did not propose to sit down to supper in that state. He excused himself politely and disappeared, returning as the others were taking their places at table with damp hair, clean face and hands, and a clean tunic. Since the Bishop of Winchester's two men had joined the party, Sir Fulk's time had been taken up by Sir Richard and with preparations for the onward journey, but everything was now ready for an early start in the morning, and he turned his attention to more social matters. He had contrived to change places at table with Sir Richard's squire, and so was between Elys and Maud. As the latter knew her place too well to presume to indulge in idle talk at table, he was able to give his full attention to Elys, and kept up a gentle, undemanding conversation with her, first about Rome and the sights to be seen there.

For Elys, these had consisted almost entirely of churches, for she and her mother had been there for one purpose only, and that involved long hours of prayer in as many of the sacred buildings as possible, with daily visits to the shrines of St Peter and St Paul, in St Peter's basilica and St Paul-without-the-wall respectively.

'If you were unable to see much of the city, at least you must have observed the fashions,' he said when she had explained this. 'What did you think of them?'

'They were much the same as the fashions anywhere else, save that more people were wearing silk. I'd heard that the ladies of Rome are considered great beauties. Did you think them so?'

Sir Fulk seemed remarkably pleased by such a simple question, leaned closer to her and murmured, 'I forget. A nearer beauty to me now has driven all memory of others from my head.'

Elys, who had not, even unconsciously, been fishing for a compliment, was taken aback, but had the presence of mind to reply, 'You flatter me, sir,' in a cool tone, but she felt an internal shiver of excitement that such a handsome knight should pay her a compliment.

'Indeed I do not!' he said caressingly, leaning even closer. 'I protest, I tell but the bare truth, and would be happy to serve you in any way that I might.'

Elys glanced cautiously around to see if her mother or her uncle had noticed Sir Fulk's behaviour, and was relieved to find that they were both oblivious of it. Nevertheless, she thought it best to change the direction of the conversation in as tactful a manner as she could. 'Then perhaps you can tell me something,' she replied, leaning a little away from him.

'Anything I may confide to you without injury to my honour!' he said grandiloquently, bending his head to look languishingly into her face.

Her eyebrows rose at this blatant piece of flirtation, and she flicked another glance at her mother, but Lady Mabilia was talking to Maud.

'It's something quite simple,' she said hastily, drawing back a trifle, and wondering if he were making advances toward her, and to what end. 'It's just that everyone calls the Empress just that, or the Lady Matilda. Even people who take her side never call her the Queen, although King

Stephen's wife is given the title by his supporters. I wondered why, that's all.'

'It's because her title of Empress is higher than that of Queen,' Sir Fulk replied, looking disappointed. 'Of course, she's either the Queen of England or the Countess of Anjou, depending on which side one takes, but no doubt she prefers the superior rank endowed by her first marriage. Also, it would be very confusing, as the King's wife is also Matilda . . .'

'There's a sounder reason than that,' said Aylwin from his seat at the end of the table. 'We don't use the title "Queen" in England. It's a foreign importation.'

It happened that this pronouncement fell into one of those sudden lulls which occasionally occur, even among a number of people, and more frequently than usual among the present company, as none of the Templars spoke during meals. Everyone looked at Aylwin, and Sir Richard opened his mouth as if he was about to speak, but quickly recollected himself and put a piece of bread into it instead, frowned, and stared at the mason in silence.

'By "we",' Aylwin went on unperturbedly, 'I mean, of course, the English, as opposed to the Normans or the Angevins, or the Scots. We have always titled the wife of our king *The Lady*. Only Aethelred II's wife was ever called Queen, and that only by her foreign relations. My grandfather told me that his father knew the wife of our last king but one very well, and he always styled her the Lady Edith.'

'Edith!' exclaimed Lady Mabilia. 'But our last king but one was Rufus . . . He had no wife!'

'*Our* last king but one,' Aylwin replied, smiling a little, 'was Eadward!'

Elys noticed that he gave the initial vowel of the name its full English value, as he had with Aethelred, and not the clipped Norman pronunciation.

'Oh, you will have your little joke,' Sir Fulk said, laughing, as the mystery suddenly became clear to him. Aylwin still smiled, but with a wry twist to his lips, and Elys wondered, for the first time in her life, how the English really felt about their Norman overlords in this seventh decade after the conquest.

43

'Your great-grandfather knew King Edward's wife!' exclaimed Lady Mabilia. 'How interesting! Was he, perhaps, working on the king's great church at Westminster?'

'He was a thane, and a member of the Witanagemot,' Aylwin replied quietly. 'What you would call a baron, with a seat on the King's Great Council.'

Once more, Sir Richard almost broke the Rule concerning speech at table as he, and everyone else, stared at Aylwin, reassessing his rank and standing in the world. Lady Mabilia must have guessed how much her brother wished to speak and what he wanted to ask, for she asked it herself.

'But how does it come about that his great-grandson is a – a mason?'

The hesitation was quickly covered, but it was there, and it brought another wry smile to Aylwin's lips. 'A master-mason,' he corrected gently. 'Something rather more than a mere artisan, my lady. My great-grandfather was killed in the battle. His lands and title were, therefore, forfeit.'

He did not need to say which battle. To anyone born in England, whether English or Norman, there was only one battle which did not need further identification. The statement caused a slight movement through the body of everyone who heard it, like the ripple in a field of barley in the lightest puff of a breeze, and the soldiers present, to a man, gave a faint sigh.

'As did my grandfather,' Sir Richard said harshly, rising to his feet. There was a sound between a gasp and a gulp from one of the sergeants at the shock of hearing the Seneschal himself break the Rule, but Sir Richard obviously thought the breach was warranted. 'I suppose it might be said that your family's loss was mine's gain, Master Aylwin.'

'It's all long past,' Aylwin replied, looking him steadily in the eyes. The knight returned the direct look, and nodded.

'I'm sometimes moved to – to establish my position in the world,' Aylwin went on, explaining but not excusing. 'Not to stir up old enmities, but to let it be known that I am what I am.'

Sir Richard nodded again, understanding exactly what he meant, and strode to the end of the high table, hand extended. Aylwin stood up, held out his own hand, and they exchanged a firm clasp, each smiling with understanding and approval at the other.

'It's time the English were one nation again,' Sir Richard said. 'A century or more ago you absorbed the Danes, and soon your latest invaders will be English too. By the Splendour of God, I called myself Englishman in Rome, when His Holiness asked my nation, and I thought nothing of it. My father gave up his lands in Normandy when the Conqueror died.'

He returned to his place and his discipline of silence, but the discussion continued a little longer among those who were free to talk, but without any feeling of embarrassment, for Aylwin seemed quite at ease, and answered the questions put to him with good humour.

'Where did your family hold lands?' asked Lady Mabilia, wondering if she might know who had been granted them by the Conqueror.

'We *owned* estates near Winchester and in Essex,' Aylwin replied, with a slight stress on the verb, for no-one had owned lands in England since the Conquest save the king. 'My great-grandfather was with the King much of his time, and it was convenient for him to own lands near the main royal palaces.'

'Own?' queried Sir Fulk. 'You mean, he held them as tenant-in-chief?'

'No. He was *given* them by the King. We had no vassalage and tenure by service. The land was ours, to hold and inherit by right, or to buy or sell as we chose.'

'And your great-grandfather supported Earl Harold, then?' Elys asked.

'Of course. He was our rightful king, elected by the Witanagemot and crowned with the consent of the three estates.'

'But I thought – didn't King Edward promise the crown to Duke William?'

'If he did, he had no right to do so. The crown of England passed by election, not by blood or inheritance. Stephen of Blois might have established his own right to be king by

45

the same method, and thereby won the support of the native English – or so might the Empress, for that matter!'

'Are you suggesting . . .' Sir Fulk began, looking puzzled, but Aylwin cut in smoothly, 'I suggest nothing. I take no interest in great affairs, being a mere Englishman! No-one listens to us, so we ignore them, as much as we're able, and get on with the business of living. It's one of the advantages of being a conquered people, you know – you're not required to think, suggest, advise or take responsibility!'

Sir Fulk laughed heartily at the joke, but Elys considered it seriously, frowning a little, and decided that it was not a joke at all, but a bitter, heartfelt observation, and she regarded Aylwin with more respect thereafter.

CHAPTER THREE

'Given that the Serpent tempted the Woman, and the Woman then tempted the Man,' said Master Aylwin slowly and distinctly, 'who was, then, the most to blame?'

They were riding through the Vale of Aosta, deeper and deeper into the mountains, and Sir Fulk, who found riding for hour after hour tedious, had proposed that they should each in turn choose a subject for disputation. By 'each' he had, of course, meant Sir Richard, Aylwin and himself, assuming that all the other members of the party lacked the wit and ability to dispute anything in the formal manner of the Schoolmen.

Despite the young knight's assumption, Lady Mabilia had already joined with effective vigour in the discussion of Sir Richard's chosen subject, which had been the thorny old problem of whether or not a knight was right to take another's life in defence of his overlord. The debate on that had been, of course, entirely academic, as neither of the knights had the slightest doubt that one's feudal duty to one's lord justified any amount of killing. It was, in fact, even more academic for Sir Richard, who, as a Templar, was forbidden to engage in any fighting save for the defence of pilgrims and the Holy Places.

Elys, who had listened with interest, noting the holes in the arguments put forward but prudently keeping her mouth shut, thought that Sir Fulk and Master Aylwin had sharp, well-ordered minds. They had both quoted the opinions of great men in their arguments, and she suspected that both could and did read, or else had frequently joined in such disputations in the past in good, intelligent company.

'The Serpent, which originated the temptation, I would say,' replied Sir Fulk, concentrating and mulling over his words before he uttered them. 'Had he not done so, neither of the others would have been tempted.'

'You could say,' replied Aylwin, gazing up at the wall of

47

mountains which rose ever higher on either side of the valley, and apparently paying little attention to what he was saying, 'that, had there been no ban on eating the fruit, there had been no ground for temptation, which would be to lay the blame on God, which would be heresy.'

Sir Richard took this argument up with a strong counterblast, which caused Aylwin's lips to twitch, as Elys guessed that he had intended this to happen. He had his notebook in his hand as usual – or, rather, one of his notebooks, for the baggage he had loaded into the wagon had consisted of a small bundle of clothes and three sacks of such notebooks – and he quickly sketched a ploughman at work in the fertile valley, complete with plough and oxen, all in a few swift, sure lines. He seemed to let his horse go its own gait, and paid more attention to what was happening around him than to where he was going.

'And the Serpent being the Devil himself, who cannot help but be evil, I say the Woman was to blame, for she not only succumbed to the Tempter herself, but then tempted another – to wit, the Man – to his downfall!' Sir Richard concluded.

'And what says the Lady Elys?' asked Aylwin suddenly, turning to look at the ladies, who were riding between the two knights.

There was a moment's silence, Sir Richard being rendered speechless by the idea of his niece having an opinion at all, let alone one worth hearing, and Sir Fulk, who was a trifle less bigoted, looking first surprised, and then mildly interested, as if his horse had been invited to speak.

'I think,' Elys said, collecting her startled wits, 'that the Man was most to blame.'

'What nonsense! How could that be?' cried Sir Richard scornfully.

Elys lowered her chin a little and scowled, determined not to be browbeaten out of her opinion. 'Because he was supposed to be the master, the stronger of the two,' she went on. 'The Woman, who was weaker and his inferior, needed the wiles of the Devil himself to persuade her to do wrong, but the Man was led into sin by the weak Woman, where he should have been able to stand against her tempting, and show her that she had done wrong. Instead of that, he ate the fruit and then blamed her for his own weakness!'

'Well argued!' cried Aylwin, his face alight with merriment. 'I own Lady Elys the victor!'

'But the Woman did evil first,' Sir Richard persisted doggedly.

'Because she was tempted first!' retorted Elys. 'Knowing her to be the weaker, the Serpent would expect to succeed with her. I doubt if even he expected that she would be able to seduce the strong Man so easily.'

Sir Richard frowned and rode in silence, apparently considering the matter. There was a lengthy silence, and then Sir Fulk said tentatively, 'Shall I propose a subject now?'

'Aosta is a bare half-mile ahead,' replied Sir Richard. 'I trust we'll find a suitable lodging there. In which direction lies the road from there to the great pass?'

'Over there,' Sir Fulk pointed to the right of the walled town ahead of them. 'You can see it, following that torrent that pours down the mountainside. It climbs up to the saddle there, where you can just see a tiny village, and then runs on the far side of that peak until it turns north to go over the head of the pass.'

'That peak?' Elys gazed, awe-struck, straight ahead to where a great snow-covered ridge towered halfway to Heaven.

Aylwin followed the direction of her eyes, and said reassuringly, 'We go round the high range. Fulk means the little mountain on the right, just above Aosta. We'll not take you over the high Alps in the snow. Only the chamois go there.'

'What are chamois?' she asked.

'Wild goats. I expect you'll see some when we pass amid the mountains. Ah, look at the great arch! Over a thousand years old, and as solid as a rock. Why can we not build to last as well as the Romans could?'

He was admiring the triumphal arch which spanned the road on the far side of the stone bridge they were crossing, and hardly had they passed through it than he was exclaiming again about the massive triple gateway in the town wall.

They found lodging in the guesthouse of the Priory of St Orso, which, they discovered, had been founded by

49

Archbishop Anselm, and set out early the next morning on the difficult and dangerous mountain crossing. The monks of St Orso assured them that there was no danger of robbers since Bernard of Montjoux, a former canon of Aosta cathedral, had cleared them all away eighty years since, and that they would find safe and clean lodging and a guide (if they needed one) at St Rhémy village at the halfway stage to the top of the pass.

'And at the top? Is the hospice still there?' asked Sir Fulk.

'Indeed, the hospice of St Nicholas is newly repaired and ready to receive you,' they were assured, 'and you will find a good inn at Martigny on the far side. The road is plain – you'll not mistake it.'

'Did you notice,' Elys asked as the track up the steep mountainside narrowed and forced them to go in single file, 'that everyone in Aosta spoke French?'

Aylwin had fallen in behind her, and he answered, although she had spoken to Sir Fulk, who was in front of her. 'They consider themselves to be more French than Italian,' he said, 'although it makes little difference to me – it's just as foreign a tongue as Italian.'

There was that little tinge of bitterness in his tone, and Elys, letting her palfrey pick his own way up the rough track, wondered how it must feel to a man whose great-grandfather had been an important landholder, a member of the King's Council, to be reduced to the status of a mere artisan – and yet, she reflected, could he really be dismissed as a mere anything? He was an educated man, skilled in argument, able to read and write, a remarkably talented artist, not just a cutter of stones . . .

She was shaken out of her thoughts by her horse suddenly stumbling and almost coming down as loose stones turned under his hooves. For a moment which seemed an eternity, she clung to the animal's mane and looked down at the sheer drop to her right, down a rough cliff to the rock-strewn torrent of angry white water far enough below to warn her that she would have little chance of surviving such a fall without terrible injuries. Then, suddenly, Fulk checked and backed his horse, turning in his saddle to catch her bridle close to the bit and steady her mount, while

Aylwin came up from behind and pushed his own horse between hers and the edge until it could regain its balance.

'Thank you,' she gasped.

'Sit easy and let the horse find his own way,' Sir Fulk advised over his shoulder, unaware that she had been doing so.

'I could wish you were properly mounted,' Aylwin said, sounding anxious. 'That side-saddle's unbalanced, and when the drop's on the other side, a stumble like that could pitch you down the cliff. Can you ride astride?'

'I expect so,' Elys replied, although she had never tried.

He said no more about the matter for the moment, but when they stopped to rest the horses, he told Sir Richard, as if speaking to an equal, that he thought the ladies' necks were being risked unnecessarily by their being expected to ride side-saddle on mountain tracks. Sir Fulk supported him, giving a graphic and frightening description of how a stumbling horse might pitch either lady down a cliff if it happened to be to the left.

Sir Richard, naturally, objected that it would not be decent for ladies to ride astride, but his argument rapidly dwindled in force as he considered the matter and saw the sense of the suggestion. Then he said grudgingly that there was, he thought, a spare saddle in the baggage-wagon, which one of the ladies might use if she chose.

Naturally, Lady Mabilia was offered it, and, being a sensible woman, she accepted. It was put on her horse, and she managed to dispose her long, full skirts quite decently, both while mounting and when actually seated astride. Her palfrey raised no objections, as all the horses had been broken for normal riding long before they were trained to take a side-saddle.

'Lady Elys may have my saddle,' Fulk said, as if there was nothing much involved in the offer, and he had it off his horse before anyone could point out that he was condemning himself to a long and difficult ride bareback.

The changeover was made, and Elys found she was much more secure mounted astride, although her skirts would keep sliding up to reveal her legs to quite six inches above her ankles, which drew some indignant clucks from her uncle. She was very conscious that Master Aylwin, riding behind her, had an excellent view of her calves, albeit shrouded in decent cloth hose, and it was as well for her peace of mind that she did not know that half a page of his current notebook was soon devoted to drawings of the unusual draping of her skirts, and of her ankles and feet.

The rest of the crossing of the St Nicholas Pass was uneventful. They passed an uncomfortable and expensive night at St Rhémy, were made very welcome and much more comfortable by the canons at the hospice for the next night, and descended the long, narrow valley to Martigny, then on to the upper Rhône valley, without mishap and in clement weather. The ladies returned to their side-saddles as soon as it was safe to do so, which relieved the men of the party of the necessity to gaze woodenly in any direction save the forbidden ones which might give them a glimpse of (oh horror!) a female leg!

Elys had expected to be impressed by the mountains, but they were far higher and grander than she had realized, and correspondingly more frightening. The scenery seemed to her to be wild, barren and foresaken, more than beautiful, although Aylwin, who seemed to know how she felt without her saying anything, told her that she should ride among the mountains in the early summer, when the alps were thick with wild flowers, to see them at their most beautiful. The green richness of the Rhône valley was a relief to her, and by the time they reached the shores of Lac Leman, she had ceased to look up at the snow-clad wilderness at all, sparing even the Dents du Midi no more than a glance. The days seemed to merge in one long, interminable journeying, punctuated only by restless nights in inns of varying size and cleanliness, and the daily observance of Mass in little country churches, where Aylwin would occasionally touch her arm and point silently to a carving or a well-proportioned arch.

Lac Leman was so long that she thought they would never reach the far end of it, and, in fact, they never did, for Sir Richard decreed that they should take the harder road over the mountains towards Clairvaux, which he was certain they should visit.

'What great saint's relics lie there?' asked Lady Mabilia eagerly.

'No relics, but a living saint,' replied her brother. 'The great Abbot Bernard. If he will pray for Matthew, the lad's recovery is assured. Pray God he will grant me an audience, for he has a great love for our Order, and wrote movingly in its support in the early days of our foundation.'

'Clairvaux!' exclaimed Aylwin in a disgusted tone. 'Abbot Bernard may be all you say he is, but his abbey's an abomination to stone-masons. He'll allow no carvings, no ornaments. Everything must be of the plainest . . . I've no wish to go near the place!'

'It's on our way to Paris . . .' Sir Fulk put in placatingly.

'It is not!' retorted Aylwin. 'I'm surprised you want to go there, for it was his opposition that stopped our master from becoming Archbishop of Canterbury. Go there if you must, but don't expect me to come with you. I'll press on to Paris, and wait for you there.'

Despite Sir Fulk's attempts to persuade him to change his mind, he stood firm, and when they turned down the side-road to Clairvaux, he went on alone on the more direct route towards Paris, promising to wait there for them. Sir Fulk had felt himself obliged to go with him, but Aylwin said, quite gently, that he had no wish to deprive him of the pleasure of seeing Abbot Bernard or of the company of his friends, his eyes flickering expressively towards Elys at the last phrase, and Sir Fulk gave in gracefully and with some relief.

Elys was sorry to see the mason go. He was the only one of her companions who ever sought her opinion on any serious matter, and listened courteously to what she had to say, and she had learned a great deal from him about man-made things of beauty by listening and looking when he spoke about the buildings they had entered together. Sir Fulk also missed him, for they had carried on their formal disputations to while away the long hours on the road, covering a wide variety of subjects with enjoyment and a complete lack of ill-temper.

Sir Richard had not joined in the discussions since the unfortunate occasion near Aosta, and, military topics of conversation having run out, he seldom bothered to talk to the young knight at all, but passed his time in prayer and meditation, or talking with his sister or the two sergeants. Sir Fulk began to give his attention to Elys, becoming more at ease with her and less inclined to talk to her as if she were a mentally deficient child.

'I don't suppose you've heard of Father Bernard before,' he began one conversation as they neared Clairvaux.

'Indeed I have,' she retorted a trifle sharply, 'I know a great deal about him.'

'Oh.' Sir Fulk looked taken aback. 'You know, then, that you'll not be permitted near enough to him for speech?'

'I know he disapproves of women, and thinks that no man or woman should marry.'

Sir Fulk gave her one of his languishing looks and sighed, 'The cruelty of it – to deny a man the comfort and happiness of wedding the woman of his heart. To condemn poor lovers to dwell forever apart. I hope – oh, most earnestly I hope – that you don't agree with him?'

Elys eyed him doubtfully, for she could not make up her mind if it would be wise to believe that any of his flirtatious conversation had any serious intent. However, it was undeniably pleasant and exciting, and she most certainly did not wish to discourage so eligible a young man if there was any possibility that he might mean what his speech and manner implied, so she replied judicially, 'I believe that some people are called to live celibate, but not all. My sister's a nun, but I feel no call to join her in the cloister. I'd rather be a good wife than a bad nun.'

Even as she spoke, she felt a flicker of hope deep within her, for Sir Fulk's face broke into what she could only interpret as a relieved smile as he replied, 'Oh, indeed – it would be wicked to waste such a lovely face and form in the cold cells of a nunnery. I'm sure even Abbot Bernard wouldn't find it easy to condemn you to celibacy.'

Elys shivered at the thought, and said grimly, 'I'm glad he hasn't that power over me, for I'm sure he'd use it. When I think of the way he destroyed Master Abelard . . .' Her voice filled with poignant sorrow at this last sentence, for she had heard of the tragedy of Abelard's great scholarship, brought low and condemned to monastic silence by Bernard of Clairvaux's bitter opposition, and of the equally tragic story of his love for his one-time pupil, whose name, Heloise, sounded so much like her own name. She did not know *all* the details of the story, so she was inclined to ascribe all the blame to Bernard.

'Abelard was a heretic,' Sir Fulk said self-righteously.

'Was he?' Elys asked coldly, and received no reply, save an evasive, 'You're like Aylwin – he admires Abelard beyond reason,' for Sir Fulk was out of his depth.

After a few minutes, he essayed a different subject. 'Your uncle admires the Abbot, I gather.'

'Oh, only because he wrote a letter to the Pope, recommending the Templars, and he drew up their Rule. Anyone who supports the Templars is a candidate for canonisation, in Uncle Richard's estimation.'

Despite her words, Elys hoped she might have a chance to see Abbot Bernard, and perhaps even hear him preach, for she had heard so much about him from various people that she knew him to be a very great man. She was disappointed, however. Bernard of Clairvaux's labours in the service of God had ruined his physical health, and he lived a quiet, retired life in a hut in the precinct of his abbey, emerging only to go on his travels, receive important guests, and attend Mass. All Elys saw of him was a distant figure, slight and frail, among the other white-robed monks in the choir of the Abbey church, so far from where she stood in the nave that she only knew which was he because Sir Richard had kindly murmured to her that the thin man following the processional cross was the Abbot.

Sir Richard was of sufficient importance, being the second in the hierarchy of the English Templars, to merit a brief audience, and he returned from it with the good news that Bernard had prayed with him for Matthew for a full quarter-hour, but had been suffering from too bad a migraine for more than a few words of conversation.

After Clairvaux, there were, to Elys's great relief, no more mountains, only the interminable dusty roads of Burgundy, and, eventually, of the Ile de France. Sir Fulk's attentions gradually became less patronising as he came to understand that she was not so very much his inferior in intellect or knowledge. Her sharp eyes often observed something which he had missed, and when she pointed out an unusual building, a fine carving in one of the myriad churches which they entered, or a different type of plough, he began to respond with genuine interest and appreciation, instead of the condescending air of one humouring a child. By the time they reached Paris, he had learned to respect Elys for her intelligence, as well as admire her for her grace and beauty, and she had grown to like him as a friend, as well as thinking him handsome and brave, and she occasionally allowed herself the luxury of wondering about the possibility of marrying him.

They stayed for several days in Paris, the men at the Templar preceptory and the ladies at the guesthouse of a nearby nunnery. This was against Elys's will, for she dreaded the very thought of a convent, and felt a cold touch of fear in her heart and a suffocating claustrophobia on entering the enclosure, however temporarily.

To make matters worse, Lady Mabilia insisted that they must rest in preparation for the last part of their long journey home, so poor Elys was allowed to go out only once, briefly, to accompany her mother to the cathedral to pray for Matthew.

The nunnery in which they were lodged was on the right bank of the river, and they had to cross by boat to the city itself, which was crammed within the confines of a not over-large island surrounded by a stone wall. The streets within the wall were very narrow and dark, for the houses were tall, to make the most of the limited space. No account was taken by the citizens of the need for cleanliness in such a crowded place, so the usual city stench was here almost overpowering. The royal palace occupied the middle of the island, but it was so hemmed in that it was impossible to form any idea of its size, and it certainly showed no outward signs of magnificence.

The cathedral also was squeezed on all sides but one by narrow, dilapidated houses, and was so small that it hardly rose above them. The one open side was at the west end, where a small *parvis* lent a little much-needed dignity to the entrance, but even this was ankle-deep in decaying rubbish, and a stout pig was fast asleep against the side of the main doorway.

Inside, the building was so dark and dank that it seemed more like a large cellar than a church, but Elys supposed that, once the lamps were lit for a service, it would appear more impressive. She had no opportunity to find out, as they stayed only half an hour.

'Could we not go to the market?' she asked her mother as they left.

'To what purpose? We bought all we need in Italy. The fabrics here will be the same as we've already seen in Italy, and much more expensive, having been brought so much further. Besides, I don't know where the market-place is, and the city has a bad reputation.'

On the way back to the convent, the boatman pointed out the bridge which connected the city to the left bank, where houses had spilled out to make a *faubourg* where the students lodged and the Schoolmen held their classes and disputations, but that was all Elys managed to see of the famous centre of learning. She had a better view of the Templars' great fortress, for that was set back behind the marshes on the right bank, and then they returned to the convent, and she was shut up again until it was time to leave Paris.

There was, at first, no sign of Aylwin, but Sir Fulk, following his nose and his knowledge of his friend, soon found him working at St Denis. He seemed quite pleased to see his comrade, and enquired, 'Did you see the noble Bernard, then?'

'No,' Sir Fulk replied with a shrug. 'He had a migraine.'

'Poor soul,' said Aylwin with so little expression that it was difficult to tell whether he meant it or not. 'Come and see what I've been making.'

It was an elaborately carved capital, depicting a devil happily chewing the head off a monk. There was no indication that the monk belonged to any particular order, but Aylwin, showing his work to Fulk, commented, 'That should cure his migraine!' which made the knight laugh, albeit in a guilty fashion.

Elys was pleased to see Aylwin again, but confined her greeting to a cool 'How do you, Master Aylwin?' and a gracious smile, to which he responded with a courtly bow and a polite 'Well, I thank you, and how does your ladyship?'

They left Paris for Calais the next morning, Sir Richard having found the French Templars a deal too worldly for his liking, and Lady Mabilia, who had been so intrepid and uncomplaining on the long overland journey, began to express doubts about the sea-crossing ahead.

'This is the last time I shall venture overseas,' she announced. 'I grow too old for the perils of sea-voyaging. If Matthew be not cured by this pilgrimage, we must go again to all the English shrines, but no more overseas!'

'Mother, you don't doubt he'll be cured, do you?' Elys asked, her voice and face troubled, for Lady Mabilia had seemed so confident that the visit to Rome would bring about the miracle.

'No – no! Of course not!' she replied a little too hastily, and began a sharp-voiced conversation with her brother, drawing ahead of Elys to ride beside him.

'She's tired with the long journeying,' Aylwin said quietly. 'Weariness depresses the spirits, and makes hope seem vain. Don't be troubled.'

Elys twisted in her saddle to look at him in surprise, for he was riding on her right. 'You think that's all it is? I wonder if perhaps she's losing hope. We've made so many pilgrimages, and come home sure that we'd find Matthew healed, only to be disappointed. I'm afraid poor Mother is losing her faith after so many failures. Do you really think that it's just that she's tired?'

'That and the little runnel twixt Calais and Dover!' he replied.

'Pray God it be not rough!' Elys exclaimed.

But it was. The weather seemed fair and calm enough when they reached Calais and embarked in a ship which Sir Richard had personally inspected for seaworthiness and suitability for conveying the precious destriers, but he seemed little concerned about the human passengers. There was good stabling for the horses in the hold, with ropes to hold them steady if the sea turned rough, but the ladies were allocated a tiny cabin, with only a rough canvas curtain across the doorway for privacy, and three straw palliasses on shelving along the ship's side for beds. It was damp, stuffy and uncomfortable, and smelt abominably of horses and worse things.

Lady Mabilia and Maud took to their beds at once, and steeled themselves to endure. Elys, thinking they knew better than she did, went against her own instinct to stay on deck, in the fresh air, and reluctantly joined them. By the time the ship sailed, she felt decidedly queasy, and Lady Mabilia had already been sick twice. Things did not improve when they left harbour, for the sea was choppy, with the wind blowing across the tide. After a bare half-hour, Lady Mabilia and Maud were moaning and praying by turns, and Elys felt so ill that she made no protest when the curtain was thrust aside and Aylwin lurched into the cabin.

'Your pardon, ladies,' he said, 'but Sir Richard sent me to enquire if you need anything.' The only reply was a hollow groan from Lady Mabilia, and, after a momentary hesitation, he went on: 'I assure you that you'd feel much better on deck, in the fresh air. Can I not persuade you . . .'

'Go away, young man!' Lady Mabilia interrupted tersely. 'Leave us to die in peace!'

Aylwin stared at her for a few seconds, then at Maud, who was moaning, shrugged, and turned his attention to Elys, who was sitting on a large chest which was fastened down to the deck, holding on to it with both hands and willing herself not to vomit, at least not until this importunate fellow had gone.

'You must be mad!' he informed Elys sharply. 'Come along, out of this!' and he seized her, hoisting her to lie over his shoulder as if she were a loosely rolled bolt of cloth, and made his way out, along the narrow way between the horses' stalls, timing his steps more or less to the roll and pitch of the vessel, but lurching about fairly frequently, as the motion was irregular. He reached the companion ladder safely, mounted it, and emerged on the open deck.

The stiff breeze flung a capful of spray into Elys's face, making her gasp, and she clapped both hands over her mouth in desperation, but Aylwin was ready for her, and

59

had her against the leeward bulwark in a trice, where she could hang over the side in safety, and he held her firmly until the paroxysm had passed.

'Better?' he asked.

She nodded weakly, and he pulled her down to sit on the deck, sheltering her with his own body and wrapping his cloak round her.

'You should have stayed on deck. It's fatal to go below, unless you've a particularly strong stomach!' he said. 'Are you cold?' She nodded miserably, so he put a brotherly arm about her shoulders and drew her close to him, treating her like the child he probably thought she was.

After a while, she began to feel less cold and wretched, and looked about her. They were sitting on the deck, under the lee of the bulwark, in the afterpart of the ship, close against the shelter of the aftercastle. There were sailors busy about the deck, coiling ropes or hauling on them as their master commanded, but no sign of any of their party.

'Where is my uncle?' she asked.

'With the horses. So is Fulk, and the squires and the sergeants. The men-at-arms are in the forecastle, playing nine men's morris – but not gambling, of course,' he said, ironically.

Elys was sufficiently recovered to give him a suspicious glance, for he sounded sarcastic, but his face was blandly innocent. She suddenly became aware that she was sitting far too close to him, within the circle of his arm, and she drew away slightly. His arm dropped from her shoulders quite naturally, and he, too, moved away a little.

'Do you feel better?' he asked, and when she said cautiously that she did, he produced a clean bundle of cloth from his wallet, and unwrapped two manchets of bread from it. 'Nibble this,' he said, giving her one, and set to work himself on the other.

Elys began, quite literally, to nibble, pausing after every few crumbs to see what her stomach would say about them. She felt better as soon as she had eaten a little, and finished the manchet almost as soon as Aylwin swallowed the last of his.

With a favourable wind, the journey was soon over, and

Elys, by staying on deck in the fresh air, wrapped in a warm cloak, even managed to enjoy it, although she wished that there might have been another manchet of bread or two, for she was now very hungry.

Night had fallen by the time they entered Dover harbour and tied up alongside the quay. The great deck-hatch was removed, and the horses led out up a ramp, all the men being engaged for a time in walking them up and down on the quay until the four legs of each beast returned to their owner's control. Only when he was satisfied that all were well did Sir Richard look about for the womenfolk.

Elys was already ashore, and had even taken a turn at walking her own horse, but it required four strong men and two covered litters to bring the older ladies out of the ship, Lady Mabilia feebly demanding a good inn, hot water and a firm, unmoving bed.

Sir Richard accepted with grim resignation that they would not be leaving Dover before the next day, despite his haste to return to London and discover the situation in the country. He gave rather curt orders to that effect, and then his eye lighted on his niece, and he said, 'What's this, Elys? You don't appear to be ill!'

'I'm quite well, thank you,' she replied brightly. 'Will there be supper soon? I'm so hungry.'

There was, indeed, supper quite soon, and Sir Richard watched his niece make short work of her portion with a bemused expression on his face.

'Extraordinary,' he murmured. 'I'd assumed that all females were seasick. The world is full of surprises.'

'It is indeed,' agreed Sir Fulk. 'I'm happy to see that Lady Elys hasn't suffered from the elements. It would distress me very much if she were to be indisposed.'

Sir Richard gave him a hard look, and said curtly, 'You'd do well not to concern yourself about her, sir. As soon as her brother is recovered, she and her mother will join my other niece in the nunnery at Wix.'

'I will not enter a nunnery,' Elys said in a quiet, determined voice. 'I've told you before, my lord Uncle, that I will not be a nun, and you can't force me to take the veil!' She made her protest deliberately, knowing that the more

61

witnesses she had to her refusal the better if it came to a matter of her family trying to insist on her entering the nunnery. She cast a hasty glance at Sir Fulk as she spoke, and was mortified to see that he looked like a man who had just received unwelcome news, for he was frowning down at his platter. She bit her lip in mortification, and felt the blood rise to her cheeks.

'Nobody will force you,' Sir Richard replied calmly. 'Your dowry is already paid to the nuns, so you'll have no choice in the matter! No man will wed you without a dowry, and I can do nothing for you, so how can you live outside the cloister?'

'I'll keep house for Matthew,' she replied, chin up and voice unfaltering, although she knew that he was quite right. Again her eyes flicked to Sir Fulk, and found that he was staring in her direction, but past rather than at her, biting the end of his index finger and looking very thoughtful. A lead weight suddenly seemed to materialize in her stomach, and she felt very much inclined to lose her temper or to dissolve into tears. Having been trained all her life to control herself, she did neither, but merely tightened her lips and hoped that her colour would be ascribed to anger rather than shame at Sir Fulk's obvious reaction to the news that she had no dowry to offer a husband.

'Matthew will enter the Order and go to the Holy Land,' Sir Richard replied. 'Some more beef, Sir Fulk? Come, squire! You neglect your duty!'

The two squires, not being sure which of them he was addressing, each hastened to serve his own knight, and while they did so, Elys had abandoned the remains of her supper and retired to the room where Lady Mabilia and the poor gentlewoman were sleeping off the after-effects of their voyage.

Afraid to waken them, she tried very hard to stifle her angry tears, for she had begun, very tentatively, to hope that Sir Fulk might be thinking of marrying her, but her uncle had effectively put paid to any chance in that direction. Sir Fulk had become more and more attentive and friendly as they had crossed France, and the words of concern which had brought that cruel speech from her uncle would surely

62

not have been uttered unless he had formed an intention to . . . After all, an experienced man of his rank would never express a personal concern about a lady in the presence of her guardian unless he had the most honourable intentions!

It did not, of course, occur to her to wonder if she might be in love with Sir Fulk. Love was for peasants, if for anyone at all! It would be enough for her that he was young, good-looking, pleasant company and of good birth and breeding. No man or woman looked for more than that in a marriage-partner, and most settled for much less, but no man who had so much to offer would ever consider marrying a girl without a dowry.

These bitter thoughts occupied her as she undressed swiftly in the cold room and slipped into her narrow bed. It had clean sheets, a featherbed, and plenty of blankets, but she hardly noticed the luxury. She felt cold and desolate, and lay in a huddled ball, shivering and praying desperately to every saint she could think of for help to avoid the narrow, enclosed world of the nunnery. She had little hope that any would listen, for all the saints she could think of had been celibate, and would have no sympathy for a girl praying to be the bride of a human man, and not a bride of Christ.

She fell asleep at last, and woke in the morning feeling wretched and hopeless, knowing that her prayers had fallen on indifferent ears. Oddly enough, at breakfast, after Mass, when she had hardly forced a mouthful of bread down her throat, which ached with unshed tears, a word of hope suddenly sounded in her ear. It was not uttered in celestial tones, but in the soft Wessex burr of Aylwin, who said, very quietly, 'A good broideress can always find work and support herself.'

She gave him a startled look, and glanced round quickly to see who else might have heard, but the others were all standing about the table, making a hasty breakfast of bread and ale before setting out towards Canterbury and their next night's lodging. Sir Richard, in particular, was enquiring, in the tones of one expecting a favourable reply, of his sister whether she was intending to continue in a litter.

Lady Mabilia, who looked old and grey this morning,

63

replied grimly that she would ride. Nobody asked Maud, who looked even worse than her mistress, and she was too timid to protest at having to ride on the baggage-wagon on the rough roads.

'But how?' Elys breathed, turning back to Aylwin.

'Keep some samples of your best work, of all kinds, and go to any great church, be it minster or cathedral; show them to the sacristan, and ask for work,' he replied, but had no time to say more, for Sir Fulk was calling to him that the man in charge of the baggage wanted to know if he had anything more to go in the cart, and he had to go and check his belongings to make sure nothing had been overlooked.

Elys soon noticed, as they plodded along the old Roman road, that Sir Fulk was markedly less attentive to her. He did not ignore her, nor was he at all lacking in courtesy, but he no longer put himself to the trouble of thinking of topics of conversation which might interest her. She had expected it, and was determined not to let it upset her, so she thought instead about Aylwin's suggestion, and began to plan which forms of embroidery would show her skill the best, managing to keep her spirits up fairly well.

Lady Mabilia had recovered by the time they reached Canterbury, and did not neglect to visit the Cathedral to pray once more to St Wilfrid and the other saints whose relics were honoured there. Elys accompanied her, but went her own way in the church, and prayed by the tomb of Archbishop Anselm. He was not canonised, but he had been a good man in life, and she begged him to intercede for Matthew, that their long journey, passing through his birthplace, might not have been in vain.

Another day on the road brought them to Rochester. Sir Richard said nothing about any possible danger on the road as they drew nearer to London, but Elys noted that their escort rode armed and surrounded them on all sides, and both the Templar and Sir Fulk wore their ringmail hauberks and helms, and rode their destriers after they left Canterbury.

'Who controls London now?' she asked before supper that night.

'The sheriff and the justiciar, of course,' replied Sir Richard, frowning. 'If you mean who controls England – the answer is still in doubt. Stephen has London and the East, the Empress and Robert of Gloucester the West Country.'

'Thank you,' Elys said meekly, which drew a suspicious glare from her uncle.

They reached London the following afternoon in the early dusk of a miserable sleety day, just two days before Christmas, clattering over the dilapidated wooden bridge past a guard of watchful citizens, who eyed the Templar's white cloak and his men's black ones with neither hostility nor enthusiasm, as befitted the Temple's neutrality in the civil war.

'It's about time this bridge was rebuilt in stone,' Aylwin said with unwonted irritability. 'It's a disgrace to have nothing better than this tumbledown affair in England's second city. It's never been fit for use since the Danes tried to tow it away.'

'Who has time to care about a bridge, with the country torn by civil war?' replied Sir Fulk sourly, and no one else bothered to answer at all.

CHAPTER FOUR

Despite the many fine cities she had seen on her travels, Elys still thought London the finest of all, and her preference was not entirely based on chauvinism, for it was truly a fine and fair city, prosperous despite the troubles of the country of which it was now considered by most people to be the capital.

A severe fire had destroyed most of it in the early days of Stephen's seizure of the throne – an omen, many people claimed. It had swept away most of the thatched wooden houses, built too close together and grown insanitary and dangerous with age, and the commonalty, led by the sheriff, had resolved to build a better city on the ruins. The well-to-do had stone houses, and a regulation requiring party walls to be of stone had, in the main, been well enforced, so that those who could not afford stone had built detached wooden houses, lessening the risk of fire spreading as rapidly as it had in the past. All but the poorest houses had gardens where vegetables and fruit might be grown, and few of the narrow streets were without at least a glimpse of trees between the houses. The streets were paved, and kept clean by gutters of running water, as well as by the usual kites and ravens which roosted amid the thatch and tile, or in the towers of the many churches.

It was these last which Elys thought made the city look like a fairytale place from a distance, and lent beauty and interest from within the walls, for at every street corner, in at least one direction, a tower could be seen piercing the sky.

'How many churches are there in London?' she wondered aloud as the party passed St Magnus and ascended Fish Street Hill.

'One hundred and twenty-six,' replied Aylwin promptly. 'Including St Paul's, of course, although that's in a poor state at present.'

He sounded so unexpectedly dismissive of the cathedral, which Elys had thought to be the beginnings of one of the largest in Europe, that she asked, 'What's wrong with the cathedral? I thought it looked magnificent when we were last in London, despite the damage.'

'Bishop Maurice should have let the old one stand,' Aylwin replied. 'It was well built, and big enough, but he would have a far larger and grander house for his throne. A twelve-bay nave . . . ! Even London can't afford so great a quantity of stone, so the work's scamped. It would be better to build six bays set on solid stone pillars, instead of twelve on pillars built hollow of small, thin stones and filled with rubble! They'll not bear the weight. When the church caught fire in '36, half of them cracked and spilled their filling.'

'Is that not the usual method of building pillars?' enquired Sir Richard, who had seen the erection of several large stone buildings, here and in the Holy Land, during his Templar service.

'Yes, and it's good enough for small buildings of inconsiderable height, but not for a great cathedral with stone vaults,' Aylwin replied. 'They should at least have mixed the infill with mortar. They'll collapse in a hundred years or so, and our descendants'll scorn our poor workmanship, instead of blaming the ambition or meanness of the founders.'

He spoke with feeling, his voice deeper and his Wessex accent more pronounced, in contrast to his usual light, quick manner of speech in only slightly accented French, and Elys looked at him curiously, a little puzzled. He spoke as if it mattered very much to him what future generations might think of the work done by his fellow-masons. He must really care about fashioning buildings and carvings from stone, although, without really thinking about the matter, she had always assumed that a working-man regarded his work as nothing more than a means of earning a livelihood.

'Would you like your great-grandchildren to scorn your needlework as poor work done with inferior materials?' he demanded, catching her eye.

She thought fleetingly of the long hours spent with her

needle, and the many little sacrifices she had to make to afford real gold spangles, silk thread and fine linen or damask for her altar frontals. 'No, I would not,' she said, with as much feeling as he had shown in talking of the future collapse of great churches.

They picked their way along West Cheap, through the crowded market which, despite the lateness of the hour, was still busy, with so little time left before the great feast of Christmas. Stalls had been set up even in the main thoroughfare, which was normally kept clear, and careful housewives were buying their roots, worts and meat now, when the stallholders had dropped their prices to be rid of their perishable goods before trading ceased for the day. Foodstuffs normally sold only in the streets allocated to them had spilled out into the main market, and there was even a woman milking a cow on one corner, squirting the warm liquid straight into the pitchers or wooden buckets of her customers as they waited their turn. Flaring torches and horn lanterns lit the lively scene, casting strange shadows and illuminating the faces, anxious, excited, joyful or wretched, of buyers and sellers alike. The noise was tremendous, for vendors were shouting, geese cackled, the cow lowed as if to advertise her own produce, and itinerant musicians sang or piped or plucked with more enthusiasm than art, while the myriad London dogs, who were almost as numerous as the people, all seemed to be barking at once.

With difficulty, Sir Richard's party picked its way through to the quieter thoroughfare beyond West Cheap, then left the City by the new gate. They went on down the hill, over the bridge, and up again to Holborn Bars, where the Templars were to lodge in the cramped and inadequate buildings which were their quarters in England. They came to a halt before the gatehouse.

'I regret we have no room for guests,' Sir Richard informed Sir Fulk, his voice made even harsher than usual by the embarrassment of appearing inhospitable.

'Aylwin and I must go on to Westminster, to find the Bishop,' Fulk replied. 'We thank you for your company and your escort, which have made our long journey so much more easy and pleasant. We're sorry to have to bid you all farewell, but, God willing, we may all meet again at some time.'

It was a correct and courteous speech, but Elys felt that the young knight's mind had already left them, and was occupied with thoughts and plans for his own future. She exchanged the kiss of peace in farewell with him with no particular feeling, for she had schooled herself, during the journey from Dover, to accept that what plans he might have half-formed concerning her were no longer worth his consideration, now he knew she had nothing to bring him. There seemed to be a block of ice in her breast, where her heart should have been, and she felt afraid and hopeless.

Sir Fulk, brushing his lips against her cold cheek, felt a sense of relief that he had not committed himself before discovering the girl's ineligibility. She was pretty and pleasant company, but a female who received even a formal kiss with the unyielding stiffness of a statue would hardly be likely to make an entertaining bedfellow.

Lady Mabilia had hesitated slightly before lifting her face to signal that Aylwin might kiss her as he approached to make his formal farewell, but, with his usual quiet assumption of equality, he kissed her weather-beaten cheek as of right, with no sign of awareness of her condescension, and moved on to Maud, who happened to be standing next to and a little behind her mistress, setting her in quite a flutter, for Sir Fulk had overlooked her, as most men tended to do. He gave her a hearty kiss, and thanked her for darning his shirt for him on some half-forgotten occasion, and then turned to Elys.

'If you need help at any time, send me a message in the care of my lord Bishop,' he murmured. 'I'll receive it within a week or so, wherever I may be in England. Don't let them force you into a cage.' He took both her hands in his, and leaned forward to kiss her cheek, but, by some chance movement of her head, or his, his lips arrived on hers, and dwelt there for a moment, at first in a light, formal fashion, then, suddenly, more firmly.

Elys gave a little gasp, her lips parting, and he took the opportunity to kiss her properly – or improperly, she was not sure which. It made a strange tremor run through her, like the shiver of a breeze across water. Her immediate reaction was one of indignation that he should be so presumptuous, then regret that it was the English craftsman who had presumed, and not the eligible Fulk.

Before she could pull away, he had released her hands and turned away to bid farewell to Sir Richard, who gave him the formal kiss without hesitation, and they exchanged a few words about the new buildings which the Templars were beginning to erect on the site they had recently acquired, down by the river, Aylwin advising that the foundations be made adequate, as the site might be marshy. Then he and Fulk and the squire, with a few general words to the sergeants and men-at-arms, remounted and clattered off westwards, towards Westminster.

'Why should they expect the Bishop of Winchester to be at Westminster?' Elys asked absently, slipping the small object which Aylwin had left in her hand into the purse hanging from her girdle. She did not really care very much, but she felt she had to say something, or dissolve into tears, she felt so wretched and lost.

'He'll be with the King, his brother, of course,' replied her uncle curtly. 'Now I'd best see you to your lodgings, Mabilia, before curfew sounds.'

The ladies were to lodge at a nearby inn, which boasted cleanliness as its sole virtue, for it was small, the beds were lumpy, and the whole building smelled of boiled cabbage, which proved to be the main ingredient of every meal except breakfast. There the ladies were to spend Christmas, recovering, Sir Richard said, from their journeying, before setting off for Wix and, they hoped, a healed Matthew.

It was not until she was undressing for bed in a tiny cupboard of a room next to her mother's chamber, which itself was not big enough for more than Lady Mabilia and Maud, that Elys had a chance to see what Aylwin had given her. She took the little package, which was wrapped in a piece of blue silk, from her purse and put it on her pillow while she said her prayers in the dim glimmer of the rushlight, and then, wrapping her nightrail about her and shivering in the unheated room, she tunnelled under the blankets

70

and unwrapped the fabric with some excitement, for she had received few·gifts in her life.

The piece of silk was bigger than she had expected – big enough to make her a head-veil, for it was very fine. She thought as she unrolled it that she would embroider flowers – daisies, perhaps – along its edges. Then the last fold slipped away, and she forgot the silk as she gazed in wonderment at the little bird lying in her hand. It was a sparrow, only about a quarter of its natural size, carved in wood, with the grain of the wood used skilfully to show the feathers and markings typical of the bird. It was sitting, as if on its nest, and its clawed feet had been cleverly shown under its body, tucked up against its feathers, even the scales on its legs indicated by tiny cuts. She held it in her cupped hand and it seemed to look up at her, its bright black eyes, which were two tiny pieces of polished stone, gleaming in the dim light.

'Oh, but you are beautiful,' she exclaimed softly, and kissed it, almost expecting to feel feathers against her lips, it was so lifelike. 'How kind of Master Aylwin! It must have taken him a long time to make you! How clever he is.' She snuggled further down into her bed and lay there, turning the little bird to and fro to look at it until the rushlight finally guttered and went out. For a while, the bird had lightened the burden of fear and misery which weighed her down, but in the lonely darkness it seemed to her to be a toy for a child, not a gift for a woman.

On Christmas Eve, Sir Richard took supper with them – or, rather, sat with them, picking at dry bread while they ate, as he was keeping a strict fast, but did not expect mere lay-women to do so – and enquired where lady Mabilia wished to attend Mass in the morning.

'I shall be in our own church, of course,' he went on, 'where females are not admitted, but there are several parish churches nearby. You could go to the cathedral, of course.'

'Is not Christmas Day one of the days on which the King wears his crown?' asked Lady Mabilia thoughtfully.

'Yes. Why do you ask?'

'Presumably, as he's at Westminster, he'll attend Mass in St Peter's Abbey. We shall go there,' she stated firmly.

'I've never seen a king wearing his crown, and we can pray at King Edward's tomb while we're there. St Paul's has no saint of any great merit.'

Elys, who by now had an extensive knowledge of which churches contained the shrines of which saints, opened her mouth to protest at this casual dismissal of several very worthy ones, and to point out that King Edward had not yet been canonised, despite Stephen's application to the Pope, but closed it again as it dawned on her that her mother knew that, or she would not have referred to *King* Edward's *tomb*, and that the Bishop of Winchester was said to be at Westminster with the King, and no doubt would take his knights to church with him . . .

'You realize that I cannot accompany you,' Sir Richard was saying, frowning. 'Quite apart from it being my duty to attend our own church, the Temple is neutral in this contest over the succession to the English crown, and I may not, therefore, show favour to Stephen of Blois or to the Empress by attending the crown-wearing of either.'

'The Empress hasn't been crowned, so she won't be having a crown-wearing,' replied Lady Mabilia, who had little sympathy with neutrality. 'We'll hire a couple of men-servants from the inn for escort.'

'Indeed you will not!' her brother exclaimed indignantly. 'I shall send three of our lay-servants to attend you, but without any identifying badges.'

And so, early the next morning, the ladies set out on horseback in a light fall of snow, escorted by three stout men, to follow the bank of the Fleet river to the bridge below Ludgate, where they turned right along the strand of the Thames to Charing village, and thence to the walled enclosure of the royal palace and St Peter's Abbey on Thorney Island.

Crossing the bridge over the Tyburn reminded Elys a little of the approach to the other St Peter's in Rome, for, although this was only a small structure over a shallow stream, it was crowded, and progress was slow until they had passed through the gate into the enclosure and followed the broad gravelled road to the west end of the church, where they could tether their horses under the watchful eyes of the king's guards and enter between the twin towers into the minster.

'Yet another church!' Elys thought wearily, who had entered so many in the past few years, always with the hope that the saint whose earthly remains lay within might prove to be the one who would obtain healing for her brother. She had been here, before, of course, for although Kind Edward was not yet officially a saint, he had been revered throughout England and Normandy ever since his death, and many pilgrims to his shrine ascribed their cures to his intercession. As in Rome, the crowd filing into the church was made up almost equally of pilgrims and local people from London and the surrounding villages.

Lady Mabilia flung back her cloak to reveal her fine clothing, and that, combined with her confident and proud bearing, ensured that she and her companions reached places near to the nave altar and to the central aisle, where they would have as good a view as the darkness of the building would allow of the great men processing through the *pulpitum* to the monks' choir and the chancel beyond.

They had come early in order to secure these positions, and had quite a long time to wait, but Elys, at least, was content to stand quietly and look discreetly about, trying to make out the features which Aylwin had taught her to look for in the churches she had visited with him. It was several minutes before Lady Mabilia noticed that she was not praying, and drew her attention to her duty with the usual sharp elbow. Soon after that, distant chanting heralded the entry of the monks into the choir, invisible beyond the bulky, elaborately-carved *pulpitum*.

Moments later, a procession began to move up the nave from the west door, and Lady Mabilia turned her head a little to her right, just enough to be able to see the great men as they passed, and both Elys and Maud assumed that they might do the same. The servants, who were across the aisle on the men's side, turned round and gaped openly at the approaching lords.

The various barons who supported Stephen, and were not employed elsewhere, came pacing solemnly, two by two, in their finest clothing, each pair between two pages carrying candles in tall holders. As it was a very dull morning, and what little daylight there was had to filter into the building through small windows in the clerestory, Elys thought that the pages' candles were probably necessary for the barons to find their way through the church. The only other light came from the side chapels in the aisles, where all the altar candles were lit, but little of that reached as far as the centre of the nave.

After the barons came the clergy, accompanied in the same way, all robed in magnificent chasubles and copes which glimmered with gold and precious stones where the light caught their folds, and made Elys long to examine their decoration more closely. The last of the priests, the officiant for the Mass, was a tall, strikingly distinguished man with a heavy black beard, wearing a purple gown under his chasuble instead of the usual white alb, which made Elys think that he must be the Papal Legate, Sir Fulk's master, Bishop Henry of Winchester. To her disappointment, he was attended only by acolytes, not his knights.

Behind the clergy came another smaller group of barons, surrounding a mitred priest, who must be the Abbot, and another man who was tall enough to stand out among his companions, even if he had not been wearing a stiff robe of cloth of gold, and a jewelled crown which sparkled as he turned his head from side to side, smiling and nodding affably to anyone who caught his eye as he strode slowly along, sceptre in one hand and orb in the other.

Elys stared after him as he made his splendid way round the nave altar and disappeared through the arch of the *pulpitum*, and wished that she could have seen more of his face than his profile as he passed her. Perhaps she would see him full-face when he returned after the Mass. She thought to herself that her mother, despite her usual unruffled calm, must have anticipated a feeling of excitement at actually seeing the King in state, wearing the crown. She leaned forward to look at Lady Mabilia's face, but her expression was as detached as ever, and she looked as if she had never felt the bubbling excitement which had welled up in her daughter at the magnificent display.

For another long interval, there was nothing to see, and

only the distant chanting to be heard as Mass was celebrated at the high altar beyond the monks' choir. Elys followed the service with half her mind, but allowed her eyes and some of her thoughts to wander as she looked at what little was visible to her of the church and the congregation. The church was long, she knew, and had a stone vault which was quite high compared with most others she had seen. The pillars were thick and heavy, the arches carved with elaborate patterns, and the vertical surfaces, wherever the light caught them, were covered with painted figures, presumably of saints and biblical figures, which wavered and seemed alive in the flickering candlelight.

A sharp nudge told her that she had been careless in looking about her too freely, so she abandoned her intention of trying to see some of the people's faces and kept her gaze strictly before her, where her eyes fell on the nave altar, which was well-lit by the candles massed on either side. She peered at its white and gold frontal and noted that the embroidery on it looked well-drawn and finely worked, but she thought, with all proper allowances for modesty, that she could do as well, and felt a lifting of her spirits. Perhaps, if her family disowned her for refusing to go into Wix nunnery, she might get employment in one of the broidery workshops in the city and support herself with her needle . . .

At that point, the closing chant of the service drew to an end, and the procession began to emerge from the *pulpitum* arch and move back down the nave in the same order as it had come. Elys watched for the Bishop, and studied his face as he came, his hand moving from side to side as he blessed the people he was passing. He had a piercing gaze which seemed to miss nothing, a firm, thin-lipped mouth within the frame of his beard, and he looked very alert and capable.

When the King appeared, she compared the two faces in her mind, and saw a clear resemblance, but Stephen's face lacked the alert intelligence of his brother's. Instead, he looked amiable, good-humoured, kindly, and perhaps a little weak about the mouth and chin. She felt that he might be a very likeable man, but she was far from sure that he would be a good, strong king. 'He's just as I should expect, after all I've heard about him,' she thought, and turned to look after the procession, and then let her eyes run swiftly over what faces were visible on the men's side in the hope of seeing Fulk, but there was no sign of him. She thought she did catch a glimpse of Master Aylwin's head and shoulders. He was standing by one of the pillars, looking up at its capital, and some light from an unseen source just in front of him caught his features and his fair hair. She had no doubt that he was drawing the capital in one of his notebooks.

'Come along, Elys, and stop mooning about, or we'll be here all day!' Lady Mabilia hissed, and led the way to the north aisle, where a lay-brother was waiting to admit pilgrims to the tomb of King Edward.

The aisle was almost pitch dark, so that when they emerged beyond the choir into the crossing, the blaze of light which greeted them was all the more dramatic. The King's last resting-place had been constructed to look more like a shrine than a founder's tomb, and rose in two tiers of ornamented stonework in the very centre of the crossing, where light could fall on it from the lantern of the tower, and from the dozens of candles about the high altar, as well as those about the tomb itself and the votive tapers before it. Over it hung a rich pall, which the lay-brother told them in a bored tone had been given by the first King William in honour of his predecessor. He then directed the pilgrims to kneel by the tomb and make their petitions through the arches cut into the sides of it.

Elys waited her turn with her mother, and eventually was able to stand close to one of the little arches and whisper her request for healing for her dear brother. Then, under her breath, she added, 'And, oh please! freedom for me!' It occurred to her that freedom was an odd thing to request, for what did it mean? Nobody was *free*. Everyone owed duties to someone else, so why had she chosen that word?

There was no time to consider the matter, for Lady Mabilia, duty done, was now anxious about the horses waiting in the cold, worried that the snow might be falling more heavily, and conscious that it must be near dinner-time. As they hurried back down the nave, Elys ventured to ask, 'Did you not think the procession was very grand, Mother?'

'A gross extravagance of candles,' Lady Mabilia replied non-committally. 'Using *wax* ones just to light their way. Do hurry, Maud. You're forever falling behind!'

The days passed quietly as they rested after their long travelling and waited for the weather to improve, and New Year's Day came. Aylwin's bird was not the only gift Elys received, for, on New Year's morning, after Mass, her mother gave her one of the precious needles which she had bought in Mantova, and a little wooden case in which to keep it, and Sir Richard, to her amazement, gave her a silver thimble, with a sententious speech about using it in the creation of fine needlework for the greater glory of God. She remembered Aylwin's opinion that she might earn her living with her embroidery, and took the two gifts as a good omen, or a talisman to help her keep her freedom and not be caged in the nunnery.

Sir Richard had also a little gift for his sister, a gold and ivory crucifix to wear on her girdle or about her neck, which he had bought in Rome. It had been blessed by the Pope himself. Even better, he had brought a letter from Matthew.

Unlike most men of the knightly class, Matthew was lettered, for he had learned to read and write a good hand in the past three years, when his injured foot had become too painful to allow him to put it to the ground, let alone walk on it. His mother, of course, could not read what he had written, nor could his uncle or his sister, but Sir Richard had thought to bring a priest with him, who agreed to read the letter aloud to them, so they sat down round the table in the little parlour where the ladies took their meals in private, and composed themselves to listen.

They had expected that Matthew would send the good news of his recovery, but he began, after the usual formal greetings to them all, with the unexpected news that he had left Wix with his younger brother Crispin, and gone to Waltham, which was also in Essex, but on the west side of the shire, and less than twenty miles from where they were sitting.

'But why has he done that?' exclaimed Lady Mabilia. 'He

shouldn't travel, with his poor foot . . . unless . . . unless . . . Does he say if . . . ?'

'I would prefer that you do not interrupt,' said the priest severely. 'I am not accustomed to reading secular writings, and this is in French. He should have written in Latin.'

'But then you would have to translate it as well,' Elys pointed out.

'Writing should not be demeaned by being used to record a barbarous common tongue,' the priest replied reprovingly. 'Do you wish me to continue, or shall I return later, when you have finished discussing the first sentence?'

Elys thought him very rude, but Lady Mabilia humbly begged his pardon for interrupting, and asked him to continue. From the rest of the letter, it emerged that Matthew had heard that the minster at Waltham housed a great crucifix, which was famed among the English for the many cures granted to sick people who had been to pray before it, and he had decided to make the great effort to go there himself, having come to the conclusion that pilgrimages made by others on his behalf could not effect the healing of his foot.

'The ulcer grows wider and deeper, month by month,' he continued. 'I feel it eating into my flesh and bone, as if it were a live thing. The canons here at Waltham are kind. They have found us a house near the church, and servants to look after us. Crispin is content to remain here with me, as he can continue his studies for the priesthood with the canons – they have an excellent school and library. I trust you will join me here, and add your prayers to mine, for I feel sure that at Waltham I shall find what I seek.' The letter ended, as it had begun, with great formality.

There was a brief silence after the priest had finished reading, and then Sir Richard said to him, 'Thank you for your trouble, Father. Do you know aught of this Waltham? What manner of place is it? Is it true that this crucifix has effected cures?'

'Certainly not,' the priest replied angrily. 'That is mere superstition! It is, however, true that some articles are imbued very strongly with God's love, and prayer in their vicinity seems the more readily channelled to the Divine

Presence. I have heard of this crucifix, and of the minster at Waltham.'

There was something in his voice which caught the attention of all three of his hearers, and Lady Mabilia said sharply, 'What's wrong with the place?'

The priest closed his eyes for a moment, then said, 'Nothing. It's a small town – hardly more than a village – with a great church, recently rebuilt by our late king's successive wives, but not, I think, finished yet. There had been a place of worship there for centuries, but it was refounded some eighty or so years ago by – by Earl Harold, the usurper, and his body is said to be entombed there, behind the altar, but without any memorial, of course. That may perhaps indicate where the fault lies in the place, that the canons of the college he placed there should have dared to inter a foresworn man, a perjurer, within their church! And that is not all!'

He paused dramatically, then, assured that their eyes were fixed in horrified expectation on his face, he continued, dropping his voice to an effective, hollow whisper, 'The canons are seculars, of the old, unreformed kind, and many of them . . .' He paused again, as if he had to force himself to speak the unspeakable. '. . . Many of them are *not celibate*!'

'Not . . . ?' prompted Lady Mabilia, mouth agape with expectancy and forgetting that Elys was present.

'Married,' he hissed.

'Oh.' Lady Mabilia sounded a mite disappointed. 'Well, many priests of the old foundations are still married, even today. The English were accustomed to having married priests, I believe, until Archbishop Lanfranc brought in the new rules.'

'But we are three generations on from Lanfranc's time,' pointed out the priest. 'There should be no married parish priests in England by now, let alone a whole college of them.'

'But you have heard of pilgrims to Waltham being cured?' Sir Richard interrupted impatiently.

The priest admitted reluctantly that he had, and that several other apparently miraculous events had occurred which appeared to be connected with the presence of

Waltham's great crucifix. 'Were those sinful pretence priests replaced by Canons Regular of my own Order, the Augustinians, no doubt there would be far more cures and miracles,' he added, doggedly determined not to allow any good to be thought of married canons.

'The important thing is that Matthew seems to believe he'll find healing there,' Elys said quietly. 'He's never been sufficiently convinced that he would be thought deserving of a cure to make the effort to go himself to any other shrine.'

'The boy is too modest!' exclaimed his loving mother. 'I'm sure there is no more deserving lad in the whole of Christendom.'

Elys made no reply to that, but Sir Richard sniffed disparagingly, having a deep, inborn distrust of any emotion not inspired entirely by religion, and no high opinion of the judgment of any woman, particularly a doting mother. 'You'd best go to Waltham and find out what's to do,' he said.

And so they did, setting out as soon as Epiphany brought the end of the twelve days of Christmas. It was bitter cold, with a few inches of snow on the ground, and a lowering, yellowish-grey sky threatening more, but Lady Mabilia scoffed at Elys for suggesting that they should wait a few days in the hope of better weather. Sir Richard did not accompany them, having much to do, after his long absence, about the affairs of the Temple, but he sent an escort of twenty men-at-arms and three sergeants to escort his sister and niece, which, to Elys, conveyed how disturbed the country had become, after seven years of a disputed succession. To think that a simple journey of a score of miles from Westminster and the King's presence require so much larger an escort than that which had brought them safely all the way from Rome.

There were rumours in the City, it appeared, about the activities of the Earl of Essex, the infamous Geoffrey de Mandeville, who had made himself thoroughly hated by every right-thinking man and woman in England. He had insinuated and bullied himself into the confidence of first

Stephen, then of the Empress, and had gained thereby his earldom and the constabulary of the Tower, as well as the office of sheriff in two or three shires, changing sides whenever it seemed to be to his advantage, bargaining secretly with one claimant to the throne while openly supporting the other, plundering the frightened townspeople and villagers in the eastern counties and browbeating the Londoners, generally earning himself the reputation of a devil incarnate. If he and his men were anywhere on the route to Waltham, twenty-three armed men would hardly be a sufficient escort.

Fortunately Earl Geoffrey was occupied elsewhere, but the journey to Waltham was made as hurriedly as the weather would allow, with everyone in the party keeping a sharp lookout for a possible ambush, approaching every copse – almost every bush – in a wary fashion, and hardly daring to speak above a whisper as they passed through the villages on the road, for fear of attracting attention.

At last, after a long day's journey which had begun well before dawn and ended as the sun was setting behind a bank of cloud stained an angry crimson, they clattered across the causeway over the Lea marshes, and entered the town of Waltham.

It was a very small town, with no protective wall, nor even a palisade. It consisted of a great stone church, surrounded by a huddle of thatched roofs, like a hen amid a brood of chicks. The main street began a few hundreds yards to the west of the church, spread out a little short of it round a market-place on the north side of the road, then drew together at a ford and a rickety wooden footbridge over the millstream, which ran across the road just before the two stumpy western towers of the church, and then curved round the south side of the churchyard, to peter out at the top of the rise up from the ford, level with the churchyard gate.

'We'd best go to the priory and ask my son's direction,' Lady Mabilia said to the sergeant in charge, who knew the area, having been born not far away.

'There is no priory, my lady,' he replied apologetically. 'The good fathers have each a house amid the townsfolk.

81

They don't live in common, like the Canons Regular. There's just the church, the school, and a few other buildings.'

Lady Mabilia gave a little cluck of annoyance, and looked about her, at a loss to know what to do. The party had come to a halt after crossing the ford, and were crowded together on the small forecourt of the church. There was nobody of any apparent importance about, only peasants on their way home from work, and Lady Mabilia assumed they would hardly have enough sense, and she enough English, to be of any help.

Elys, who was cold and weary, hardly lifted her eyes from the imaginary point between her palfrey's ears at which she had been gazing for the past hour in order to retain her balance on her insecure saddle. The sudden sound of a bell made her start and look up to see where it was coming from, her eyes going first to one tower then the other. She noticed how square and sturdy they were, and that the building between them, where the west door and window should be, was only a temporary wooden structure, for the nave of the church was unfinished. The bell, now into its stride and ringing steadily, was further east, and must hang in either a central tower or a separate campanile. She had been so lost in her own depression and weariness as they crossed the river that she had not looked at all at the approaching view of the church, and had no idea of its length or height, or of the position of the other tower.

One of the passing peasants paused and looked curiously at this large party of black-cloaked soldiers guarding three women and a baggage-wagon, and then came closer, in an odd, uncoordinated fashion, and asked confidently, 'Be you looking for Father Brian?'

'Who's Father Brian?' asked the leading sergeant.

'That's in charge of the minster, do the Dean be absent,' the man replied, eyeing the sergeant's hauberk and cloak with interest. 'Be you a Templar?'

'Yes,' the sergeant replied, with a touch of superiority.

'Ah, I thought you be, with yon black cloak. Knights wears white and ordinary fellows wears black. I seen some on 'em down Chingford way.'

'Where is the Dean of the college?' asked Lady Mabilia sharply, for it seemed to her that a great deal of time was being wasted on trivialities, and this homespun fellow at least seemed to have a grain of sense and a tongue in his head.

'Oh, that be with the King – or the Count, according to which way you looks at it, lady, being as that's that's brother.'

Everyone looked blank at this curious speech, for most of them had only a very basic knowledge of English, quite inadequate for understanding such a complicated statement, but Elys, pulling herself together and thinking hard about what he had said, exclaimed, 'Oh, you mean that the Dean is the King's brother.'

'That's right, my lady,' the man said, grinning. In the gathering darkness, it was difficult to see him clearly, but he looked an odd fellow, with a long nose and chin, little deep-set eyes, and a thatch of fair hair sticking out from under a conical cloth cap which was pulled down over his ears. 'Bishop Henry don't have time to come to Waltham much, so Father Brian, being senior canon, be in charge, and that lives over there.' He pointed to a neat little cottage tucked in beside the northern of the church's twin west towers.

'Thank you, my good man!' exclaimed Lady Mabilia, fishing in her purse. 'Here, take this for your trouble,' and she held out the smallest piece of a penny which her cold fingers could find. It could hardly have been more than an eighth of the small silver coin, but it was probably still as much as the man could earn by a day's work.

He had been standing with his hands tucked in his sleeves for warmth, and he kept them there, saying with dignity, 'Lord bless you, my lady, no need for that. If you want anything while you're in Waltham, Lukin Dulpain's the man to ask, being as I'm reeve here.'

'Do you know my son, Matthew de Wix?' Lady Mabilia asked, suddenly realizing that this was no mere peasant.

'That I do! That lives opposite the churchyard gate,' Lukin replied. 'That's brother to Father Crispin. Go on up by the churchyard fence, and you'll find that in the last house on the right,' and he wriggled his hands further up his sleeves, made a series of bobbing bows all round, like a pied wagtail, and went off across the ramshackle foot-bridge in a curious manner, almost as if he were dancing.

The last house on the right seemed larger and more solidly built than most in the town, but it was quite dark by the time they reached it, and it was difficult to see anything much of the outside. A neatly-dressed serving-man opened the door when they knocked, and bowed the ladies in as soon as he heard who they were. The escort, its duty done, remained outside conferring for a few minutes, then departed to find lodging for the night in one of the inns.

The outer door of the house opened into a screen pass-age, which ran through to the yard at the back and the kitchen, which they later found was, as usual, a separate building. A door on the right opened into the hall, which occupied most of the house, being open to the roof. The servant ushered the new arrivals into it, and they stood for a moment, blinking in the light, for half a dozen torches flared in sconces on the walls, and a good fire blazed on the hearth in the middle of the rush-strewn floor. By the hearth stood a small table, a few stools, and a curious piece of furniture, shaped like a high-backed chair, but with the seat extended in front and padded with straw-stuffed cloth.

A young man with curly brown hair, dressed in a deacon's plain black robe, sat on one stool and the chair was occupied by another, slightly older man, much like him in features, but with lank hair, a pale, drawn face, and dark shadows beneath his eyes and in the hollows of his cheeks. His legs rested on the extended seat in front of him, the right foot swathed in bandages. He had an air of pain and exhaustion, as if he could hardly bear to go on reclining there, yet had not the strength to do anything else.

'Matthew!' exclaimed Lady Mabilia, flinging wide her arms and swooping across the hall to him. He flinched, as if afraid she would touch him, but she stopped a few feet from him, then very gently took the last three or four steps to his side and bent to kiss his brow.

'Mother!' he said, managing a wan smile. 'I'm so happy to see you safely home. And Elys.' He stretched out a hand towards his sister, and Elys moved forward to take it in both of hers, for he hardly had the strength to hold it out to her.

'How are you, dear Matthew?' she asked, kneeling beside him.

He sighed and shook his head slightly, and then said, with an effort at brightness, and with a certain note of confidence which Elys could not recall hearing in his voice before, 'But I shall be healed here, I'm sure of it, and so is Crispin. There's a holiness, a peace, in this place, a wholesomeness, which is healing and calming. Crispin feels it too.'

Crispin, who had risen from his stool and stood waiting patiently for his mother and sister to remember him, smiled and nodded.

'A blessed place,' he said. 'I shall stay here, come what may, and complete my studies, and then, God willing, become a member of the college.'

'Crispin, my dear boy.' Lady Mabilia held out her hands to him, but did not offer to kiss him, for he was already a deacon in holy orders. He barely touched her hands, but smiled and murmured a blessing, then did the same for Elys.

'Matthew looks tired now,' he said. 'The journey here was very trying for him, and he's been in the church all the afternoon, meditating and praying. But you must be weary yourselves, and hungry. We have a room prepared for you, a solar above the back room there, where you may be private. Would you like to go there now, to refresh yourselves, and then we'll have supper, before I go across to Vespers.'

Lady Mabilia owned herself hungry, for they had only eaten pottage for dinner in a poor little inn that had nothing more to offer. Elys felt too cold and tired to be much concerned about food, but she followed her mother and Crispin, first through a door at the back of the low dais across the far end of the hall, which led to a room shared by Matthew and Crispin, then up a wooden stair in the corner to the room above. Crispin had brought a lighted candle, which he used to light other candles and rushlights put ready earlier, and revealed their bedchamber before leaving them rather hastily, as if he had found himself in an improper place.

It was a large room, with plenty of space to accommodate three ladies in comfort, and three narrow wooden beds equipped with sheets, blankets and fur covers. There was a window in each side wall, with well-fitting shutters and the luxury of oiled linen stretched across a frame to let in light during the day, yet keep out wind and rain. Two long rails for clothes ran along the back wall, and there was a small table with a ewer and basin, a close-stool behind a curtain in the corner, and two stools with padded seats. A couple of servants came bumping and puffing up the stairs with the travelling trunks, and a stout, sensible-looking serving-woman brought a jug of hot water.

Washed, changed out of their damp travelling-clothes and feeling warmer, the ladies soon returned to the hall, where the tables had been set up and laid for supper. There were eight servants visible, but Crispin said that the kitchen staff ate in the kitchen. Four boys served the gentry at the high table on the dais with plentiful, well-cooked food, and Lady Mabilia remarked that the servants appeared to be eating the same as their masters.

'They are all freemen, working for a money wage and their food,' replied Crispin. 'Our needs are simple, so I would say, rather, that we eat the same as our servants – good, wholesome, simple food.'

The two brothers were anxious to hear about their mother's and sister's travels, and, most particularly, about Rome, but Lady Mabilia told them only a little, saying that there was plenty of time for the rest later, and she would rather hear how her two sons had been faring.

Crispin explained how they had heard about the Holy Cross of Waltham from a pilgrim who had passed through Wix on his way to Harwich to take ship to the continent.

'Matthew dreamed about it that night, and for several nights after, and felt called to come here. I came with him, and as soon as we arrived, we knew we had made the right choice.'

'But how did you bring Matthew so far?' asked Elys, who knew how much Matthew dreaded being moved, even a few yards, for the slightest jolt caused great pain in his damaged foot.

'I came in a wagon,' Matthew replied grimly. 'It was – unpleasant, but I arrived, eventually. Father Brian and the other canons have been very kind and helpful. Father Radulf has knowledge of wounds, and his wife makes excellent simples and unguents . . .'

'His wife!' Lady Mabilia exclaimed. 'It's true, then! These canons are of the old English kind. Married!'

'Only three or four of them,' Crispin protested. 'They find their wives of great help to them in their work, and I think none the worse of them. The rule here is that a canon may choose to marry or be celibate when he enters the college, but he may not change his mind later if he chooses the better course.'

'Rome is set against non-celibate clergy,' Lady Mabilia protested.

'But Rome is far from England, as you know only too well, and always has been,' Crispin replied with a faint smile. 'The English ever went their own way. Besides, Mother, it's only in these past fifty years that even Rome has insisted on a celibate priesthood. Remember, St Peter himself was a married man.'

'How can you know that?' snapped Lady Mabilia. 'I'm sure Scripture doesn't say so. Quote me the text that says that St Peter had a wife.'

'I can quote you one which says that he had a mother-in-law,' replied Crispin, with his calm, unruffled smile. 'These are good men here, and good priests, dear Mother, and learned, too. They have a fine library, and an excellent school.'

'How many are they?' asked Lady Mabilia, surprised that a church in so small a town should have a library, let alone a school.

'Twelve. They hold several parishes hereabouts, taking turns to serve the churches, and provide vicars for others further afield. There's a Dean of the college as well, who normally resides here and is the priest of this parish, but the present Dean, unusually, holds other, more important offices, and is seldom able to come here, so Father Brian is in charge of Waltham.'

'The Dean is the Bishop of Winchester,' Elys said quietly, finding that merely to say the words aloud gave her an odd feeling of comfort, as if it were good news. Yet why should it be? Henry of Blois, Papal Legate and Bishop of Winchester, was a remote, important figure, frequently heard mentioned, but Elys had seen him only once, and knew little about him, save that he was said to be wise, clever, ambitious, and not particularly saintly, although not considered bad, either as a man or as a bishop. She had heard some men whisper that he would make a better king than his brother, but none of this meant anything to her, so why should the mention of his name make her feel less wretched and fearful of the future?

'Indeed, and a generous benefactor,' Crispin said. 'King Henry's queens began to rebuild the minster here, but it was left unfinished when the – the troubles began, and Bishop Henry has decided to finish the work.'

Perhaps he'll send Master Aylwin to help with the work, Elys thought, and perhaps Sir Fulk will come with him, or at least visit him sometimes . . . But she kept her thoughts to herself.

CHAPTER FIVE

Elys woke early in the morning, while her mother and Maud were still asleep, and crept from her bed to the nearer window, where she gently eased open one leaf on the shutters and tried to see out through the oiled linen.

Fool! she thought. It's still dark out there! How can you expect to see anything? She slipped back between the crisp linen sheets and snuggled down into the warmth and began to drowse, thinking disconnectedly about her present situation.

She felt guilty about the persistent thought which would keep coming to the surface that, with Matthew's foot still not healed, she was in no immediate danger of being carried off to the nunnery, and she prayed for forgiveness that she should find anything pleasing about her poor brother's suffering and her mother's disappointment.

Last night, Lady Mabilia had said little about the long pilgrimage to Rome and back. Elys knew that she had hoped for so much from it, and had come back tired out, only buoyed up by the belief that it must have gained the longed-for cure for her dear son. The shock of finding him not only no better, but, to judge by his hollow cheeks and dark-ringed eyes, worse than before, must have been a bitter blow.

Even as Elys lay thinking about Matthew, she heard a low moaning sound coming from the room below, and then Crispin's quiet, calm voice saying softly, 'Drink this, Matthew. It will ease the pain.'

'You gave me a stronger draught last night again, didn't you?' she heard Matthew reply. 'How long can I go on like this, Crispin? The time will come when the draught must be so strong to ease the pain that it will kill me.'

'That won't be for a good while yet,' Crispin answered. 'Hush now, brother – there are only the boards between us and our mother, and we mustn't wake her.'

Elys bit her lips, turned her face into the pillow and wept silently, wretched enough to consider offering in her prayers to go without protest to the nunnery and endure the life, if only Matthew might be healed, but she remembered someone saying that one cannot make bargains with God . . . Who was it? Of course . . . Master Aylwin!

Trying to stop herself fretting over Matthew, she concentrated on remembering some of the interesting things she had seen on this latest and greatest pilgrimage, until Lady Mabilia woke suddenly and demanded to know why she was still slugabed when she should have been up and dressed by now.

The January day was cold and dull, but Lady Mabilia was determined to go to Mass with Crispin, and Elys must go too. She was not averse to the idea, for Matthew's talk of the great crucifix had filled her with curiosity, so, wrapped in her warmest cloak and hood, she was the first of the three to step out into the street, where she stopped suddenly, arrested by the view before her.

The street was narrow, and she was looking across it, over a wooden fence, to the snow-covered churchyard, where a few black trees stood stark between the snow and the grey sky. Between, a warm golden grey in the mist, stood the bulk of a great stone church, its horn-covered window-spaces glowing with candle-light. A stubby central tower rose above the crossing, where the short transepts projected, but it was a little higher than the twin western towers she had seen last night. The church looked, she thought, like a great animal, crouching in the snow, and something about its quiet solidity made her feel an immediate affection for it.

'Why must you stand in the way, Elys?' demanded her mother irritably, trying to push past her. 'What are you staring at?'

'I was looking at the church,' she replied.

'Well, what of it? You've seen bigger and more beautiful churches than this. Do come along – it's too cold to stand about staring at nothing.'

Crispin led them across the street and a little to their right, so that they might enter the churchyard by the lychgate, which had a peaked roof where mourners might stand in shelter during the first part of a burial service. From there, a stone-flagged path ran down the churchyard towards the west end of the church, with a short branch off to the south door, by which they entered the building.

Elys looked about her at the great stone pillars, which supported massy arches, a triforium above, and, somewhere up in the dark shadows, surely a clerestory as well. Every part that she could see of the stonework was plastered and painted with grape-bearing vines, twisting about the figures of saints, all in soft, clear colours. It was indeed a great minster for so small a town, and very impressive, despite the last two bays to the west being unfinished and blocked off by a wooden hoarding.

Crispin silently pointed them to the northern side of the nave, where a dozen or so women stood waiting for the service to begin. There were even fewer men on the south side, for most of the townsfolk would be at their work by now. Lady Mabilia led the way to a charcoal brazier, well forward near the nave altar, and stood close to it, pulling her cloak tightly round her against the draughts. Maud, a silent and unconsidered presence, as usual, would have stood behind her, but Elys, feeling sorry for the poor creature, took her arm and moved her nearer to the brazier, then stood beside her, blocking her natural tendency to move back again.

Lady Mabilia closed her eyes at once and began to pray, but Elys could not resist looking about her discreetly, noting that the frontal of the altar, which had once been a very fine one, was faded and in need of repair. Beyond the altar and the crossing, she could see the stalls of the canons' choir. They appeared to be made of plain oak, with no carving or other ornament. Beyond them, the High Altar gleamed with silver in the light of a dozen large candles, and everywhere, looking down from the walls and arches, the faces of angels and saints gleamed amid the twisting stems of the painted vines.

Crispin had gone off somewhere to the east, but presently reappeared, robed in a white alb, carrying a taper, with which he lit the candles on the nave altar, seeming to intensify the shadows in the nave and aisle by contrast. Elys turned her eyes upwards, without moving her head, but still could not see the full height of the building.

A bell had been ringing in the central tower for the past five or ten minutes. It now ceased, and the priest who was to sing Mass entered in a veritable cloud of incense and acolytes, for there were a dozen boys, all very earnest and important, half with thuribles and the other half bearing candles. They paced solemnly to their places and, at the same time, the choir entered two by two, from the south transept into the stalls beyond the crossing, took their stands, and the service began.

It occurred to Elys that there was something miraculous in the very words of the Mass. She had heard the familiar Latin in so many different churches in half a dozen different lands, but they were always the same, and would be wherever she went in Christendom. It gave her a sense of warm security, a feeling that the Church would always be there, wherever she might wander, to protect and comfort her. She was no Latinist, but she had learned the words and their meaning in her childhood, and she need never fear that she might enter a church and not understand what was being said and sung. Why, at this very minute, the same words were rising from hundreds and hundreds of churches throughout England, as already they had come from those in the Low Countries, in Normandy, Anjou, France, as the sun had risen over the Christian lands from the farthest reaches of the Empire. Her uncle would be hearing them in the round church of the Templars at Holborn, and Sir Fulk and Master Aylwin would be listening to them at Westminster, perhaps even being sung by Bishop Henry.

For an unguarded moment, she visualized the tall, handsome knight with his dark curls and charming smile, and felt a pang of sorrow. She was sure he had been almost about to offer to marry her, but had been forestalled by her uncle's bald announcement that her dowry had already been given away. She bit her lips, blinked hard, and forced herself to turn away from vain regrets for an attractive way of escape, and concentrate on the service, fixing her eyes on the priest, who was a tall, burly man with hair which was that odd colour, between gold and grey, which made guessing his age difficult.

To Lady Mabilia's unconcealed pleasure, Crispin read the Gospel, intoning in a clear, tuneful voice, which carried the Word easily to every ear in the great building, cutting through the echoes from the vaulted side aisles and ringing up into the shadowed height above the great arches, where Elys could almost imagine winged shapes might be hovering. There was certainly a sense of warm and listening presence in this church, which she had rarely felt in any other of the many churches in which she had prayed. She wondered if it was generally present throughout the building, or if it emanated from some particular place.

Something made her look up, not towards the roof above her head, but to something in the shadows above and beyond the nave altar, and suddenly, she became aware of the great crucifix which seemed to hover there in the shadows. It was black, and gleamed faintly in the candle-light, but the figure of Christ, which must have been almost life-sized, was white, and seemed to hover, unsupported, framed in the far arch of the tower. That, surely, must be the Holy Cross of Waltham! She had imagined something much smaller, made, perhaps, of gold or silver, and set on an altar, but the reality was so different – a great black cross, reflecting barely enough light to be visible, and that luminous pale figure . . . Was it silver or white?

A sharp nudge in the ribs from her mother recalled her attention to the service, and she dared not let her attention wander again, but when it was over, and she was waiting with her mother for Crispin to rejoin them, she made her way discreetly, by way of the north aisle, to the crossing, and looked up at the Cross.

The light had increased by now, and she could see it much more clearly. The figure of Christ was covered with silver, and had, oddly, a sword girded about the waist, a golden crown of thorns on the head, and a great gem glowing redly on the breast. It was not beautiful, but she felt awed by its majesty.

'That is our Holy Cross,' said Crispin, coming silently to stand beside her. 'Nobody knows how old it is. It was found a hundred years ago, buried in a hilltop in Somerset, and brought here by miraculous means. The Christus is carved in stone and mounted on a wooden cross, but the man who had it brought here, a great lord, had the figure covered with silver, and gave his own sword to hang about its waist, and his wife gave her jewel to adorn it, and her gold necklaces to make the crown. The silver is dark with age now, and some of the canons think it should be cleaned.'

'Of all the great and wonderful things I've ever seen,' Elys breathed, 'I've never felt anything so holy, so powerful . . .'

'Yes. It has great power for good,' Crispin agreed.

'What are you staring at?' Lady Mabilia asked, having abandoned the brazier and come to find them. 'Oh – is that the Holy Cross? It's very large, and looks quite barbaric. Are you sure you were right to bring Matthew all this way for – for that?'

'Don't you feel it, Mother?' Elys asked, puzzled.

'Feel what?'

'The . . . I don't know . . . I feel a great sense of quiet and peace, and power – a great power.'

Lady Mabilia shrugged. 'The church has a pleasant atmosphere. It's kept clean, and the people behave reverently, the service is well-sung, and the boys kept under discipline. I can't imagine what else you mean. I trust you're not becoming fanciful and – well – mystical, Elys. Mother Prioress has no patience with would-be mystics, I assure you.'

Elys made no reply, feeling that the retort she would otherwise have made would be out of place here. Lady Mabilia, having made her point, got down on her knees on the cold stone floor, clasped her hands, fixed her eyes on the Cross, and began once more to pray, so Elys, Crispin and the gentlewoman joined her, all praying earnestly to the Lord portrayed here in His agony to have mercy of Matthew, who also suffered.

They were all cold and stiff when they rose, and went out of the church as they had come, silent and thoughtful, but their mood was broken outside the south door, for an odd figure trotted up to Lady Mabilia and bowed low before her. He was a short man, with thin, nobbly legs, ears project-

94

ing like jug handles, a long nose set in a narrow face, and a thatch of fair hair which stuck out straight all round his head.

'Lukin Dulpain at your service again, dear lady,' he said, presenting a small bunch of snowdrops to Lady Mabilia. 'A reminder that spring will certainly come, and hope may dawn in the darkest hour. How is Master Matthew today, Father Crispin?'

'My brother is – is much the same,' Crispin replied, smiling at the odd little man. Lady Mabilia was staring at the snowdrops in blank astonishment, but, as Crispin spoke, she recovered her wits and smiled graciously at their giver. 'How very kind!' she said. 'My thanks to you, Master Dulpain, and also for your assistance last night.'

Master Dulpain flourished his conical cap airily, beamed at everyone, and pranced away down the path with satisfaction apparent in every line of his odd little body.

'Who on earth is he?' asked Lady Mabilia.

'The canons' reeve,' replied Crispin. 'A very popular man, and as good-hearted as any you'll meet – and very efficient in his work. He gets better results by goodwill than other reeves manage with threats and blows. This is a town with several interesting characters, you'll find.'

'But it's such a small place,' Lady Mabilia said, looking about her. 'I wouldn't call it a town. It's no more than a hamlet.'

'There are eighty houses in all,' Crispin replied. 'I happen to know, because I've been helping the Almoner compile a list of householders. Over there, beyond the ford, there are more cottages set behind those you see, around the market-place, and round the corner from our house, along the edge of the fairground, there's another dozen, and then there are three streets running southwards behind Church Street, where we live.'

'But it has no wall. Towns have walls,' insisted his mother.

'The folk have never felt a need for a wall. It's a place of peace, set between the river and the forest, on the way to nowhere, and with nothing to attract marauders.'

'Forest?' asked Elys. 'What forest?'

95

'The Forest of Essex. It begins a mile or so to the east, where the road into Essex rises up from the valley, and stretches – oh, half across the shire, I suppose, although not all of it is covered with trees – much of it is open land.'

'Is it another of the Conqueror's creations?' Elys asked, for she had seen the New Forest and knew how bitterly the people there hated it and the Forest Law.

'No. It's so old that nobody can tell how long it's been here. Edwin the Warrener says that it's been here since the Creation, and he may well be right. He lives nearer to it than anyone else in Waltham, for his cot and his warren are at the very edge of it.'

'Is he not afraid to live so close to it? There must be wild animals . . .'

'He knows them all too well to fear them. He lives up there with a baggage of ferrets and a dog, and wouldn't change his home for a palace. He often calls to see Matthew, so you'll meet him before long, and ask him yourself about his animal friends.'

Elys met a number of people in the next few weeks as she found her way about the small town and settled into her new home. At least, she thought of the house in Church Street as a new home, but Lady Mabilia spoke of it as only a temporary lodging, and still talked confidently of Matthew's return to the Order of the Temple and the Holy Land. It appeared that she had somehow forgotten that she had returned from every pilgrimage, and particularly the most recent one, certain that she would find Matthew cured, and said now that she could see a great improvement in his health and appearance, and that the wound in his foot was obviously beginning to heal.

Hardly knowing how to respond to such statements, Elys held her tongue until she had met Father Radulf, the infirmarian, and even then, she waited until she had seen him come four times on his regular thrice-weekly visits before she ventured to waylay him in the passage as he left and ask what he thought of Matthew's wound.

'The substance continues to eat away his flesh and bone,' the canon replied bluntly. He was an austere, grave-looking man, with a gaunt frame and face and shining silver hair.

'I must admit I've never before seen a wound caused by Greek fire, and it looks to me more like a canker. I've seen such ulcers resulting from no more than a blow on the leg. However, the effect is much the same, whatever the cause.'

'My mother believes it's beginning to heal.'

Father Radulf looked at her steadily, but made no reply.

'Can it be cured?' Elys tried again.

'Do you believe in miracles?' the canon asked, apparently conversationally.

'Yes, of course.'

'You believe that God can alter the natural progression of events, if He chooses?'

'Yes. He created the world, and everything in it. It must be easy for Him to alter a little bit of it, when he made it all.'

Father Radulf's face broke into a singularly pleasant and warm smile. 'Dear child!' he said. 'The Lord bless your faith and bring you that which you most desire,' and he went on his way, leaving Elys convinced that Matthew was no better, but, as she had suspected, growing steadily worse. She went into the hall, intending to ask Crispin, on whom fell the main burden of caring for Matthew.

She found them both in the hall, sitting at the table on the dais, busy copying an old document. Crispin read out the words, one or two at a time, while Matthew, who had learned to write well during his enforced idleness, wrote on a sheet of vellum which had been carefully ruled with straight lines and margins.

'What are you copying?' she asked.

'It's a charter given to the college by King Edward when Earl Harold founded it in the last century,' Crispin replied. 'It's difficult, as some of it is in English. Shall we go on, Matthew?'

'No. I can't concentrate on it, and I don't want to make any mistakes,' Matthew replied wearily. 'I always feel so tired when Father Radulf has been. I think I'll just go and sit by the fire. It's so cold today.'

Crispin silently put away the parchments and the pens and ink, and called a servant to help him move Matthew in his chairbed nearer to the hearth and then he went out.

Elys fetched her needlework and sat where the wintry sunlight fell on it, then began to talk about the journey home from Rome.

'You said that both the young men serve the Bishop of Winchester?' Matthew asked presently. 'An odd friendship, surely, between a knight and a mason?'

'I thought so at first,' Elys replied, stitching industriously, 'but Master Aylwin is of gentle birth. I think he's a mason from preference, for he loves stone and fine carving . . . I wouldn't say they're exactly friends, in any case. It seemed as if the Bishop sent Sir Fulk to fetch Master Aylwin and bring him safely home!'

'Where is Mother?' Matthew asked, shifting in his chair as if he could not get himself comfortable.

'Gone to the church to pray.'

'God must be tired of her constant begging,' he said bitterly.

'Matthew!' Elys exclaimed, shocked. 'How can you?'

'Be so ungrateful? I suppose that's how it sounds, but I am grateful, really. It's just that this goes on and on, ever growing a little worse, and I find myself increasingly longing for it all to be over.'

'Then all the more reason for all of us to pray.'

'But you all pray for the impossible. Who am I to expect, or even hope for a cure? I mean that I wish it were all over in the more likely way.'

Elys felt as if her heart had stopped for a moment with the shock. She had never thought that Matthew's wound might eventually kill him, and yet he spoke as if he expected that it would. She sat quite still for what seemed a long time, unable to find anything to say, and then she heard the street door open and close, and two men came into the hall, robbing her of the chance to say anything at all.

'Good morrow, Master Matthew,' said the smaller of the two men, who was Lukin Dulpain. 'Here's Edwin Warrener come to bring some conies for your supper and a parcel of ferrets for your entertainment.'

'Baggage,' said the other man, who was tall and lanky, with a handsome face marred by a severe frown. 'It's a *baggage* of ferrets, not a parcel.'

'But a baggage do be many ferrets,' argued the odd little man, drawing up two stools to the fire and sitting on one of them without waiting for an invitation. 'As you've only brought two, that be a small part of a baggage, and a small part of something be a parcel, do it don't, Lady Elys?'

'I suppose so,' Elys replied. 'Oh, do sit down, Master Edwin, and may I offer you some refreshment?' It seemed odd to her that a reeve and a warrener should come visiting her brother, but the expression on Matthew's face made it clear to her that they were welcome friends.

'A cup of mulled ale?' added Matthew, sitting up a little straighter and looking much less drawn and weary. 'Call one of the men, Elys. We always have mulled ale when Lukin and Edwin come visiting.'

The warrener, meanwhile, was looking about for somewhere to put the bunch of furry bodies which he held in one hand, and which Elys was trying to avoid looking at, for she always felt sorry to see dead conies although she was not averse to eating them when they appeared, roasted or in a pie, at the supper-table. The problem was solved by the entry of one of the servants, who must have heard the visitors arrive, for he brought a jug of ale, a spice-box and some cups on a tray, which he put down on another stool nearby, collected the conies from Edwin and took them away to the kitchen.

'They'm drawn but not skinned,' Edwin called after him, and sat down on the stool which Lukin had set for him, while Lukin got up and put the poker in the fire to heat while he poured the ale and dropped tiny pinches of the precious spices into the cups, stirring busily.

'You'll take a little ale, Lady Elys?' he asked, poised with a stick of cinnamon between finger and thumb, knobbly knees bent and head cocked, so that he looked like a large, inquisitive bird.

'Yes, please,' Elys replied gravely, determined not to laugh at him.

Edwin, who was wearing a curiously baggy-looking open-fronted supertunic secured by a leather belt, delved inside the garment, and brought out two wriggling bundles of creamy fur, which he handed across to Matthew, one by one.

'Don't you go poking of them,' he said. 'They don't like poking fingers, and they bite.'

'I'll be careful,' Matthew promised, putting the two animals carefully in his lap and circling his forearms round them like a low fence. There was a deal of squirming and wriggling, and then the ferrets settled, content to be in a warm place, and peered over Matthew's arms at the outside world, showing little bright eyes and delicate rounded ears.

'They're very pretty,' Elys said doubtfully, looking at them from a safe distance.

'Pretty, ay!' Edwin replied, frowning more than ever, 'but fierce and hard-working, mind you.'

Watching the sinuous, graceful bodies moving about on Matthew's lap, Elys thought how Aylwin would love to draw them, and perhaps carve them as well, and she gave a little unconscious sigh, remembering once more how her uncle's unfortunate intervention had stopped the mason's friend from proposing marriage to her . . .

'I hope you had no trouble on your way here, my lady?' Lukin asked her when he had handed her with a comical little flourish a cup of hot ale.

'No, none at all, neither between Dover and London, nor between London and Waltham,' she replied. 'We were nervous, but my uncle gave us a good escort.'

'You were lucky, nonetheless,' Lukin assured her. 'Such dreadful things do be happening these days. They say God and His angels do be sleeping, and I can well believe it, the tales we hear of robbery, rape, murder and torture! Some of the barons do be using the foulest tortures on innocent folk to get their money, and let them die in agony, do they have none. Pray God continue to keep us safe here. We're lucky that Queen Adeliza be our patron and good lady, and her husband, Earl William, keeps watch and ward on our affairs. Of course, we're known to be far from rich, and that do help.'

'Ay, we be poor folk in wordly goods!' Edwin confirmed gloomily. 'Even the minster's poor, compared with other great churches. Red William saw to that.'

'You mean William Rufus?' Elys asked.

'Yes, the black-hearted villain!' exclaimed Lukin. 'That robbed our church to enrich the two abbeys in Normandy as his parents founded to assoil their sins. That took our gold altar as King Harold gave us, and our crosses and candlesticks, and the gold and silver covers of our gospellers. That even took the copes and altar-cloths that had any gold in them, and one cope as was worth sixty marks. That said they were all to go to the abbeys, but I've often wondered why that took gold things, and not any of our precious relics. You'd think abbeys would want relics more nor gold, wouldn't you now?' and he tapped his long nose with one finger, winking and capering about, flourishing the hot poker as he mulled a cup of ale for Edwin.

'You would indeed,' agreed Elys, sipping the ale, which was pleasantly hot and flavoursome on this cold morning.

'Well, I'll tell you what I think that done with them,' Lukin said, leaning confidentially towards her, but he was not able to do so, for the street door banged, and Lady Mabilia and Maud entered the hall.

'What's this?' she asked, surveying the group by the hearth. 'Should you not be resting, Matthew? Who are these men?'

'My friends, Master Lukin Dulpain, the college reeve, whom you have already met, and Master Edwin the warrener,' Matthew replied, sounding a little aggressive. 'They're kind enough to visit me and pass a little time with me, when their work allows it.'

Lady Mabilia looked disapprovingly at the visitors, no doubt thinking them hardly fit company for a young man who held a good manor, and would be a knight as soon as his health permitted. 'You mustn't let them tire you, nor keep them from their work. No doubt they have a great deal to do.'

'May I pour you some ale, gracious lady?' Lukin enquired, prancing across to the jug and the tray of cups. He seemed unable to move in a normal fashion, but walked with his knees bent, picking his feet up very high, his arms and hands flourishing about him, making him look more like a dancing jester than a sober reeve. Elys came to the conclusion that there must be a physical reason for it – perhaps the result of an accident or a strange illness.

'You must be cold after kneeling so long in the church,' he continued, adding little pinches of spices to the cups and plunging the hot poker into the result so that a cloud of fragrant steam arose, wafting under Lady Mabilia's cold and reddened nose and magically softening her mood. She accepted the cup graciously, despite the fantastic bow which accompanied its presentation, and was too busy sipping its hot contents to notice that Maud received equal service from the reeve immediately afterwards.

'Edwin has brought two of his ferrets to show me,' Matthew said. 'Aren't they beautiful?'

Lady Mabilia advanced to peer a little short-sightedly at the furry mass in Matthew's lap, caught an unexpected glimpse of a fierce little eye and a mouthful of sharp teeth, and exclaimed, 'Ugh! What dreadful teeth. Be careful, Matthew. They'll bite.'

'Only if they gets upsettled or poked,' Edwin defended his charges with a ferocious scowl. 'Or folk shriek at 'em. They'm well-trained fitchets, and keeps their biting for conies, so be they ain't upsettled nor shrieked at.'

'That's as may be,' Lady Mabilia replied, drawing herself up to her full, if inconsiderable, height and glaring at the warrener, intending, no doubt, to put him in his place. 'And what are these fellows and their fitchets doing here in the first place?'

'I told you, Mother; they're my friends, and they're kind enough to visit me when they have time,' Matthew replied, a touch of steel entering his normally gentle tones. 'In my own house, I receive whatever friends I choose, together with their animals. Master Edwin has kindly brought conies for our supper. Shall we have them in a pie, or roasted?'

'Conies!' Lady Mabilia exclaimed, eyeing Edwin in a more friendly fashion. 'How kind. I trust it's in order – I mean . . .' She sounded a little anxious, for rights of warren were strictly limited, and conies were a luxury.

'The warren belongs to the college,' Edwin replied, taking her point without resentment. 'Father Brian lets me take a moiety as part of my wages, to eat or sell or give, as I choose. A fellow can get sick of rabbit pie.' His frown softened and he grinned a little at the last statement. 'Well, I mun get back to me warrening. There's a fox somewheres about, and I needs to see what the rest of me baggage is doing about him.'

'Can a ferret tackle a fox?' asked Elys, looking at the two sinuous animals as Edwin took them back from Matthew and stowed them away inside his supertunic.

'Three or four on 'em can, working together. They'd not kill Master Reynard, but they'd give him a regular fright,' Edwin assured her. 'Coming, Lukin?'

He nodded his farewells in a solemn and dignified fashion, but Lukin must bow and make a proper speech of thanks and goodbye with ceremony.

'What an odd little man,' Lady Mabilia commented after the two visitors had gone, 'yet he seems a kindly soul, and he mulls ale well!' She sipped gratefully at the remains of the hot drink, for the church had indeed been very cold and draughty in its uncompleted state. 'Is it time for dinner yet?'

Crispin, who had been about his duties, came in then, and dinner was served soon after. While they were eating, he asked his mother and Elys if they would like to ride out during the afternoon and see something of the countryside. Lady Mabilia declined, thinking it too cold, but Elys, who did not relish spending whole days indoors, accepted the offer, and they set off soon after the meal, Elys on her palfrey and Crispin, as befitted a candidate for the priesthood, on a mule of considerable size and, it appeared, above average mulishness, for when Crispin attempted to turn left down Church Street, the mule insisted on turning right, and set off at a brisk clip across the nearer end of the fairground, and along the road which led eastwards, towards the Forest.

'I'm sorry!' Crispin exclaimed, laughing. 'I'd intended to take you up the valley by the cornmill stream, but Apuleius thinks otherwise.'

'Apuleius?' Elys queried. 'What an odd name.'

'He was an old Roman author, who wrote a book about a golden ass. I've not read it myself, for it's not considered fit reading for a churchman, but Father Brian knows of it, and he named this fellow because of his bay coat – it was quite red-gold when he was foaled, I'm told.'

The mule flapped his long ears, as if in agreement with the statement, and continued to trot along by the boundary fence of the churchyard and the canons's orchard, as if he knew where he was going. After a quarter-mile or so, they reached a crossroads, where they crossed the road which ran down the length of the valley, and went on, rising steadily, towards the Forest, which loomed above them on the ridge, filling the horizon as far as they could see on either side.

'The canons have a vineyard here,' Edwin pointed out a hedged enclosure amid the great fields on either side of the road. 'The grapes are small, but they ripen well in a good year, and make a palatable wine, but only enough for use at Mass. Edwin's warren lies over there, on the slope below the edge of the trees. Do you see the deer-fence? The canons had it made to keep the deer out of the crops, much to the delight of the townsfolk, but they had no permission from the King, so they'll probably have to take it down again if he finds out. Kings regard their peoples' crops as food for deer rather than people.'

'Crispin,' Elys said, having hardly spoken so far on their ride, for she had been wondering what she should say to her brother, 'I hadn't realized that Matthew might die of his wound.'

Crispin's face, usually so calm, changed subtly, and he looked suddenly older and very weary. 'Did he tell you so?' he asked.

'Not in so many words, but he said that sometimes he wishes it were all over, in the most likely way . . .'

'He's in constant pain, which grows worse by degrees. He can't sleep without poppy-juice, and needs ever more of it to have any effect. I fear that may kill him in the end, before the – the thing on his foot.' Crispin stared straight ahead between his mule's ears. 'He's changed since we came here. At Wix, he used to talk of recovering, and he was angry and impatient about the wound, but here, at Waltham, he's become much more patient and ready to accept God's will in the matter. He seems to have found peace of mind here, which is in itself a great improvement.'

They had entered the Forest by now, and were riding more slowly up the steep ridge, between great beech and hornbeam trees, whose huge trunks and pollarded crowns showed signs of great age. Apuleius, following his own wishes, turned off the road and trotted along an invisible path across the carpet of beechmast, and came to a stand on the edge of an open running, where a small herd of red deer was grazing. They looked up, startled, but moved away slowly, as if they were aware that the new arrivals meant them no harm.

'Beautiful creatures,' Crispin said softly. 'The one good thing about this interminable war is that it leaves Stephen and his court no time for hunting. Elys, pray for Matthew – even pray for a miracle for him – but try to accept that nothing but a miracle can save his life now, and death will be a welcome release for him.'

'I'll try,' she said sadly, 'but shouldn't Mother be told?'

'She knows,' Crispin replied, 'but she won't accept it.'

CHAPTER SIX

By the end of February, Elys felt quite at home in Waltham. She had explored deep into the Forest and some way both up and down the valley, cut by the seven streams of the river, riding out on every fine day with Crispin, who loved to show her the birds and animals, and promised a wealth of wild flowers later in the year.

The direction of their rides was usually determined by Apuleius, who set off in whichever direction he fancied as soon as he emerged from the arch which led from the yard at the back of the house into Church Street, but neither Elys nor Crispin could find fault with his choices, which were always fortunate. Oddly enough, on the few occasions when Crispin insisted on going a different way, they always found a cold wind blowing in their faces, or impassable mud on the road.

It was on their return from one of these rides that Lady Mabilia suddenly raised a matter which Elys had assumed had fallen into abeyance for the time being.

'I don't think Elys should be idling away her time like this,' she said. 'Quite apart from the danger of riding without a proper escort in these dangerous times, she's doing no good here to Matthew or herself.'

'There's only danger from de Mandeville's men on the high roads,' Crispin said quietly. 'I see that we keep to the little local lanes and the forest glades. What harm is it doing for her to be here? She prays assiduously, and attends Mass with you every morning, and she needs fresh air and exercise for her health's sake. I'm sure Matthew is glad of her presence to cheer his long days.'

'That's as may be,' Lady Mabilia retorted sharply. She was not accustomed to meeting with argument or discussion of her decisions, least of all from one of her own children, and did not seem to have assimilated the fact that her sons were now grown men. 'I think it past time that she went to Wix.'

'But our house there is shut up,' Matthew stirred himself to protest. 'We brought the servants with us, and there's no one there but my reeve and his family. Elys couldn't live there alone.'

'To the nunnery at Wix,' Lady Mabilia amended in an exasperated tone. 'She's to go there eventually, when . . . when I do . . .' She had meant to say 'When you are healed', but could not quite manage the words. 'And I think she might just as well go there now. She's becoming far too worldly in her manner and opinions for a nun.'

'I will not be a nun,' Elys said firmly, trying to make it sound a calm statement of fact rather than defiance.

'You'll do as you're told, you silly child,' Lady Mabilia snapped. 'I can't imagine why you have to be so troublesome! It's not for you to say what you will or will not do, but for *me*, lacking the guidance of a husband, to decide what is best for you, and for the family. Your sister Judith went gladly enough, giving herself as a free-will offering for her brother's good. I'd have thought you would be equally glad to do the same, as you profess to be a loving sister to dear Matthew.'

'Judith wanted to be a nun,' Elys said patiently. 'I don't know why, for I don't feel that I've ever really known Judith – she's so much older than I. I'm sure, however, that it had less to do with sacrificing herself for Matthew than following her own inclination, and I'm even more sure that God doesn't want me for a nun.'

'Elys is right,' Crispin said in his calm, gentle way, before his mother could gather her indignation into a reply. 'Judith was – is – older than Matthew by eight years, and twelve years older than Elys. I can't recall that she ever showed any affection for the three of us, or even any interest in us. My impression is that she disliked family life, the world in general, and men in particular, and always wanted to enter the cloistered life. Elys is not in the least like her.'

'That is immaterial,' Lady Mabilia retorted angrily. 'It is her plain duty to enter the nunnery. I promised that she and I would join Judith as soon as Matthew was healed, and her dowry is already paid to the nuns. I think she should go *now*, before these foolish worldly ideas take any stronger hold on her.'

'I will not go to a nunnery now, or at any future time,' Elys said clearly and very firmly. 'I'm sorry, Mother, but I don't believe that you had any right to make such a promise on my behalf, and I'm very sure that God does not want an unwilling nun.'

'*No right?* How dare you, you wicked girl! You're my daughter and I have every right to decide what is to become of you.'

'That may have been true when Elys was a child, but she's a grown woman now,' Matthew said, looking troubled. 'If anyone has a right to make decisions on her behalf, it's I, as head of the family, and I certainly wouldn't wish my sister to feel that she should sacrifice herself for me. Your promise was made, Mother, as an offering of thanks for my healing, and I'm not healed yet, so there is no reason why Elys should be sent to Wix now, if ever. I would rather she stayed here until . . . for the time being.

Lady Mabilia shrugged, unwillingly admitting defeat for the moment, but Elys remained alarmed and wary, sure that her mother would not let the matter rest for long. It was time to start making firm plans for finding a means to live respectably in the world without a dowry and, presumably, without help from her family.

A few days later, she encountered Father Warmand, the Sacristan, leaving the church on some errand as she was about to enter it, and she asked tentatively, 'Father, would you tell me, please . . . what do you do when you need something for the church?'

'How do you mean?' he asked, frowning. 'What sort of thing were you thinking of?'

'Well . . . say you need a new altar-cloth . . .'

'We'd send Lukin to London, with an escort, of course, to buy one. Perhaps you've noticed that our linen, frontals and vestments are old and shabby? Sadly, we've no gentlefolk hereabouts, our Lady of the Manor being the Dowager Queen, who lives at Arundel, so there is no lucrative work for fine ladies to attract a professional broiderer or a mercer to settle here, and we've no nunnery nearby with sisters willing to do our needlework, so we must needs buy from the broiderers in London. I sometimes envy sacristans of churches no greater than ours, which happen to be in wealthy towns, with mercers and broiderers by the dozen to work for them. Why do you ask?'

'I'm – I'm thinking of turning professional broiderer . . .' Elys replied so nervously that she sounded thoroughly childish and unconvincing in her own ears. 'I'm good with my needle . . .'

Father Warmand was a kindly man, and he did his best not to show his amusement at the fanciful ideas of this well-bred lady, hardly more than a girl, who thought that her amateurish essays at home-taught needlework could ever be worthy of gracing the altar of a great minster like Waltham. He replied, in a gentle tone to soften his words, 'Work for the Church is work for God, and only the very highest standard is good enough. I'm sure you try hard to do good work, and perhaps, if you really intend to be a broiderer, your brother might be able to persuade a London workshop to take you as an apprentice, but no doubt they'd expect payment for their trouble.' Being a busy man in a hurry, he did not wait for her reply, but gave her a blessing and walked on.

Elys felt her eyes pricking with tears of humiliation and disappointment. He didn't even ask to see my work, she thought angrily. He's just said that he needs a good broiderer in the town, but he didn't even stop to think whether I might just be what he's looking for. He must think I'm a conceited, spoiled brat who thinks her botched, grubby cobbling the equal of the best professional work. I'll wait until I have something really good to show him, and then make him look at it, whatever he says! The mason thought my work good enough for a professional, and he knows about such things. At least he's seen it, and he's not a man to say something's good if it isn't. The thought was some comfort, but she was still left smarting at her own ineptitude in putting her case, and the sacristan's well-meaning condescension.

March brought Lent, wild daffodils, and the masons sent

by Bishop Henry to complete the building of the church. They erected their lodge-house between the cornmill stream and the market-place, laid their plaster drawing-floor, and began to erect scaffolding about the half-finished columns at the west end of the church. Elys, on her daily visits to the minster, eyed them covertly, hoping to see a familiar face among them, but she was disappointed. Crispin brought the master-mason, William of Norwich, home to supper one evening, and it emerged that the whole lodge had come down from Durham, where they had been working on the cathedral, although many of them were natives of the Norwich area.

'When do you expect the stone to begin to arrive?' asked Matthew, who had been roused to interest by the arrival of a new visitor.

'Any day now. The wind'll dry the road nicely,' William replied. He was a big, burly man with disproportionately heavy muscles in his arms and shoulders.

'Won't it come on the river?' asked Crispin.

'There's ten mills, I'd guess, between here and Bow Creek,' William replied. 'It's quicker and less bothersome to haul the stone on the road, it bein' still good, even if it's adunnamy hundred year since it were mended!'

'Where will the stone come from?' asked Elys.

'Some from Caen and some from Kent,' the mason replied. 'They'll be for load-bearin' and outside work.' He treated her question seriously, even if it did come from a female, for it dealt with the sacred material. 'Much of the rest is comin' from Merstham, in Surrey. I'd have liked some Barnack, but Bishop Henry's man thought otherwise. There's one great block comin' up from the Isle of Purbeck, but that's for a special thing, and the Bishop's man's to work on that.'

'But are you not all the Bishop's men?' asked Lady Mabilia.

'Faith, no!' William exclaimed, looking shocked. 'We work together in a group – a lodge, we call it, with masters and journeymen, and we take on apprentices to learn our mystery. We hire ourselves out to whoever needs our services and will pay our price. We belong to no man, bein' free and independent craftsmen. We've been workin' for the Bishop of Durham, and now we've hired our services to the Bishop of Winchester. The Bishop's man is a good few steps higher than any of us, a'cause he's a great artist in the carvin' and ranks with a knight, holdin' land from the Bishop, like any gentle ... He hired us in the Bishop's behalf, and specifies what we're to do, and what we've to use, but he'll leave the doin' of it to us. He'll come to carve, not to interfere. I've known him some years, and he knows his work, and he knows ours, and knows we know it too.'

'That sounds a very satisfactory state of affairs,' Matthew commented, his thin, pale face animated by a smile.

'Ay, it is that. Wish we'd had the same dealin' at Durham – nowt but interference there! No, Bishop Henry don't believe in hirin' a dog and barkin' hisself, nor do Master Aylwin – he's the carver, by the way. Choose your dog well, they reckon, and let him get on with it.'

'So Master Aylwin will be coming here, then?' Elys said, trying very hard to keep her voice calm and level, thinking it was possible Aylwin might bring news of Fulk, but not entirely succeeding, for Crispin looked at her as if something in her tone had caught his attention.

'We met him in Italy and travelled part of the way back with him in our company,' Lady Mabilia graciously informed the mason. She had become used to meeting some surprising people at her son's table, and had discovered that even people of low rank could be agreeable and interesting, provided that their table manners were not too uncouth.

'Italy!' exclaimed Master William in the awed tones usually reserved for reference to Paradise. 'Oh, by the Temple of Solomon, what would I give to go to Italy! Did you see Rome?'

'Yes.' Lady Mabilia sounded slightly puzzled, for she had not thought very highly of Rome as a city – it had merely appeared to be full of ruins.

'Did you see St Peter's?'

'Yes.'

'I heard tell there's some columns there round the high altar, all grooved and filled with gold. We cut some of our pillars in spirals in memory of them, and put them nearest

111

the altar, to mark the holiest part. We've done it at Durham and Wymondham, and other places we've worked.'

'And it's done here, too!' Elys exclaimed. 'I've noticed that the two pillars nearest the nave altar have spirals cut in them, and the next two are cut in chevrons.'

'My father worked here – he were master of our lodge twenty year since, when what's standin' here now were built. His father before him too, and *he* went to Rome and saw the pillars there. I got a drawin' he made of them.'

The news that Aylwin – and, therefore, possibly Fulk – would be coming to Waltham made Elys decide to attempt to talk to her mother about her plans to earn her own living, but first she thought she must make a more determined effort to interest Father Warmand in the possibility of giving her work. She had just finished the altar-cloth intended for the nunnery at Wix, so she took it, together with some other samples of her work, wrapped in a square of clean linen, and went to find the Sacristan.

He was in the vestry at the end of the north transept, sorting out some of the altar linen and looking depressed. He greeted her courteously, but with an air of patient resignation when she put her bundle of work on the table and asked him to inspect it.

'My dear daughter,' he said, putting aside the old stained cloth which he had been examining, 'I will not deny that we have need of needlework here, and that it's both inconvenient and expensive to have to send a score of men to London so that Lukin may go to buy what we need in reasonable safety, but I repeat that the work must be of the very highest quality, and I hardly think that an amateur like yourself, however well-meaning . . .'

'But please do me the justice and courtesy of looking!' Elys interrupted. 'This is not just an idle display of vanity, Father; I have been told by another sacristan in Italy, and by a great craftsman, that my work is of a very high standard, and I must seek employment. If my work isn't good enough, I'll accept your judgment and not trouble you again, but you could at least look at it.'

Father Warmand bowed his head and said quietly, 'You do right to chide me, daughter. I apologize. Yes, I will look, and I'll judge without prejudice. What do you wish to show me?'

'I have an altar-cloth here which I've been making for my sister's nunnery at Wix, so that you can see my white-work, and these girdles, so that you can judge my satin-stitch and laid-work. I know they're secular things, but the designs are my own, and two of them have some gold-work . . .' She unwrapped and spread out her samples.

Warmand carried the altar-cloth carefully across to the small barred window which provided the only daylight in the vestry, and peered at it very closely for what seemed a long time, inspecting the whole length of it – some fifteen feet – and occasionally making a little murmuring sound to himself. Then he returned to the table and carefully refolded it before carrying the girdles to the window to look over the coloured and gold work.

'You've used good materials. Where did you get them?'

'In Italy. My mother bought a stock of fabrics and silks for her own use, and gave me some.'

'And how much help did she give you with the work?' He looked very hard at her as he spoke and she answered.

'None at all. I was taught by the nuns at Wix, not by my mother. She does little fine work herself.'

'And who drew your designs?' He held up a girdle which had a pattern of intertwined dragons along its length, their heads forming the shaped ends.

'I did. I copied that one from a carving I saw in Worcester cathedral.'

After another long scrutiny, he returned to the table and folded the girdles, one by one, looking thoughtful, then eventually said, 'I'll admit that your stitchery is a great deal better than I expected, but I've no means of telling whether you will maintain your standard throughout a long piece of work, or if you'll grow tired of it and leave the work half-done and expensive materials gone to waste. I'm prepared to pay you to make an altar-cloth, using your own design; but it must incorporate the five crosses, of course, and some fine work on the falls at either end. The college will supply the linen and thread. I shall also give you a piece of damask, silks, gold, haircloth and silk for the lining, to make a burse,

113

again to your own design. I'll not conceal from you that these two articles will be test-pieces, particularly the burse, as your girdles are really not sufficiently rich or elaborate for me to judge your gold-work, or how you put such an article together, which is as important as the embroidery. I shall pay you half the reward in advance, as is the custom, and the other half on completion, subject to the work being acceptable. Is that agreeable to you?'

'Yes, thank you. That's very fair.' She wished he had given some indication of how much he intended to pay her, for she had no idea of the usual rates of pay to broiderers.

'I would estimate that there is about the same amount of work in each of the two articles, so I shall pay you a mark and a half in silver for each. I'll look out the materials from our store now, if you can wait a few minutes, and then we'll go to Father Brian to obtain his consent and have the first amount of silver weighed out.'

Elys gave a happy little sigh, and sank down on to a stool which he placed for her while he delved into store-chests for materials, saying, 'As you see, we have a good stock of linen, and some oddments of silk and threads, but we'll have to send to London for more if your work proves satisfactory.'

'It will,' Elys said fervently.

'Now, tell me,' he said, bringing the materials to the table to check them and fold them in a neat pile, 'why you feel it necessary to keep yourself with the needle, when you have two brothers to be responsible for you, and your upbringing can hardly have been that of a craftswoman.'

She sighed. 'My family has decided that I must be a nun, and I cannot. My whole being rebels against the idea, but I know that if I refuse to do as they wish, my family is bound to cast me out, so I must try to earn my own living.'

Warmand frowned. He did not offer an opinion, but merely said, 'I would not have thought that either Matthew or Father Crispin would cast out his younger sister into the world. I must admit we're in sore need of a really good broiderer. All our burses, banners, copes, chasubles, frontals and hangings are old, and some of them shabby, for I think we've had little new since King Harold died. I expect you've heard how the second William – er – took many of our vestments and furnishings? Queen Maud gave us some replacements, but not of such richness, for she was spending a great deal on the rebuilding, and with all the upheaval of that, the dust and the many moves of the altars, we've put off buying new until now, when there's only the west end left to be finished; but now, of course, we have to consider whether it's fair to Lukin to ask him to journey to London, carrying the necessarily large amounts of money, when the highroads are so dangerous . . . If your work does prove satisfactory, I can promise you plenty of employment. If it does, perhaps you'd care to draw a design for a cope, for example, and I'd be willing to consider it . . .'

'I'll do my best,' Elys promised, her eyes shining with pleasure that she had won her chance to prove herself, and Father Warmand, despite his 'ifs' spoke as though he expected that she would succeed.

'I'm not promising,' he added warningly, perhaps inter- preting her expression correctly. 'I still find it hard to believe that a lady can produce work of a professional standard, and, even more difficult, perhaps, keep up the long hours that the professional has worked from childhood.'

'You're giving me a chance to show what I can do,' Elys replied, 'and that's all I ask at present.'

Elys went home as light in heart with relief as she was heavy in purse. If only she could maintain a good standard of craftsmanship, it seemed that she could earn a very good living – enough to be independent and live in comfort, with enough over to save for times of illness or old age. She recalled that she had heard that some people deposited money with the Knights Templars for safe-keeping, and she resolved to ask her uncle, when she had a few pounds saved, if she could do the same herself. Crispin would write the letter for her, if she did not see Sir Richard, and no doubt he would be able to find someone to carry it to Holborn.

Her mind busy with plans, she entered the house, pushed open the door into the hall, and was well inside, wondering how to break the news of her good fortune, when she realized that Crispin, Matthew and her mother were sitting by the hearth with two guests. One, tall and dark-haired, was talking to Lady Mabilia, and the other, broad-should-ered and fair, was apparently drawing a portrait of Matthew. The former turned his head, smiled at her, then rose to his feet in a lithe, controlled movement which reminded her of a cat.

'Lady Elys!' he said, advancing to meet her with out-stretched hands. She took them in her own, dropping her precious bundle of linen and thread, and exclaimed, 'Why, Sir Fulk, we wondered when you would come!' She was conscious of a warm glow of pleasure at seeing him again, remembering her romantic dreams wistfully.

'I hadn't realized that I was expected, although I'd heard from your uncle that you were in Waltham!' he replied, pulling her closer and giving her the formal kiss of peace on her cheek. 'I expect you remember Master Aylwin?'

Aylwin had also risen, and came a trifle hesitantly to greet her, his lips barely brushing her face and his hands hardly touching hers when she offered them. Elys took the oppor-tunity to thank him for his New Year gift, which he acknowl-edged with a smile and a nod.

'Are you here to see that Master Aylwin doesn't wander off somewhere else, or to safeguard him?' she asked Sir Fulk teasingly.

'Oh, to guard him. He's one of Bishop Henry's most prized possessions,' Sir Fulk replied. 'Even more precious than his ostriches, I believe.'

'Just as well,' Aylwin commented. 'They died this last winter, poor creatures. We actually had to fight our way here, I'm sorry to say. I spent two years in Italy, and met not so much as one robber, but encountered a swarm of them on the road out of London.'

'You would come by way of Stratford by Bow and Wood-ford!' exclaimed Sir Fulk. 'I told you we should use the Cambridge road, but you insisted on coming through the Forest.'

'What robbers were they?' asked Crispin anxiously. 'I don't like the thought of any so near here. This is supposed to be the safest part of the kingdom.'

'We gathered that they were mercenaries in the pay of

116

the Earl of Essex,' Sir Fulk replied. 'They demanded way-geld in his name.'

'Did you pay?' asked Matthew, who looked more alert and well than usual, with the excitement of new visitors.

'We argued the matter, and I rapped one on the head with my best mallet,' Aylwin replied, grinning. 'Fulk swung his sword about, and his horse kicked a couple into the ditch. They lost interest after that – there were only six of them!'

'Geoffrey de Mandeville, the *former* Earl of Essex, is in disgrace with the King,' Crispin said, still looking anxious. 'He's changed sides so many times that neither party trusts him, and the King found out recently that he'd been plotting with the Empress while professing loyalty to Stephen. I heard that he's been deprived of his lands and titles and declared an outlaw. The last I heard of him, he'd seized Ely and Ramsey, and was terrorizing the country between Cambridge and Ely. God help us if he decides to come into this part of the country!'

'I doubt it,' said Sir Fulk soberly. 'He stays in the Fens because it's well-nigh impossible for the King to attack him there. He'd not risk raiding in force near London, or so far from his stronghold. The most he'll do is send a few mercenaries to attack the lands of his worst enemies.'

Crispin opened his mouth to say something more, but shut it again without speaking, glancing instead at his mother and Elys, who thought to herself that one of the few things she knew about the enemies of Geoffrey de Mandeville was the name of the one said to be the greatest of his foes, William d'Aubigny, Earl of Arundel, the second husband of Queen Adeliza. As nearly half the town of Waltham belonged to the Queen, and therefore, by right of marriage, to her husband, she was not surprised that Crispin thought it best not to continue the conversation in their mother's presence.

'Where do you mean to lodge while you're here?' Matthew asked suddenly. He had not appeared to pay much attention to the talk about de Mandeville, apparently having been more interested in his own thoughts.

'Fulk is to return to Westminster in a day or two,' Aylwin

replied. 'I shall find lodging in the town somewhere. I suppose there are inns for the pilgrims?'

'I wish you would stay here,' Matthew said. 'You could tell me so much about the places you've seen, and about your work. I would like to learn to draw. I can write well enough to be a scribe, but I need to be able to draw as well, to do the miniatures in the great letters . . . We've a bed to spare, haven't we, Crispin?'

'Yes, of course,' Crispin agreed at once. 'We'd be very happy to have you here, Master Aylwin. You'd be close to your work, and not likely to be disturbed by rowdy revellers at night, as you might be at an inn . . .'

So it was agreed that Aylwin should lodge with them, and Fulk too, until he had to return to Westminster in a day or two.

While the guests were being settled in the men's room by Crispin, Elys picked up her bundle of cloth and guiltily inspected it, fearing that her own work, or, more importantly, the linen and damask belonging to the college, might have been soiled by being dropped on the earthen, rush-strewn floor. To her relief, the wrapping was still firmly in place.

'What have you there, Elys?' her mother asked.

'Cloth for some work I'm to do for the college,' Elys replied in as matter-of-fact a tone as she could manage. 'I took some samples of my work to show the Sacristan, and he's asked me to make an altar-cloth and a burse, and he wishes me to draw a design for a cope . . .'

'He wishes!' Lady Mabilia exclaimed indignantly. 'Does he take you for a common craftswoman, to receive orders concerning your work?'

'Yes,' Elys replied firmly. 'Precisely that. The work I'm to do is a trial. If it's good enough, there'll be more, and I'm to be paid for it – well-paid, at that. I already have some silver in advance for the trial pieces. You need not concern yourself any more about how I shall live in the world, for I can keep myself very well with my needle.'

'You mean you'll receive a pittance for weeks of work, and you think you can live on that!' Lady Mabilia retorted scornfully.

'Is a purse of good silver pennies a pittance for an altar-cloth and a burse?' Elys replied defiantly. 'Mother, please try to understand,' she went on, softening her tone to something near pleading, 'I cannot be a nun! I'd rather die than be shut up in a convent. I've no wish to be a burden to anyone, and I mean to prove that I can earn my living in a very respectable trade, using the talent God has given me.'

'Mother,' Matthew put in quietly and unexpectedly, 'at least consider what she says. I've no wish for my own sister to be forced into a nunnery against her will for my sake, and you know that she'll not be accepted if she's unwilling. She can serve God with her needle in the world, and earn a respectable living as well.'

'The world's too full of danger for a woman alone,' Lady Mabilia said, looking troubled. 'A convent is safe, and a nun's life untroubled. Why are you so different from Judith and myself?'

'I'm not so different from you, though I may be from Judith,' Elys replied. 'You had a husband and children, and that's what I want.'

'You don't know what you're talking about.' Lady Mabilia suddenly looked old and worn. 'Married to a rough stranger, subject to his every whim, an object for his satisfaction, but no more important than his hawk, and less than his horse! And children! Borne with trouble and ill-health, brought forth in pain, and half of them dying, despite all your prayers and love! Judith was my eldest, and she saw the others come, five of them sickening and dying, and only three to live . . . She made the wise choice, poor dear, knowing the alternative. You, the youngest, have no idea what you are talking about.'

'Many women marry and have children and are happy,' Elys countered, thinking privately that at last she had some inkling of the reason for Judith's cold detachment, which she had always found so hurtful as a child, and a great deal more understanding of her mother. Why had they never talked like this before?

'You've no dowry, so you'll have no husband.' Lady Mabilia sounded less sharp and decisive than usual.

'I have the means to earn myself a dowry, with my needle,'

Elys replied, stifling a niggling fear that her work might not prove satisfactory after all . . .

'A couple of silver pennies, and you think yourself rich!' her mother scoffed.

'Two hundred and forty silver pennies,' Elys retorted, 'and that's only the advance payment. There'll be another mark and a half when the work's finished, and a pound is as much as you get from the rents on your widow's portion in a quarter-year.'

'Two pounds . . . Merciful Heavens!' Lady Mabilia was astounded. 'Is that what a broiderer receives for a few weeks' work?'

'I believe the king pays his broiderers ten pounds each a year,' Aylwin volunteered, coming back into the hall with Fulk and Crispin as she was speaking. 'That's besides their allowances for materials and candles, of course. My master pays much the same, with extra for ecclesiastical work. You've made a start on your profession, then, Elys?'

'I've two trial pieces to make for the college, and a promise of more if I'm good enough,' she replied, noting that he still called her by her name, without a title, and thinking that she must get used to that from a fellow-craftsman, 'and Father Warmand wishes me to draw a design for a cope.'

'You'll need a frame to make a cope,' Aylwin said thoughtfully. 'Do you have one?'

'No, not a table-frame – only tambours in various sizes. If I get the work of making a cope, I'll have to have a frame made.'

'One of my friends is the carpenter sent here by the Bishop to advise of the furnishings,' Aylwin said. 'I'll ask him to make you a frame – it's a simple job and he'll not charge much. I'm glad you thought to ask if the minster here needs any needle-work.'

'I have to thank you for the suggestion,' Elys said quietly. 'I'd never have thought of it for myself, for I'd no idea it was such well-paid work!' She glanced at her mother, but Lady Mabilia's attention was on Matthew, who, having inadvertently jarred his foot, was gasping with pain. Elys started to her feet as soon as she realized what had happened, but she could only watch helplessly while Crispin ran to get his small phial of poppy-juice. Taking in the situation with remarkable quickness, Aylwin ran to the kitchen for water, while Fulk sat looking bewildered, not sure what was going on.

Water and poppy-juice arrived almost together, and Crispin carefully stirred a few drops of the opiate into the cup, then held it to Matthew's lips. He drank, pausing from time to time to bite his lips and draw a shuddering breath, until the cup was empty, then lay back, his face pasty and sweating.

Lady Mabilia sat watching him, blinking back tears, until the drug took effect and he began to relax.

Then she said, 'I must go across to the church to pray. Excuse me.'

'Shall I come with you?' Elys asked.

'No. You stay here and attend to our guests. I'd rather go alone.'

She returned just before supper, by which time Matthew was recovered, although still a little pale and drowsy, content to lie back in his chair and listen to the conversation, which was mostly a dialogue between Crispin and Aylwin about the minster building and the work still to be done on it.

'Master William is in charge of the building,' Aylwin explained. 'My part is only to make a new font, and to provide any carvings required. I doubt if there'll be many, for it's a remarkably unadorned building in that respect! I noticed while I was in it, before we met you, that there are only two carved capitals in the whole place, and they look old-fashioned enough to have come from King Harold's church. Otherwise, there are just half a dozen heads of imps, peering down from the triforium.'

'Why are they there?' asked Elys. 'I'd have thought angels would be more appropriate!'

'If you observe them closely, you'll see that they're being crushed by the weight of the stones above them,' Aylwin replied, treating her question as seriously as he had always done. 'It's a charming conceit, I think.'

'There are a few corbel-heads outside, under the eaves,' Crispin said.

'Yes. I'm to do some more, to complete the row along

the south side, if I have time, but my master wants me back at Winchester by the end of the summer, so I'll not have time to do very many. The font is the more important work, as the old one leaks quite badly. Bishop Henry seems to have a habit of giving fonts to churches in his charge. He's just presented one to each of eight churches in his diocese, to my knowledge, all of Tournai marble, but it's to be Purbeck this time.'

He wasted no time in setting about the making of the font, the stone for which had already arrived in the first cart-load to come up from Bow Creek. The very next morning, he set up a roofed work-shed for himself, with the carpenter's help, in the angle between the southwest tower and the south aisle wall, and during the afternoon, the great block of Purbeck marble was hauled round from the masons' yard and set up ready for him. Elys, who happened to pass soon after, looked in and asked, 'Am I interrupting you?'

'Not at all,' he replied. 'Come in and look.'

Elys took a few steps into the shed, then realized that someone else was there, sitting on a stool in the darkest corner. 'Oh, I'm sorry,' she said, 'I didn't realize you were busy.'

'We were just exchanging news,' Aylwin reassured her. 'This is my old friend Galien, a master carpenter. I've known him for years, but we meet only occasionally, when we happen to be working in the same place. I've asked him to make you a table-frame, by the way.'

Elys smiled and greeted Galien, who made no move, except to duck his head in acknowledgement, and said nothing at all.

'I'd be very grateful,' she said, 'but I haven't been granted the work of making a cope yet. Perhaps it would be better to wait until I know if I'm to make it or not.'

'I'll make the frame anyway, while I'm here and have suitable wood to hand,' the carpenter said so quietly that she could hardly hear him. His voice had a curiously thick, sibilant quality and a slight accent which she could not place. 'I'll be going now,' he added, getting to his feet. 'We can talk later, Aylwin. Good day to you, lady,' and he slipped past Elys and out of the door before she could reply. As he went, she caught a glimpse of a swarthy, beak-nosed face framed by beard and hair which were curly and glossy, and of the raven's-wing black which has a blue sheen.

'Is he very shy?' she asked when he had gone. 'He doesn't sound English or Norman – perhaps he finds the language difficult . . . ?'

'He was born in Nazareth, which is as good a place for a carpenter's home-town as any I can imagine,' Aylwin said lightly.

'In the Holy Land? Surely he's not a Saracen?' Elys was shocked at the thought.

'No. He's as Christian as you or I, but folk often think otherwise, so he's learned to be as near invisible as possible, for fear of being attacked.'

'Why should anyone attack him?'

Aylwin made a sound which might have been amusement or exasperation. 'Surely you've travelled about in Christendom enough to know how bitterly most folk hate the Jews!' he said. 'Even to look like a Jew is enough to bring accusations of ritual murder of Christian children, quite apart from the sin of being one of the race which crucified Our Lord!'

'Yes, I know, but you say he's a Christian . . .'

'Do you imagine that the ruffians who stone Jews in the street stop to enquire about their victims' faith? Suffice it to say that even his appearance is against him, so he chooses to remain unnoticed. He'll make you a good frame, but you may not even set eyes on him again, unless you happen to stumble on the quiet corner where he's working.'

'But if Father Warmand doesn't think my work good enough to make a cope . . .'

'The first thing you have to learn when you're a craftsman – or -woman – is to have faith in your own ability. Do you think you can make a cope worthy of Waltham minster?'

'Yes.'

'Then you'll need a good frame. Galien will see to it as soon as the shuttering is down at the west end, to let the

123

masons start building. He'll find enough spare wood in the remains, I expect.'

Elys thanked him, and then asked, 'What sort of a font are you going to make?'

Aylwin, who was already making the first tentative chips with chisel and mallet, gestured with the latter towards the bench by the door, where one of his notebooks was lying open. 'It's there, in the book. You may look, if you wish.'

She went to the bench and studied the drawings carefully. The first showed a font on a drum-shaped base, with a square top, supported at each corner by a small round column, the whole standing on a stepped base. The four sides of the top were drawn in detail on the following pages, and she wondered how he would be able to show so much detail in hard stone. The first side showed the Ark, with Noah counting the animals in, two by two, and Noah's wife standing at a distance, refusing to come into the Ark. The second side showed Jonah being dropped over the side of a small ship into the toothy maw of a very large fish. On the third side was Moses as a baby, floating in a cradle among the bulrushes, his hands held out, trying to catch a bird, and the fourth showed the baptism of Jesus, with John the Baptist in his goatskins bowing before him, fish swimming about their feet as they stood in the Jordan, and a dove hovering over the head of Jesus.

'Can you really show all that in stone?' she marvelled.

'To be honest, no! It will be clumsier, and lack the finer detail. I suppose that one day someone will manage to carve in fine detail, but at present our tools are just not good enough. Have you thought any more about the design for your cope?'

'I thought perhaps the burning bush . . .' Elys replied hesitantly, for she had been too busy planning the altar-cloth and the burse to consider the cope in any detail. 'King William took – stole – a cope from here which they called "The Lord Spake Unto Me", and I thought it would be suitable to make a new one, with the words in the orphrey – in Latin, of course – and the bush, all gold and reds and yellows, growing up the back, from a meadow of wild flowers . . . It depends what colour they want it to be. It it's green, that would be best, but they may want white or gold if it's to be for festivals . . .'

'Best find out,' Aylwin replied a trifle absently, for he had just found a small flaw in the stone and was working out how best to allow for it in his carving.

Elys realized that he was concentrating on his work, so she silently turned the pages of his book, finding trees, faces, animals – there was a very beautiful head of a horse, which she recognized as Sir Fulk's destrier – a sketch of St Paul's, which she also recognized, and, on the page before the font, a crucifix. It was so beautiful, the figure of Christ depicted so movingly, that her eyes filled with tears as she looked at it. On the facing page was a larger drawing of the face, which she thought quite marvellous. It was a strong, rather ugly face, with heavy brows and a large aquiline nose, but the most beautiful melancholy dark eyes. Gazing at it, she realized she had just caught a fleeting glimpse of that face in life. It was Galien.

'Have you ever carved this?' she asked.

Aylwin stood up, having just found the answer to his problem, and crossed over to the bench to look at the drawing.

'Oh – the crucifix. No, not yet. I think I might do it in wood, or even ivory. That's Galien, by the way.'

'Yes, I recognized him,' Elys exclaimed. 'I didn't realize that you would use the face of a real person for something like that – for holy statues, I mean!'

'Why not? Yours would make an excellent Madonna. Who better for Christ than a carpenter?'

'Does the Church allow you to use ordinary faces as models for such things?'

'I don't use *ordinary* faces. I use faces which have something of the character that I want to portray. Galien has suffered a great deal, and known rejection in his life, and it shows in his face, particularly in his eyes. Your face has an unusual combination of innocence, strength and courage, which our Lady would have needed to bear the Christ-child and endure the sorrows of the Crucifixion. See Noah in the font drawings? That's Bishop Henry.'

Elys studied the drawing of Noah again, with half her

mind on what he had said about her own face – innocence, strength and courage! That was quite the greatest compliment she had ever received in her life, yet it had not been spoken in a flattering manner, but as a simple statement of fact. Aylwin must consider her no more than a young girl with an interesting face . . . She concentrated on the figure of Noah, seeing a well-built man with a handsome face and a heavy black beard, which she recognized without difficulty.

'Why?' she asked.

'He loves animals – he keeps a menagerie of them at Bishop's Waltham. He loves carving, too, but in miniature. Did you see any cameos while you were in Rome?'

'Yes. My mother bought one – of St Paul, I think, with the saint in white on a pink background.'

'Bishop Henry collects them, and carved gems as well, but old Roman ones. He has hundreds. I've learned a great deal about carving fine detail from studying them . . . Have you designed your cope yet?'

'Only in my head.'

'Why don't you draw it?' He produced his precious silverpoint from his purse, picked up a knife from the bench and cut out a page from the back of his notebook, and gave both to Elys, who tentatively began to draw.

She started with the outline of the half-circle of an outspread cope, then, gaining confidence as she found that the unfamiliar tool was easier to manage than charcoal, began at the bottom of the centre back with the short trunk of a bush, spreading out the branches as she progressed upwards, pair by pair, so that they covered the back and would flow over the shoulders when the cope was worn. Once the skeleton was drawn, she filled in the side-shoots, ending each with a leaf shaped like a flame.

'Why, it's coming out just as I imagined it!' she exclaimed, and boldly drew in a formalized coney, half behind the trunk and peering out, and perched a few birds in the branches. Then, drawing the shape of the hood between the shoulders, she filled it with a dove, wings outspread, appearing to be about to alight on the topmost twig.

'That's a good design,' Aylwin commented, looking over

her shoulder. 'What do you usually draw with? Charcoal or chalk?'

'Charcoal. It's so easy to come by, but much clumsier than this. When I've earned enough money to have some to spare, I'll buy a silver-point.'

'If I were Father Warmand, I'd want you to make that. I know he has an eye for anything unusual, so be it's well-designed. How do you put the drawing on the cloth?'

'I prick the parchment, then rub chalk through it, but it wears off so easily that I have to keep doing it over again.'

'I'll show you how to paint over the chalk-marks when the time comes.'

'How kind you are!' she exclaimed, clasping her drawing to her breast and turning to look up into his face. 'You've been so helpful and encouraging, ever since I met you. I wish I could do something for you.'

'You can give me back my silver-point,' he said, plucking it from her fingers, 'and do your best work on that cope, for I've told Father Warmand that I think you can equal any London broiderer, and I have a reputation to keep. I'll be interested to see how that drawing is transformed into another form of art and another medium, other than parchment, stone or wood.'

Meanwhile, Elys still had a fair white linen cloth and a burse to make. With the days slowly lengthening and the weather growing warmer, Elys could sit for hours by the window, stitching and talking to Matthew and his frequent visitors. On his better days, she had some time to herself while he was carried in his chair to the church to pray before the Holy Cross for an hour or two, and she did not neglect to take exercise, either riding with Crispin and Sir Fulk or walking about the town. On most days, she found time to stop for a few minutes at Aylwin's workshed, to see how the font was progressing.

Sir Fulk's stay in Waltham lengthened to three weeks, which he spent hanging about between Matthew's house and Aylwin's workshop or riding in the Forest, unashamedly idle, rarely speaking directly to Elys, but often watching her at her work while he talked to her brothers or her mother, and somehow she felt that, although he did not talk to her very much, it was not because he was no longer interested. There was a tension about him, an impression that he was having difficulty in preventing himself from saying or doing something forbidden. Eventually he received a curt note from the Bishop, who required his presence 'two weeks since', as he expressed it, and he had, perforce, to prepare to depart.

Before he left, he returned to the house in Church Street at a time when he knew, having been watching from the door of Aylwin's shed, that Elys was alone in the house, apart from the servants, Crispin being engaged in assisting at Mass, and Matthew and his mother at their prayers. He complimented Elys on her fine needlework, remarked on the weather, which was fine and mild, reported a flowering of primroses in the churchyard, and, eventually, after a long pause, said abruptly, 'I expect you realized that I nearly offered for you when we were in Dover?'

'Did you?' Elys replied calmly, hiding a resurgence of the anger and despair which had engulfed her that winter's night, which now seemed a long time ago. 'I suppose my uncle dissuaded you,' she added, hoping her voice sounded no more than mildly interested.

'Well – in a way. He said you'd have no dowry . . . You see, my family would never allow me to marry a lady, however suitable she might otherwise be, unless she would bring lands or influence to the family . . . or even money . . . I regret it bitterly, for I'd like very much to marry you . . . I don't suppose you'd consider . . .'

'Consider what?' Elys asked when the hesitation had become uncomfortably long. She looked at him enquiringly, genuinely having no idea what he meant.

'I don't suppose you'd consider becoming my mistress?' He got it out in a rush and looked at her in what was meant to be a beseeching fashion, but which looked to Elys to be merely quizzical.

'No, I would not!' she said decisively, her indignation overcoming her embarrassment. 'If my lack of a dowry condemns me in the eyes of your family, and you're not prepared to defy them, I suggest you go away and forget all about me. I, too, have a family to consider.'

Fulk sighed deeply. 'I can't forget you,' he said gloomily. 'What can I do?'

'Go to Winchester, and busy yourself with your master's ostriches!' Elys snapped. 'I believe they are said to bury their heads in the ground when they see something which upsets them! You might emulate them when you're beset with thoughts of my dowerless state!'

'I'm not sure that's true,' he replied gravely. 'I've never seen them do it, and anyway, they died in the winter. I'm sorry I've made you angry. I hope you find a husband more worthy of you. Goodbye.'

'I'm sorry,' Elys exclaimed to his retreating back. 'I shouldn't have spoken so unkindly.'

He turned at the door, smiled sadly, and said, 'It's I who should apologize. I had no right to ask such a thing of you and I deserve your anger. A true knight would defy even his family for his lady, but I lack the courage, or perhaps the singlemindedness, to do that. I shall never forget you, and I hope you'll think of me sometimes – kindly, if possible!' He made her a courtly bow, and went out.

Elys listened to the bang of the street door behind him and his footsteps retreating down Church Street, staring unseeingly at her work. So he had, in fact, loved her, not merely thought of her as a suitable bride, but not enough to take her without that dowry! She sighed, feeling empty of any emotion save an arid hopelessness, tinged with bitter disappointment. She had thought, even dreamed, of Fulk, mistaking him for a fine example of Norman knighthood, but he had turned out to be nothing but a spineless popinjay, too afraid of his family to risk displeasing them.

If I had a dowry, I might have married him, she thought, and not found out until after that he's a – a *nithing*! The English word came into her mind unbidden, surprising her, but she could not think of a more fitting epithet. Well, thank Heaven I found out what he's really like! I'll not waste any more dreams on him, but find a better man, who won't care if I have a dowry or not. A brave resolve, but her common sense made her add forlornly, if such a man exists. Perhaps, if she worked hard and saved all she could of her earnings, she might eventually gain a dowry for herself, but how old would she be by then? At seventeen, she was already growing too old for many men to consider marrying her. She sighed again, and then resumed her work, her needle passing in and out of the fine linen in a regular, precise sequence of stitches, each one perfectly in place, small and neat, and each representing a moment of her life. How many years would she stitch away like this, without a husband or a child to love?

The street door banged again, and Aylwin came in, his hair tousled and full of stone-dust, and a cut on his cheek marked by a little dried blood.

'Fulk's on his way, then,' he said. 'Did he come to bid you goodbye?'

'Yes.'

'His father has the temper of the devil, and it's not improved by his lands all lying in the west, in the territory still held by the Empress, so, he being for the King, he has no income from them. He wants a rich bride for Fulk.'

'Yes. I understand,' Elys replied expressionlessly. 'I suppose you know he made me an – an offer . . . of sorts . . . ?'

'I told him he'd be a fool if he did, but he was desperate enough to risk it, apparently. I'm sorry, Elys. He'd have made you a good husband . . . I won't mention the matter again, unless you bring it up first.'

'Thank you.' Elys managed a bleak little smile. 'Tell me, did Bishop Henry's ostriches ever bury their heads in the ground?'

'Not that I ever observed. They'd have found it difficult, though, for he kept them in a grass paddock, along with the peacocks. I must go and stand under the pump – I'm filthy. I've been helping Galien take down some of the temporary woodwork, and it's amazing how much dust it's collected in the past seven years!'

He went through to the room which he shared with Matthew and Crispin, returning with a bundle of clean clothes, then went out to the yard, whence Elys heard the sound of the pump clanking as one of the servants sent a

130

stream of icy water pouring over the mason, who could also be heard exclaiming as he rotated in it, washing the dust from his hair and body. Elys wondered if he was wise to risk washing himself so thoroughly, particularly in cold water, but supposed he had enough sense to realize how dangerous it could be. He returned presently, damp and cleanly dressed, just as the rest of the family came home to supper.

A little later that evening, Father Radulf came to change the dressing on Matthew's foot. He found his patient and Aylwin playing chess, Crispin watching, and the ladies sitting by the window, catching the last of the daylight on their sewing, so he sat down quietly to wait until Matthew had finished his game, assuring him that he was glad of a chance to rest after a busy day.

'We had a poor old woman in the church today,' he told Crispin. 'She went up to the altar of the Holy Cross just after a lady from Enfield, who had laid an offering – a gold piece – on it. The woman – Edith, her name is – tried to steal it by picking it up on her tongue as she pretended to kiss the altar, and hiding it in her mouth. Just as she was walking away, she started to choke, but luckily Father Antony was nearby. He thumped her hard on the back, and the coin was dislodged in a great gout of blood! The poor creature seems to have hurt her neck somehow in her choking, and she's unable to hold her head normally, but has it bent back, so she can only see upwards!'

'A judgment on her for her wickedness,' Lady Mabilia said primly, pursing her lips and looking so self-righteous that Elys could not resist saying, 'She must have been desperate for money to steal from the altar.'

'Indeed, yes,' Father Radulf replied, 'and more desperate now, for she can't go about as she is. We have her in the infirmary.'

Matthew, who had been concentrating on his game, gave a triumphant cry of 'Checkmate!' and sat back, flushed and pleased, and Aylwin smilingly accepted defeat. There was a little shifting about to make it easier for Father Radulf to treat the injured foot, and then he set to work.

'How is it this evening?' asked Lady Mabilia, sounding confident that it would be better.

Father Radulf made no reply. He had removed the outer layer of bandages, and was gently unwinding the inner layer, and an unpleasant, sickly-sweet smell began to spread across the hall.

CHAPTER SEVEN

When Father Radulf had finished redressing his foot, Matthew, white-faced and with traces of blood on his bitten lips, said briefly that he felt tired and would go to bed. He was taken there swiftly and easily by Crispin and Aylwin, who had already grown used to working together in such matters. The invalid was left in peace in the sleeping-chamber, with the luxury of two wax candles and one of Aylwin's notebooks to look at. It happened to be the one containing the sketches for the font.

When Crispin and Aylwin returned to the hall, where Father Radulf was taking a goblet of wine with the ladies in uneasy silence, Crispin said abruptly, 'Is it as you feared, then?'

Radulf nodded gravely. 'Necrosis has developed in the toes,' he replied bleakly. 'I know of no remedy.'

'But surely,' Lady Mabilia said, 'there must be something . . .' Her usually decisive tone was lacking, however, and her voice tailed off, quavering. Elys, looking fearfully at her face, saw that she looked old, tired, and, for the first time, hopeless.

Radulf shook his head. 'I know of only one course of action, and I may not use it. It's seldom successful, I believe, and usually only hastens . . . the inevitable.'

'Why may you not use it?' demanded Lady Mabilia. 'Is it witchcraft of some sort?'

'No. Amputation. A priest may not shed blood.'

'How long?' asked Crispin, voicing the thought in all their minds.

'I don't know. Weeks, perhaps, or maybe only days. I'm sorry.'

There was nothing more to be said, so Father Radulf gave them his blessing and went away. Presently they all went to bed, even before the curfew had sounded from the church. Elys hardly slept at all, but lay still, trying to avoid sobbing aloud as tears ran down her cheeks. Somewhere in the dead hours of the night she heard her mother creep out of the room and descend the stairs. She did not pause there, in the men's room, but went on, presumably out of the house and across the road to the church.

In the succeeding days, Lady Mabilia spent most of her time in the church, kneeling for long hours in the shadow of the great cross, and Elys and Crispin were often with her, but Crispin had his duties about the church, and preferred to spend most of his free time with his brother, as did Elys, who would sit with him by the fire, working on the embroidery of the burse.

Once it was done, she wrapped it up with the altar cloth, and took both to Father Warmand, who unfolded the cloth first and inspected it minutely, in silence, for so long, that Elys, already depressed by the news of Matthew, felt her hopes fading like mist on a summer's morning.

'And the burse?' he asked eventually, laying the cloth aside carefully, but without commenting on it.

'I've done the embroidery, but I'd like your opinion before I make it up, because you won't be able to see the back of the work then,' she said nervously, handing him the piece of damask on which she had drawn a cross fleury and filled it with couched gold thread. He barely glanced at the front, but turned it over and carried it to the window to inspect the back.

'Your couching just pulls the gold through the fabric,' he commented. 'I've not seen that before. Is it done for a purpose?'

'Yes. It makes a tiny hinge in the gold at every stitch, so the finished work is flexible. I saw it done like that in France. I'll do it flat if you prefer, but it will be stiffer, and won't wear so well.'

'It also allows the light to catch the gold at a variety of angles, making a richer impression,' he observed, looking at the right side. 'I like it – it's more interesting than a flat surface. Have you thought at all about the cope?'

She produced her drawing, suddenly feeling a little more hopeful.

'What does it represent?' he asked, 'The Tree of Life?'

'The burning bush,' she replied. 'With the leaves done in laid work in various flame colours, it will appear to be on fire, but the birds aren't consumed. The trunk and branches will be gold.'

'And the dove is the Holy Ghost entering it . . .' He held the drawing at arm's length, turning it to the light. 'All the colours of flames and of autumn leaves . . . You've not drawn the orphreys.'

'I thought I might do those plain, with the words *Dominus dixit ad me* in gold . . .'

' "The Lord spake to me" . . . You've heard that we had a cope which was called by that name, but William Rufus took it from us? It was stiff with gold, they say, and extremely valuable, so I doubt, somehow, that it ever reached Caen and his parents' foundations . . .'

'Lukin told me about it.' She hesitated, longing to know what he thought of her work and her design, but afraid to ask.

'Green silk, I think . . . twill, not damask . . .' he said, as if to himself. 'We've a length would do very well. The flames would show well on it . . . Do you agree?' She nodded dumbly, surprised that he had guessed her own preference so closely. 'I must consult Father Brian about sending Lukin to London for more thread and gold, but we've enough to start you on the work meanwhile . . . and we must send to Lord Aucher about borrowing an escort . . .'

'Lord Aucher?' she asked, still afraid to ask the more important question.

'A friend of the college. He holds land in the Forest and lends us men at arms when we need them, which is whenever we must send Lukin or one of our brethren on an errand. Without his help, we'd not have managed to do our duties in our daughter churches these past half-dozen years and more. There's the matter of a pound due to you for the altar-cloth as well. Wait here, and I'll fetch it for you.'

'You mean . . . my work is good enough?' she blurted out at last.

He looked surprised. 'I thought it was I who doubted that, not you, child. Yes, it's as good as any I've seen, and

I'm sorry I doubted you,' and he went out of the vestry without waiting for her fervent thanks.

He returned with Father Brian, as well as the pound of silver pennies due for the altar-cloth, and gravely showed the work Elys had done and her drawing. Father Brian disclaimed any knowledge of needlecraft, but said the stitches were incredibly small and neat, and approved the design for the cope, and asked, 'What are you thinking of paying? The last one we bought from London was twelve pounds, as I recall, but it was fairly plain . . . The thread for this will cost more than that.'

'I'd say six pounds for the work, and we to supply the materials,' Father Warmand replied after some thought. 'Perhaps a little more, if it turns out as well as the drawing promises.'

Elys left the church feeling comforted and satisfied, her anxiety about Matthew overweighing the elation she would otherwise have felt. Nevertheless, she stopped at Aylwin's workshed to tell him the good news, and he was obviously pleased, but not surprised.

'I told you you'd need that frame,' he said. 'Galien's nearly finished it, and it'll be ready by the time you finish putting the burse together. Well done, craftswoman.'

Elys laughed with pleasure at the last three words, and was still smiling when she reached home, but the sight of her brother's pale face soon sobered her again.

Matthew seemed unaware that anything in his situation had changed, and he neither mentioned nor questioned the smell of his foot when Father Radulf dressed it, but Elys was sure that he knew that death was drawing near to him. He would sit still for long periods, staring into the fire, occasionally looking up to smile at whoever was with him. His friends from the town were not told of his condition, but they seemed to sense it, and came often, but stayed only for short visits, not wishing to tire him. They talked quietly, even Lukin reducing his fantastic prancing and gesturing to a muted pantomime. There was a general feeling of depression in the house which worked on everyone's spirits, already brought down by the fasting of Lent and the long sleepless hours when each member of the family lay awake, praying or fearing for the doomed man.

Lady Mabilia had sent word to her brother and her other daughter that they should come to Waltham, without saying why. Judith arrived within the week, much flustered and upset because, although her prioress had sent her with an escort of six reliable men, she had been stopped on the road by some of de Mandeville's mercenaries, who had robbed her of her silver crucifix and ivory-covered psalter, and thoroughly frightened her by their lewd looks and speech as they openly discussed whether or not they should rape her.

'Godless barbarians,' she said with unaccustomed asperity. 'What is England coming to when a fully professed nun may not travel the width of a shire in safety? Obviously, I should not have left the cloister, but I thought it my duty to come and pray for my poor brother. I take it that he is dying, or you would not have summoned me from my duties.'

'We do not speak of such a possibility!' Lady Mabilia replied curtly. 'He requires our prayers, of course, but for healing, not for the passage of his soul.'

Judith gave a faint sniff, murmured something to the effect that she could equally well have continued praying for that at Wix, and withdrew to a corner of the dais, where she knelt in prayer for a considerable time, ignoring everyone else.

Sir Richard came the next day, arriving in mid-afternoon, just as Aylwin was helping Elys to set up her new table-frame, which was a large rectangle, the long sides made as rollers, held by the side-pieces at each corner in forks tightened by thumbscrews. It stood on trestles, so it could be taken down and leaned against the wall, out of the way, when not in use, and it was big enough to take the quarter-circle of half a cope with ease.

'What on earth is that?' enquired the Templar after greeting his niece in a perfunctory fashion, and Aylwin with surprise and restrained pleasure. He had not forgotten the respect he had learned to feel for the mason.

'An embroidery frame,' Elys replied.

137

'You can think of such worldly matters at a time like this?' Sir Richard asked coldly, for he had guessed why his sister had summoned him, 'and in Lent, at that.'

'I have a commission to make a cope for the canons of the minster,' Elys replied calmly. 'My skill with the needle meets their approval, so I'm turned professional broideress.'

Sir Richard's mouth dropped open for a moment, and his normally reserved, inscrutable face showed his amazement, but he soon recovered. 'I had observed that you appear to be gifted with your needle,' he said stiffly, being unused to having anything good to say of Elys. 'I'm glad you've decided to dedicate your gift to the service of Our Lord and Holy Mother Church. No doubt you'll find many opportunities to do so at Wix.'

'I shall never return to Wix,' Elys replied, lowering her chin and looking up at him in a manner in which Aylwin's observant eyes saw a resemblance of a bull about to charge. He hastily interposed himself, before she could say anything she might repent. 'Lady Elys has decided to stay in the world and earn her living by her needle. Matthew's asleep at present, and perhaps you'll think it better not to wake him. Lady Mabilia, Crispin and Sister Helen are in the church. Shall I fetch them, or will you join them there?'

'Sister Helen?' Sir Richard looked blank for a moment, having forgotten his other niece's name in religion. 'Oh, Judith . . . I'll take a cup of ale and a little bread, if it won't be too much trouble, and then go over to the church.'

One of the servants, who had been hovering outside the hall door, expecting a summons, was sent to the kitchen for ale and bread, and Sir Richard walked to the table on the dais and began his sixty Paternosters, leaving Aylwin and Elys to spread the beautiful green silk twill across the frame, ready for Elys to fasten it with firm stitches to the stout linen strips nailed to the wood. She had already marked on it, using white paint and a sparrow's feather, the outline of the half-cope, with turning allowances and the width of the centre seam, for it was not possible to obtain fabric wide enough to cut a cope in one piece.

'I must thank Master Galien for making the frame,' she said.

'Best not. I'll convey your thanks to him.'

She looked at him enquiringly, and he went on, 'Galien's a shy man, afraid, in a way, of being noticed, or even of talking to strangers. I've known him for years, and I think he trusts me, but he prefers not to have anything to do with most other people.'

'Why?'

He hesitated, and glanced towards Sir Richard, who was now sitting at the high table, eating his bread and a bowl of vegetable pottage, a goblet of ale standing out of his reach until he should have finished eating. 'What do you think of the Jews?' Aylwin asked.

Elys looked blank, and replied, 'I don't think I know any. I've seen them, of course, in the towns, but they keep to their own quarters, and I've not actually met one, except perhaps to buy something . . . It's difficult to tell what a foreign merchant may be if he speaks English . . .'

'As I mentioned before, many folk hate them for their wealth, their usury, their foreignness, and, of course, their religion, but, above all, because they brought Our Lord to his death,' Aylwin said. 'Most of them hate the Christians equally, but a few are made miserable by the hatred . . . Such a one was Galien's father . . . He turned Christian.'

Elys had experienced some of the problems of being a stranger in a foreign land, but she had always had her religion in common with the people there, and had been secure in the knowledge that she was still in Christendom, within the mantle of Mother Church. She had never considered what it must be like to belong to a religious minority, let alone to be hated by the majority. She thought about it now, and, gropingly, began to understand a little why Galien, born of a people whose religion was linked to their race, yet, presumably, brought up in an alien faith, might feel insecure and afraid of his fellow-men.

'So he doesn't just look like a Jew,' she said. 'But you said he's a Christian? He must be, to be working for the Church . . .'

'Yes, but he's always afraid that someone will realize that he's a Jew by race . . . I could be putting his life in your hands by telling you . . .'

'I'll not mention it to anyone,' Elys replied, glancing at her uncle.

'What are you whispering about, down there?' asked Sir Richard, pushing away his bowl and reaching for his goblet.

'We were talking about the design for the cope,' Elys replied, lying without compunction. 'Master Aylwin has kindly offered to help paint the design on the cloth for me.'

'Why whisper about it, then?'

'We didn't wish to disturb you, Uncle.'

'Hm. Well, Master Aylwin – will you be so kind as to take me to my sister?'

'By all means,' Aylwin replied with easy courtesy. 'I must, in any case, return to my work. We'll start to paint the cope after supper, if you have the cloth on the frame by then,' he added to Elys.

'Thank you. Oh – how much should I pay Master Galien?'

'Have you a fourthing? It's all he'll take.'

Elys searched in her purse for a quarter of a penny, but could not find one, so Aylwin broke a whole penny for her, carefully doing it on the lines of the cross marked on its surface for that purpose, his strong fingers snapping the silver easily, where she would have found it necessary to use shears. He took one quarter, and promised to add her thanks when he delivered it.

By the time the rest of her family returned for supper, Elys had the heavy silk securely fastened and stretched on the frame, and Matthew was awake and had been brought back to the hall by the servants. He greeted his uncle without much enthusiasm, and his bitter statement, 'So now you're all here to take your leave of me!' made it clear that he knew he could not expect to live much longer.

'It's time to make your peace and prepare yourself for a better life,' replied Sir Richard in a stiff and formal fashion, which made Elys wonder if he were unfeeling, or perhaps unable to reveal his deeper emotions. She decided to give him the benefit of the doubt, and smiled gently at him when she caught his eyes, but drew no response.

'Will you not join us at table?' his sister asked when he made no move to take the place prepared for him.

'I've eaten once today,' he replied. 'I never take more than one meal a day in Lent.'

'But you had only a little soup and some bread,' Elys protested.

'That's more than Our Lord had in the wilderness,' he answered brusquely. 'I shall go and see that my men are well lodged. We are to stay in the minster guesthouse.'

'Not you as well,' protested Lady Mabilia. 'We have room here for you.'

'If you mean I may have a bed in the room where my nephew will be trying to rest, I must tell you that I think it better that he be left in peace to consider his – his position, and that Crispin and Master Aylwin should sleep elsewhere, perhaps by joining us in the guesthouse.'

'No!' Matthew protested sharply. 'I need Crispin and Aylwin with me.' He looked from his brother to his friend, his face troubled and afraid.

'We shall be with you, never fear,' Crispin replied soothingly. 'Come, eat your supper, there's a good lad.'

Father Radulf had given Matthew dispensation from fasting during Lent, advising him to eat well and keep up his strength, so he was served with meat and eggs, but ate little of either, toying with his food as if he could hardly bring himself to swallow it. The others had vegetables, bread and ale, except Sister Helen who took only bread and water, despite her mother's mild protest that there was no need to fast so stringently.

'I follow the Rule of my house,' the nun replied reprovingly. She seemed to Elys to have become very cold and aloof since taking her vows, and had shown no emotion, once the agitation of her encounter with de Mandeville's men had subsided.

To Elys, she was almost a stranger, for it was ten years since Judith had entered the convent, and although Elys had spent some hours almost every day during her childhood being schooled in the same nunnery, she had seen hardly anything of her sister. She remembered her only as a detached, incomprehensible person, who seldom smiled, and took almost no notice of her young sister.

After supper, Aylwin arranged half a dozen candles, provided by Father Warmand, to shed a good light on the silk, but set at a safe distance, so that no wax might drip on it, and watched as Elys marked the outline of half the burning bush with chalk. For a smaller piece of work, she would have pricked the design on parchment and then rubbed chalk through the holes on to the cloth, but this was too large a design for that. When she had the main outlines measured and marked, Aylwin showed her how to use a little brush made of four or five stiff hairs from a squirrel's tail to paint over the lines and shapes just enough to guide her in placing her stitches. The only part which needed any detail was the back end of the coney at the foot of the bush, which he painted when she expressed some doubt about being able to place its tail correctly.

'I'll have to be careful to match the two halves well,' she commented. 'Edwin will be annoyed if the coney is deformed through my carelessness.'

Father Radulf came again the next day to look at Matthew's foot, and looked sad and disappointed at what was revealed when the bandages were removed. 'I had hoped it might begin to dry,' he said. 'Sometimes it does, and the putrefied part becomes mummified, but . . .' He shook he head instead of finishing the sentence.

'Is there nothing you can do?' asked Sir Richard, looking at the wound with a black, set face, for he had seen such sights before and knew the answer already. 'I've known cauterization with iron or vitriol work wonders in serious wounds . . .'

'I did think of that, when Matthew first came here, but the bone was already infected, and such measures aren't effective in such a case. As the wound was caused by a sort of burning, I doubt if further burning would do aught but increase the patient's suffering.'

Aylwin, who was standing nearby, looked across at Crispin, who was kneeling beside Matthew with an arm about his shoulders. They exchanged a long look, and Crispin nodded slightly. A few minutes later, Elys, who was sitting by the fire with her mother and sister, felt a sudden slight draught, and turned just in time to see the door to the screens passage close. Puzzled, she looked about her, and realized that Aylwin must have gone out, but she could not imagine why he had left so quietly, almost surreptitiously, unless, perhaps, the sight and smell of Matthew's wound had sickened him.

He returned later, saying nothing about why he had gone out, and gave Crispin a little nod, which Elys noticed and fleetingly wondered about, but there were more important things to occupy her mind, for Radulf had gently told Matthew that he should begin to compose himself and attend to any matter of consequence or obligation which he would not wish to leave undone.

'How long have I?' Matthew asked in a weary voice.

'A few days, and then you'll probably fall into a fever,' Radulf replied.

'And there is no hope?'

'There is always hope, my son! Don't cease to pray for a miracle. I've seen worse cases than yours brought back from the very threshold by faith and prayer.'

After the infirmarian had gone, the family sat in depressed silence, not looking at one another, and no one seemed to have anything to say, until at length Crispin said, 'Let's all keep vigil in the church all through the night. If we pray with true faith, we may yet bring Our Lord's healing mercy for my brother.'

'Yes,' Lady Mabilia agreed firmly. 'There'll be a miracle, I'm certain. We mustn't lose faith. Immediately after supper, we'll go, all the family, and do as Crispin suggests. Oh, but who will stay with Matthew?'

'I will,' Aylwin said at once. 'I know how to look after him, if he needs anything. I'll stay and talk to him, and help him to bed when he's ready. Is that agreeable to you, Matthew?'

'Yes, thank you.' Matthew shifted in his chair, and then said, in a tense, nervous voice, 'I don't want to die, with so much left undone that I longed to do in my life. Please do as Crispin suggests and pray for a miracle. I don't mind if it's not a cure – I don't hope for that. Even if I'm always in pain, it won't matter, or if I'm crippled. I just want to live . . .'

'The Holy Cross has brought healing to a great many

who were thought beyond recovery,' Crispin assured him. 'We'll keep vigil tonight, and every night, as long as it's necessary.'

Immediately after their frugal Lenten supper, Lady Mabilia, her daughters, Crispin and Sir Richard wrapped themselves in warm cloaks, kissed Matthew, and went across to the church. Compline was just about to begin in the canons' choir, and several of the townsfolk were standing or kneeling in the nave. Crispin spoke privately to Father Brian by the nave altar, and then beckoned his family to go with him into the crossing, where they knelt in the shadow of the great Cross, a little apart from one another, and began their vigil.

After praying with her eyes closed for some time, Elys opened her eyes and looked about her, moving her head as little as possible, and that very slowly.

Her mother and Judith were sitting back on their heels, hands clasped in their laps and heads bowed, but Sir Richard knelt bolt upright, his face upturned and his eyes fixed on the Cross, which gleamed softly in the light of the candles on the two main altars. Crispin was lying on his face, his arms outspread. Compline was almost over, and presently, after the final prayers were sung, the canons filed out in silence and the folk in the nave left, shuffling their feet and whispering among themselves.

Time passed. The canons returned presently to sing Vespers, and again left, the candles were extinguished, and darkness, like great black wings, closed abut the little group of praying figures.

Elys was usually a little afraid of the dark, but not tonight, not here, for, of all the great and small churches she had visited, this one seemed to her the most holy, the most welcoming and safe. The darkness here was not threatening, but comforting, and those great wings which she had imagined were not black with evil, but only lack of light. She looked up, into the dark height of the tower, and was not surprised to catch a glint of gold, nor was she startled when a pale, soft light gleamed through the unshuttered windows in the transept, making faint pools on the stone floor and gently glimmering on the figure on the Cross.

144

'Is there hope?' she thought, and, almost as if a quiet voice had spoken in her head, knew that there was, there would always be hope, that all would be well, even if it might not be what she desired or expected. She closed her eyes again, and lapsed into a curious, trance-like state, between waking and dreaming, hardly conscious of the cold stone under her knees, or the little eddies of icy air which occasionally ran through the building.

At some time during the small hours, she rose stiffly to her feet and crept away to relieve herself, going out through the little wicket in the south door. Before she came in again, she stood for a moment in the shelter of the porch, looking out at the sleeping town. The moon was nearly full, and rode the sky, seeming to skim along through the few clouds. A handful of scattered stars shone like jewels, cold in the velvet blackness. It was mild for March, and she could see clumps of daffodils between the grave mounds. A great barn owl drifted across from one tree to another, startling her with its weird cry, and a dog fox loped along the churchyard path, paused to look at her, then trotted on its way, intent, no doubt, on some poor housewife's few hens.

She looked across to the house in Church Street, and saw a light gleaming through a crack in the shutters of the hall window. She wondered for a moment if something was amiss, that Aylwin should be defying the curfew law, but she decided that he was probably getting something for Matthew. If anything was wrong, he would surely have sent across to the church to fetch Crispin, at least. The owl hooted again, and she shivered, huddling her cloak about her, and went back into the church.

Sir Richard had moved from his upright position, and was lying full-length, like Crispin, feet together and arms outstretched, in imitation of the crucified Christ. Judith was standing, but she sank to her knees again as Elys slipped back into her former place and position, and the long vigil went on.

She must have fallen asleep eventually, but she was suddenly jerked awake by the loud clang of the bell as one of the deacons began to ring for Matins. She looked about her, bewildered and uncertain of her whereabouts, and saw

145

her mother on her hands and knees, vainly trying to get up, her limbs grown stiff and cramped with the long kneeling.

Elys herself had some difficulty in getting to her feet, for one leg had become quite numb, and it was Crispin who helped Lady Mabilia to stand, and held her while she stamped her feet and shook them to recover feeling in them. Sir Richard got up, slowly and painfully, but Judith rose as if she had only been kneeling for a few minutes.

They stood, all five, looking about them in the grey light which filtered through the deeply-embrasured windows, the clangour of the bell above their heads making speech impossible, and then Elys swung around, thinking she heard a strange noise coming from the south door. Crispin turned too, obviously also having heard it, and Lady Mabilia said 'What is it?' pitching her voice above the sound of the bell.

At that moment, the chiming of the bell slowed, and, after a couple of odd clangs, stopped, and the church was filled instead with the sound of someone banging on the south door, and calling out in a loud voice.

'What is that unseemly noise?' demanded Sir Richard irritably, but he made no move to find out. It was Father Warmand who, emerging from his sacristy, hurried to investigate, opening the wicket, which the knocker had not realized was unlocked.

'A miracle,' a breathless voice panted, and a man stumbled in, almost incoherent with excitement. 'It's a miracle! It's Master Aylwin! He says to come and see!'

'What's happened?' Warmand said, taking the man by the shoulders and shaking him a little. 'What precisely is the miracle?'

'Master Matthew's cured!' the man announced, flinging his arms wide and grinning all over his face, then bursting into tears.

There was a stunned silence for the space of a few heartbeats, and then Warmand turned on his heel and ran back the way he had come. Within minutes, all the bells were ringing, the canons had all come into the church, Father Brian already robed for Matins, and the choir boys and acolytes, with the schoolmaster, were gathered in an excited bunch in the south transept.

146

In all this hubbub, Matthew's family stood silent and stunned, until Crispin suddenly gave an exclamation and ran from the church. Judith crossed herself and sank to her knees again, her face utterly calm and unmoved, and Elys started after Crispin. She walked until she was outside, then gathered up her long skirts in both hands and ran as fast as she could, her light metal coronet falling from her head unnoticed and rolling across the path behind her.

The bells had roused everyone in the town, apart from the many peasants who were already up, and even, in some cases, at work. Lights were appearing in windows, and the first tentative puffs of smoke were rising from the louvres in thatched roofs, but Elys noticed none of this. Every thought, every nerve in her body, strained towards the house in Church Street, and she arrived there, out of breath, only a little behind Crispin.

As she entered the hall, he was just falling to his knees beside Matthew, who was still fully dressed and half-lying in his chair, with Aylwin behind him. The few servants who lived in and slept in the penthouse at the back, next to the kitchen, were standing about, in various states of dress, gaping in amazement at their master. The fire was burning well, and a dozen candles had been lit, for it was barely light outside.

'Matthew! Is it true?' Elys cried, running to kneel on the other side of him from Crispin.

'My foot is gone. That's true enough...' Matthew replied in a faint, remote voice, as if he were half asleep. He looked very white, drowsy and confused, but he was quite clear about the most important thing. 'Look.' He pointed to where his right foot should have been. His leg ended at the ankle, which was neatly bandaged with clean linen. There was nothing beyond that.

'But how? What happened?' Elys demanded, wondering why Aylwin and Crispin were silent. She glanced at their faces, and saw that they both looked pale and anxious. They exchanged one intense stare, then deliberately looked away.

'I don't know what happened,' Matthew said vaguely. 'I've not long been awake, and I'm still confused... I

147

think I took too much poppy-juice . . . Someone came . . . I thought it was a dream . . .'

Before he could go on, his mother and uncle came in, both a little flushed from walking as quickly as they could and their exclamations and questions pushed Elys's enquiries into the background. Indeed, she was even set back physically, for her mother pushed her out of the way to get to Matthew's side, and she had to rise and move away to make room. Sir Richard stood directly in front of his nephew, and stared at the bandaged stump in astonishment.

'You won't be able to ride a destrier,' he said, sounding disappointed. 'That means you can't be a knight of the Order.'

'No matter, as long as he lives,' cried Lady Mabilia. 'Oh, my dear, dear boy.' She dissolved into tears, burying her face in Matthew's shoulder and sobbing her heart out, while Matthew, still looking puzzled and bemused, patted her back and murmured disjointed phrases of comfort.

Before Lady Mabilia had recovered, the outer and inner doors opened again, and a procession entered which soon filled the hall. It was led by Father Brian, still in his robes, preceded by a crucifer with the minster's great processional cross, and followed by the half-dozen canons who happened to be at home and not serving the outlying parishes. Behind them came the deacons, and then the acolytes, including no fewer than seven thurifers with their censers, which filled the hall with the scent of their incense. After them came the precentor and the choir, with the schoolmaster behind them, and then a number of townsfolk who had either not yet started work, or were able to leave it as they pleased.

'What has happened, my son?' asked Father Brian in a powerful, carrying voice, which effectively silenced everyone except Lukin Dulpain, who quite clearly remarked, 'Isn't it exciting? I've not been so excited since the Queen came to visit us.'

'Hush,' said Father Brian sternly. 'Let's all listen to Master Matthew, and discover what's happened.'

Matthew looked even more confused and sleepy, taken aback by this sudden invasion, but he did his best to tell what he knew, which was muddled and did not amount to a great deal.

'Aylwin and I were sitting here, talking,' he said. 'We had some wine, and I remember Aylwin putting the cover over the fire when the curfew rang. Then I felt very sleepy, but I was warm and comfortable, and I didn't want to be bothered to go to bed, so I sat here and drowsed, and I suppose I fell asleep. I dreamed – or I thought it was a dream – that I opened my eyes and there were many lights, more than just the lantern we'd been using. A man in white was standing there, by my feet. I thought I knew his face, that I'd seen him somewhere, but I didn't know his voice when he spoke. It was deep and strange – foreign . . .'

'What did he say?' prompted Father Brian, for Matthew had stopped and seemed to be thinking.

'He asked me if I wanted to be healed, if I would serve God and lead a good life. I promised I'd try, and then he – he did something to my foot. It hurt a great deal, but it seemed as if it was a long way away . . . I can't exactly describe it, because I thought I was asleep, and I couldn't wake up . . . Then I think he put his hands round my ankle and did something else, and that hurt too, but not as much, and then everything went a long, long way away, and I think I fainted. When I woke up, there was just a dull aching instead of the usual pain, and I looked – the lantern was still alight, but the other lights had gone – and my foot wasn't there.'

There was an awed silence, the crowd in the hall gazing open-mouthed at Matthew, or glancing at one another. Most of them crossed themselves, and several dropped to their knees to pray.

'Where were you while all this was happening?' Father Brian asked Aylwin.

'Asleep in that chair there,' he replied, nodding towards where he had been sitting when Matthew's family left to go to the church. 'Matthew woke me when he found his foot had – well, whatever happened to it.'

'May I ascertain exactly what *has* happened to it?' asked Father Radulf, stepping forward and kneeling by Matthew's legs. Sir Richard drew back out of his way, but everyone else seemed to take a step forward. Radulf waved them back, then gently unwound the bandages, and gasped at what was revealed. The dreadful, half-rotten foot had gone, and the skin had been drawn over the stump and fastened with a few ligatures of tarred twine.

'Amputated!' exclaimed Radulf, Sir Richard and Father Brian as one.

'You say you recognized the man who did this?' Father Brian asked, frowning. 'Can you tell us who he is?'

Matthew was gazing at the stump with a bemused expression on his face. He seemed scarcely able to keep his eyes open, but he made an effort to reply and said, 'I felt that I'd seen him before.'

'Where?'

He closed his eyes and his head fell forward, but he said drowsily, 'On the cross. That was it. It was his face . . . The man on the cross.' His head dropped still further, and he was asleep.

'The Man on the Cross,' breathed Father Brian, his face alight with joy. 'It is indeed a miracle. Let us return to the church and sing Te Deum. Quietly, now. Master Matthew is exhausted. He must sleep.'

Two of the thurifers, the sixth and seventh, despite the solemnity of the occasion, had been surreptitiously pushing one another, and now the seventh, who was the smallest, piped up nervously, 'Please Father – there's something in the corner there . . .' He pointed to the shadowed corner at the back of the dais furthest from the door to the sleeping-quarters, where something gleamed faintly in the candlelight.

Sir Richard stalked across to the corner, looked, and said in a shaken voice, quickly mastered, 'It's the foot! Bring a cloth to cover it, and take it away! It must be buried before it befouls the air!'

The servants engaged in a subdued battle of reluctance, and eventually thrust forward the backhouse boy, the lowest member of the household. One of the others pushed a piece of rag into his hands, and he had the unpleasant task of gathering up the terrible thing, but then he stood looking about him helplessly, not knowing what to do with it.

'Take it to the infirmary and leave it with my assistant,' Father Radulf told him. 'I'll see it's properly buried in the morning.'

'Why ever was it left?' Lady Mabilia asked tremulously. The strain of the past weeks and the shock of this sudden reponse to all her prayers and pilgrimages, just when she had finally given up hope, had completely unnerved her. 'Why didn't it simply disappear?'

'Would you have your son maimed for all eternity?' Father Brian asked reprovingly. 'Of course it must be given Christian burial, so it may be reunited with Matthew on the Last Day, when all will be made whole again.'

'Of course,' Radulf confirmed, with no expression at all. Elys noticed that he seemd to be the only person present, other than Matthew, whose face was not lit up with wonder and joy. He did, however, smile as he continued, 'I think everyone except the family should leave now. The amputation has been excellently carried out, and, all being well, the young man should recover well, but he must be allowed rest and quiet.'

The procession reformed itself in reverse order, there being no room to do otherwise, and filed out, the seventh thurifer grinning with delight at having taken a leading role in the proceedings (in his own estimation, at least), and swinging his thurible with enthusiasm. He gave a little skip as he reached the door, and the precentor made a long arm and tapped him sharply on the head with one bony finger.

'That'll need crutches,' Lukin Dulpain could be heard declaiming outside, 'and you're just the man to make them, Alvin Bisemare! That must be the finest pair you ever made, to be worthy of a man who's been healed by a miracle!'

'Tain't the first time, and, pray God, 'twon't be the last!' replied a dry, creaky voice in the flat tones of one refusing to appear excited.

Father Brian turned in the doorway to pronounce a long benediction in flowing and sonorous Latin, his face beaming with joy and goodwill, and then he was gone, and sudden silence fell on the group left in the hall.

'Are we not to break our fast today?' demanded Lady

Mabilia, rising to her feet and glaring at the servants, who scuttled out of the hall. 'Cover your head, Elys!'

Elys put her hands up to straighten her veil, and found that it was hanging loose over one ear, and her coronet had vanished. She wondered vaguely what had become of it. Sir Richard walked a trifle unsteadily to a chair and sat down abruptly. Aylwin went out through the door to the bed-chamber, and returned presently, shaved and in his work-ing-clothes. Crispin followed him, but returned before him, just as Judith came in, quiet and composed, her hands hidden in the wide sleeves of her black habit and her face as expressionless as marble within the shade of her volumin-ous veil.

'You are indeed blessed,' she said to Matthew, who was fast asleep. She glanced at his leg, which Radulf had just finished rebandaging, and went to sit at the table, where she waited impassively for food to arrive.

Elys, puzzled and confused, caught Radulf's eye as he turned to go, and said, 'Father – did the Figure from the Cross come here and . . . and take Matthew's foot off . . . ?'

Radulf looked at her kindly and said, 'A miracle isn't an easy thing to adjust one's mind to accept, let alone under-stand.' He paused, then went on, seeming to pick his words very carefully, 'Some power, some skill, in some form, was here tonight, and removed your brother's foot, saving him from certain death. It seems that the – the power appeared in a form which your brother could recognize and accept – that of the Figure on the Cross, but that, of course, is only a man-made thing of stone, which represents Our Lord. Accept the joy of knowing that your brother has a good chance of life now, and don't trouble yourself about the means. Whatever that means was, it came from God, and that is all that matters. My only concern is that the ligatures will need to be removed in a few weeks. But if all goes well, I think his leg will now heal completely – thanks be to God.'

CHAPTER EIGHT

As soon as bread and ale arrived on the table, they all broke their fast, and then went to Mass, except for Aylwin, who stayed to sit with Matthew.

The latter slept all day, a peaceful and apparently natural sleep, and the family crept about for fear of waking him. They were all very quiet and subdued, for, despite having lived in hopes of a miracle for so long, they were overawed and confused by its actual happening.

During the afternoon, Sir Richard and Crispin rode out for exercise, Lady Mabilia sat with Matthew, weeping silently, now that there was no longer a need to maintain a calm and cheerful appearance, Judith went to the church, and Elys worked on the burse. She sat by the window, from which she had taken down the oiled linen screen, so she could sit at her work in a good north light, and occasionally look out across to the church.

There was a happy glow deep inside her to think that at last Matthew was free from the terrible pain of his injury, and that he could expect to live his normal span, provided the ankle healed properly. It hardly mattered that he would be unable to walk without crutches – surely it was better to be without a foot than in constant pain, or dead. All those weary miles of travelling, the difficulties and dangers, the uncomfortable inns, bad food, cold, wet, heat and dust, had been worthwhile, as her mother had always insisted they would be. It was ironic that Matthew's miracle had come, not from the pilgrimages to far places of his mother and sister, but by his own journey of a mere three days' slow travel from Wix to Waltham. But who was to say that the pilgrimages had been unnecessary? Surely it was the cumulative effect of all the pilgrimages and prayers which had brought this wonder to pass? It was odd, though . . .

She stopped the course of her thoughts by a deliberate

effort, afraid that she had been about to fall into the sins of doubt and ingratitude, and turned her mind to the future.

As soon as her mother was sure that Matthew would be well, she would go to Wix, and Elys was sure that considerable pressure would be put upon her to go too. She must be strong and resist, or she would find herself shut up in the nunnery for the rest of her life. She must be confident that she could earn her living, not allow doubts to creep in and weaken her resolve. It would be hard, but she must hold fast to her freedom, or lose it . . .

'Is this yours, my lady?' asked a conspiratorial voice.

She looked up, startled, to find a freckle-faced boy of about twelve looking at her through the window. He was holding up her lost coronet.

'Why, yes! Where did you find it?'

'It was lying in a clump of daffydillies in the churchyard. I thought first off it was fairy gold, but Master Peter says there aren't any fairies. He's our schoolmaster, and he knows almost everything!'

'Only *almost* everything?' Elys asked, smiling.

'He doesn't know about ferrets,' the boy replied seriously. 'Master Edwin knows about them, and a lot of other things, but I'm going to be a priest, so it's what Master Peter knows that matters to me. The Queen sent me here when I was little, to be educated, you know, because I'm an orphan.'

'And now you want to stay and be a canon?' Elys asked, feeling anxious that one so young should already be committing himself.

'Yes. Father Brian says I can change my mind as much as I like in the next eight years, but I know now that's what I want to be. I don't expect you remember me, but I was here this morning. I was the seventh thurifer.'

'I remember you,' Elys assured him, not untruthfully, for the eager tones of his voice had sounded vaguely familiar.

'Wasn't it exciting? It's the biggest miracle I've seen, so far. We have little ones quite often, but nothing as grand as this – not in my time, anyway. What did they do with it?'

'With what?'

'The foot. I s'pose they buried it. It wasn't something anyone'd want to keep.'

'No.' Elys shuddered.

'It must feel strange, having a miracle happen to your own brother. I felt all shivery, and I wanted to laugh and jump about! You should have come back to the church with us.'

'Yes, I suppose we should, but we were all so – so overcome . . .'

'Yes – well – you would be . . . Fancy Our Lord coming down from the Cross and visiting your own brother. We all went back into the choir, candles, torches and all, and started Matins, only we had the festival one, not the Lenten penitential, and then Father Radulf came and sang the *Te Deum* – he's got a lovely voice, all rich and strong, like a thrush in a rainstorm. And Master Dulpain – you know Master Dulpain?'

'Yes.'

'Well, he played the trumpet *at the same time*. The two together sounded like – oh, I don't know what, but it was grand. Here, you'd better take your little crown. It's not broken or anything.'

Elys took her coronet from him, and he asked, 'Why do some ladies wear them and not others? Is it because ordinary ladies aren't allowed to have them?'

'No, it's more to do with birth,' Elys replied seriously. 'A noble lady wears one, because it's the fashion, but an ordinary housewife or a farm girl wouldn't, because she couldn't afford it, and, in any case, it would get in the way when she was at work. Would you like a cake?'

The boy's face, already beaming with pleasure and excitement over the day's events, lit up even more, so Elys let him in at the street door and took him through the screens passage to the kitchen.

This was a separate building in the yard behind the house, ruled over by a stout matron called Matilda Mayngod, known to her underlings, behind her back, as the Empress, for obvious reasons; for she ruled her little kingdom in a single-minded fashion aimed solely and entirely towards the production of good, satisfying food. She looked suspiciously at Elys and the boy, planting large hands on

155

massive hips and staring at them over a table half-covered with pastry.

'Good day, Mistress Mayngod,' Elys said placatingly. 'This boy has been kind enough to bring me something which I lost this morning. I wondered if perhaps you might spare him a little cake . . .'

'Little cake!' exclaimed the cook. 'Much good a little cake'd be to a boy. Boys need more than little cakes. Here, boy. Mind your fingers – it's hot,' and she picked up a large pasty, big enough for a ploughman's bevers, and thrust it into the boy's hands.

He looked at it, awe-struck, and said, 'Thank you, mistress! Oh, but . . .' His face dropped and he looked suddenly sad and wistful. 'Is there meat in it?'

'In Lent? Don't be a fool, boy!' the cook roared, sounding wrathful, but with little twinkling eyes in her fat face. 'There's a mite o' cheese, maybe, but nothing more but roots and worts.'

The boy's face lit up again, and he made a polite little speech of thanks to both Mistress Mayngod and Elys, and said a short Latin grace in a whisper before biting into the pasty, an expression of bliss crossing his face at the hot tastiness of it. Elys tried to give him a coin before he left, but he declined it with good manners and great firmness, saying that the pasty was more than enough reward.

Elys had not been back at her embroidery an hour when Lady Mabilia came out into the hall, looked at her work, and then said, 'Don't spend the entire day on it, or you'll grow bent and pale and unhealthy! Time now to go out and take a little walk for your own good! You may go to the cordwainer in West Street with these shoes. They need patching.'

Elys was surprised, for her mother normally despatched a servant on such errands, but Lady Mabilia, seeing her expression, added, 'If you mean to earn your bread as a craftswoman, you mustn't expect to behave like a lady, my girl. Off you go.'

Taking her cloak and the worn shoes, Elys left the house and walked down Church Street to the millstream, and crossed it on the rickety wooden bridge, pausing to watch half a dozen ducks enjoying the spring sunshine in the shallows by the ford, and to stroke the glossy black and white cat which thought he owned the mill, and often came to sit by the end of the bridge and watch for fish in his millstream.

The cordwainer's was almost at the far end of West Street, and she walked towards it slowly, looking at the neat little houses which lined the street. Some were in excellent repair, with no chinks in their plastered walls, and good thick thatch on their roofs, but others looked neglected, with old, decaying thatch and plaster falling from their walls, revealing the laths underneath. The former belonged, she already knew, to the college, some being the homes of the canons, who lived among their flock, not in enclosure. The others mostly belonged to Queen Adeliza, and Elys had already learned from some of Matthew's friends that these had once been as well-cared for as the others, but since the Queen had married again and her property had passed to her husband, no help had been forthcoming to keep them in repair, and the folk who lived in them, being the poorest in the town, had neither the time nor the money to do anything about them for themselves.

Elys had noticed a few days before that her own shoes were badly worn. They were simply made, as were all shoes, each consisting of a single piece of leather, which wrapped round the foot and was cut and stitched to fit. There was no heel, and extra soles were only stitched on to heavy shoes for people who worked in the fields or walked long distances. She wondered if the cordwainer might have any to fit her at a reasonable price.

His shop was also his workshop, smelling of leather, which hung, ready for use, in a mixture of whole and cut skins, from hooks in the crossbeams of his front room. Shoes awaiting repair were piled in one corner, and those already mended in another, and his workbench sported, at one end, a dozen pairs of new shoes – or, rather, two dozen shoes of various sizes, which might be worn as pairs, for there was no difference in shape between a shoe for a right foot and one for a left.

'Fine workmanship and good leather,' the cordwainer

said, inspecting Lady Mabilia's shoes. 'Not made in England, I think?'

'My mother bought them in Rome,' Elys replied.

'Ah!' The cordwainer handled them reverently. 'They've trodden holy places, then. Did they ever walk on the pavement of St Peter's, d'you know?'

'Yes, they did.'

'There now. To think a pair of shoes may go to such a blessed place, but I expect I never shall. Ah, well. They're worn through here, but I can patch them.'

'Yes, please, and I thought I might buy myself a new pair, if you've any to fit me,' Elys said, looking at the stiff oxhide ones piled on the bench.

'Oh, they're too coarse for your little feet,' the cordwainer exclaimed. 'Take a seat if you please, my lady, and let me show you my better work.'

Elys sat down on a stool which was obviously set for customers, and wondered how she could tell him that she could not afford anything expensive, but the shoes he brought out from a chest were plain and serviceable, made of smooth, supple leather, without fashionable pointed toes or ornament. Two which fitted her comfortably and matched in colour and shape were soon found, and cost only one of her silver pennies.

'If they chafe your heel at all, rub a little goosegrease into the place on the shoe – and on your heel, for that matter. Good for a' many things, is goosegrease. And how does the young gentleman now, my lady? Your house must be full of rejoicing. Of course, we have many little miracles here, but we still rejoice over even the smallest of them. God's good to Waltham, my lady, and gives us great cause to praise Him – why, He even keeps us safe in these troublous times.'

'Long may He continue to do so,' Elys said soberly, paying for her shoes and promising that someone would collect her mother's before the end of the week. Then, on an impulse, she asked, 'Do you know anyone in the town who would take a lodger?'

The cordwainer looked a little surprised, and thought for a moment before he replied, 'There's old Widow Miller, round by the fairground, sometimes takes in a pilgrim or two, or Mistress Chich, by the ford. She's a widow too, but a cut above most of us, being as her husband was one of the canons, but she sometimes takes in a pilgrim of the – well, of your own rank, you know . . . Was it for one of your friends, or a servant, my lady? It would make a difference, you see . . .'

'It was just a thought I had,' she replied vaguely, thinking that it might be possible to find somewhere to live in the town if it became necessary. So far, no one at home had raised the question of where she would live if she did not go to Wix, and Matthew and Crispin had been less opposed to her determination not to be a nun than the rest of the family, but that did not mean that they would be willing to go on giving her a home, so it would be as well to think about possible alternatives. She walked back along West Street with a feeling of contentment and achievement, for had she not just made her very first purchase with money which she had earned by her own work?

It seemed such an important landmark in her life that she longed to talk to someone about it, but whom could she tell? Not her mother or Judith, nor even Crispin or Matthew, who could not be worried with such trivial matters at this time. She tried to imagine her uncle's face if she told him, but meanwhile her feet led her to the right place, and she entered Aylwin's workshed with the shoes clasped in both hands.

He looked up as her shadow fell across his work, but she moved to one side of the door, out of his light, and he continued tapping gently on the blunt end of his chisel, putting in the neat formal curls of Noah's beard.

'Why do you carve the pictures first, before you've finished shaping the font?' she asked.

'In case I'm struck by lightning, or something equally final, before it's finished. I want my ideas to be here, in stone – any competent craftsman could finish the font, once the panels of figures are done.'

'I've been to take my mother's shoes to be mended,' she blurted out, 'and I bought myself a new pair while I was in the shop.'

'Did you need them?' he asked, looking at her, his mallet arrested between strokes.

'Yes. I have only two pairs, and these are almost worn through on one sole. They've been patched a dozen times. The other pair is too fine and soft for everyday wear.'

'One of the things you must learn, if you're to earn your bread in the world, is not to buy things you don't really need until you're sure you can afford them.'

'Yes, but I do need shoes . . .'

'I accept that. In any case, Father Warmand will pay you something each week while you're working for the minster, so you can afford them at present. Besides, G . . . someone once told me of an old saying in the east. If you have only two loaves in the world, you should sell one and buy something beautiful with the money to feed your soul, for your soul needs beauty as much as your body needs food.'

'Was that your friend Galien?' asked Elys, struck by the truth and wisdom of the saying.

'Yes.'

'I wish he would let me thank him for making my frame. It's perfect, and I find it so much easier to work with the cloth stretched on it. It's the right height, too, and I can sit at it perfectly comfortably to work. If I just went up to him when he's alone and said, "Thank you for making the frame. It's just what I wanted," surely that couldn't draw attention to him or do him any harm?'

'He wouldn't like it. In any case, he's gone.'

'Gone? Gone where?'

'Away.'

'But when? I thought he was here to do some work in the minster?'

'He's finished it. He left early this morning.'

'Oh.' Elys felt flat and disappointed, and turned away, meaning to leave.

'However, I'll tell him next time I see him that you're very happy with the frame,' Aylwin went on, 'and I haven't yet wished you joy of your new shoes. I remember the thrill of buying something with the very first of my own earnings.'

'What did *you* buy?' she asked, turning back to him, feeling suddenly much happier.

160

'Something for my soul, I'm afraid, despite all the good advice I've given you. It was a little carved ivory angel.'

'Do you still have it?'

'Yes, but my mother keeps it for me. It's too fragile to carry about on my travels.'

There was a sudden sound of pounding feet on the churchyard path, and a dishevelled youth came running into the shed, barely stopping himself from cannoning into Aylwin's font. Elys recognized him as one of the apprentices of William of Norwich.

'Where's Master Galien?' he panted. 'We need him, quickly.'

'What's happened?' asked Aylwin, putting down his tools and frowning.

'We were unloading stone from a cart, and a block slipped and fell on Walter. It's broke his arm badly, and Master said to fetch Galien.'

'I'm sorry, but Galien left early this morning,' Aylwin replied. 'You'll have to see Father Radulf in the infirmary.'

The boy looked worried and disappointed. 'But Galien's better nor anybody,' he said. 'He can set a broken limb, if 'tis possible at all, or take it off, if it ain't possible . . .'

'Be quiet!' Aylwin said peremptorily. 'Learn to hold your tongue, boy, before you put a man's life in jeopardy. Galien has gone to London, and you'll not get him back in time to be of any help. Go to the infirmary and fetch Father Radulf.'

The boy looked chastened and mumbled an apology, then ran off towards the infirmary. Elys stared after him for a moment, then turned to Aylwin and asked, 'What did you mean?'

He picked up his tools, looked at his work, and said quietly, 'Don't you know what happens to a man who maims another?'

'Yes. He's maimed in the same way.'

'And if his victim dies, he'll either hang or lose hands and feet. All cases where one man causes physical injury to another go before the King's Court. If the offence is committed against a Norman, the matter's more serious, of course. In any case, there's seldom any allowance made for

161

the reason for the maiming, even if it were done to save life. Added to that, Galien is . . . I told you about his origins. They suffer the penalties to the greatest degree the law allows, and beyond, simply because they are what they are. We'll say no more about the matter, if you please.'

'But he said that Galien could take the arm off . . . Aylwin, I don't think Father Radulf believes that Matthew's healing was really a miracle . . .'

'Did he say so?'

'Not in so many words.'

'Then why do you think he doubts it?'

'Something he said . . . I can't recall exactly. Aylwin, when Matthew said that it was the Figure from the Cross . . . He'd been looking at your notebook earlier that day.'

'He likes looking through my workbooks. He's seen nearly all I have with me.' Aylwin's face was watchful and his voice sounded cautious.

'It was the one with the font drawings, and the two pictures of Galien.'

'You've spent years praying for your brother to be healed, and travelled hundreds of miles on pilgrimage to the same purpose. Now you have what you asked, do you want a man to be maimed or killed for it?'

'No, of course not.'

'Then don't speculate. Yes, Father Radulf has too much experience of bodily ills and accidents not to wonder what sort of miracle leaves sutures of tarred string, and Crispin knows . . . something. They both have the sense to be silent on the subject – do you the same, Elys, and don't pry any further.'

'Very well. I hadn't realized . . .' Elys said unhappily, shocked by the severity of the punishment which might be imposed on a man who amputated another's shattered limb in order to save his life. Of course, if someone like Father Radulf did it, apart from the breach of his priestly vows, a court would understand and no doubt acquit him, but a member of the hated race, even if he did not follow the faith of his ancestors . . . 'I'm sorry,' she added, then, not entirely inconsequentially, 'Father Radulf thought that amputation would be the only way to save Matthew, but he wouldn't do it, because he's a priest. He didn't say anything about the penalty.'

'He's a Norman, and an infirmarian,' Aylwin replied rather curtly. 'So your work is going well? I'm glad. Did the lad who found your crown bring it to you?'

'Yes, thank you. I suppose I shouldn't wear a coronet any more.'

'Why not?'

'It's hardly suitable for a working craftswoman.'

'You wear it because it's fashionable among women of noble family. The fact that you're of noble birth doesn't alter because you choose to use your skills to earn your living, does it?'

Again, he spoke rather curtly, and Elys, instead of answering, pondered the point and his manner, and decided that he must be sensitive about it because of his own position. Eventually, she said, 'No, I suppose not.'

'One of the things you'll have to learn, if you really mean to support yourself, is that you can't afford to waste the daylight hours in gossiping,' he said after another lengthy silence, during which he had finished Noah's beard and moved on to the folds in his robe.

Elys took the hint, said, 'I'll see you at supper, then,' and went back to her work, which employed her hands, but left most of her mind free to think, and she found that Aylwin's unusually cold manner had left her depressed and anxious. She told herself that what he had said was true, but she had come to count on his support and sympathy more than she realized, and she felt a helpless, confused sorrow when she remembered how he had snubbed her for not realizing that Galien's apparent reputation for treating injuries could lead to the loss of his own limbs, and even his life. She could accept his implied reprimand for that, but she thought he had been a little unfair in being annoyed with her for thinking she should dress more plainly now she was a working woman. She supposed she had angered him by assuming that a craftswoman or man could not be considered noble . . .

She was startled out of her thoughts by the sudden arrival,

163

via the window, of a large tabby cat with grey-brown stripes, which steadied itself momentarily on the narrow sill, and then jumped clear over her frame and landed with a plump on the floor, promptly sitting down to wash its paws, face and tail, completely ignoring her.

'Well,' she said to it, twisting round on her stool, 'pardon me for putting my work in your way, Sir Cat.'

The cat paused briefly in its toilet to give her an enigmatic stare, then blinked deliberately at her, as if winking with both eyes, and continued to pass its rough tongue over its thick fur with a faint tearing sound. As it seemed disinclined to indulge in conversation, Elys turned back to her work and forgot about it, lost once more in a vague, unhappy wondering about whether Aylwin was offended or annoyed with her. She was reminded of the cat's presence after a few minutes, however, for there was suddenly a warm, heavy weight leaning against her right ankle, and a loud throbbing sound of feline pleasure.

She leaned down to rub the cat behind its ears, which was apparently approved, and then went on placing her neat bars of couching across the gleaming gold, working steadily before tapering off the gold until one last pair of fat threads curved round to form the final stitch in the pattern. It formed a satisfyingly sweeping, sinuous line, and she leaned back and looked at it with pleasure. The cat, as if sensing her feeling, purred all the more.

By the time Crispin and Sir Richard came in, she had made a deal of progress and the cat had fallen silent and still. The sudden entry of the two men disturbed both of them, particularly as Sir Richard, who habitually wore riding boots, tended to have a correspondingly heavy tread, to which the cat took exception, for it uttered a brief and derogatory remark, and left as it had come.

'That was Tigrus,' Crispin remarked, coming to look at his sister's work. 'That's very fine, Elys. Your stitches are so fine and even, I don't know how you can do it so quickly.'

'It's finding a rhythm,' Elys explained, feeling a glow of pleasure at praise from Crispin, for she was a little in awe of him, although she loved him dearly, for he was not only a deacon, but a skilled calligrapher. 'I expect you do the same in your writing,' she added with a sudden glimmer of enlightenment.

'Yes. It must be, in some ways, a similar activity.'

'Why Tigrus?' asked Sir Richard, looking over Elys's other shoulder. 'Oh – because he's striped, I suppose. That's coming along quite well, Niece. To whom does he belong – or should I say, who does he own?'

'The latter, I think!' Crispin replied with a smile, which, in any lesser person might have been called a grin. 'It's Mistress Mayngod, our cook. He lives in the kitchen and storerooms.'

'A good mouser, I should think,' Sir Richard observed with the air of a connoisseur. 'An essential official in any good kitchen, storeroom or granary!' Both his niece and his nephew looked at him with some surprise, for his voice sounded unusually gentle, lacking its normal brisk, commanding tone.

'I didn't know you liked cats, Uncle,' Elys ventured.

'Not a matter of liking,' Sir Richard replied gruffly. 'Common sense. Treat a horse or dog or cat well, and you'll get better service. Besides, they're good, faithful companions. Someone to talk to who doesn't argue or betray confidences.' With that, he stumped away towards the far end of the hall, intending to look in on Matthew, Crispin went about his duties, and Elys continued with her work.

Presently, the hall door opened and Elys looked towards, surprised, for the street door had not banged as it usually did if anyone entered the house. Judith was standing there, looking at her with no discernible expression on her face.

'You startled me, Judith!' Elys exclaimed.

'Sister Helen,' Judith corrected sharply. 'I try to avoid unnecessary noise in my movements.' She glided across to stand by Elys, looking down on her work.

'A burse, I believe?' she said. 'One might suppose that the price of that gold would be better spent on relieving the poor, and your time in prayer. I suppose we must be thankful that at least you are using what skill you have in the service of Mother Church,' Judith said reflectively. 'But surely you could do such work better in the quiet of a

165

nunnery, where you would be free from constant distraction?'

'I will not enter a nunnery,' Elys replied firmly, the constant repetition of the phrase giving her voice a certain note of dogged grimness. 'I have no wish to be a nun!'

'Wish?' Judith appeared to consider the word. 'What have wishes to do with it? There are but two ways of life open to a female – marriage or a nunnery. Surely you cannot prefer the brutal carnality of marriage?'

'Many women find happiness with a husband and children,' Elys said a trifle defensively. She had always found difficulty in talking to Judith, and to do so was no easier now that her sister seemed to have become even more austere and detached.

'And many do not. The cloister is the better place.'

'Better, or safer?' Elys asked, looking sharply up at the pale face framed by the black head-veil, and surprising a faint increase in the colour of Judith's cheeks.

'I shall be glad to return to Wix as soon as possible,' Judith replied indirectly, turning away. 'I shall be in the bedchamber if I am needed,' and with that, she left the hall, gliding silently over the rushes. Elys watched her go, noticing how stiffly she held her shoulders, and wondered, not for the first time, exactly why Judith had been so ready to take the veil.

Lady Mabilia came from her son's bedside a little before supper, and said that he was awake and in a little pain, but he said it was nothing compared with the constant nagging torture of his foot.

'I think he should stay abed for at least a few days more, and take nourishing broth,' she went on. 'He still has the dispensation, so I've ordered beef broth for him for supper, and eggs beaten up in milk.' She looked a little defiantly at her brother and son, as if she expected the combined displeasure of the Church Militant and Pacific at her statement, but Sir Richard merely said, 'Yes, he needs to build up his strength,' and Crispin added, 'Good, strengthening dishes, both of them. Perhaps he'd like some fish tomorrow, for his dinner. I'll ask Father Antony if I may take a carp from the fishpond for him.'

Matthew insisted on sitting up to eat his carp. He looked tired and weak, but was obviously so relieved to be free of his foot that the shock and weakening effect of its removal were considerably counteracted by the comparative freedom from pain and the knowledge that he now stood a good chance of living and having an active life again.

During the afternoon, Lukin Dulpain's long nose came round the door, followed by his head, and he said, 'I do but enquire how Master Matthew be faring, and – oh, there he is!' and he came completely into the hall and over to where Matthew sat in his chairbed by the fire.

Matthew was pleased to see him, and when Lady Mabilia said sternly that he should go back to bed and not let idle fellows tire him, he replied, 'But Lukin's such a pleasant companion, Mother. I'd like him to stay a little while, and tell me what's to do in the town.'

'There do be nothing spoken of but the Miracle,' Lukin exclaimed, sitting down on the nearest stool and launching into conversation at once. 'Such excitement! We've had people suddenly get better from all sorts of ills, of course, and bad wounds and ulcers begin to heal, though more slowly, but there's never been one like this, with Our Lord appearing to someone in – can you say in the flesh, do you think? – anyway, appearing, and doing such a – an extraordinary . . . There's some say as the foot'll grow again from the stump, as do a worm when that's cut by the spade, it being Our Lord's work, but do it do or do it don't, it be a great miracle.'

Elys, working by the window, turned and called across, 'So you haven't always lived in Waltham, Master Dulpain?'

'I was born and bred in Suffolk, my lady,' Lukin replied. 'How did you know?'

'I've been to St Edmundsbury,' Elys replied, 'and I heard people say "do it don't" while I was there.'

'Ay, there's many an odd saying comes out of Suffolk, and even odder from Norfolk!' Lukin said, grinning. 'I've lived in Essex so long I've lost near all my Suffolk speech, but sometimes it do slip to my tongue when I'm excited, and this great matter's exciting to all on us. You must feel greatly proud and humble, Master Matthew.'

'Humble, and very, very grateful,' Matthew replied. 'I can't really remember exactly what happened, for I felt so strange and drowsy. I expect I'd have been terrified otherwise, to think that He had appeared to me . . . I shall serve Him as best I can all my days, friend Lukin.'

There was a glow of happiness and peace in his pale, drawn face, and Elys, still turned round on her stool, wondered what it must feel like to be so certain, so contented, to know exactly what one wanted to do with one's life. She supposed that he would become a monk, for that must be what he meant, and he was obviously filled with joy to speak of it, whereas she, who was meant by her family to be a nun, hated and rebelled against the idea, and Judith, who had already taken her vows, seemed to have found no happiness in the nunnery, showing only a cold austerity, and no joy at all. She sighed, and turned back to her work.

'Did He really look like He does on our Cross?' asked Lukin eagerly.

Matthew frowned a little and gazed into the fire, obviously making a great effort to remember exactly what he had seen.

'It's all so confused and hazy, like a half-remembered dream,' he said at length. 'I remember looking at Him and thinking that I'd seen His face before, and there was a picture in my mind of a crucifix, with the man before me on it . . . I suppose it must have been our Cross, for that's the one I've been gazing at so much lately. I'm sorry, Lukin – I wish I could recall every detail of it, but the more I try, the more uncertain and confused my memory becomes.'

'Seen through a glass darkly,' Lukin said sagely, using the Latin words of the Vulgate, 'but then, face to face. Do it won't be face to face for a long time, God willing, after this, and that's the real miracle, isn't it, for we all thought you'd not got above a few days, once the rot started. Well, I mustn't keep you talking here, tiring you out. Everyone sends you their best wishes, from Father Brian to Edwin's littlest fitchet. I'll come again when you're a bit more recovered. Thank you for letting me stay, my lady.' This last was addressed to Lady Mabilia as the little man stood up and made a bow which brought his nose near to his nobbly knees, and then, flourishing his cap, he bowed less low to everyone else and moved towards the door, pausing as he passed Elys to say, 'I be off to London in the morning, to fetch the silks and gold you do be needing, Lady. I'll mind to get the best I can.'

'Could you look for some thread to match this, for sewing the pieces together?' Elys asked, pulling a few loose ravellings of silk from the spare corner of the fabric.

Lukin came back into the hall to take them from her, twisted them into a thread, and tied them round the middle finger of his left hand with surprising dexterity. 'I won't forget that so be that's tied to I,' he said, and went out again with a farewell flourish.

Elys smiled to herself at the thought of the quaint, kindly little man, and went on stitching steadily, right hand under her work and left hand over, the needle passing smoothly from one to the other and back again through the heavy silk. Matthew yawned, and said that he thought perhaps he would go to bed for an hour as he was a little tired.

Once he was settled, the household split up, each going about his or her affairs, and Elys went on working, alone in the hall, until, an hour or so later, she stretched, easing her back, and decided to take a short walk.

It was almost the end of March, and the day was mild and sunny, so she did not bother to take a cloak, but walked out of the house as she was. Tigrus accompanied her to the street door, then turned about and stepped lightly along the screens passage, tail erect and a little bent over at the tip, towards the kitchen.

Elys crossed the road and walked down the churchyard path, thinking to speak to Aylwin, as she had not had an opportunity to see him alone since the day before, and she wanted to apologize for any annoyance she had caused him.

The door of his workshed was ajar, but he was not there, and his bag of tools was gone too, so she assumed that he was working somewhere in the church or the mason's yard today. She went in to look at the font and admire his skilled carving, and then saw one of his notebooks lying on the bench.

Hoping it was the one with the drawings for the font, she

opened it, thinking it would be interesting to compare the drawing of Noah with the carving. It was the right book, and she stood for a while, looking from drawing to stone, observing how cleverly he had adapted the details which were so easy to draw with a silverpoint to the much more difficult work in obdurate stone. Then she turned the pages, looking for the drawings of Galien, but they were not there, and the neatly cut edges, almost hidden in the binding, showed where the pages had been taken out.

CHAPTER NINE

A shadow suddenly fell across the book, and Aylwin's voice said coldly, 'What are you looking for?'

Startled, and with a feeling of guilt, Elys replied defensively, 'I'm sorry – I didn't mean to pry, but I wanted to compare your drawings with the finished work.'

'Far from finished,' he said, looking critically at his carving, 'and neither matches what was in my head. You're several pages too far on in the book.'

'I also wanted to look again at your drawings of – of your friend,' Elys confessed, feeling thoroughly embarrassed.

'Oh, those! I gave them to him before he left, as a gift for his wife. She sees little of him in the flesh, as she doesn't choose to travel with him.' He said nothing more, but stood looking at her, his face shuttered.

'I – I'm afraid I offended you yesterday . . .' she began, closing the book and putting it down where she had found it.

'No.'

'But you seemed annoyed . . .'

'Did I?'

There was an awkward silence, and Elys bit her lips, unaccountably feeling near to tears, and eventually said, in a low, uncertain voice, 'I value your friendship. I'd not wish to lose it because I said something foolish.'

He gave a little sigh, and said quietly, 'You've not offended me, nor lost my friendship. It's just that it would be easier for me, and safer for – for others, if you ceased to speculate about . . . recent events. You understand? Your brother stands a good chance of recovery – let that satisfy you.'

'It does. The miracle is that he was dying, and now he'll live. How or by what means, is unimportant.'

He nodded, looking searchingly into her face, then nodded again, as if what he found there satisfied him, and gave her a little crooked smile. 'Your own work goes well,' he offered as a token of peace. 'Does it satisfy you?'

'It's something near to what I imagined. I must go back to it. I only slipped out for a breath of air.'

She was careful after that to make no mention of Galien, and gave no more thought to the means whereby Matthew's foot had been amputated, contenting herself with the knowledge that no infection appeared in the wound, which healed well, and Matthew grew stronger each day now that he was free from the pain and suppuration of the great ulcer. She thanked God several times a day for what was still a miracle, however it had happened, and did not forget to pray for the welfare of a certain carpenter who was not the One of Nazareth.

She went out early the next morning to see Lukin set off for London, wishing she could go with him to choose her materials for herself, but reassured by the fact that those which Father Warmand had given her from his store were just what she would have chosen had she been able to, so she was confident that Lukin, who had purchased those on one of his earlier visits to the city, knew exactly what quality and sorts to bring.

She found him outside the church, checking the harness of one of the college's horses, which was to draw the stout cart in which he was to travel and bring back the goods he was to buy – not just her threads, it appeared, but other supplies for the college.

'Where will you go for the silks?' she asked him when he had made his usual elaborate greetings, which appeared to interest the horse, as it turned its head to watch.

'We do patronize a mercer in Westcheap for thread, but another by St Botolph's for cloth,' he replied grandly, 'and the gold thread and purl from a goldsmith in Eastcheap . . . I've to buy currants too, and linen and . . . Hannibal, do thou get thy hoof off'n my foot, gurt clumsy brute!' he added lovingly to the horse, which tossed its head and obeyed unhurriedly.

'You'll take care on the road,' Elys said anxiously. 'It can be so dangerous these days.'

'Bless you now, don't you fret none!' Lukin was quite

embarrassed by her concern. 'Us'll go acrost the river here, and down Ermine Street to Bishopsgate. 'Tis a busy way, plenty folks about, and I'll be well looked after. See, here that comes now!'

There was a clattering and jingling down Church Street, and eight mounted men-at-arms came riding, two abreast, round the churchyard fence to where they were standing. Father Warmand came hurrying out with two purses in his hands, gave the larger to Lukin, who caused it to disappear immediately somewhere inside his clothing, and the smaller to the leader of the soldiers, adding to his greeting the information that it was for his men's subsistence and trouble for the day, followed by a few courteous words of thanks for their help.

'M'lord sends his best regards,' the captain replied. 'We'll aim to be back latish this evening, if your reeve does his business speedily.'

'Ar,' said Lukin, climbing on to his cart and sorting out his reins. 'I'm not one to loiter, so let's be off!'

Father Warmand had only time for a brief blessing before the cart gave a lurch and set off through the ford, the mounted men hurrying after it to take up positions around it.

They returned safely after dark, and Lukin brought Elys her materials the next morning. He was full of breathless description of the beautiful fabrics in the mercer's booth, but to Elys there was beauty enough in the skeins of lustrous silk, shimmering with a score of shades of brown, orange, yellow, red and green, and the gold, thin strips of pure gold foil wrapped tightly round a core of natural silk, and delicate spirals of gold wire, called purl, which she would use for the lettering.

'And here's a hank of the silk for sewing up,' Lukin said, adding it to the pile. 'That did give a little trouble, as the mercer had none that shade, but that sent out for that to that's brother-in-law's mother's cousin, and that did have just the thing!'

'Thank you, Lukin. They're just what I wanted,' Elys said gratefully, 'and you had no trouble on the road?'

'Apart from a horse what shies at pigs, none at all,' Lukin

assured her. 'Happen, when times be better, you'll be able to come with I and choose for yoursen.'

The rest of Lent passed swiftly, and the sadness of Good Friday was lightened by Matthew making his first outing on his new crutches to go across to the church for the long series of services, where he was allowed to sit while everyone stood or knelt. He had a slight adjustment made to the length of the crutches the next morning, when Alvin Bisemare called to see how they suited him, and then went swinging about the town, seeing the houses and shops he had only heard about before. After an hour's rest, he was up and about again and accompanied his family to the midnight service when the Paschal candle was lighted, followed by the first Mass of Easter.

Elys had always loved that service, with its great air of rejoicing after the long, hard, dark time of Lent and the sorrow of Good Friday. She walked in the procession which wound round the town from the church and back again with a full heart and a radiant smile on her face, and greeted her family and all her acquaintances afterwards with a heartfelt 'He is risen!' and a kiss of peace, from dear Matthew to the seventh thurifer, who seemed to regard her as his particular friend. When she returned home in the cold grey light of dawn, she even gathered Tigrus up in her arms, kissed his nose, and told him the glad news as well.

The cat suffered the embrace with dignity, and, noting that the fire had been uncovered and stirred into a cheerful blaze, went to sit by it, blinking golden eyes at the flames. The family sat round the hearth, sipping mulled ale and warming themselves, and presently Tigrus flowed up in one sinuous movement on to Sir Richard's knees. The Templar frowned severly at his nephew and nieces and said nothing, but presently he might have been observed to be rubbing the animal in various delectable places behind the ears and under the chin, but in a detached, absent-minded fashion.

Aylwin, who by now was regarded as a member of the family, was sitting, as usual, with a notebook propped on his thigh, and Elys saw, craning her neck, that he was drawing the knight and the cat, catching the ecstatic lift of

174

the cat's head and the remote expression on the knight's face, and she smiled to herself.

'I shall return to Wix tomorrow,' Judith said abruptly, 'there being no further need of my presence here. I've instructed my escort to be ready after morning Mass. Do you come with me, my lady?' She had never addressed Lady Mabilia as 'mother' since she entered the convent, reserving that title for the Prioress.

Lady Mabilia hesitated, weighing the inconvenience of departure at such short notice against the advantage of travelling with Judith's escort, but before she could reply, Sir Richard said, 'Pray, Sister Helen, delay your departure until the following day, and I'll escort you and my sister myself, with my own men, in addition to those your Prioress provided. I mislike the idea of your travelling with so few men in these troublous times.'

Judith bowed her head in assent, and looked deliberately at Elys, but without saying anything, leaving it to Lady Mabilia to ask, 'And do you go with us, Elys?'

Elys noted, with a spark of encouragement, that she was being asked, not told, and she replied, 'No, Mother. I have no vocation for the life of a nun. My calling is to work to God's glory with my needle.'

'Think well, Niece,' Sir Richard put in weightily. 'Do you feel no obligation to fulfill the promide made on your behalf that you would take the veil when your brother should be healed? The healing has been accomplished. What of your side of the matter?'

'Needlework may be equally well done in the cloister,' Lady Mabilia objected, but in a half-hearted fashion, and Judith for the first time spoke.

'I wish to speak to Elys alone,' she said in a voice which discouraged argument. 'We shall walk in the churchyard.' She rose, gesturing impatiently to Elys, who had not moved, and went out, so Elys perforce followed.

Once across the road in the seclusion of the far corner of the churchyard, she turned and said coldly, 'Why are you so obstinate, Elys?'

'Because I feel no call to be a nun,' Elys replied patiently. 'Surely you remember how wretched I was when I stayed those weeks in the nunnery before? I couldn't bear to be shut in like that! I want to stay in the world, to do my work, perhaps marry and have children.'

Judith sighed. 'How foolish you are, child! Fear of being shut in can be mastered, in time, and do you really imagine you can support yourself by embroidery?'

'Yes,' Elys replied firmly. 'People who know about such things say my work is good enough, and broiderers are well-paid. I shall save some of my money, and presently have a dowry to offer.'

Judith drew herself up, a black, stiff figure in the early morning sunlight, and snapped, 'You've no idea what you're talking about! Have you ever heard a woman in childbed?'

'No. Have you?'

'Of course. You forget that I am the eldest of the family. I saw our mother forced to yield her body to our father whenever and however his lust required, and that's all marriage is, you ignorant girl! A legal way for a man to do as he pleases with a woman, with no thought for her feelings or sufferings! And children! Conceived in shame, humiliation and pain, brought forth in agony, and for what? I saw five children born to our mother, learned to love them, and then saw them waste away and die! I say it's better to have no children at all, to love nothing and no one of this world, but give all your love, your body and soul to the worship of God, and live in peace of mind and heart in the safety of the cloister!'

Elys stared in shocked silence for a moment, then faltered, 'Oh, Judith!'

'Sister Helen.'

'Sister Helen, then. Do you really mean that? Don't you feel any love at all for Mother, for Crispin and Matthew and me? Is that why you've always seemed so cold and distant?'

'I've learned from bitter experience that it's the only way to avoid futile misery.'

Elys shook her head. 'Yes, it is painful to love someone sometimes, I know. I've been desperately unhappy about Matthew, especially when I saw him in pain and I thought he was going to die, but I wouldn't, even then, choose not

176

to have loved my dear brother! You have to accept the pain and the unhappiness, but you have the times of joy as well. Are you happy, Ju – Sister Helen?'

'Happy? Happiness is for the next world, not this. I've learned to feel nothing, but to be at peace, waiting and serving until I can die, and hope that I've earned the right to real happiness in Heaven.'

'I can't be like that,' Elys said firmly. 'I'd rather take the risks and find happiness where I can. I'm sorry, but I can't go to Wix with you, and nothing you say will make me change my mind.' She did not add that she felt a deep pity for her sister, for she knew that Judith would not understand. 'Shall we go back to the others?'

'I shall pray that you'll learn sense before it's too late,' Judith said calmly, and followed Elys back to the house.

They found the others as they had left them. Judith said nothing but returned to her seat and fixed her eyes on her hands folded in her lap.

'Well?' asked Sir Richard. 'Has your sister persuaded you to see sense and acknowledge your obligations?'

'I was not party to that bargain,' Elys replied in a quiet and reasonable tone, resuming her seat.

'I did not speak of bargains – one does not bargain with Our Lord!' Sir Richard said irritably. 'I spoke of a promise! Promises are meant to be kept!'

'Indeed!' said Lady Mabilia, looking troubled. 'I promised that Judith, you and I would serve Our Lord all our days when Matthew was safe and well. I can't rest easy, thinking that my promise hasn't been kept!'

'May I, as an outsider, express an opinion?' Aylwin asked. Everyone looked at him, and he went on. 'You may well feel that this is none of my business, but you're all so closely involved that it may be easier for one who isn't so close to the problem to see it more clearly.'

'True enough,' Sir Richard allowed judicially.

'Aylwin is a sensible and thoughtful man. Let's hear his opinion,' said Crispin, and Matthew nodded agreement.

Lady Mabilia hesitated, then said, 'Very well. Let him say what he thinks.' Judith said nothing, but gave Aylwin a cold, considering look, and then bowed her head with an odd mixture of pride and submission.

'I value Master Aylwin's opinions and advice,' Elys said firmly, determined to have her say in all matters concerning her future.

Aylwin looked at each speaker in turn, then thought for a moment before saying slowly, weighing every word, 'Each of us here serves God in his or her own way. Crispin, Sister Helen and you, my lady, have chosen the greater way of the religious life, but Sir Richard also serves Him with the sword, as Matthew once meant to do. Matthew has now chosen to serve Him through his skill with a pen and by teaching. I, too, serve Him with the gift He's given me, of carving rough stone into things of beauty and edification to His greater glory, and that's the manner of service which Lady Elys wishes to choose. Surely all these forms of service are pleasing to God? He gave each of us a gift, and did not Our Lord bid us to make good use of our gifts in His service? We have another thing in common, I believe. We all chose our manner of serving for ourselves, under God's guidance, yet it seems that Lady Elys may not be allowed that choice. If the promise Lady Mabilia made on her daughter's behalf was that she should serve God, surely it's right that she should do so by the means which God has given her, following the vocation to which she feels He has led her?'

He stopped, made a little gesture with his hands, and looked again at each of them with an enquiring humility that seemed to beg each to consider his words, however poorly expressed they might have seemed.

There was silence for what seemed to Elys a very long time. Lady Mabilia closed her eyes, Judith sat as still and remote as a statue, Sir Richard absent-mindedly stroked Tigrus and stared at the floor, while Crispin and Matthew, after a pause, looked at one another, nodded slightly, then waited for their elder to speak first.

At length, Sir Richard said, 'Well-reasoned. I agree. Our method of service should be determined by our talents. Elys is clearly gifted with her needle.' His answer was possibly influenced by the ingrained sense in every Templar that the religious considered them inferior, because their service necessarily involved violence and bloodshed, but it was, nevertheless, sincere.

'As head of the family,' Matthew said, somewhat unexpectedly, for his long illness had prevented him from taking that, his rightful position, 'I say that Elys has the right to determine her own way of keeping the promise which our mother made on her behalf. Crispin and I can gladly offer her a home until she marries, as, no doubt, she will, and a place to work. I gather from Father Warmand that there's enough for her to do here to keep her employed for several years. In any case, with so many barons and knights salving their consciences by founding monasteries, there'll obviously be much work to be done in supplying their needs for several generations.'

'But she has no dowry,' Lady Mabilia wailed softly.

'I dare say that Crispin and I can make shift to find her something when she needs it,' Matthew replied. 'I still have my manor of Wix, and, besides, a broidress is a craftswoman, and is paid accordingly. I've no fear that Elys will be a drain on our resources,' and he smiled across at his sister in a warm and encouraging fashion which filled her with affection, making her eyes brim over with emotional tears.

Sir Richard, retrieving his position as the senior man, and, therefore, the most important person present, collected their attention with a stern eye, and announced, 'The matter is settled, then. My sister and elder niece will return to Wix under my escort on Tuesday, and my younger niece will remain under the wardship of her elder brother. I think I speak for all of us in thanking you, Master Aylwin, for your helpful intervention. It's quite true that those most closely concerned in these matters see the situation the least clearly.' He bowed slightly to Aylwin, who returned the courtesy with calm dignity.

Elys, who was sitting nearest to Aylwin, leaned towards him and added her own thanks with an intensity which reflected her relief at having the matter of her future resolved at last, and to her satisfaction. He looked at her, his blue eyes looking a little concerned and surprised, and said, 'I did nothing, except put the discussion on a less emotional footing. Your mother has already accepted that you'd not take the veil! Hadn't you realized that?'

Elys shook her head, surprised and confused by his certainty, but when she thought about it, she realized that he was quite right. Ever since she had come home with two pounds in good silver and a commission to make an altar-cloth, her mother had not mentioned the subject of her becoming a nun, until today, and then only to ask *if* she would go, not to tell her that she must! She looked at Aylwin through a mist of relief and gratitude, seeing how golden his hair was in the firelight, how blue and candid were his eyes, how handsome his face, and something inside her body seemed to lurch and turn over, so that she could hardly catch her breath for a few moments. How good and kind and beautiful he is, she thought.

Crispin and Matthew gave a feast on Monday night, after a consultation with Matilda Mayngod. The day was occupied with much scurrying to and fro of servants, who swept up all the rushes from the floor, together with all the rubbish which had accumulated among them, and polished the stools, chairs and tables until the whole house smelled pleasantly of beeswax and lavender. The scullery-maids and boys seemed to spend the day running in and out of the street door, which banged every few minutes, fetching more eggs, begging a pinch of this or a sprig of that, or another jug of cream, from Mistress Mayngod's many friends among those who cooked, in cottage or inn, throughout the town. She even went herself at one point to purchase some oysters from the innkeeper at the Swan, who was rumoured to have received a couple of barrels fresh from Colchester.

Judith declined to attend the feast, and spent the evening in the church, but the rest of the family gathered in the hall to receive the guests, who arrived one by one from about four o'clock onwards, as they finished their work. Father Warmand and Father Radulf were the only canons who were free of duties here, or in the outlying parishes, that evening, and they were the first to arrive, followed by Lukin Dulpain, Master Peter the schoolmaster, Alvin Bisemare, and many other of the townsfolk, including, of course,

Edwin Warrener, who brought what could only be described as a bouquet of conies and daffodils, all arranged in one great bunch, for Mistress Mayngod, towards whom, according to Lukin, he nurtured certain intentions.

Sir Richard's two sergeants were also bidden to attend, although they cast rather a damper on their end of one of the long tables by refusing wine or ale and eating only the plainest dishes, in silence, being under the watchful eye of their master.

There were, in all, about twenty guests crammed into the hall, and a great deal of merriment as the ale and wine were passed in jugs up and down the tables and the good, plentiful food appeared, to be admired and then consumed. Many of the guests were among the poorer folk in the town, who could rarely afford to eat meat, and they tucked in to the beef, chickens, sucking-pigs, coney pies and steak pies with oysters with great enjoyment, but everyone was pleased with the generous helpings after the long austerity of Lent.

When Mistress Mayngod's masterpiece, a great castle of marchpane and blancmanger, had been brought in with ceremony, admired to everyone's satisfaction, and demolished with the reverence due to its novelty and tastiness, it was the turn of those guests who had the ability to provide the entertainment.

Elys, sitting at the high table between Matthew and her uncle, thought with interest that here was an unusual gathering of people from all ranks of society, and from both nations in the kingdom. Most of the guests had the fair colouring and the speech of Englishmen, and only her own family, Father Radulf and perhaps William of Norwich, were Normans. This fact became more obvious when people began to take turns at singing or reciting, for one poem or song after another was in English, and, for the first time in her life, she heard something of the beauty of English verse, with its alliteration and metaphor, its vivid word pictures and its subtle rhythms. She realized, also for the first time, how supple and versatile the language was, and how great the poets who had used it to make these poems. She knew enough English now to follow most of it, for she had fallen into the habit of speaking English with most of the people she encountered in Waltham, adding greatly to what she had learned as a child from her English nurse.

Lukin Dulpain recited a number of riddles, each a short poem, all of which were obviously familiar to his audience, who cheerfully roared out the answer as soon as he finished declaiming each one. William of Norwich recited a poem in such a thick Norfolk accent that nobody could understand it, but they all applauded none the less, and Edwin Warrener sang in a sweet tenor, a sad, haunting lovesong, accompanied on a pipe by a shepherd called, appropriately enough, David.

Gradually, the turns moved up the hall, until it became obvious that the high table would be expected to make a contribution. Lady Mabilia whispered something to Matthew, who replied, 'No, Mother – ladies aren't expected to perform!' The sergeants, when their turn came, each replied apologetically that their Rule forbade them, at which Sir Richard's eyebrows rose a trifle. Father Warmand recited part of a long poem about St Helen and the discovery of the true Cross, which was applauded because it reminded them all of the finding of their own Cross in far-away Somerset. Father Radulf, who had been to English feasts before, had learned the first few lines of Caedmon's great Hymn of the Creation, and always sang it on such occasions, getting most of the words more or less right and earning applause because he, a Norman, had made the effort.

Aylwin's turn came next, and he sang in a true and pleasant baritone. He chose a Latin song, which much impressed his audience, most of whom did not understand the words, but appreciated the scholarship. Elys, who had a little Latin, understood the first lines to be about going into the woods alone and loving solitary places, and the last couplet to mention the singing of the nightingale and something about love in the heart, and she felt that strange, melting sensation inside her again.

She was brought back to her surroundings by the unexpected sound of Sir Richard's voice uplifted in song. He had, in fact, quite a melodious voice, and sang a Templar marching song, more of a hymn than a soldier's song, although it spoke of slaying the Saracen to the Glory of God. The words were Norman-French, lacking the smooth flow of either English or Latin, but it was a good, rousing tune with a chorus which the sergeants, and then everyone else, joined in, thumping fists or cups on the table in rhythm, and Sir Richard received a hearty cheer when it ended and he sat down, which made his smile a little self-conscious.

The merriment and feasting went on until well after curfew, but the hall was so full that nobody minded that the fire had been covered and only a few lanterns provided a dim light. Most of the folk, however, faced a hard day's work in the morning, and had the sense to drink moderately and leave early, but not before Matilda Mayngod herself came in with a great tray of patties stuffed to bursting with chopped meat, raisins, suet, spices and currants, all of which quickly disappeared, not so much into mouths as into purses or wallets, to be treats for the children or wives left at home.

Lukin Dulpain was one of the last to leave, prancing up to the dais to make his formal farewells to Lady Mabilia and Sir Richard, wishing them well on their journeyings, and begging that Lady Mabilia might occasionally remember him, a poor, sinful reeve, in her prayers, which she promised to do with a suspiciously moist shine gleaming in the corners of her eyes in the lanternlight. Lukin then made a further speech, regretting that he had not been able to wish Godspeed to Sister Helen. He had been clutching a bundle of something to his chest during his speechmaking, but Elys, who had noticed it, could not make out what it was in the dim light. All was revealed however, when he made yet another speech, this time to Mistress Mayngod, praising the products of her kitchen, and ending by presenting the bundle to her, when it proved to be a somnolent and over-full Tigrus, who had spent the greatest part of the feast on Lukin's lap, being fed tidbits. Mistress Mayngod uttered a shriek of surprise and amusement, Lukin made one of his deep bows, flourished his conical cap, and capered out of the door with a last 'Goodnight!'

Father Radulf was still there, as he had promised to make

an examination of Matthew's stump, in order to give Lady Mabilia the latest news of it.

'Healing excellently well,' he pronounced. 'I should be able to remove the ligatures in a few days. It fills me with wonder to see how marvellously well it was done. I've often felt that, despite my vows, I should attempt to amputate when it might save a life otherwise doomed, but never could I do it so well, of course . . . Truly miraculous.'

He gave the intending travellers a particular blessing, and pronounced a general one on the household before he left, meeting Judith at the door as she came in, and pausing to bless her and wish her well, to which she responded with an unemotional inclination of her head. She then went straight upstairs to bed without a word to anyone, which Elys thought very cold and strange.

Lady Mabilia, once the guests had gone, said briskly that she intended to retire at once, in view of the journey to be started in the morning, and Elys could hardly do other than go up with her. They found Judith at her prayers and the harassed Maud struggling to close the lids of her mistress's four travelling chests, all of which were a little too full.

'You'll not manage it,' Lady Mabilia informed her. 'Let me see what may be left behind.'

In a few minutes she undid all Maud's careful packing, pulling out garments, pilgrim tokens, carvings, fabrics, shoes and a variety of odds and ends acquired on the long journey to Rome and back, and tossed every item on one or other of three piles.

'There!' she said eventually. 'Those will go with me, those may be given to the poor, and those I shall leave with you, Elys. Do as you please with them. No doubt some will be of use to you.'

Elys stared at her pile in amazement, for it included several lengths of expensive silks and brocades which Lady Mabilia had bought in Italy, and her jewel-case.

'But, Mother . . .' she began.

'They'll none of them be of any use to me in the nunnery,' Lady Mabilia pointed out. 'The fabrics will make you some decent gowns, for I'd not wish you to go about all the time dressed like a peasant, or you can use them in your work.

As for the jewels – keep some of them in case you fall ill, or have no work to do. Some of the oddments might do to adorn a cope, or something of the sort.'

Elys thanked her mother with a sudden rush of tears, for she had just realized that she might never see her again. Lady Mabilia embraced her and bade her be a good girl and work hard, 'And then I'll be satisfied,' she finished, turning away to watch Maud pack the few things she had decided to keep.

Judith had risen from her knees, and she now remarked, with no apparent emotion, 'Nobody asked me if I wished to enter the nunnery. It seems strange that one sister should be allowed to choose, but not the other!'

'I thought you longed to be a nun!' Lady Mabilia protested.

'What if I did, and do? I was never given a choice in the matter. It makes no difference that I would have chosen to be a religious. I should still have been asked.'

'I don't see why,' Lady Mabilia replied calmly. 'Elys wasn't. I told her she was to take the veil, and she refused. You could have done the same, if you felt strongly about it.'

Judith made a sound which, if she had not been a precise, well-mannered and self-contained person, might have been mistaken for a snort, turned her back on the room, removed her veil and outer robe, slipped into bed and apparently immediately fell asleep. Lady Mabilia exchanged a look with Elys, raised her eyebrows, and set about her own preparations for bed.

'M-my lady,' Maud ventured timidly, 'what – please – what am I to do?'

'Do?' demanded Lady Mabilia, startled. 'In what respect?'

'W-when you enter the nunnery.'

'Why, come with me, of course. Good heavens, my dear girl,' (Maud was well past forty) 'you don't imagine I mean to abandon you? My arrangement with the Prioress included you, of course.'

'But I've no dowry,' the gentlewoman faltered.

'No matter – they don't expect one, in your case, as I've made over a substantial gift to them. Besides, they have

Lady Elys's dowry, and that must more than satisfy them. You can begin as a lay-sister, and perhaps you may even aspire to be a nun, in time. Now, stop chattering and go to bed.'

The poor woman obviously wanted to express her thanks, but was too nervous to disobey, so she contented herself with kissing her mistress's hand before creeping away to her pallet in the corner.

Elys, before settling down to sleep, thought about her conversation with Judith, and tried to imagine how she would have felt herself if she had been the first-born, and had grown up knowing that her mother was unhappy in her marriage, aware of all that her mother suffered in bearing children, and then seeing them each die in turn, after only a few brief years or months of life. Perhaps she, too, would have been glad to take refuge from such a life in a nunnery. She also thought about poor Maud, unconsidered and unloved for so long that she was actually grateful to be called someone's dear, and to be allowed to assume the drudgery of life as a lay-sister. For a few horrifying moments, she saw herself in that position, if she failed to make her way as a broiderer, and did not find a husband. Would she end up, estranged from her family, old and unwanted, glad to be at the beck and call of some wealthy lady, even becoming a servant with gratitude if the alternative was to be cast out, homeless and destitute, into the world? It was a sobering thought, and she prayed hard that she might be spared such a fate, but also made the prudent resolve to seek a lodging somewhere in the town before her brothers told her to leave their house.

Despite it being April, the next day showed every sign of being dry and even warm, and suitable for travelling. Lady Mabilia and her family attended Mass with Sir Richard and his Templars, and Aylwin joined them, just before the Elevation, in his working-clothes and holding a small bundle, which he gave to Lady Mabilia after the service.

'It's not a cat!' he assured her when she looked at it dubiously. It was wrapped in a piece of cloth, which she unwound, to reveal a wooden carving of Our Lady. It was a lovely figure, showing Her as a young woman, and Aylwin had used the grain of the wood very cleverly to show the folds and shadows of Her robe.

'You've caught a likeness of Elys!' she exclaimed in a pleased tone. 'I suppose you did it from that drawing you made it Mantova. What skill you have, Master Aylwin. I'm very grateful to you for this – I shall treasure it, although I must, of course, give it to the nunnery, but I shan't tell them that it resembles my daughter.' She gave Aylwin her hand in a warm clasp, and actually smiled at him with more warmth than she normally allowed herself to show even her own children.

Her farewells to them were brief, consisting only of a blessing and a swift embrace, and then she mounted her horse, which was waiting with the others and the baggage-wagon at the churchyard gate, and rode off without waiting for anyone else. Elys, with a wordless cry, ran a few steps after her, but Lady Mabilia went on, a stiffening of her back the only response. Elys halted, and stood looking lost and lonely until Crispin went to put a comforting arm about her shoulders, saying, 'It's not easy for her, my dear. She doesn't expect to see any of us again in this life.' She nodded dumbly, and let him guide her back to stand between him and Matthew.

Judith merely said, 'Goodbye' to nobody in particular, and followed her mother, but Sir Richard made his farewells in a proper and more leisurely form. As Elys rose from receiving his blessing, she asked if he thought it likely that he would encounter de Mandeville's men on the road, but he replied, 'Little matter if I do. He's a member of a lay fraternity of the Order, so he won't dare to let his fellows trouble us! I have to visit our property at Cressing, but I'll try to find time to call here again on my way back, or, if not, some time during the summer.' With that, he, too, mounted and rode off, leaving his men to scramble on to their mounts and follow as best they could.

Feeling somehow disappointed and a little tearful, Elys went home to her work, feeling uncertain and apprehensive about her future without her mother's sharp tongue and acute mind to guide her. Presently she began to feel guilty, wondering if she was wrong to refuse to fall in with her mother's wishes and take the veil with her. Although Lady Mabilia had not reproached her for refusing, she must feel that her daughter had failed her . . .

Crispin and Matthew had not come home, but had gone about their work, Crispin to his studies and Matthew to the scriptorium, and she wished desperately that one of them would come back, for she felt a great need to talk to someone about her anxieties. Eventually, she could bear it no longer, and went across to Aylwin's workshed, then hesitated in the doorway, not wishing to interrupt him if he was busy.

'Come in, then,' he said, looking up from his carving, which had now progressed to Jonah and the Whale, the latter already taking shape under his chisel. 'You're blocking the light there. I suppose you're tormented by doubts and feelings of guilt?'

'How did you know?' she asked, moving to one side and leaning against the bench.

'It's natural to feel like that when you go against your parent's wishes.'

'Perhaps I was wrong to refuse to go with her,' she said, half to herself. 'She did promise Our Lord that all three of us would go to Wix when Matthew was better, so perhaps I have no right to refuse. He did heal Matthew, and it'd be wicked and sinful if I refused to serve Him after that . . . What must I do, Aylwin?'

He was kneeling by the font, peering at the whale's fine set of teeth, but he sat back on his heels, giving her his full attention, and said kindly, 'It's not for me to tell you what you must do. You must make up your own mind about that. I can only repeat that there are more ways of serving God than in entering religion. If you really want to go to Wix after all, I'll take you there, but don't go simply because you feel guilty.'

'We stayed there, in the nunnery, for a month once,' Elys said, staring unseeingly into space. 'It was dreadful. I felt shut in and suffocating all the time, and at night I'd lie in my cell, longing to open the door, to run out and away from the enclosure. I couldn't sleep, because the walls seemed to be closing in on me, and I couldn't breathe. I couldn't pray, and they made me eat, but I was sick after every meal. I thought I'd go mad if I had to stay there any longer. The day we left, I felt as if I'd been released from a cage. It was so wonderful to feel the wind and rain on my face and to see the trees, the great fields, the whole arch of the sky, instead of just a little square over the cloister.'

'What use would you be in a nunnery, feeling like that?' Aylwin asked. 'God's churches need your work, just as they need mine.'

'But I could do needlework in a nunnery.'

'Not if you were ill, or mad, and it sounds to me as if you'd be one or the other, or both, within a half-year. Your mother agreed that your choice accorded with the intention of her promise, so I don't think you need worry – but I'm only a craftsman. You should talk to a priest about matters of conscience. To my mind, you were put in the world to do embroidery and be a wife and mother, not a nun.'

'Thank you.' Elys managed a little smile. 'You're so kind and helpful, Aylwin. I'm glad we met you in Mantova.'

'What do you think of this whale? It looks more like a codfish to me,' queried Aylwin, smoothly changing the subject.

Elys went to look more closely at Leviathan sporting in the waves, and said that she thought it looked very like she imagined a whale might be, although she had never seen one. Aylwin said neither had he, and he preferred to carve things he had actually seen.

'Why did you choose to put Jonah on your font, then?'

'I didn't, Bishop Henry told me what was to be on it, and I believe the canons had expressed some wishes to him. He particularly wanted Jonah, Noah and the baptism of Jesus, but he was rather vague about Moses.'

'Is he a man of definite ideas?'

'Usually. He's very intelligent and able. Fulk said it's a pity he was the youngest son, for he'd have made a better Count than his brother Theobald, and a better King than . . . It's the teeth that make it cod-like! I'll take a few of them out. I think he might still be Pope eventually, for he's not much past forty. The trouble is, Bernard of Clairvaux dislikes him intensely, and Rome seems to dance to Bernard's tune in everything.'

He concentrated on his work for a while, and Elys watched in silence. When eventually he sat back and said, 'That's better,' she asked inconsequentially, 'Aylwin, are you married?' and had no idea why the question had entered her head, let alone passed her lips, for she had only been watching him and thinking not only how skilful he was, but how very kind he was to talk to her when he had so much to do.

He looked up, and their eyes met. For what seemed a long time, he regarded her steadily, and she felt her colour rising and her breath coming with difficulty. She could read nothing in his blue eyes but a mild curiosity, and then something kindled in their depths for a brief second.

'Only to my work,' he replied lightly, turning his gaze back to the whale. 'Do you think that's less cod-like?'

CHAPTER TEN

Neither Matthew nor Crispin had said anything so far about where Elys was to live and work, but she was sure that, sooner or later, they would tell her, however sorrowfully, that a sister who so boldly flouted her family's wishes was no longer welcome in their home, or that they were both to be housed by the church. Her pride would not allow her to wait for that humiliation, so she set out next morning to look for a lodging.

Of the two places mentioned by the cordwainer, Widow Miller's was the nearer, so, feeling very nervous, she went there first, and found, after asking directions of a passing housewife, a very small hall-house of one storey, with an even smaller two-storeyed cross-wing at one end. Repeated knocking on the battered door eventually brought an old bent woman in a drab gown and a grubby head-veil to open it. She peered up at Elys with watering eyes almost opaque with cataracts, and said, 'What do you want?'

'I'm looking for a lodging,' Elys replied. 'I was told that you might have a room to let.'

The woman looked beyond her and asked, 'Who's with yer? I see nobody.'

'I'm alone.'

'Where's yer 'usband?'

'I'm not married.'

'Yer father, then?'

'He died when I was a child.'

'You mean ye're *on yer own?*'

'Yes.'

'What do yer take me fer? A brothel-keeper?'

'No, of course not! I'm a broiderer, and I'm making vestments and altar-linen for the college here. I need somewhere to live and do my work.'

'A likely tale!' the woman sniffed disbelievingly. 'I take in pilgrims, single men of religion, or respectable married

191

couples, not flighty girls with brass coronets pretending ter be fine ladies, on the look-out fer gullible young fellers! Be off with yer, yer Norman Jezebel!' She slammed the door forcefully in Elys's face.

This was worse than Elys had expected, but she told herself that Mistress Chich, as a priest's widow, would be more ready to understand her problem, so she went, still very nervously, to the larger house which she had already identified on the other side of the ford, and again knocked at the door.

It was opened by a thin little girl of about ten, wearing an old and shabby gown which had obviously been made for a much larger person, but had been adapted for its present wearer by having the excess material cut off the ends of the sleeves and the hem, which had then been very inexpertly turned up again.

'Wot yer want?' demanded the child, with a piercing sniff for punctuation.

'How many times, Martha, have I told you what to say to visitors?' demanded a cold and somewhat affected voice from within the house.

'Me name's Edith. Don't like Martha,' the child returned sulkily. 'Goo' mornin' did yer want to see Mistress Chich please ter come in,' she then recited without pause for breath.

'Thank you,' Elys replied, and stepped inside as the child stood back, then banged the door shut behind the visitor, scuttled past her and disappeared down the screens passage, helped on her way by a sharp slap from a large and very imposing lady who was standing a few yards further into the house.

'I am Mistress Chich,' she announced in the same affected tones which Elys had heard before. 'How may I assist you?'

'I am Elys de Wix,' she replied. 'I'm a broiderer by profession, doing some work for the college.'

'Work? What kind of work?' Mistress Chich pronounced the word as if it were something distasteful.

'At the moment, I'm making a burse and an altar-cloth. I hope after that to make more vestments and altar-linen.'

192

'Very commendable, I'm sure. You do this sort of thing for a living?'

'Yes.'

'And what has that to do with me?' Mistress Chich had been a little condescending when the conversation began, but she now sounded haughty. 'If you seek assistance with your work, I assure you that I have not descended to sewing for a living! My dear lamented husband, Canon William de Chich, had noble connections, and would have regarded such a suggestion as an insult!'

'I have noble connections myself, madam,' Elys returned a trifle edgily. 'I think it no shame to earn my living by means of an honourable craft for which God has given me a talent. I understand that I might find a lodging here, and perhaps also rent a room in which to do my work.'

Mistress Chich drew herself up, thrusting out a massive bosom, and declared in a rich contralto of even greater affectation, 'I occasionally provide a lodging for minor clergy in attendance on great men of the Church who come on pilgrimage or on business to Waltham, and for whom there is insufficient suitable accommodation in the college guest-house or the canons' residences. I do not take in travelling seamstresses!'

'I am not a seamstress,' Elys replied mildly, curbing her temper and trying to speak pleasantly. 'I'm a skilled broid-erer, and I can pay for a good lodging. If you're doubtful about me, Father Warmand will vouch for the truth of what I tell you, and I dare say you know my brother, Father Crispin.'

'Father Crispin and his brother have a house with far more room in it than this,' Mistress Chich snapped. 'If you are indeed their sister, which I doubt, you should be living under their protection, like any decent single lady, and not traipsing about talking of earning your living like some common slut. You should be ashamed of yourself, behaving so disgracefully, young woman! A respectable girl stays at home with her father or her brother until she marries or enters a convent, and doesn't go wandering about like a common vagrant, working with her hands. Be off with you, out of my house, before I box your ears, which your own mother should have done to knock such foolishness out of you!' With that, she seized Elys by the arm, pushed her out of the house, and slammed the door after her.

Elys stood in the street, staring irresolutely at the door and trying not to dissolve into tears, then turned and walked slowly away towards the footbridge, where the miller's black cat looked up from its contemplation of the water in expectation of at least a word of greeting, but she was too dejected even to notice it, and went on over the bridge, round the scaffolded west end of the church, and in through the south door, even passing Aylwin's work-shed without looking to see if he was within.

It was peaceful in the church, apart from a group of pilgrims praying silently beneath the Cross, and some subdued discussion from the masons, who were fitting *voussoirs* to the frame of another arch of the nave arcade. Elys made her reverence to the altar and the Cross, and stood for a few minutes, trying to pray, but unable to find the words. Then she walked round to the north transept and knocked gently on the door of the sacristy.

Father Warmand opened it with a jerk and exclaimed, 'What, are you back already . . . Oh, Lady Elys! Good morning. I thought you were the boy I've sent to the chandler for candles. Is something amiss? You look distressed . . . Not the work?'

'No, the work goes quite well,' she replied absently. 'Oh, Father, I don't know what to do. I've been looking for a lodging – the cordwainer told me of two places where I might get a room – but they said such unpleasant things to me. They seem to think that there's something shameful about a woman trying to earn her own living.'

'Well, no doubt that's because it's outside their experience,' Warmand said comfortably, ushering her into the sacristy and clearing a stool of its burden of laundered linen for her to sit down. 'In a little place like this, girls work at home helping their mothers, or in the fields helping their fathers and brothers, until they marry, and then they're busy in their own homes . . . It's only a few enterprising widows, like Mistress Mayngod, or Widow Godwin who does our laundry, who make a living for themselves after they lose their husbands, if they've no sons to keep them in their old age. But why do you need a lodging? I thought your brothers were settled here? Father Crispin has asked to be considered for the next vacancy in the college after he's priested.'

'Yes, but I'm not sure they'll be prepared to let me go on living with them,' Elys said sadly. 'My mother vowed that she and I would enter the nunnery where my sister is if Matthew were to be healed, and he was, and I've refused to go, so I've upset the whole family, and I can't expect Matthew and Crispin to go on treating me as if nothing's happened.'

'Have they told you to leave?'

'No, not yet, but I'm sure they will sooner or later. I wanted to find somewhere to live and work before that happens, to save them, and myself, the embarrassment . . .'

'If I were you,' Warmand said briskly, suspecting that she was about to start crying, 'I'd wait until it happens, if it ever does. I don't think either of those young men would be so lacking in charity as to turn their own sister out of doors, or condemn her for having a strong feeling about her own vocation! If I'm wrong – well, come back to me, and we'll make shift to find you a workroom and a lodging somewhere – perhaps in the guesthouse. It wouldn't be very comfortable, but it would serve until you can find something better. Ah, here's the lad with the candles. Now I must sort them and put them away, and then prepare the altar for High Mass. You go home and get on with your work, daughter, and don't worry about things until they happen. The Lord bless you and keep you.'

Elys went home uncomforted, and tried to work, but the unkind reception she had met with from the two widows, and Father Warmand's sublime lack of concern, had thoroughly upset her. Her eyes kept filling, and eventually she had to turn away from her work, for fear of tears falling on the silk. She put her hands over her face and sobbed, full of desolation and fear for the future.

Crispin entered, light-footed, a little ahead of Matthew, who had not yet mastered his crutches well enough to move quickly, and found her still weeping. He stopped in the doorway and said, 'Why, Elys, you're crying. I'm sorry – I should have thought how much you must miss our mother and stayed with you this morning.'

'It's not that,' she sobbed, wiping her eyes on the heel of her hand, having nothing better available. 'I've been trying to find a lodging, and they were so unkind . . .'

'A *lodging*?' Matthew asked, pushing in behind Crispin and coming to stand over her. 'Why do you want a lodging? Aren't you comfortable here?'

'Y-yes, but you won't want me here now, not when I've disobeyed Mother and Uncle Richard, and people think it's a disgrace that I've turned into a-a common vagrant!' The phrase, which had been the most shaming to her, had burned itself into her memory and slipped out unbidden. 'I didn't think there was anything dishonourable about using my gifts to earn a living, but other people do, and I shall drag you down . . .'

'Oh, come now,' Crispin said coaxingly, putting his arm about her shoulders, 'there's a world of difference between a skilled craftswoman and a vagrant. The good folk here-abouts know very little of the world outside their own town, so perhaps they don't realize – you mustn't be upset by what a few ignorant women say. Matthew and I have talked this over, and we've decided that you have as much right as either of us to decide your own way of serving God. As you feel so strongly opposed to being a nun, we respect your decision to earn your own living, don't we, Matthew?'

'Indeed,' Matthew said, giving his brother a slight frown for starting on a statement which he felt should have come from the head of the family. 'We've decided that we must support you in this, and provide a home for you here as long as you're working in Waltham. When you've finished here, we shall have to discuss what's best to do for you, but that won't be for some time yet. As if we'd turn our only remaining sister out of her home. My dear little goose, don't be so silly!' he finished, in startling contrast to the pomposity of the earlier part of his speech.

Elys felt a great wave of relief flood through her, and said unsteadily, 'Oh, bless you both; I've been so worried! I'd no idea that it would be so difficult to find somewhere to live. Later on, I expect I'll be able to buy or rent my own house wherever I'm working, but if I could stay here until then, I'd be so happy.'

'Stay as long as you wish,' Matthew said kindly. 'At least until your work in Waltham's finished.'

With the greatest of her worries resolved, Elys turned her mind to a lesser one. She found it very strange to sleep alone in the upper bedchamber, for, apart from the cell in the nunnery, she had seldom had a room to herself before. It seemed too quiet and very lonely, and she was unable to sleep well for the lack of the sound of someone else breathing, stirring, even snoring. She lay awake worrying over all sorts of things which she would normally have put out of her mind after a brief consideration.

She was anxious about her mother and sister on their journey, and fretted over the possible dangers they might encounter, then chided herself for foolishness, for had they not both the escort provided by the convent and the Templars to guard them?

That led her to worry again about her refusal to go with them, to fears that she might fall ill, might fail to work well enough to get new commissions, might injure her hands, or lose her sight . . .

By some curious process which had nothing to do with reason, she then went on to worry about having asked Aylwin if he were married. What had he thought about her question? Did he think she was suggesting that he might . . .

He held land from Bishop Henry, and was of noble descent. Even an ordinary master-mason, like William of Norwich, ranked as an esquire, and Aylwin was superior to him . . . But why was she thinking about it? Aylwin had been kind and helpful, but always in the manner of a man to a child, as if she were his daughter, although he could not be as much as ten years older than she.

Oh, Fulk! Why didn't you offer before Uncle Richard told you I had no dowry? It seemed so hard that a man should actually have grown to care for her and might wish to marry her, to be eligible in every respect, and even be someone she liked, and yet be unable to become her husband because she had neither land nor money, and then

197

had turned out to be such a worthless creature after all. What if he had found the courage to defy his father and marry her? What would have happened? Would his father have forgiven him in the end, or would they have lived in poverty, perhaps depending on what she could earn with her needle? Oh, Fulk! That a man could be so handsome and charming, that such a man should have fallen in love with her, like a prince in an old tale, and then prove more afraid of his father than devoted to his love. She shed a few tears of vexation and frustration over it, and went on tossing and turning for what seemed most of the night, although, in fact, she must have fallen asleep eventually, for the bell for Lauds woke her in the early morning.

During the day, she spoke to both Matthew and Crispin, and as a result went to see Matilda Mayngod in the kitchen. After a little talk about this and that, she asked her where she slept.

'In the loft,' she answered, indicating that half of the kitchen roof which was closed off by an inserted floor. 'It's warm and dry, but the smoke hangs about there when the wind's in the south or west.'

'I wondered,' Elys said hesitantly, 'if you would care to share the bedchamber with me. It's quite a large room, and it seems wrong that I should have it all to myself.'

Mistress Mayngod, a freewoman of good family, her father and grandfather having been sokemen, holding their land from the college by payment of a rent of firewood and eggs but no labour requirements, was obviously delighted at the thought of having somewhere to keep her property away from the eternal smell of food in the kitchen. She was shrewd enough to guess the main reason for the invitation, but said nothing about that, nor did she value the honour any the less for the fact that it was a matter of mutual benefit. Elys slept better thereafter, and had no cause to regret her decision, for the cook was a quiet, well-mannered and clean woman.

Easter once over, the whole town began to look forward to May, and the coming events of the month seemed to be the main topic of conversation. As Elys sat at her window working, every passer-by who stopped to greet her seemed to have something to say about which was the best part of the Forest to go a-maying, or what they hoped to buy at the fair which would follow two days later. The canons had the right, granted them by Henry I's first wife, to hold a fair on each of the two feasts of the Holy Cross, in May and September, and both were major events in the town's year. After that would come Pentecost, and there was always a church ale after haymaking, which was another great event. Those women who could afford new clothes usually had them then, to wear demurely to church on the feast, and to peacock in at the ale.

These conversations at the window were an unexpected bonus to doing the work she enjoyed, Elys found. Whenever the weather was fine enough to allow her to take down the screen from the window, a succession of people would pause there for a few words. They did not interrupt her work, for they expected her to go on stitching while they gossiped, and the fact that she was a lady was mitigated by her being also a craftswoman, so even quite humble folk were not reluctant to talk to her. Elys, who had expected her working life to be lonely, was delighted to find it quite otherwise, and she soon knew most of what was going on in the town, although she had the sense to keep it to herself.

She was invited to go a-maying by the daughters of the miller and the blacksmith, but found when she set out, well before dawn on May morning, that the unmarried girls and young men of the town all went, in two separate bodies, ostensibly to different parts of the Forest, but they usually managed to meet during the course of their collecting flowers and green branches.

The girls took with them a great basket and a statue, about the length of a man's forearm, of the Virgin, which usually stood in a niche above one of the altars in the south transept of the minster. It was wooden, old and a little battered from many May-morning excursions, and most of the blue paint was worn or chipped from the robes, but it had been carried in Mayday processions as long as anyone could remember, even by adding the memories of great-grandparents to their own. It was set in the middle of the basket in a block shaped to hold it upright, and then the

199

sides of the basket, one of which rose up in a protective arch over the statue, were decorated with flowers, particularly hawthorn blossom, Mary's own flower.

On this particular Mayday, there was little hawthorn blossom out, and the girls roved far and wide along the edge of the Forest seeking its white glimmer in the darkness, and generally managing to find amorous young men looking for them as well as branches of greenery. Elys went at first with her two companions, but soon lost them, one to the cordwainer's son and the other to the hayward, and so wandered on alone, finding half a dozen sprays of hawthorn and many clumps of primroses, shining palely in the grass, with which she filled the small basket she was carrying.

Suddenly she spotted several bunches of hawthorn blossom above her head in the branches of a very old, gnarled tree. She put her basket down and balanced on the roots, reaching up as high as she could, even attempting to climb a little way up the trunk, which was leaning away from her. So busy was she in her efforts that she did not notice someone creeping up behind her, until suddenly she was seized from behind in a tight embrace and a voice whispered in her ear, 'Oh that the sun might rise and show me your pretty face, my fairy! Will you vanish away when it does?'

'Let me go!' Elys said indignantly. 'I don't even know who you are.'

'Don't you?' the voice whispered so close to her ear that she could feel his breath tickling her neck.

She twisted her head away and tried to lean back far enough to see his face, for the sky was growing lighter by the minute, and she could see the tree and the blossom quite clearly now, so she would be able to recognize him, if only she could catch a glimpse of his face! He put a hand behind her head, stopping her from moving it, and kissed her ear, then her jawline and her cheeks, but still she could not see his face. However much she struggled, he held her easily, seeming to have great strength in his arms and hands.

Eventually, having taken his time over showering her neck and the sides of her face with light kisses, he pulled her round a little, so that he could reach her lips, and his kissing changed, becoming far from light, so that she gasped, and

200

his tongue darted between her lips in a flash. He went on kissing her, turning her and gently pushing her back against the tree-trunk. She was trembling, half-afraid, half-excited, never having experienced anything like this before. His kisses became harder, more demanding, and she suddenly became thoroughly frightened, not, oddly enough, of the man or his kisses, but of the tumult of feeling they aroused in her. She began to struggle in earnest, pounding his shoulders with her fists, and he stopped, raised his head, and stepped back, releasing her so suddenly that she almost fell over.

'How dare . . .' she began, furious with herself as much as with him, but she broke off abruptly, for she had looked up into his face as she spoke.

He was Aylwin.

'You!' she exclaimed.

'I thought you'd guessed,' he said, looking puzzled. 'Did you think it was someone else?'

Elys stared at him, speechless with surprise, confusion, emotion. Was this really the man she thought treated her like a child? Was this really the calm, rather serious man who was so kind and helpful, yet so cool and detached?

'I didn't know who it was,' she said. 'I'd no idea. I never thought it might be you.'

There had been the remains of a smile on his face, but it vanished suddenly and he said, 'Then I'm very sorry if I frightened you. It wasn't my intention.'

'Then what did you intend?' she asked, covering her confusion with a show of hauteur, and looked down to see where her basket had got to, for she did not wish to tread or trip on it. As a result, she missed seeing the expression of longing on his face. By the time she had located the basket and looked up again, he was his usual calm, impassive self.

'No more than a little Mayday revelry,' he replied. 'It's the whole point of the festival, you know.'

'No, I don't know,' she said sharply. 'I thought all that sort of thing was for villeins and peasants, not for – for gentry.' She almost said 'nobles', but changed it just in time.

'Oh? Well, I'm sorry if our humble English peasant customs offend my lady! If I'd realized that you didn't expect anyone to presume to kiss you, I'd not have ventured. Was it very disagreeable?'

The last question sounded genuinely interested, as if he had asked her if she had found Rome a fine city or enjoyed crossing the Alps. She looked at him a little suspiciously, wondering if he were laughing at her, but it did not appear so, so she replied seriously, 'No, but it might have been if it had been someone I disliked, or didn't know.'

'I wouldn't harm you, or frighten you, for the world,' he said quietly.

'I know,' she replied, after remembering all his kind words and actions, and she wondered what it would have been like if Fulk had been here. Would he have taken advantage of the English custom, or would his Norman pride have prevented him? On the whole, she thought he would have taken the opportunity. There was a little silence, an oasis in the midst of a great deal of noise, for the dawn chorus was in full cry, and there were shrieks and giggles and wild halloas coming from all directions in the Forest.

Suddenly Aylwin stepped forward, reached up, and picked the bunches of may blossom which had been beyond her reach, and handed them to her. She thanked him, and they walked back, side by side, along the Forest edge to where the basket and the statue were now being adorned with flowers, mainly by the smaller girls who were not yet old enough to join in the chasing and kissing among the trees.

Presently the sun rose above the Forest, and the serious business of the day began. The basket, now Our Lady's bower, was decorated, the girls wove garlands of flowers for their heads, and the boys crowned themselves with leafy twigs twisted into coronets. Aylwin took Elys's garland from her as she was about to lift it to her head, and crowned her with it, looking critically to see that it was on straight. She half-expected he would kiss her after that, but he did not, and she had to tell herself severely that her feelings were not disappointment, but relief.

By now, most of the young people were gathered together.

The bower was hoisted on to the shoulders of two strapping young men, and the rest made an informal procession as they all set out down the long hill back to the town, carrying bunches and baskets of flowers or branches. These were mostly of hawthorn, for every cowshed must have a branch above the door, and every house must have a twig laid in its rafters by someone who was not a member of the family which dwelt there, to give Mary's protection from evil in the coming year.

As they walked down the hill, laughing and still larking about, they began to sing a song so old that the words had become garbled, and nobody really understood them, but everyone knew them, and the tune, for it had been sung every Mayday, probably since Waltham was first settled. Elys soon picked up the tune and hummed it, but Aylwin seemed to know it already, for he said it was much like the song he had learned at home.

When they reached the town, they gathered on the fairground, where a large hawthorn of great antiquity grew. The bower was hauled up into its branches, and everyone joined hands in a series of concentric circles, and they danced round the tree, still singing, each circle moving the opposite way to the one outside it. At the end of each verse, they changed direction, and so danced on for a dozen verses or more, by which time they were out of breath with singing and dancing together, and broke up, laughing and chattering.

The bower was lowered from the tree, and carried round the town, and then to the church in procession, entering by where the great west door would be when the minster was finished, William's masons having moved their scaffolding and tools out of the way for the morning. The procession moved solemnly now, going in silence up the nave. Everyone made a reverence to the nave altar in passing, and another to the great Cross, as they made their way to the transept, where Father Brian received the bower and placed it on the altar below the niche where the Virgin normally stood.

A few prayers were chanted, a blessing given, and then the revellers went out of the church, still in solemn silence, to break up outside into chattering groups, going with their burdens to the various houses to deliver the protecting branches and gifts of flowers to their neighbours and friends.

Aylwin carried his branch to the house in Church Street, where Crispin fetched a ladder and held it while he climbed up and tied the branch to one of the rafters, and Lukin came in later with another, which was placed with equal care on the other side of the hall. A succession of visitors followed, each bringing flowers and wishing them a merry May. Most of them really came to see Matthew, for it was generally believed that, as the beneficiary of a miracle, he had some power within him which would bless anyone who spoke to him or touched him.

Mistress Mayngod had baked a number of little cakes, so that everyone who called might have one, and Tigrus walked calmly and nimbly amid their feet, while they stood about eating and talking, and kindly cleared up any crumbs which they dropped in the clean rushes.

The day was regarded as a holiday, but in fact there was no such thing as a whole day's holiday in a community which lived mainly by farming. Birds still had to be scared off the growing crops, animals must be tended, the sheep in the pastures, and the cows and pigs, at this season, in the Forest. Weeds still grew on Mayday, and must be hoed, and stones also, it was believed, grew in the fields, and must be collected, either for road repairs or, at present, mainly for conversion into rubble-filling for the walls and pillars of the minster.

After dinner, Aylwin went back to work, and Elys resumed her embroidery, but she was constantly looking out of the window all afternoon, for the merchants were arriving for the fair, clattering up Church Street with their carts and wagons, and setting up their booths round the corner, on the fairground.

During the next day, more traders arrived, swelling the normal traffic of pilgrims until the roads into the town could hardly take any more. Goods were laid out in the booths, and apprentices left to guard them while the merchants joined the townsfolk and the pilgrims in the church for the service held on the eve of the minster's patronal festival.

Elys, Matthew and Crispin had particular reason to attend, and Matthew was given a place of honour at the front of the men's side of the nave, for his healing was the great event of the year, and special thanks must be given for it. Elys joined in the prayer of oblation as heartily and sincerely as anyone, for she had come to the conclusion that, whoever had removed her brother's foot, it was indeed a miracle, and it had happened because he had come to the Holy Cross of Waltham to pray for it.

There was festival High Mass in the morning, and after it, the canons went in procession to the fairground, where Father Brian blessed the merchants and their customers, and Lukin Dulpain, as reeve, read out the regulations for the conduct of the fair in a loud, carrying voice, pausing to frown severely after each item. As soon as he had finished, down came the shutters of the booths, and trading began.

Elys had consulted Mistress Mayngod about her intended purchases, seeking advice about which traders would have the best goods and most reasonable prices, and she accompanied the cook on her purchasing round first of all, for various household items must be bought now, the only opportunity which there would be until the second fair in September. Elys had no experience of buying such things as spices and dried fruits, which were only sold in shops in the great cities, and she thought she should learn about that sort of shopping for when she had her own household.

There were several stalls selling exotic foodstuffs – dried apricots from Cyprus, dates from the Holy Land, spices from the lands of the East – and they went the rounds of all of them, examining the goods and enquiring the prices, before Mistress Mayngod decided which trader she would patronize. Even then, she haggled with spirit and good humour to get true bargains – not the cheapest, but the best quality at a reasonable price, explaining to Elys how to tell which raisins would keep and cook up plump and juicy, how to tell freshly imported cloves and cinnamon from last year's leftovers, and it was some time before Elys felt free to leave her and seek the things she needed herself.

The most important were needles. Few women owned more than one good sewing needle, for the best were steel,

fine and sharp, and even the poor quality ones were expensive. Elys knew how to judge the quality of those on offer,
and what was a fair price for them, and she spent several
of her silver pennies on half a dozen of the best available,
for she was afraid to rely on one or two, in case they broke
and left her without the essential tool for her work. There
were other things – fabrics, fine leather and threads, which
attracted her, but she bought only those which she would
need for her embroidery, telling herself that she had more
than enough clothes, and the materials to make more among
the things her mother had given her.

The whole town seemed to have turned out to visit the
fair, but many of the poorer folk only looked at the goods,
or stood watching the dancing bear or the tumblers, enjoying the bustle and the unusual sights, but spending nothing,
having no money to spare. Most of them received no wages,
but had their share of the produce of the fields in exchange
for their labour on the lands held by the canons and the
two or three other tenants who held a hide or two in the
manor. The only things they bought were essentials which
they could not produce themselves – iron goods, footwear,
salt, and, rarely, fine cloth, such as linen, which they could
not grow or spin and weave for themselves.

By dinnertime, Elys had bought all that she intended,
and went home, satisfied that she had obtained value for
money. She put away her precious needles before sitting
down to the meal. To her surprise, there were three little
parcels waiting by her wooden platter – one from each of
her brothers, and the third, it presently appeared, from
Aylwin, for each of them had bought her a fairing.

Matthew's gift was a small pair of very sharp shears, a
miniature of those used for shearing sheep or cutting cloth,
for her to use to cut her threads. Crispin's gift was a dozen
turned wooden spools on which she could wind her threads
to keep them from tangling. Aylwin had bought her a silver
chain with a pendant which was a good example of what
she knew was a typically English form of ornament – an
interlacing strap-pattern of great complexity. She examined
it carefully, expecting to find animal or bird heads concealed
in it, with the straps forming their attenuated but recogniz-

206

able bodies, but there were none. This pattern was a continuous ribbon, forming an extremely complicated endless knot.

'How kind you all are to me,' she exclaimed, delighted with the thoughtfulness her brothers had shown in their choices. 'It's not satisfactory to cut threads with a knife – the little shears will be much better, and the spools will be so useful. Oh, and Aylwin! Such a lovely pendant – what does it signify?'

Aylwin gave her a quizzical look, realized that she genuinely did not know, and replied evasively, 'It's just a peace-offering for startling you the other day.'

'But there was no need for a peace-offering,' Elys said earnestly. 'I was only startled because it was unexpected. I wasn't offended. Thank you very much. It's such a very pretty thing,' and she fastened the chain round her neck and adjusted the pendant to hang straight on her breast.

Aylwin made her a little bow, his lips quirking in a crooked smile, and went on eating, aware that both Matthew and Crispin, more worldly-wise than their sister, were regarding him thoughtfully, and, perhaps, speculatively.

Mistress Mayngod had also received a fairing, which she showed to Elys at bedtime, with a certain not unbecoming coyness.

'Look what that Edwin bought me at the fair,' she said, exhibiting a brooch in the shape of a running coney, its body enlivened with blue enamel, and a tiny garnet for its eye. 'All that man ever thinks of is his conies and his fitches! Well, he'll not get me to live on the edge of the Forest with nubbut deer and conies for company all day long.'

'Does he want to marry you, then?' Elys asked, having suspected that Edwin had something of the sort in mind, as so many coney pies appeared on the dinner table.

'Well, I don't know that it's a church-door matter he's thinking on,' Mistress Mayngod replied, admiring her brooch in the rushlight. 'More like a handfasting, Danish fashion, I expect. He'll not be lucky, though! One husband in the churchyard's enough for me, God rest him.'

Having received the cook's confidence in the matter of fairings, Elys felt obliged to show her own, which Mistress

Mayngod admired in her turn, snipping the air with the tiny shears and feeling the smooth yew-wood of the spools, commenting that there were no rough places to snag the threads. She looked at the pendant in silence for a moment, then her eyes moved to Elys's face, looking speculative and merry, and asked, 'What bold lad gave you this?'

'Master Aylwin,' Elys replied. 'We had a little misunderstanding a day or two ago, and he said it was a peace-offering.'

'Peace, is it? Some might say it's more an invitation to warfare,' Mistress Mayngod said obscurely, handing it back. 'He's a good man, and a skilled one. He'll never lack for bread, or clothes to his back.'

Her comment about warfare puzzled Elys, and she wondered about it in the quiet darkness of the bedchamber before she went to sleep. It was pleasing to know that the shrewd cook had a favourable opinion of her friend, for she felt that he was a truly good, kind man. All the more surprising that he had behaved so strangely on Mayday! She shivered with a peculiar, half-frightened, half-excited feeling as she recalled those kisses, and the strength and warmth of Aylwin's body against her own. Was that what a husband did, she wondered, before coupling with his wife?

She knew about coupling, of course, for animals did it openly, and she supposed that humans behaved much the same under the decent cloak of darkness or privacy. It was something a wife must put up with as part of her duty and the need to get children, but what if the husband had foul breath, or a stiff beard, which would make kissing unpleasant? There had been little affection between her parents, and she could never recall having seen them kiss, except formally, so she was only now, belatedly, beginning to realize that a husband might, if he liked his wife, wish to kiss and fondle her as Aylwin . . .

It had not been unpleasant . . . In fact, she had to admit that, apart from the surprise and momentary panic, once she knew who had hold of her, she had quite enjoyed it . . . No, that was not exactly true! At the time, she had been shocked and frightened, and it was only in restrospect, now she knew it was only what the English of all ranks did on

Mayday, that she could remember the enjoyable aspect of it. Had it been a stranger, she would have hated it, but she knew Aylwin, liked and trusted him, and it must be that which made it all right.

The fair lasted for three days, and Elys went again on both second and third, spending a long time there on the last day, walking from booth to booth, enjoying the bustle and air of excitement, looking at the goods for sale and listening to the haggling. Father Warmand had been to see the cope a few days before, and had paid her some more money, being pleased with its progress. She had offered it all to Matthew towards her keep, but could only persuade him to accept a few pennies as a token amount, so she felt that she could afford to be a little less careful with her money while she had the chance to buy at the fair.

She saw Widow Miller there, bargaining for a woollen cloak, calling the merchant a robber in her shrill, cackling voice, offering half what he asked, walking away and coming back again, forcing him down a fourthing at a time, until, exasperated with her chaffering and anxious to attend to other, less parsimonious customers, he said, 'Oh, very well, rob me of my livelihood, and never let it be said I give nothing in charity!' and agreed to her latest offer.

'I don't want it now – it's the wrong colour,' the woman said triumphantly, and hobbled off cackling, bumping into Elys, but clearly not recognizing her.

Elys caught the merchant's indignant eye and could not help smiling, which set him to turning over his wares in the hope of attracting her custom. She did stop to look while he was distracted by another customer who really wanted to buy, but she found that the cloak which Widow Miller had spurned was not a particularly good one, and neither were the others, and she was just about to turn away when a heavy hand was laid on her shoulder. She turned, startled, and came face to face with a bear.

'Oh!' she exclaimed, shocked to find dark fur, little red-brown eyes and a black leathery nose where she had expected to see a human face. She stepped back involuntarily, but found that her back was against the cloak-seller's counter and she could retreat no further.

'Don't be afraid, lovely lady!' cried the bear-leader, drawing his charge away by its chain. 'He won't hurt you. He only wants to see your pretty face.'

Elys smiled uncertainly, and edged away, not at all sure that the bear was as harmless as the man said. There were some wicked-looking black claws attached to the paw which it had laid on her shoulder, and its muzzle looked inadequate, being only a thin leather strap.

The bear moved on, lumbering on its hind legs and dancing a little to the pipe which the leader played with his free hand, and Elys moved in the opposite direction, pausing to look at a selection of bone combs and little polished bronze mirrors. These latter intrigued her, for she had never owned a mirror, and had rarely been allowed to take a look at her own face in her mother's silver one. She needed a comb, for some of the teeth had broken in her old one, so she bought one, then, on an extravagant impulse, bought a mirror as well, telling herself that she needed it to see if her crown and veil were on straight.

The next stall sold braids and ribbons, and she looked them over with interest. The braids were woven in many colours, and some of the ribbons were embroidered, and very expensive. She was encouraged to think that she could do similar work herself of at least as good a standard, and perhaps might find employment in that work if she ever needed it.

The tapping of a tabor and some inexpert tootling on a trumpet drew her to another part of the ground, near the hawthorn tree, where a cart stood, propped up and tied so that its bed lay horizontally, and three people in garish, ragged costumes were dancing about on it, singing. Elys, with a great many other people, stopped to watch, and presently the tabor and trumpet fell silent, and the brightly-dressed trio acted out a little story, narrated by the tabor-player, about a fair maiden, a wicked knight and a handsome squire. It was not easy to follow, as the narrator kept turning his head from side to side as he spoke, and the actors made long speeches in such a gabbled fashion that hardly a word could be distinguished. It was by no means well done, but most of the audience had never seen better, so they applauded and paid cheerfully for the entertainment with buns, bread, vegetables, and even a little money.

A fight broke out then between a man who claimed his purse had been stolen and the lad he accused of taking it, but it was speedily broken up by Lukin, who arrived with two stalwart supporters and a bucket of water. He threw the contents of the bucket over the combatants with an economy of effort which told of previous experience, and the drenched pair were hauled off by the stalwarts to answer to Father Brian, *vice* the absent Dean. Elys, who had kept a firm hand on her own purse, paused for a few friendly words with Lukin. He looked tired, but said he enjoyed the excitement of the fair if there was not too much of the fighting and thievery. A dispute between a merchant and a customer soon called him away to arbitrate, and Elys walked on among the booths.

'Figs! Fine figs from Italy!' bellowed a voice from a little further on. Elys had eaten and enjoyed fresh figs in Italy, so she hastened eagerly to look, and found that the booth had a good show of dried fruits of various kinds, including the figs, which still retained a little of the succulence she remembered, so she bought a poke of them, and looked at the other wares, remembering Mistress Mayngod's words about judging raisins. These, she thought, were quite good, but the currants were too dry. Some little dark orange discs puzzled her, but the merchant said they were apricots, and she could then recognize them.

As she moved away, she encountered Mistress Chich, with little Martha in attendance, sailing through the crowd with the majesty of a loaded hay-wagon. Elys gave her a civil 'good-day', and the lady responded quite graciously, then recognized Elys and looked disconcerted.

'Oh! Er – yes . . .' she said, then, to Elys's surprise, went on, 'I fear I misjudged you when you called at my house. Father Warmand has explained to me that you are, in fact, quite a respectable person, and that many women in the larger towns do actually earn money by handiwork. I must say that I was quite relieved to hear it. One does not care to encounter the other sort of female – so unpleasant . . .' and she swept on without waiting for a reply. Martha, following in a surly fashion with a massive shopping-basket, gave Elys a wink and pulled a grotesque face as she passed.

Chewing a fig with remembered enjoyment rather than present pleasure – it was a little leathery – Elys wandered on to look at swords and knives, rush baskets, buns and pies, leather goods, and eventually came to a booth selling tools of various kinds, where she found Aylwin bargaining for some chisels. He broke off to greet her, but resumed his chaffering at once, while she stood listening and taking in his appearance, for he was quite splendid in a new blue supertunic and a pair of soft leather boots.

When a satisfactory price had been agreed, he paid for his chisels, tied them in a bundle with a length of twine, and turned to her, asking if she were enjoying herself.

'Yes, very much,' she replied, offering him a fig. 'Did you really need new boots?' she added mischievously.

'Desperately,' he replied, acknowledging the allusion with a grin. 'I haven't had a fig since we left Italy. They're not as good dried, but they bring back some memories . . .'

'Of what?' she asked, interested. 'Churches, I suppose, and carvings . . .'

'And dark-eyed Italian girls, and . . . Do you remember the market in Mantova? Have you bought as many things here as you did there?'

'It was Mother who bought things there,' she reminded him. 'I've only bought a few things I need, not fine clothes and boots.'

'I dress as becomes a master craftsman,' Aylwin replied gravely. 'Not extravagantly, but as befits my standing in the world.'

Mistress Mayngod also indulged in a luxury before the fair packed up and the merchants departed. She bought Tigrus a narrow blue leather collar, to signify his standing as a house-cat, not a half-wild farm animal. It had a tiny crotal bell on it, and seemed to please the cat, as he wore it without attempting to be rid of it. There was discussion about it over supper when he appeared wearing it, for Crispin said he thought the cat was meant to catch rats and mice, and it seemed unfair to hamper him by making him wear a bell.

'Surely the mice know he's about, with or without the bell?' Matthew replied. 'They must catch his scent, and hear him moving. After all, a gazehound can run down a deer which knows full well it's being pursued! The cat moves faster than the mouse, and the bell makes no difference!'

They were sitting at table on the dais, after the servants had eaten and cleared the rest of the hall, and Tigrus was by the hearth, gazing into the flames with lazy eyes. Elys, who had seen the cat walking about all afternoon in the new collar, smiled at her brothers' innocent observations, and said 'Listen!' She called Tigrus, and held a tidbit of meat below the table, where the cat could see it. He turned his head at the sound of his name, then ran swiftly to take the meat.

'What did you hear?' Elys asked.

Matthew laughed. 'Nothing,' he said. 'The bell didn't ring.'

'But how can that be?' Crispin asked.

'A cat can move without disturbing his own whiskers if he chooses, let alone a clumsy bell,' said Aylwin, and, as if in agreement with him, Tigrus stalked back to his place by the fire, bell tinkling merrily, and settled down to wash his face and paws.

During the next week or so, there was much activity among the women of the town as they helped one another to make new clothes for Pentecost. The day before the feast, the minster was decorated with flowers, some from the few gardens which had room for a rosebush and a row of pinks among the vegetables, but most from the meadows and the banks between the ploughlands in the big fields. Elys went along by the millstream and picked lady-smocks and forget-me-nots to fill a clay pot, which she set among many others at the sides of the nave altar. Mistress Mayngod packed a tray with damp moss and made a fine display in it of harebells and young beechleaves, picked in the verge of the Forest behind the warren.

Elys had a new gown to wear, but it was one she had made before she went to Rome, and not worn until now. It was made of a fine, light brown woollen cloth, which intensified the colour of her hair and eyes, and she had embroidered the neck and sleeves with a pattern of intertwined branches and leaves in bright silks. Her fine lawn veil had a border of the same design, and her girdle was also decorated to match. She put her fairing round her neck, and went to Mass feeling happily aware that she looked well, that the long winter was truly over, and summer coming soon, that her work was going well, Matthew's stump was fully healed, and her uncle had sent word via one of his sergeants, from Cressing, where he was still busy, that Lady Mabilia and Judith were safely settled at Wix. He also said that he had heard no more news of de Mandeville's depradations anywhere in Essex, whatever mischief he might be about elsewhere.

It was a beautiful, clear sunny day. Swifts darted and screamed about the eaves of the minster roof, where they were building their nests. Work on the building was going well, and the masons trooped in a procession, all in their best clothes, across the stream from their stoneyard, headed by a proud 'prentice carrying a pole with a trowel and a bunch of flowers tied to its top. They entered by the gaping hole where the west front would soon be built by their efforts, but the townsfolk used the south door, according to their normal custom, and stood in their usual places in the nave, the masons filtering along the aisles or standing at the back, in recognition that this was not their church, even if they were finishing the building of it.

Father Brian sang Mass, this being a great festival, and Crispin sang the Gospel, a great honour, as it was usual for a priest to do so on festival days. Bishop Henry had sent a letter of encouragement and blessing, which was listened to, as Father Antony read it, with as much reverence as if it had been a *Papal Bull*, and the choir sang a *Te Deum* in a fine new setting devised by the precentor.

After the service, most people found time to stroll about the churchyard, or cross the little bridge and walk slowly down West Street and back, all ostensibly enjoying the sunshine and the holiday atmosphere, but really showing off their new clothes. Those who, through poverty, had none hurried home shamefacedly, for poverty was considered shameful, but there were few of them, the canons having made a charitable distribution of pieces of cloth after the fair among the deserving poor of the town, enabling them to produce at least a new tunic or cloak for each member of the family.

Matthew and Crispin had again invited friends for supper, although only a dozen or so this time, and once more a pleasant evening was spent eating, drinking, telling stories, reciting verse and singing, even Tigrus contributing a few loud miaous while requesting bits of carp or beef from his friends.

CHAPTER ELEVEN

Now that the growing season had started in earnest, there were fewer passers-by to stop and talk to Elys as she worked by the window, for everyone was out in the great fields, hoeing and weeding, picking up stones, pursuing swarms of bees, shearing sheep, sorting the fleeces, and all the other manifold tasks of getting a living from the land, which occupied every man, woman and child in the peasant families.

With fewer interruptions and longer hours of daylight, the embroidery advanced rapidly, but Elys was free to think as she worked, to worry and to puzzle. Her conscience still troubled her occasionally about her refusal to enter the convent, but she had made an arrangement with herself that if she found a husband, she would accept that her decision had been right, and if not – well, no doubt the convent would still accept her, however belatedly, for she had a talent to offer to add to the dowry which the nuns had already received.

Her worrying was mostly to do with the problem of finding a husband, for in noble families such matters were always arranged by the lady's parents or guardians, but she could not imagine Matthew entering the marriage-market on her behalf, especially as she would bring no dowry, save what she earned with her needle. Besides, however much she refused to allow herself to think about it, Aylwin's odd behaviour on Mayday still disturbed her deeply, and, unless she was very careful, she tended to find herself remembering his kisses and pondering over why he had bought her a fairing. It even entered her mind, one wet morning, when the screen was up at the window to keep out the rain and she could not distract herself by looking out, that it would be very pleasant to be married to Aylwin, who appreciated her skill with a needle, and travel about with him wherever his work took him. She would make her own contribution to their finances, and he would kiss and caress her . . . It was a tantalising picture which she forced herself to dismiss from her mind, because had he not said he was married to his work?

As the days lengthened, she took to working in the evening, and had the first half of the cope finished by early June. Father Warmand came to see it before she took it off the frame, bringing Father Brian and Father Antony with him, and they were full of praise for her work. She received another payment from the sacristan, which made her carefully-hidden bag of savings bulge very satisfactorily.

When the second piece of silk had been stretched on the frame, she painted the outline for the other half of the cope on it, carefully allowing for the centre seam and matching the meeting points all the way up the middle. The completion of the coney was the most difficult, and that was put in place in the silence of deep concentration, but Aylwin came in and talked to her while she outlined the sweeping curves of the branches and the curling leaf-shapes, which he said were taken from an age-old pattern, based on a plant called acanthus, which the ancient Greeks had much favoured for decoration. She painted the dove on the piece which she had cut for the hood while she was about the work.

Aylwin had almost finished the font, and he talked about the corbel-heads which he would soon be starting to carve, for Bishop Henry had ordered a row of them to go along the outside of the nave walls, just under the eaves.

'Most of them will be lions,' he said, 'but Lord Henry did say "other animals", so I'll add a horse and perhaps a sheep and a cow, as well as the usual dragons and eagles, and perhaps a portrait of Tigrus. I shall make them all different – not that two of anything ever turn out quite alike, stone having a mind of its own. It makes the work more interesting, both for me, and for those who will look at them.'

'But nobody will be able to see them very well, so high up,' Elys protested, for the eaves of the nave roof were sixty feet above the ground.

'No humans, perhaps,' Aylwin replied in his usual matter-of-fact fashion, 'but I don't only work for human eyes, you know! Things within the sight of a man are intended to remind and instruct, but the things which only God and His angels see are more to amuse and give pleasure. I had a letter from Fulk this morning. You remember Fulk?'

'Yes, of course.' Elys felt a little revulsion at the memory of her last conversation with the knight. 'How is he?'

'Well, but in disgrace with his family. His father's found three brides for him, one another another, and he's refused to consider them. I suppose he still hopes, by some miracle, to marry you.'

He did not look at her as he spoke, and she was busy wiping her little brush on a piece of old linen and critically surveying her own painting. 'There, that's finished,' she said, putting the brush and oyster-shell palette in the box in which she kept them. 'Will it do?'

'Very well. Don't forget to give the coney some fine golden whiskers, or Edwin will be disappointed! I'm going for a stroll along by the cornmill stream to see how the haymaking goes. Why don't you come, while the paint is drying?'

It was a lovely sunny June day, and Elys went willingly enough, and with a good conscience, for she could do nothing to the work while the paint was wet. She moved the frame away from the window, put up the screen, and went out with Aylwin, down Church Street and over the rickety bridge by the ford, where the mill-cat was, as usual, fishing and, also as usual, catching nothing.

' "Trees and stones will teach you things which you can never learn from masters," ' Aylwin said, looking at the oak which grew beside the mill and the alders leaning across the stream above the sluices. 'Bernard of Clairvaux wrote that in one of his interminable letters. Much as I dislike him, I have to admit that he has more than a grain of sense.'

'My uncle thinks he'll be canonized,' Elys said gravely.

'Not before he's dead, surely?' Aylwin exclaimed quizzically. 'Yes, I expect he will be. Any monk who could devise a Rule for a band of knights and make them obey it deserves the scent of violets and a glory about his tonsure. I'm sorry – I shouldn't speak lightly of such things, but the man's sickening self-righteousness sticks in my gullet! He ruined the life of one man I respected and revered, and thwarted the justifiable ambitions of my master, so don't expect me to love him, saint or not. Look how the briar twines through the hawthorn. I'd like to carve that in stone, and make it look as fine and delicate as the real thing. It's beyond my skill, with the tools I have, but perhaps my great-grandson will manage it.'

'You haven't even a son yet, let alone a great-grandson,' Elys said thoughtlessly, then put her hand to her mouth, appalled that she had said something which he might interpret as a suggestion ...

'True. I must get me a wife before I'm too old to persuade one to have me, I suppose. Shall I try Mistress Mayngod, do you think?'

'Edwin Warrener already has a claim there,' Elys replied, relieved that he had turned the subject into something of a joke.

'She's a good cook,' he said thoughtfully. 'Look, the haymaking is going well.'

They had just passed through the open gateway into the first of the hay-meadows, which lay between the artificial cornmill stream and one of the lesser streams of the river, a little higher than the marshes. The grass was tall and thick, and bright with wild flowers and butterflies, but already, on the far side of the field, it was cut, and the men were bent over their sickles, well out in the field, cutting the grass in great handfuls, the women and children following, raking it into haycocks.

A hare ran between Aylwin's feet, almost tripping him, and a kingfisher flashed into the river from a willow not five yards from where they stood, then rose again with a fish in its beak, and darted away into the clumps of sedge growing against the far bank.

'He must have a nest in the bank,' Aylwin remarked. 'Such a beautiful bird. Look, there's a heron!'

They walked along the stream for a mile or so, seeing several more hares and any number of birds, all going about their business with a wary eye on the passers-by and the haymakers, who were turning yesterday's cut in the next meadow, under the watchful eye of Lukin Dulpain, who came over to greet the walkers.

'A good crop, Lukin?' Aylwin asked.

'Good enough, do it don't rain in the next few days. We've never enough, however good the crop. The canons're bound to supply a deal of that for the King's horses, and we must bring in more from the other manors to make up the weight. It do take a mortal amount of hay to fill a wagon. Be you without work this day? I can find plenty for you to do here, and a penny a day to pay you.'

'No, we're not without work,' Aylwin replied, smiling. 'My chisels and adzes are at the smithy, being retempered, and Lady Elys is waiting for the paint to dry on her work, so we're taking an hour in the fields, to see how the birds and beasts fare.'

'That do be faring well enough,' Lukin said grudgingly. 'I seen that damnety heron take a good carp out of the fishpond, and there's a 'fisher about to, flashing his fine coat like a popinjay. I'd set a lad with a slingshot to that, do that weren't so pretty.' And he pranced away across the meadow, shaking his head lugubriously.

'I wonder why he walks like that,' Elys said quietly.

'It's a sad tale. His father, I'm told, was a great Hercules of a man, tall above average, and strong as a horse, and his mother something of a beauty, and an Amazon to match her husband. Lukin was their only child, and a fine baby, but when he was a year old, he was stricken by a terrible illness. It lasted for many weeks, and after it, he grew more slowly than other children, and he had little command over his arms and legs. His father felt it was a disgrace of some kind – men are seldom rational about weaknesses in their own offspring – and he abandoned wife and child when Lukin was ten. His mother brought him to Waltham, hoping for a cure, and Father Radulf had the care of him. He hadn't managed to walk alone until he was past six years old, and that only by sheer determination. He has to lift his feet in that exaggerated way, or he trips over them, and what starts as a normal gesture with a hand ends as a great sweep of his whole arm. I admire him for his courage in persisting in trying to make his limbs work, where another lad might have given up and turned into a cabbage. He has a good brain, and the best of natures, which must be hard when he sees his own awkwardness against the easy movement of others.'

'Is his mother still here? I've not seen her,' Elys asked.

'Not long after she brought him here, she was found early one morning in the mill-pond. They assumed that she'd missed her footing in the dark during the night and fallen . . .'

'Oh, poor Lukin!'

'And poor woman. Lukin was taken into the school, and became reeve when his predecessor died. He'd been helping with the work for some time, and was nigh twenty by then. Father Radulf is very proud of him for turning out such a good scholar, and such a sensible, kind-hearted man.'

'Who told you about him?'

'Father Radulf. He came a few weeks ago to see how the font was shaping, and somehow we got into conversation about Lukin, among other things.'

'It's a wonder he didn't turn bitter and envious of people more fortunate. He was so pleased about Matthew's healing, when he might have begrudged that Matthew was blessed, but the Cross did nothing for him,' Elys said.

'Perhaps the Cross did help him, by giving him a home and work he can do so well. Healing comes in many forms, and in many ways, as it did with Matthew. Lukin acts the clown sometimes, but it's to make people laugh with him, instead of at him.'

'I like him very much, and I do hope that one day he'll find a good wife to love him and make him happy,' Elys said. 'Thank you for telling me about him. I think I should go back now. The paint will be dry by the time I reach home.'

Aylwin turned back with her, and strolled along at her side, looking at the ground and apparently lost in thought. She glanced at him from time to time, and wondered what he was thinking about, but did not presume to ask. When they reached the footbridge, he said, 'I must go over to the smithy and see if my tools are ready. I'll have to resharpen them all before I can use them – I never trust anyone else to do it. What shall I tell Fulk, then?'

'I don't know,' she replied, caught unawares by the question.

'Do you want to marry him?'

She hesitated, and eventually said reluctantly, 'I don't know. If he offered, I suppose I'd agree, if Matthew approved. I can't afford to pick and choose.'

'What you must consider is whether you could live happily with him for the rest of your life,' Aylwin said, looking, not at Elys, but at the mill-cat, which was gingerly sniffing his boots, 'and also, whether there's anyone else you'd rather marry. If there is, it would be better and more honest to say no. You can't marry one man while you love another, and expect to be content.'

'Love,' Elys said blankly. 'Love never seems to have anything to do with marriage.'

'Not among the knightly class, perhaps, but humbler folk marry for love as often as not. Is there anyone?'

Elys hesitated for a very long time – much too long, but Aylwin did not seem to notice. He squatted down and stroked the mill-cat, which obligingly rolled on its back and offered its stomach to be smoothed and gently scratched. Eventually, she said 'Yes' so quietly that she wondered how he could have heard it, but he obviously had, for he stood up, saying, 'I won't encourage him, then. I'll see you at supper,' and he swung round and strode away towards the smithy, which was on the north side of the market-place, down-wind of the houses for fear of fire.

The haymaking finished a few days later, the last wagon-load being brought into the town, attended by all the hay-makers carrying bunches of flowers tied to their rakes. The wagon was driven into the church, where Father Brian blessed all the workers and gave thanks for a good haysel, and then the procession escorted the load to the haybarn, to be unloaded and stacked with all the other loads which had come before it.

Next day was, of course, a normal working day, but everyone contrived to finish early, for the church ale was to be held in the evening. The canons had distributed various

222

joints of meat, chickens, capons, conies, eggs, milk, honey, flour, almonds, and other raw materials among the housewives, who had added what they could, and a great fragrance of roasting, baking and boiling hung over the town during the afternoon. A fire-pit had been dug in a bit of waste beside Father Brian's house and two spits set over it, one with an ox and the other with a fine buck, which roasted slowly all day. The deer was one which the canons were entitled to receive from the foresters under a grant from the late king, and the townsfolk appreciated their generosity in allowing them a taste of the forbidden venison. Any ordinary man who dared take a deer would lose a hand, or even his life, if he were caught, and all who lived on the borders of the Forest suffered the depredations of the deer which broke into their fields. Their rights to pasture their animals or collect firewood in the Forest were hedged about with limitations to suit the convenience of the deer, and even their dogs suffered, every one having its front paws 'lawed' by three claws being pulled out, to prevent it chasing the deer.

By about five o'clock, long benches and trestle tables had been set up in the nave and transepts, the tables covered with white cloths and decorated with pots of flowers. People carried their own knives and spoons when they went to eat away from home, but wooden platters with a thick slice of trencher bread on each, and a horn cup, were set at every place. A continuous stream of housewives brought in cauldrons of pottage, worts and roots, pies and puddings, dishes of sliced meat and fish. The butchers were busy slicing the ox and the buck, with boys running back and forth with full platters between the pit and the tables. Several barrels of ale had been set up, with an innkeeper in charge of them, he having collected money from the townsfolk ever since the last Pentecost to pay for them, and there were plenty of jugs to carry their contents to the tables.

When all was ready and every place taken, Father Warmand sang a grace, his rich voice climbing about the great arches of the building.

It was a fine church ale, everyone agreed. Vast amounts of food were eaten and enjoyed, and afterwards, the tables were stacked away, and there were games and amusements. The choirboys sang a couple of times, Lukin played a tune on his long trumpet, and someone recited a poem, which went on for a long time, until the reciter, having drunk a deal of ale, made an over-generous gesture and fell off the table. The last game, played almost in darkness as the sun was setting, was a form of blind-man's-buff, but played with several people blindfolded. For Elys, it ended with her being caught by Aylwin, whose blindfold did not appear to prevent him chasing her to and fro round the great pillars, and he, of course, claimed the usual forfeit for catching her. It was just as disturbing and exciting as his Mayday kisses had been.

In the semi-darkness and the excitement, nobody noticed the new arrivals until the laughter and chatter was cut short by a blast on a hunting horn. In the sudden silence, a harsh voice ordered, 'Bring those torches in here, and let's see what we're about!'

The startled townsfolk turned towards the west end of the church, where the temporary doors amid the scaffolding stood open, and saw two files of men in armour march in, each carrying a burning torch, and form a semi-circle behind a single figure, a tall man in a mail hauberk, carrying his helm under his arm.

The flickering torchlight seemed like a background of flames behind the man, accentuating the harsh planes of a face which might, in a more flattering illumination, have appeared handsome, but Elys, who had turned in Aylwin's arms to see what was happening, gave a gasp and a shudder, for she thought he looked like the Devil – or, at least, like the carved head of a devil which she had seen somewhere, and his whole presence struck her as an emanation of evil. Aylwin's arms tightened about her, and the townsfolk shrank back, as if they, too, felt it.

'Where is the Dean of the college?' the harsh voice demanded impatiently.

Father Brian gently made a way for himself through the silent crowd in the nave, and stepped into the area lit by the torches. 'The Dean is not here,' he replied, 'but I

224

stand in his place during his absence. Lord Geoffrey de Mandeville, I believe.'

'You know of me, priest? Then you should know I am Earl of Essex, and address me as such,' the man said sardonically. 'No doubt you also know my reputation – the spawn of the Devil!'

'I have heard you called many things,' Father Brian replied tranquilly, 'not all of them bad.'

'No man is wholly evil, or wholly good,' de Mandeville returned, sounding as if he regretted it. 'There are houses in this town which belong to the Queen, I believe?'

'To Queen Adeliza, yes, granted her by her husband, our late King Henry, of blessed memory.'

'And therefore to that upstart popinjay d'Aubigny, who calls himself her husband and Earl of Arundel.'

'Yes,' Father Brian admitted cautiously. 'He has a claim to them, by right of his wife.'

'The fool let some of his followers burn property of mine in my own earldom. I'm here to pay him back in his own coin!'

'You mean that you intend to burn his property in Waltham?' Father Brian's voice was filled with the same shock and horror which was making the townsfolk murmur frightened protests, too much in fear of de Mandeville to speak aloud. 'You can't know that the Queen's houses are not all together in one place, but scattered about the town, among the other houses which belong to private folk and to the college.'

De Mandeville shrugged. 'How unfortunate,' he sneered. 'They must take their chance.'

'So you will burn the whole town for your petty revenge, and leave these good folk, who have done you no harm and have no part in your quarrel, homeless and destitute? Mark well that you are proposing to destroy properties which belong to this college, and therefore to Holy Mother Church. Do you imagine that our Dean will do nothing when he hears of it?'

'Ah yes – your conveniently absent Dean. Who is he then? An insignificant rabbit of a priest gone snivelling to some saint's shrine to shrive himself of lewd thoughts about the Virgin's legs?'

The air in the church seemed to hiss of its own accord as all the godly folk in it drew a sharp breath of horror at this blasphemy, but Father Brian, however disgusted he may have felt, remained calm and answered steadily, 'We are honoured that our Dean is Henry, Legate in England of our Holy Father the Pope, Bishop of Winchester, Abbot of Glastonbury and brother of our sovereign and anointed King Stephen. I think, my lord Geoffrey, that you, a lay-associate of the Order of the Knights of the Temple, should mark well, and give thought to your immortal soul before you incur his wrath.'

De Mandeville gave a slight start at hearing the name and full titles of the Dean, but the rest of the speech gave him almost enough time to recover, and he replied after only a brief silence, 'My immortal soul must take its chances, being already excommunicate, but I'll make one concession to your Dean's eminence, and a bargain with you. You and your people show me which are d'Aubigny's houses, and I'll order my men to fire only those. If the rest catch fire from them, that's your misfortune, but they'll not be on my conscience.'

'And one more thing,' Father Brian said, his voice still perfectly steady and cool. 'The townsfolk shall be given an hour by our sandglass to remove as much of their own property as they can from their homes and bring it here, into the church, and you will give your word of honour, on your knighthood, that the church will not be harmed in any way.'

'You think I still have honour?' de Mandeville's face twisted in an ugly leer. 'Few would agree with you! However, for that – compliment – I'll grant you your requests. Bring your sandglass, and make sure it runs no longer than one hour.'

The sandglass was brought, set on the steps of the nave, and turned, and almost before the first grains of sand had slipped into the lower bulb, the townsfolk had rushed from the church to rescue all that they could from the coming fires, leaving Father Brian standing in prayer below the

Holy Cross, and de Mandeville, a dark embodiment of evil, leaning against one of the great grooved pillars, watching the sand.

Aylwin went home with Elys, for Crispin, after a brief word with him, went to assist the townsfolk, and Matthew remained in the church to pray, that being the one thing he could do to help. Mistress Mayngod was home before them, collecting together everything of value she could think of into blanket-wrapped bundles, with the servants scurrying to and fro to fetch each article as she remembered it.

Elys cut her embroidery free from the frame and wrapped the pieces of the cope and all her thread and gold purl into one of the few remaining blankets, before she ran upstairs to collect her own and Mistress Mayngod's treasures. She passed Aylwin in the men's room, bundling up Crispin and Matthew's manuscripts and his own tools, and he called to her not to bother with anything but those articles which the soldiers might think worth stealing.

'Why?' she asked. 'Should we not take all we can?'

'No point. All the Queen's houses lie along West Street. If de Mandeville keeps his word, the houses this side the ford are in no danger.'

'*If* he keeps it!' Elys retorted, and bundled up Mistress Mayngod's and her own best gowns and all the lengths of silk and other fabrics which her mother had given her in the sheets from her bed. As she passed the shelf on the wall, she seized the little wooden bird and slipped it into her purse for safety. Her bag of money went into the middle of the bundle, for she had worked too hard for it to risk a stray soldier finding it.

When she staggered downstairs with her load, she found Mistress Mayngod and Aylwin busy checking with each other that nothing important had been overlooked. She was surprised to see that Aylwin held an axe of a type she had never come across before, with a blade far wider than usual, and a haft so long that it came to his shoulder when he grounded the end of it.

'Whatever is that?' she asked.

'A battle-axe,' he replied. 'My great-grandfather fought with it at Senlac.'

227

Her heart gave a frightened lurch, and she gasped, 'Oh, Aylwin! You're not going to try to fight them . . . ?'

'I'm not fool enough to try that,' he replied with a wry grin. 'I thought it might be useful for cutting away timbers . . . We're going to have to fight the fires as soon as we've seen the women and children safe into the church.'

Elys thought of a great many things which she would like to say to him about being careful and keeping away from the soldiers, and actually stood for a second with her lips parted, trying to decide which would be the best words to use, but all that came out was, 'We'd best divide all these bundles among us and get them over to the church as quickly as we can. I don't think it would be wise to be caught outside the church when the hour's up.'

As they hurried across the churchyard, Lukin joined them, sobbing audibly, and Elys dropped her bundle to catch his arm, saying, 'Oh, Lukin, what is it? What's the matter?'

'I've been round with they damned Flemings of his'n, showing which are the Queen's housen, and that's marked 'em all with chalk, but, oh, my dears, once that fires they, that'll spread through all market end of the town, and the poor folk'll lose their homes. That'll blame me for showing they, but Father Brian did tell me to, and I was too scared to say I wouldn't.'

'Someone had to show them, or they'd just have set fire to all the houses. This way, there'll be a chance of saving most of the rest,' Aylwin said, sounding so confident that Lukin stopped crying and said, 'Well, I can help with that – I'm a rare hand wi' a bucket of water!' and he grabbed the bundle which Elys had dropped and hastened towards the church with it, his curious gait exaggerated by his haste and his burden.

'Come. Let's get you settled in safely, and then I must go and help the masons,' Aylwin said, seizing Elys by the arm and hurrying her along. 'They've a dozen good leather buckets, and I want to be sure the Flemings don't come across them and destroy them.'

'Flemings?' Elys gasped, running to keep up.

'Flemish mercenaries. They don't care who they fight for, or what they do, as long as they're paid.'

Father Antony had closed and barred the shutters over the church windows, and lit the candles on all the altars. They illuminated a strange scene, for already folk had carried all their portable goods – pitifully few in some cases – and piled them in heaps, one for each household, and the women and children were settling themselves in amongst their property, to guard it. The whole nave seemed to be set about with dark, amorphous shapes, weeping women and wailing children.

'Here, my lady!' called Matilda Mayngod from a little to the right of the south door, by which Elys and Aylwin had entered. When they joined her, they found Lukin and the servants piling up their bundles against the wall. Elys found her most precious bundle – the one containing the cope – which Lukin had taken from her, and settled herself down, leaning against it. The stone floor was cold, but she thought she would find another soft bundle to sit on presently. Aylwin put his toolbag down beside her, dropped on one knee, and said, 'Will you keep an eye on this for me? Matthew's somewhere in the church, and I'll find Crispin presently and try to keep him out of trouble. Stay here until he or I come for you. Don't venture outside the church before then. Are you all right? Then I'll be off.'

She caught his sleeve before he could rise, and said, 'Take care . . . Don't be tempted to use that axe on the soldiers . . .'

'I've never used it in anger, and I don't mean to start now. I'm a craftsman, a creator, not a destroyer.'

'Yes. I'm sorry.'

He leaned towards her and whispered, 'Stay safe, sweet . . .' and his lips brushed her cheek before he sprang to his feet, said 'Come, then,' to the servants, who were standing about, uncertain what to do, took Lukin's arm, and hurried from the church, the others following willingly enough.

Elys sighed, leaned back against the wall, and looked about her. There were still people coming into the building, burdened with cooking-pots, stools, bundles wrapped in blankets or cloaks, even tables. Antony, Warmand and Brian, the three oldest canons, were moving among the people, offering words of comfort and hope, settling disputes over territories, and helping the women to make themselves reasonably comfortable. Matthew appeared, swinging along on his crutches, directing the last-comers into the remaining spaces in the transepts. He waved when he caught sight of his sister, but did not join her.

In the comparative privacy of the south aisle, beside the door, Elys felt almost cut off from the scene framed between the pillars, an onlooker, but when the last families were safely in, Antony shut and barred the door, and the feeling of isolation gradually disappeared.

De Mandeville still stood against the pillar, watching the sand, and the area round him remained clear of piled belongings, for nobody cared to go near him. As the last grains dropped, he stood up straight, looked about him, laughed aloud, and strode away down the nave, lashing out at a child which wandered into his path, and laughing again as the child screamed with fright and pain.

'God curse you, and the Devil take you to hell!' a shrill voice cried from the shadows, but de Mandeville only laughed again, and disappeared through the temporary doorway at the west end, slamming the door behind him like a clap of thunder.

As soon as he appeared on the footbridge across the ford, his waiting mercenaries ran to the marked houses, shouting their battle-cries, and thrust their torches into the thatch or flung them on to the higher roofs. The men of the town stood in silent groups, watching, then ran to try to beat the flames out of pull down the thatch before it was all alight. One Fleming who paused, torch ready to throw, before an unmarked house found himself face to face with a tall, golden-haired man holding a great battle-axe at the ready. Some memory of old tales of berserker Vikings stirred deep within him, and he turned aside, looking for a legitimate target.

As soon as the marked houses were burning, the Flemings withdrew to the ford and joined their employer outside the church, where they stood watching, laughing and bellowing with excitement as the fires began to spread to neighbouring houses, and shouting jeering advice to the townsmen who were frantically trying to save their homes.

Every bucket in the town was earning its keep now, passing swiftly from hand to hand along chains of men from the ford to one or other of the half-dozen centres of fire. The masons had their own chain, and their dozen buckets moved along at nearly twice the speed of the others, for they had frequently practised the art, fire being a not infrequent hazard in their trade. Only Lukin's bucket was not in a chain, but in its owner's hand as he ran to and fro, dousing any fire-fighter whose clothes were smouldering, and hurrying back to the ford for a refill. The air between the burning houses was already so hot that no man complained if Lukin was sometimes a little over-enthusiastic in emptying his bucket.

The miller, who had intended to grind corn next day, opened his sluices, and the volume of water coming through widened the ford temporarily and reduced the distance that the buckets had to travel, but there were not enough of them to reach the furthest houses, and there the only hope was to pull down the thatch before, or at least as soon as it caught, and trample it out in the street. There were long-handled hooks for that purpose, but not nearly enough of them.

Once the timbers of a house had caught, the only thing left to do was to bring it down within its own walls, reducing it to a pile of beams, wattle and daub, the latter excluding air from the bottom of the pile and reducing the amount of flame and flying embers. It was this work which Aylwin had in mind for his battle-axe. It proved an ideal tool, its long handle giving it a greater reach and more powerful swing than the ordinary wood-chopping tools which the black-smith and his son brought out from their store and distributed among the fire-fighters.

Aylwin moved through it all like a man in a nightmare, hardly able to believe that he would not suddenly wake up. As fast as one burning house surrendered to the axes and collapsed in a pile of crackling timbers, a shout of alarm called him to another, and he began to wonder if the whole of the market end of the town would burn.

A particularly agonised cry took him to a house on the corner of the market-place, where the burning thatch had just fallen down into the upper storey. As he ran across to it, the blackmsith seized his arm and said, 'Eric – my son – he's in there!'

'Inside? Whatever made him go in?'

'He said there was a cat in there . . .'

Even as the smith spoke, a terrified ginger cat ran out of the house and vanished across the market-place, just as half the floor of the upper storey crashed down into the room below. The blacksmith ran forward, and was hauled back by three or four other men, but Aylwin dodged round them and dived in through the open door.

Inside, there was a deal of smoke, but the flame was momentarily confined to the end where the upper floor had collapsed. By its light, he saw young Eric sprawled on the floor, a thick beam lying across his legs, pinning him down and already burning only a few feet away from him. Aylwin scrambled over the wreckage to the boy's side and tried to shift the beam, but it was wedged by other wreckage, so he stood back and swung his axe time and again, his nostrils full of the acrid smell of smouldering clothing.

At last the beam shifted, almost cut through, and one last mighty blow, delivered with all the strength of muscles hardened by stone-cutting, cleaved through it. Another sinew-cracking effort shifted the stump of the beam enough for him to drag the boy out, and then he heaved him over his shoulder, grabbed his axe and ran for the door, staggering out into the arms of the men in the street just as the whole building collapsed behind him.

Luckily, Lukin returned from the ford with a full bucket just then, and doused them both before their smouldering clothing could burst into flames. Eric's arms and legs were burned, but his father carried him off to Father Radulf, and presently returned to report that the Infirmarian said he would heal. Aylwin found that he had somehow cut his head, his clothes and hair were singed, and one sleeve of his best supertunic had vanished, leaving a ragged blackened edge just above his elbow. Otherwise, he was surprised to find himself uninjured, so he patted Lukin on the back, and ran towards the next fire, conscious of a dragging ache in his arms and legs which made him wonder how much longer he and the townsmen could keep up their battle to save some of the houses.

In the church, everyone eventually settled down, the weeping and wailing died away as the women began to recover from the first shock of the sudden invasion of their quiet town, and the children were lulled to sleep.

Time passed. The sounds of burning increased, the lurid light playing on the timbered ceiling through the clerestory windows brightened and flickered, glowing red, and the atmosphere in the church became thick with smoke, until it was difficult to make out anything through the fog of it, save the candles on the altars, and the vague dark shapes which might have been goods or their owners.

Most of the women and children had worked all day in their homes or in the fields and they were tired. The three elderly canons sang their final services for the day, refusing to abandon the horarium, whatever the emergency outside, and before they had finished, most of the refugees had fallen asleep, despite their anxieties. Others sat quietly, listening to the noises from outside and trying not to disturb the sleepers. Warmand trimmed the candles on the nave and high altars, and put out the rest, then retired to the vestry in the north transept, where Antony and Matthew joined him. Father Brian went out through the wicket on silent feet, to see what he could do in the town.

A long time passed. The sounds of burning and the lurid light on the ceiling intensified, then began slowly to decline. Elys, sitting on the stone floor and leaning against the wall, wondered which of the bundles she might sit on without damaging anything inside it, but hesitated to rummage among them, for fear of waking Mistress Mayngod, who was so still and silent that Elys thought she must be asleep. She wriggled to a more comfortable position, and prayed silently that the fire might not spread, that nobody might be killed, that it might rain . . .

Suddenly, the dark shape of Mistress Mayngod beside

her stirred slightly, and Elys felt the woman's hand on her arm, then heard her breathe, 'Shhh! Look!' She took Elys's hand and pointed with it towards the area, just to their left, before the church door.

Ely looked, and saw three dark forms standing there, and the wicket door creaked faintly behind them.

'All quiet! All asleep, I reckon,' whispered one of the figures. 'Keep together, now, and look for goods where there's nobody with them, or where they're alseep, and be silent. There's good pickings here, if we're careful.'

The figures crept away, into the nave, and Mistress Mayngod breathed into Elys's ear, 'Some of de Mandeville's men – so much for his guard on the church. Watch where they go.'

'Should we cry out and wake everyone?' Elys breathed back.

'Best not. They might panic and use their swords. Wait a while,' Mistress Mayngod murmured.

She and Elys got to their feet, slowly and cautiously, and Elys crept forward to the nearest of the great columns, pressed herself against it, and slid round it until she could see into the nave. Her eyes were sufficiently accustomed to the faint light for her to make out the three men creeping from one island of goods and sleeping humanity to another, and that no one seemed to be aware of their presence.

Behind her, the wicket latch made a faint click, followed by a soft thud as Mistress Mayngod closed the door and slid the bar across to secure it. She tiptoed to where Elys was standing, and whispered, 'We must put out the altar candles and confuse them in the dark. You go to the high altar, and I'll take the nave altar. Crawl along the aisle – they'll not see you.'

Elys nodded, dropped to her hands and knees, and began to crawl eastwards, stopping to peer round each pillar as she came to it, to see what the men were doing. Mistress Mayngod had disappeared, and Elys assumed that she also was crawling, but across the nave and up the north aisle.

When she reached the crossing, she made a careful reconnaissance, and found that the men were rifling a pile of unattended bundles on the south side of the nave, so she rose to her feet, stepped round the corner into the transept, sped across it, then moved on silent feet along the aisle of the chancel towards the high altar.

Just as she reached her goal, one of the two candles on the nave altar went out. Quickly she licked her fingers, stretched up on tiptoe, and pinched out the nearest candle, then the other, thankful that they had burned down far enough for her to reach.

From behind the high altar, she looked down the length of the church, and saw a strange sight. The crucifix from the nave altar and the single remaining candle suddenly rose up together into the air and began to drift silently down the nave, the candle a little below and in front of the cross, so that, to anyone to the west of it, the cross must be illumined in the soft light. She dodged round the high altar and sped to the nave altar, crouched beside it, and watched as the thieves, intent on their plunder, suddenly became aware that the candles were out, and then that a ghostly crucifix, bathed in unearthly light, seemed to be advancing towards them. One of them gave a yelp of alarm, and all three began to back towards the south door, stumbling over people and goods in their way, but not daring to turn their backs on the cross. The light shining on its silver surface robbed them of their night vision, and they became lost and confused. They seemed to become panic-stricken after that, for when one of them staggered and fell, the others tripped over him, and, instead of getting up, all three stayed on their knees, shielding their faces with arms or hands.

'Father Warmand!' Elys shouted. 'There are thieves in the church!'

She ran to the south aisle and along it towards the south door, meaning to fling her own bundles in the way of the thieves, to hamper them if they tried to escape, but when she reached the door, she looked out into the nave and saw what the thieves were also seeing – a crucifix, gleaming in the light of a flame which had no apparent source! It made her gasp, although she half-guessed how the illusion had been created, and she crossed herself, her hand moving of its own volition

By this time, Warmand, Antony and Matthew had come

into the church, found it in darkness, and the people waking, bewildered and frightened by Elys's shout of alarm, and the first two had run back for a light. Matthew continued, swinging down the nave on his crutches, until one of them became entangled in someone's blanket, and then Antony returned with a branch of candles, followed by Warmand with another in one hand, and brandishing, of all things for a priest, a naked sword in the other.

At that moment, someone began to bang on the door behind Elys. She turned, wrestled with the bar until she had it out of its sockets, and wrenched the door open.

It was dawn outside, and the pale grey light poured in as both great leaves of the door swung open and some of the townsmen came in. They were red-eyed, smoke-blackened and exhausted, but when Elys gasped out that there were thieves in the church, they pushed her aside and crowded in, to find Warmand, sword in one hand and candles in the other, standing regarding three snivelling wretches, prostrate with fear before the nave altar crucifix, which stood on the floor, with a single candle lying, extinguished, beside it. Several yards away, leaning against a pillar, stood Mistress Mayngod, the hood of her best black cloak flung back, and an expression of ill-suppressed glee on her plump face.

There was a hubbub of voices as women, suddenly wakened, cried out to demand what had happened, children wailed, and the newly-arrived men, realizing from the dropped plunder around the thieves what they had been about, shouted in their anger, calling down the wrath of Heaven on the Earl of Essex, who had burned their homes and failed to keep his promise to guard their families and property in the church.

'Take them out and hang them!' shouted one furious man, who had fought all night against fire after fire, and failed to save his own home, which had not even belonged to d'Aubigny.

'Be silent!' roared Father Warmand as others began to echo the cry for hanging.

Startled, everyone but a few of the children obeyed. The gentlest of all the canons had a surprisingly loud voice, and he seemed to tower above all those around him, his eyes flashing with anger. The men fell back as he prodded the thieves with his sword, forcing them to their feet, and drove them before him to the nave altar, where he forced them to confess their crime and beg forgiveness. After that, he said contemptuously, 'Let them be soundly flogged and driven from the town, but do them no other harm.'

'By what right?' demanded the harsh voice of de Mandeville, who had entered the church unnoticed. 'What charges do you make against my men?'

Father Warmand still had his avenging power upon him, and he answered in a voice of authority, 'These men were caught in the act of stealing from the poor folk in the church here – the church which you undertook to safeguard. That is an offence of gravity, made sacrilegious by its being perpetrated in a consecrated building. It is therefore within the jurisdiction of the Church.'

There was a strange silence for a few moments, and then de Mandeville, who had come to the edge of the lighted area of the crossing, shrugged, his great menacing shadow, which towered up to the triforium, echoing and enlarging the movement. 'As you please,' he said indifferently. 'I'd have hanged them, but take your milder path and turn the other cheek, if you must.' He suddenly swung round on the cringing thieves, and said coldly, 'You are no longer in my service. I declare you outlawed,' and then turned on his heel, his cloak billowing round him, and stalked down the nave towards the west end, vanishing into the shadows.

The people in the church remained silent, as if spell-bound, some of them shivering at the cruel coldness of his condemnation of his men to a punishment worse than hanging. In the silence, Elys became aware that the noises outside in the town had died away, but before she could realize what that meant, there was a shouted command outside, and then the sound of trotting horses, which passed up Church Street and died away in the distance.

'He's gone,' said Father Warmand, his voice filled with the relief which everyone felt. 'Now, as I said, flog these thieves and drive them after their master, but do them no other harm.'

As the three thieves were dragged past her, Elys turned

to watch them go through the door, and saw Crispin and Aylwin standing just inside it. Crispin's face and clothes were filthy, he looked tired and depressed, but Aylwin, equally dirty, had a grubby bandage tied round his head, his right arm in a sling, and looked deathly white under the dirt. Elys gasped and ran to him, and his arms closed about her as she clung to him.

CHAPTER TWELVE

'Extraordinary!' said Lukin. 'The thieves swore that they looked up and saw a great cross advancing on them, shining with uncanny light, and they couldn't see anything else, but ran about, lost and blind, and couldn't find their way out of the church, and then they were snared by their feet until they fell and knelt before that. Folk say our Holy Cross protected their families and goods when de Mandeville, God rot that, failed in that's promise.'

It was the evening of the day which had dawned on the stricken town and the strange scene in the church, and the reeve had come after supper to see how Aylwin did after his narrow escape last night.

All day, the townsfolk had been clearing the wreckage of the burned houses, several of those in which the canons lived among them. A third of the town had been destroyed, and it was only the courage and good sense of the people, led and organized by Father Radulf, Crispin and Aylwin, which had saved the rest. Father Brian had already sent news of the attack to Bishop Henry, and, on his own authority, had given the timbers which had closed off the open end of the nave, as well as some intended to form part of the roof of the new work, towards the rebuilding. Meanwhile, the homeless were being sheltered by luckier friends and neighbours, or found lodging in the infirmary.

Nobody had said anything about Elys flinging herself into Aylwin's arms, which she blushed to recollect, for they were all more concerned about the cut on his head and his broken collarbone, which had taken a heavy blow from another falling timber at some point during the night. He had been too tired by the time it happened to remember exactly where or when, and was still sleeping off his exhaustion in Father Radulf's infirmary.

De Mandeville and his men had vanished into the Forest before dawn, having done all that they came to do, and the chastened thieves, bleeding from their flogging, shaken and frightened by their experience, and thoroughly confused after their attempts to answer Father Brian's questions about exactly what had happened, had gone limping after them. They had been pursued for the first mile or two by an angry but silent band of townsmen, prevented from hanging them only out of their respect for Father Warmand.

Elys had ventured down Church Street as far as the ford during the morning, after returning her bundled treasures to their proper places. She had stood by the footbridge for a few minutes, tears running down her cheeks, looking at the blackened, smoking ruins of a score of humble homes in West Street, where the former tenants, dazed and miserable, were searching the ruins to see if anything left behind might be salvaged. Already, William of Norwich and his men, leaving their work on the church, were helping the menfolk to clear the wreckage, testing charred timbers to see which could be scraped and reused, and using their stone-carts to haul away the ash to the fields, where it would be used as fertiliser, and to remove the debris which was past reclaim.

Father Radulf, crossing the bridge on his way back from an errand, paused beside her and said, 'It's not as bad as it looks, my child. With the timber we have, we can make a start on the rebuilding, and Father Brian's sent to Lord Gilbert de Mountfichet, the Chief Forester, to ask for more. I've no doubt he'll grant it, even if only as an advance on that which we're allowed to take from the Forest each year. No lives were lost, and nobody sustained serious injury, Our Lord be thanked.'

'How is Master Aylwin this morning?' Elys asked, feeling her cheeks flush at the mention of his name. The canon gave her a shrewd and kindly look, and replied, 'He has a headache and a broken collarbone, and can't recall how he came by either, but I expect some of the other men will have told you of his bravery. He's still sleeping – or was when I last looked in on him. He'll be home soon.'

There was nothing Elys could do to help in the work of clearance, so she went home and restitched the second half of the cope on to the frame, noting with relief that being unceremoniously rolled up had not harmed the goldwork already done. She spent the day sewing industriously, working the red cap of a yaffle, which was pecking the trunk of the bush, with only a subdued and nervous Tigrus for company.

Aylwin came back at suppertime, before the others, with his arm in a sling but without his head bandage, the cut having already begun to heal. He said he felt perfectly well when Elys asked how he did, and then looked at her work and commented favourably on the latest part of it, which overcame the embarrassment Elys felt about their last encounter and filled the few minutes before Crispin and Matthew came in.

The men were tired and dirty when they returned home, having been out all day, taking their dinner as they worked, for Mistress Mayngod, cheerful and bustling as ever, had taken hot pasties and ale down to them. They came in at suppertime, going straight to the yard to pump water over each other to clean off the filth of ash and charcoal, sending the backhouse boy to fetch them clean clothes, so that they could come into the hall clean, if damp. They sat round the bare hearth in the hall, the day being too hot for a fire, and drank a jug of ale while they waited for supper, greeting Elys, but otherwise sitting silent and thoughtful.

At length, Matthew said, 'I'm glad I was able to help. Having only one foot makes me feel useless at times, for I could do nothing last night but pray.'

'It may well have been your prayers which stopped the wind rising,' Aylwin pointed out. 'In any case, I heard otherwise. How did one of your crutches come to be entangled between the feet of a terrified thief? He swore an angel had knocked his legs from under him with a flaming sword.'

Matthew laughed, but instead of answering, said, 'I'm puzzled by their tale of the Cross pursuing them. The nave altar cross was certainly standing on the floor, close to where they fell, but it's small by comparison with the great Cross. Even so, I can't think how it got there.'

'Miracles,' Crispin said musingly. 'What constitutes a miracle? Is it what actually happens, or what people believe?

241

So be the result is good, does it matter if the agency be human or superhuman? Ah, here's supper. Thank God it's not a fast day.'

The next day, Aylwin, who had been fidgeting about with frustration, going down to the building work but prevented from doing much to help by his injured shoulder, went out after dinner, saying that he was going to his workshed, where he could smooth the bowl of his font one-handed.

'In any case, it's time I went back to it,' he said. 'I've not set foot in the shed since the day before the fire, and it'll feel neglected.'

Elys watched him go across the churchyard as she settled down to her own work at the open window, but soon became absorbed in placing her stitches, so that when Lukin suddenly spoke to her through the window, she jumped and pricked her finger.

'Lady,' he said, 'I don't know if I do right or not, but I think you should go to Aylwin. That's in that's shed, and I do think that be needing you.'

'Why, what's wrong?' she asked, seeing that the reeve's long face wore an anxious expression.

'Best you go and see,' he replied, and went on up the street.

Elys looked towards the shed, but the door was shut and there was no sign of anything untoward. She hesitated, then recalled Lukin's expression, covered her work, put up the oiled linen window screen, and went out.

There was no sound from the shed as she approached, so she gently unlatched the door and pushed it open, took a step inside, then stopped, drawing a shuddering breath in horror. Aylwin was on his knees by the font, hunched over as though he were in pain, his shoulders shaking as if in silent laughter, but Elys knew that he was crying, for the font lay in pieces, smashed beyond repair.

'Oh, my dear!' she exclaimed, putting her hands on his shoulders in an impulsive gesture. For a moment, he stiffened, and she thought he would reject her sympathy, but then his right hand came across and clasped her hand lying on his left shoulder. He was still for a moment, then turned, reached up, and pulled her down, moving at the same time

242

to prop his back against the wall, legs outstretched. She sank down, unresisting, and came to rest across his lap, her head in the angle between his neck and his uninjured shoulder. For a moment, she thought that perhaps she should have pulled away from him, but then a tear dripped on to her cheek, and she forgot propriety, put her arms round him, and wept with him.

'You're crying,' he said presently. 'You shouldn't waste your tears on dead stone.'

'You once told me that stone's living, with all sorts of wonderful things within it, waiting for a sculptor to come and release them. The font was so beautiful, and you put so much love and care into it,' she protested.

'And now it's broken and dead,' he said harshly. 'Killed by a mindless fool who cares for nothing but destroying what other men have made, and making nothing himself but a wilderness. I've wept over the waste of my broken dream, and that's the end of it. I'll go find William presently, and ask him to order me another block from Purbeck, and I'll make it again, better the second time. Perhaps I'll even get that whale to look more like a great leviathan and less like a cod-fish. Bishop Henry won't be pleased – Purbeck marble's damned expensive – but I'll pay for it myself if he won't.'

'Oh, Aylwin,' Elys could not help smiling through her tears, 'you don't admit defeat, do you?'

'Why should I when I'm not defeated? One of de Mande-ville's Flemings destroyed my work – it's not the end of the world.'

'And you went into a burning house to rescue a lad who might have been dead, for all you knew.'

'What do you expect from a man whose great-grandfather fought at Stamford Bridge and Senlac, with Hereward in the fens, and with Svein Etrithsson in Yorkshire? I'm a Wessex man, Elys. We don't give up when we've set our minds on something. Or our hearts.'

'Your heart?' she echoed. 'What is your heart set on, Aylwin?'

'Something within my reach, but perhaps beyond my grasp,' he replied obscurely. 'What made you come here just now, Elys? I left you working, looking set for the rest of the day.'

'Lukin said you needed me.'

'Lukin? Oh, yes – I thought someone came to the door and went away again. He told you what had happened?'

He was still holding her in the crook of his right arm, and she felt him start when she replied, 'No. He just said you needed me.'

'And you came . . .'

Suddenly, she was embarrassed, thinking that he sounded disapproving, so she pulled away from him and sat up. He made no attempt to stop her, but let his arm fall and sat still, looking at her, his expression impossible to read.

'I – I'm truly sorry about the font,' she said. 'I'd better be going back to my work.'

He still made no move as she got up and left the shed, hesitating a moment in the doorway, suddenly aware that she wanted him to call her back, wanted it desperately. She almost turned back unbidden, but he still sat unmoving, so she went out, closing the door behind her.

She had said she was going back to her work, and she did take a few steps along the churchyard path, then stopped and stood irresolute, one knuckle of her left hand pressed against her teeth, and her right hand clasping the fairing which Aylwin had given her. She was confused, unable to go forward, wanting to go back, yet not able to do that either.

Why? What was wrong with her? What had happened to her easy friendship with the kind, self-contained English craftsman, who should have been her inferior, yet had become her dear friend? Surely, if she heard that a friend needed her, it was natural to go at once to that friend, so why did she suddenly feel so self-conscious about it?'

The answer was perfectly obvious now that she had allowed herself to think about it, but admitting privately that she loved Aylwin solved nothing, for he showed no sign of loving her in return. He'd kissed her a few times, but there were any number of reasons why a man might kiss a woman, particularly one who was young and not unpleasing to look at. Norman men didn't, not with ladies of rank, but she

knew so little about the customs of English craftsmen . . .
He often spoke to her as if she was many years his junior,
little more than a child . . .

At this point, she was again startled by Lukin's voice
breaking into her absorption. He was returning from his
errand down the churchyard path, and stopped to ask, 'Is
that all right, then? I did think that was breaking that's heart
over the poor font. Them Flemish devils did ought to burn
for that!'

'Lukin, why did you tell me he needed me?'

The reeve looked surprised. 'When a man's upset enough
to be weeping, that needs his sweetheart,' he said, as if
explaining something perfectly obvious to a slow-thinking
child. 'And seeing as you wear that's love-token . . .'

'Love-token!' she exclaimed, her hand going again to the
silver pendant.

'Aye. That be an endless knot, a sign of eternity. If you
trace the pattern round and about and in and over and
under, that have no end, like your man's love. That were
Aylwin that gave you that, weren't that?'

Elys had a fleeting, inconsequential thought that Lukin's
speech tended to be an endless knot of thats, and then said,
'Yes. Thank you, Lukin.'

He looked a little puzzled and waited, but she said no
more, so he shrugged, replied politely, 'That do be a pleasure, lady,' and went on his way. Elys watched him go, then
sat down on the bench by the churchyard path, and thought.

If Aylwin had meant the pendant to be a love-token, why
had he not said so? Why had he shown no sign of loving
her? Surely her own behaviour, on at least two occasions,
must have betrayed her feelings to him just as much as they
had revealed them to her?

She remembered very clearly how she had run into his
arms when he returned from fighting the fires in the town
with a bandage round his head. He had held her, yes, but
only for a few seconds, and then he had gently set her aside
and walked on into the church, without another glance in
her direction.

Then she remembered the grey, mysterious dawn of
Mayday, and the kisses he had given her under the blossom-

ing hawthorn, which he had claimed were only in accordance with the old custom. That was the only time she could remember when he had ever behaved as anything more than a friend.

Then, before her courage could evaporate, she stood up, walked resolutely back to the shed, and went in.

'Lukin says this is a love-token,' she said abruptly. 'Is it?'

Aylwin was on his knees again, sorting the broken pieces of the font, setting aside those big enough to be reused for small carvings, and putting the rest in a sack. He looked up, surprised, then got to his feet, dusting his hand against his tunic, and said, 'I wondered when it would dawn on you. I didn't think you'd need to be told.'

'Norman customs differ from English ones,' she said. 'I don't think Normans are supposed to fall in love.'

'Never?' he asked, looking half quizzical, half anxious.

'No, but living in England for eighty-odd years must have changed some of us,' she replied solemnly. 'It's you stubborn English. You won't learn our language, so we have to learn yours, and you don't have our belief that marriage is only a matter of alliances and acquiring land . . .'

'But you think it might be possible for a Norman to fall in love?'

'Y-yes – I think so . . .' Her courage left her suddenly, and she stammered and blushed.

'That's a relief,' he said, reaching out his good arm and drawing her to him. 'If you'd known it was a love token, would you have worn it?'

'I am wearing it.'

'And now you know what it signifies?'

'Lukin said it's an endless knot – a symbol of eternal love . . .'

'Yes. I don't think many people know exactly when they begin to love – by the time they realize, it seems to have been for ever. I only know that, for me, it's truly an endless knot! I seem to have loved you all my life, and will do so 'til Doomsday.' He held out his right hand, and she put her own hand into its warm grasp.

'So,' he said. 'What now? Will Matthew allow you to wed me, do you think?

'I don't know.'

'And then there's your uncle, the Templar. I suppose he has some say in the matter?'

'He'll expect to be consulted.'

'Then we'd better not say any more to one another until I've seen Matthew and asked his opinion. I know and you know, but we'll leave the words unsaid until we can say them boldly and with a clear conscience.'

She nodded, and said soberly, 'That would be best,' and withdrew from his clasp, slowly and reluctantly. He let her go, and stood watching as she left the shed, then went back to work.

CHAPTER THIRTEEN

Aylwin sent word that he would not be in to supper that evening, as he had been invited for the meal by Master William. Elys told her brothers over their own supper about the breaking of the font, but did not mention why she had gone to the shed, or how she had found Aylwin.

'But that's a wicked action, to ruin a man's work!' Matthew exclaimed indignantly. 'How could anyone destroy something so beautiful?'

'Something that's taken years of learning the skill, and a God-given ability to reach such a high standard of craftsmanship,' Crispin added. 'Not to mention the weeks of work in the doing . . . He must be heart-broken.'

'He says he'll make it again, only better. He wasn't happy with the whale,' Elys replied. 'He *was* upset, though.'

'He's a fine man,' Matthew said thoughtfully. 'He has that rare ability to see through present difficulties and setbacks to what can lie beyond. I've had some foolish, ill-considered idea that all the English thanes were killed during the Conquest, but, of course, they couldn't have been. They lost their lands to our forefathers, and had to turn to another way of life. We only ever hear of the Conquest from our – the Norman – side of the tale.'

'Aylwin is a very fine man,' Elys said quietly. 'As good as any Norman baron, in my estimation.'

She kept her eyes on her platter as she spoke, not wishing to give herself away to her brothers, so did not see that they exchanged a long, questioning look, as if her words had caused them some concern. Neither replied to her statement, and presently Crispin changed the subject by saying, 'I forgot to mention that I had a message from Uncle Richard this morning. He sent his apologies for failing to call on us, as he promised he would, on his way back from the order's manor at Cressing, but he was delayed there longer than he expected, and had to hurry back to the commandery in London. He has to go again to Cressing, and hopes to call here on his way.'

'When?' asked Elys eagerly, thinking that, if Aylwin could only speak to Matthew first and, God willing, get his consent, if her uncle came soon, at least she would not have the agony of waiting to hear whether her dreams and hopes were to be realized or not. *Their* dreams and hopes, she corrected herself, still hardly able to believe that Aylwin shared them with her.

'He didn't say. In a few days, I assume,' Crispin replied, surprised. His sister did not usually appear eager for their formidable uncle to visit them.

Next day, Aylwin came home to dinner a little before the others, and, finding the servants setting the table had all, by coincidence, gone out of the hall at the same time, bent over Elys, sitting at her frame, to snatch a kiss, his lips resting lightly, yet lingeringly, on hers for a moment.

As he straightened, thinking he heard someone coming along the screens passage, he found himself looking straight into the face of Lukin Dulpain, who was out in the street, leaning on the window-sill and looking in. The little man's face was quite expressionless, but one eyelid lowered in a conspiratorial wink, and he said, 'I didn't not see a thing, and do I did, I'd not let on.' He then winked at Elys, asked her gravely if she would be so kind as to tell Mistress Mayngod that Edwin was busy with an injured ferret, and would not be bringing any conies until tomorrow.

'What – er – what happened to the ferret?' she asked, mainly for something to say, for she could feel herself blushing from the top of her head to the tips of her toes.

'That had an argument with a fox, that did, and Master Reynard lost most of that's brush!' Lukin replied, made one of his fantastic bows, and went on his way, whistling a lively tune.

'He saw,' Elys whispered, wringing her hands.

'Time for me to speak out, I think. You're sure you want me to?' Aylwin whispered back, searching her face as she turned her head to look up at him.

'More than anything in the world. I love you, Aylwin.'

'And I love you, come what may,' he replied, gave her

one more straight, clear-eyed look of reassurance, and went to wash his hands before the meal.

There was always a brief interval after dinner or supper when the servants had finished their meal and taken their dishes away, leaving the family and their guests alone at the high table for a while, to finish their wine and talk privately if they wished. Elys realized that Aylwin could not speak about their wish to be married until that time came, for it was not a matter to be discussed in the presence of servants, but it seemed an agonisingly long wait, when she knew that so much would depend on what was said in those few minutes, when they came.

Dinner was never a very long meal, but it seemed long today. The servants appeared painfully slow in bringing the food and clearing the dishes between the two courses – vegetable pottage, and fish with worts, it being a Friday. Aylwin seemed to be feeling the strain as much as she was, for he ate very little, and said even less, until the servants started clearing their own tables in the body of the hall, and then he suddenly spoke, apparently about something quite different.

'I don't know if I've ever mentioned it,' he said, 'but my family owned a great deal of land before the Conquest. We didn't have your system of holding land in exchange for service, or, at least, not in the same way. Owning land carried rights and duties, but they weren't exclusively military or financial.'

'We realize, Matthew and I, that you belong to the English equivalent of our knightly class,' Crispin replied, looking a little puzzled.

'I hold four knights' fees from Bishop Henry,' Aylwin went on, acknowledging Crispin's words with a nod. 'I supply the knights and their equipment, of course, but I don't carry out the service personally.'

Elys was startled by this statement, for it meant that he held four good-sized manors as their lord, and was, by comparison with her own family, quite rich.

'My own service to the Bishop is in my mystery. He pays me a regular sum of thirty pounds a year, with additional fees for the stonework or woodcarving I do for him, negotiated on each particular piece of work. For example, he would have paid me thirty pounds for the font.' His voice shook a little on the last word, but he corrected himself firmly: 'He *will* pay me, when I make its replacement.'

Matthew and Crispin looked interested, surprised, and deeply impressed, by turns, for they had no idea that a skilled craftsman could command such enormous sums, but Matthew said, a little protestingly, 'Why do you feel it necessary to confide this to us, Aylwin? Have we given you an unfortunate and false impression that we don't consider you our equal?'

'Not in the least,' Aylwin replied sincerely. 'I've never received anything but the kindest and most courteous treatment and true friendship from you, but that was in our direct relationship to one another, as men and friends. Matters may be different when your sister enters the picture.'

'Elys?' Crispin asked, looking quickly at Matthew, then giving his full and very alert attention to Aylwin. 'What of Elys?'

Aylwin looked to see that the last of the servants had left the hall, and then said simply, 'I wish to marry her.' He sat back on his stool, apparently relaxed, but Elys saw that his hands were tightly clasped in his lap.

Crispin and Matthew exchanged another look, and Matthew said, 'What has Elys to say to that?'

'I wish to marry Aylwin,' she replied, her voice surprisingly firm, considering how wildly her heart was beating.

'You realize,' Matthew said quietly, without any trace of surprise, 'that Aylwin's mystery means that he must travel from place to place to work, and he may not always be able to take you with him?'

'There'll be less of the travelling in future,' Aylwin put in. 'There was much damage done in Winchester during the recent siege, and also the Bishop means to build a great church and hospital in the meadows outside the city. There'll be work a-plenty for me for years to come, for he's told me this present job will be the last I'll have time for away from home in his lifetime. I own a house in Winchester – a good, stone-built one, near the Newminster.'

'Winchester is a fair city, I believe,' Crispin said musingly. 'Oh, but you know better than I, Elys. Was not one of your pilgrimages to St Swithun?'

'Yes,' Elys replied, and more from nerves than amusement, added with a tremor of laughter, 'It rained all the way, there and back.' Aylwin looked at her, and gave her a warm smile, sharing the joke.

'This is all very impressive,' Matthew said thoughtfully. 'I can see that there are many things to be said in favour of the match, and yet . . . It's a very serious matter, you understand, deciding on a husband for one's sister. I suppose you must realize that there are as many arguments against it as for it? You have a rank equal to ours, yet you are not one of us . . . I don't mean that in any derogatory sense, of course. Elys has been brought up as a Norman and a lady. You are an Englishman and a craftsman. If she marries you, she'll go out from all that's been her familiar background all her life to something quite different, among people whose ideas, language, way of life are alien . . . Oh yes, Elys – I know you think that love will overcome all these differences, but I've seen more of life than you, and I'm less sure. I like you, Aylwin, but caution and affection for my sister make me hesitate.'

'I also,' Crispin said gravely, 'and there is Uncle Richard to consider. He's been our guardian since our father died, and he must have a say in any decision as important as this. We expect him here in a few days, for he wrote to me only this week, saying that he had to visit the Templars' newly-granted manor at Cressing, and would call here on his way.'

'But he's bound to be against us!' Elys cried in protest.

'Be that as it may,' Matthew said in the tones of one who has made up his mind, 'we will wait for his opinion. I'm sorry, Aylwin, but I know that you will want whatever is best for Elys, just as we do.'

'You'll wish me to lodge elsewhere meanwhile,' Aylwin said, his face expressionless. 'I'll move out at once.'

'No, no!' Matthew protested. 'Please stay here until the matter is decided. I'd not banish you, nor lose your friendship, but ask you to bear with my wish to have time to consider such a weighty matter, and to have the advice of my uncle.'

Elys looked despairingly at Aylwin, trying not to cry. He smiled wryly, and said quietly, 'You didn't imagine it would be easy, did you? Your brother is right to ask for time, and he's not decided against us yet.'

'But Uncle Richard . . .' Elys murmured.

'Who knows? – he may favour the match,' Crispin said sympathetically.

To judge by the bleak expressions on their faces, none of his hearers thought his optimism was justified, and they awaited Sir Richard's arrival with foreboding. Aylwin tried once to raise Elys's spirits by saying to her, just before she retired that night, 'He may consent when he knows that I shan't be asking for your dowry,' but she only shook her head and said sadly, 'I think, with him, that pride of blood counts for more than lands or money.'

Fortunately, the anxious time of waiting for their doom to be decided was not too long, for Sir Richard arrived just as the tables were being set for supper the following evening. He looked tired and irritable, gave no more than the briefest greetings to his niece and nephews, nodded curtly to Aylwin, and went straight across to the church to say his sixty Paternosters in more peaceful surroundings than the hall of the house in Church Street.

When he returned, supper was served immediately, but it was eaten in silence, as Sir Richard's Rule required of him, and the others, with some idea of placating him, kept silence too. Elys was too nervous to be able to say anything sensible, so she would have held her tongue in any case.

When the last platters and dishes had been removed, and Sir Richard was free to talk and drink, he accepted a small cup of ale, settled back in the chair which he, as the honoured guest, was occupying, and said, 'Well, how are you, Matthew?'

'Very well, I thank you, Uncle,' Matthew replied. 'My leg is healed, and I manage excellently on my crutches. I've interesting work to occupy me, and feel that my life is blessed and fulfilling.'

'And you, Crispin?' Sir Richard passed on to his other nephew with no more than a nod in reply to Matthew.

'I, too, feel well settled and content. My studies make good progress, and Father Brian has offered me a canon's stall as soon as I'm ordained priest.'

Again, Sir Richard nodded acknowledgment, then turned to his niece. 'And what of you, Elys? Have you found a husband yet?'

'Yes,' Elys heard herself reply with perfect calm and assurance. 'As a matter of fact, we were waiting for your coming to ask your blessing, which I'm sure you'll be happy to give.'

Sir Richard looked taken aback for a moment, but swiftly recovered, and said, 'And does your prospective groom realize that you've no dowry?'

'I'm quite well aware of it, but it's no matter,' Aylwin replied on his own behalf. 'I mean to settle one of my four manors on Elys as her jointure, and also the reversion of my house in Winchester, so she'll have no need of anything from her family, save their love and goodwill.'

'Ah, so you have it all worked out,' Sir Richard said musingly. 'I suppose you think it suitable that a craftswoman should marry a craftsman?'

'Eminently so,' Aylwin replied steadily, looking Sir Richard squarely in the eyes.

'Tell me,' The Templar turned his attention to Elys, 'did you think of this for yourself, or did my nephews arrange it?'

'I expect you'll find it difficult to accept,' Elys replied, gazing earnestly at him and willing him to understand, 'but I've grown to respect and like Aylwin increasingly since I first met him in Mantova, and I have a deep affection for him, which he returns, so we've decided to marry . . .' She broke off and waited apprehensively for his reaction.

'Well,' he said after a few moment's silence. 'I little thought that a niece of mine would ever so forget her birth and breeding as to propose to marry a craftsman, and English at that. Think, girl! This man is the descendant of men who fought and perhaps killed your own ancestors. Also, he is an itinerant craftsman. Your life would be one

254

long round of travelling to new places, finding lodgings in dirty inns or crowded cottages, staying for a few months, then up and start again somewhere else. I've no doubt a skilled mason's well-paid enough at the end of a job, but what of the long weeks waiting for the money? What of the winters, when building stops during the frosts?'

'It wouldn't be like that . . .' Elys tried to interrupt.

'Nonsense! You think your infatuation with a handsome man will carry you through it, but it won't. When the children come, and you've to try to bring them up in squalid lodgings and constant moving on somewhere else, with no servants to help you . . . What if your man falls from a scaffold and breaks his legs, so that he can no longer work? What if he's killed? Can you support yourself and your children with your needle, and still find time to cook and clean and wash and discipline them and teach them all they need to know?'

'Sir Richard,' Aylwin cut in firmly, 'if I were a mere itinerant craftsman, that would all be true. Nay, hear me out!' as Sir Richard tried to cut him short. 'Let me make plain what I've already told your nephews. I am a master sculptor. I hold four manors from my master, Bishop Henry, and I own a freehold house in Winchester, in which my mother lives at present. After my work here is done, my master wishes me to work in Winchester for the foreseeable future. I need no dowry with Elys, which no doubt was the next objection you intended to raise, for I mean to settle more than sufficient property and money on her to enable her to live in comfort if I should die before her. I rank as a knight, although I'm a craftsman, not one of your knightly caste. If you choose to hold my nationality against me because of a battle fought more than seventy years ago, I'm sorry, but I had relations killed on that day too, yet I do not condemn all Normans for that reason. Many Normans marry English nowadays, without dire consequences.'

Sir Richard's mouth had dropped open slightly during this speech, but he now collected himself and said, 'Why did you not tell me all this before? It sheds a slightly different light on the matter. However, I am still opposed to the idea. Elys, in my opinion, should have gone to the nunnery, and made up her mind to be a good nun, whatever her purely selfish objections. If she persists in this strange conviction that she should turn craftswoman, she should at least think of her family and marry a Norman!'

'Is that your only objection, Uncle Richard?' Matthew asked, looking perplexed.

'Only? It's the over-riding objection!' Sir Richard barked, frowning. 'What could be more objectionable?'

'I'm sorry, sir, but I don't consider it a valid ground for objection,' Matthew replied. 'I've always respected your opinions in the past, but on this point I fear I must voice the strongest disagreement. I believe that it is long past time that we ceased to nurture an outdated enmity. I say that Elys may marry Aylwin, with my blessing.'

'And mine,' added Crispin promptly. I'm sorry, Uncle Richard, but Matthew is quite right.'

'Then there's no more to be said,' Sir Richard replied curtly. 'You're both of age, yet young and foolish enough to disregard the advice of your elders. On your heads be it. I shall go and attend to the welfare of my men,' and with that, he stalked out.

When he had gone, Elys ran to kiss her brothers and thank them, and Matthew, a little light-headed with relief at having at last made a decision of his own, despite his overbearing uncle, poured wine and toasted the betrothed couple.

The merriment attracted some of the servants to peep into the hall, and they were called in to take a cup of ale to the health of the couple, and then Lukin arrived, full of nods and winks and foreknowledge. Mistress Mayngod brought in a marchpane fantasy in the form of a church somewhat resembling the minster, given the limitations of what was possible in her materials. She said it had been ready for nearly a week in anticipation.

The evening turned into a merry celebration, and they were all late to bed, but before she went upstairs, Elys slipped out of the house into the summer night, and went to sit on a bench in the churchyard, gazing up at the stars and inhaling the pleasant scents of woodbine, elderflowers, eglantine, wood-smoke and mown grass, too full of happiness to sleep.

Presently Aylwin came to join her, sitting down and taking her in his arms with no more than a murmured 'Elys.'

It seemed to her that a lifetime had passed since he kissed her on May morning, but the kisses were sweeter now, even more stirring and satisfying, and it was a long time before either felt the need to speak.

At length, Aylwin said, 'I love you, Elys.'

'And I love you.'

'To think that I only went to Mantova by chance.'

'As did we! If my uncle hadn't heard there was a round church there . . .'

'San Lorenzo . . . I remember. We have much to thank St Lawrence for. Did you know the nave altar here is dedicated to him? Shall we ask to have our wedding mass said at it, in thanks?'

Elys snuggled her head into his uninjured shoulder, and said, 'And let it be on St Lawrence's day, then.'

'So be it, sweetheart,' he replied, and sought her lips again, lost with her in a private world, where both were totally unaware of the interested, watchful eyes of an owl, Tigrus, and a dog-fox, variously concealed about the peaceful churchyard.

CHAPTER FOURTEEN

A week or two later, Aylwin was in his workshed, sitting on a stool at his bench. One of his many notebooks lay open by his left elbow, and before him was a large block of carefully selected stone. Maul and chisels were ready by his right hand, and he knew exactly what he was going to conjure out of the fine limestone, for he had spent some time turning over the pages of the book, which was filled with drawings of horses' heads, and had made his choice.

There were great destriers in it, noble beasts of patrician descent, palfreys with fine bones and long pedigrees, but the open page showed a cobby pony with a lively eye and odd ears, one being larger than the other, a blunt nose and protruding teeth – a comical creature which made him smile whenever he looked at it.

At the moment, however, he was not looking at it, and, although his hands rested on the stone and his eyes appeared to dwell on it, he did not see the great mass of tiny shells and fossilized sea-creatures which concealed the carving which, in his mind, already dwelt within it. His thoughts were elsewhere.

He had passed the days since his betrothal in a state of euphoria, having achieved a goal which he had longed to attain for eight months, but had thought to be beyond his reach. Now doubt was creeping into his heart and mind. His love for Elys was certain, but he could not help but wonder if she really loved him, or had, in her inexperience, confused a longing for a husband and children with the deep, confident feeling which she would need to overcome the difficulties of marriage to him.

He sighed, and his hands moved unconsciously on the stone, feeling its texture and tracing the tiny flaws and unevennesses in its surface which might indicate greater flaws within. Their movement attracted his attention to them, and he inspected them, turning them to and fro, as if they belonged to someone else.

They were lean and strong, with calloused palms and a myriad of fine scars, for no man could work for years with stone and chisel without repeatedly chipping and cutting his hands. Surely they would feel hard and rough on her fine, soft skin . . .

'I'll not offer you a penny for your thoughts, for that don't look worth a fourthing, to judge by the look on your face,' said Lukin, who had been standing in the doorway waiting for Aylwin to notice him. 'Do you don't look like a happy bridegroom, so happen you're wishing you'd not spoken?'

'No,' Aylwin replied with a wry smile. 'I've no regrets. I'm just a mite afraid that Lady Elys may come to regret accepting me. It seems an unlikely pairing – Norman with Englishman, lady with craftsman, destined nun with itinerant mason . . .' He shook his head a little, and tried to smile as if he were joking, but only succeeded in looking as he felt, uncertain, anxious and filled with foreboding.

'That knows that's own mind,' Lukin said sagely, wrinkling his long nose to indicate sympathetic understanding. 'It do take courage to go agin the expectations of a whole family, especially when one of 'em be a Templar – powerful strong-minded, they Templars. Once a woman do make up that's mind to stand not be beat, that'll go through wi' it all the way, no matter what – you'll see if that don't. If that has to follow you all over Christendom to wherever there be stone waiting to be carven, that'll roll up that's broidery, kilt up that's skirts, and carry your chisels, like as not.'

'Have you never married, Lukin?' asked Aylwin. 'You seem to know a deal about women.'

'I got ears and eyes,' Lukin said drily, 'and a powerful funny face and body. Women don't mind me guessing their thoughts and feelings, not counting me a man. Man's as big a mystery to woman as woman is to man.'

'You think so?' Aylwin was surprised. 'I've always felt that women know what a man thinks and feels, because we're simple folk by comparison. A woman's such a complicated creature.'

259

'That's right, so that be,' Lukin nodded vigorously, 'but that don't believe a man can really be the simple child that seems. I'll tell you what, though. Happen your lady don't know all a woman ought to know afore that's wed. Could be that's mother never told that, thinking that'd not need to know, being shut up in a nunnery. That be youngest, too, so that never saw a brother or sister birthed, or that's mother carrying.'

Aylwin said nothing, feeling embarrassed that Lukin had expressed some of his own fears, and there was an awkward silence.

'Not my place to speak of it,' Lukin said eventually, nodding to himself. 'Still and all, I'll say this – you did best be sure that knows what to expect. Matilda Mayngod's your best help there. That be best midwife in the town, and knows a powerful lot. Won't be the first time that's told a maid her business, and set her on the right road to a good bedding.'

Aylwin gave him a thoughtful look, and said gruffly and self-consciously, 'Yes, you're right. I'd not thought of Mistress Mayngod.'

'Everyone did ought to think of Mistress Mayngod,' Lukin replied gravely. 'That be a woman worth the thinking on. Edwin Warrener do think of that whenever that's not thinking of conies or ferrets, which ain't often, and I do think on that myself most days. And nights,' he added, sounding a little wistful. 'An I get a chance, I'll mention the matter to that, do you want. That'll box my earen, like as not, but do that do, that'll make up wi' a pie, and maybe a hug. Tes worth a boxed ear to get pie or a hug, let alone both!' He nodded again, his little eyes twinkling below raised eyebrows, then, with a sudden change of subject, said, 'That's a good strong bench.'

'It's called a bencher,' Aylwin replied.

'A bencher? I'll remember that, and I'll remember to speak to Matilda about that other, and that'll put your maid right.' And he was gone before Aylwin could say anything.

For a moment, the mason considered going after him, but then he shrugged, thinking that Lukin was probably right, and set his mind to his work, having wasted a good part of the morning over his doubts and fears. The cobby pony's head was waiting inside that block of fine creamy-gold stone, and the row of corbels was only a quarter-done. His collarbone was healed, but Father Radulf had not yet given him leave to start work again. He was, however, impatient to begin on the new carving, and thought he could manage to work for an hour or two, at least.

First, he must decide where to start, which would be the best side of the block to face out on the world, so he pushed and pulled, turning the stone and studying its grain, for it was composed of many fine layers of those shells and fossils, and would split like wood if he made a wrong choice. It took patience and time, feeling, looking, tapping and listening, occasionally making a mark with his scriber, but, after more than an hour of absorbed, concentrated study, he found that those marks and lines already indicated the places where ears, nostrils, eyes and forelock lay, somewhere below the surface.

He put down the scriber, picked up a newly tempered and sharpened chisel and the maul, then closed his eyes and prayed silently for several minutes. When he opened his eyes, he crossed himself and the stone, the maul still in his right hand, and said aloud, '*Ad maiorem Deo gloriam!*' in a clear, almost challenging voice, then carefully struck the first blow.

The vibration of maul on chisel on stone ran up his arm and jarred his injured shoulder, making him wince, but the chisel remained steady, and exactly the right size and shape of chip flew off. With a nod of satisfaction, he moved the chisel and struck again. This time, he was prepared for the jar, and it seemed less painful. Perhaps, if he held his arm a little more stiffly, it would not hurt at all . . .

That was, he discovered, a false hope, but the pain was bearable, so he continued, working his way steadily over three sides of the block, leaving the back alone, for that needed to be big enough to key the corbel firmly into the wall.

'Aylwin! Has Father Radulf said you may do that?'

It was Elys, who had sensibly waited until he had completed a stroke, knowing that he was too absorbed to have noticed her arrival in the doorway, and that it was unwise to startle him while he was actually striking stone.

'I'm being very careful,' he replied, sounding absent-minded, for his attention was already on the positioning of the chisel for the next cut.

Again, Elys waited, then said, 'Won't you come home for your dinner? The tables are set, and my brothers are waiting.'

'I hadn't realized it was so late,' he exclaimed, putting his tools down and caressing the stone, feeling the shape beginning to emerge already, as he glanced past her to see that the sun was, indeed, casting the shadow of a tree directly towards the workshed, indicating an hour before noon as well as any sundial.

'What is it this time? Another lion?' she asked, coming to stand by him and look at the open notebook. 'Why, it's the miller's pony! He's such an odd-looking creature, with those ears and teeth.'

'I thought he might amuse the angels,' Aylwin replied, at least half-seriously. 'Besides, he belongs to Waltham, and deserves a place on his own parish church more than any strange horse.'

'Of course, he does,' Elys agreed, smiling and putting a hand shyly on her love's shoulder. 'Will you put one of Edwin's ferrets up there, and perhaps Apuleius?'

'His ears would be difficult,' he replied thoughtfully, putting his own hand over hers. 'I'd have to lay them back, close to his neck, as he does when he's annoyed. They'd be too vulnerable sticking up in their natural position, being so long. There's the dog-fox that haunts the churchyard at night, too, and any number of creatures in the fields and Forest. I thought I'd put some of them alternately with the lions. Bishop Henry didn't specify that all the corbels must be lions.'

He twisted on his stool so that he could put his arms round her, and stretched up to kiss her lips, but she pulled away a little, and said, 'Dinner, Aylwin. It will be cold, and Mistress Mayngod'll be annoyed.'

'Yes, of course,' he said at once, and set his bencher-top tidy with a few quick movements, covered the carving with

262

a square of cloth, and followed her along the churchyard path, but he could not help wondering if she had really failed to respond to his attempted kiss for fear of delaying dinner, or for some other reason.

The doubt having once taken root in his mind, he found himself watching Elys while he was with her, and mulling over every word she uttered, and even more, the silent messages of her expressions and actions, when he was away from her. Even his work failed to distract him from his anxiety for any length of time, for he found that his shoulder demanded a rest after a couple of hours' jarring, and he would find himself, in those enforced intervals, staring towards the window of the house in Church Street, where he could just see Elys's head bent over her work, his mind running to and fro over his doubts like one of Edwin's ferrets in a cage.

During the first few days, he tried to convince himself that he was tormenting himself unnecessarily. Torment it certainly was! The very idea that Elys might be slipping away from him filled him with a sick wretchedness, an aching desolation, which seemed to settle in the base of his throat, making his food taste like damp sawdust, and robbing his life of every sensation of pleasure, so that even the good progress of his carving meant nothing to him, and the beauty of the ripening countryside, basking in the heat of high summer, the pristine shine of precisely-cut ashlar, the curve of the growing arches of the church, no longer filled him with the old surging joy in the work of God or his fellow-masons.

Each day increased his fear that she was turning away from him, for he saw repeatedly that, where once her face had lit with pleasure at the sight of him, there was now doubt in her soft brown eyes, and when she touched him, she was hesitant, where, in those first happy days of their betrothal, she had been confident and eager. As a result, his own confidence ebbed, and he, too, hesitated to touch, even to reach out, fearing to see her shrink away from him. By the end of a week, he no longer seized every opportunity to steal a kiss or give her those little caresses which conveyed so much while still contriving to appear casual to anyone else. It seemed as if an invisible barrier were forming between them, and they each regarded the other across it with increasing uneasiness.

In another week, he saw that she would no longer meet his eyes when he looked at her, but turned away, and he found himself doing the same, gazing longingly while her attention was elsewhere, but immediately looking away if her eyes turned in his direction. He saw also that Matthew and Crispin were aware that something had gone wrong, although neither said anything.

It was Father Radulf who eventually mentioned the matter. He appeared one morning in the workshed, and said brusquely, 'I didn't give you leave to work again, but I assume you're the best judge of how much you can do. Does your shoulder trouble you at all?'

'It grows tired after a couple of hours,' Aylwin admitted, 'but a short rest sets it right again.'

'Let me see.'

Obediently, he stripped off his tunic and shirt, and Radulf inspected his left shoulder, which still showed the fading stains of bruising. He pulled the arm about, twisting it to several unnatural angles, which made Aylwin wince, but eventually said grudgingly, 'Well, I suppose you're doing it no great harm. I trust you'll have the sense to rest it when it aches, and it's healed well enough to stand reasonably cautious use. Now, tell me – what's troubling you?'

'Why should anything be troubling me?' Aylwin asked warily, pulling his shirt over his head and tucking it inside his braies.

'A month ago, you were a happy man with candles in your eyes,' Radulf replied bluntly. 'Now you look like a month of dull, wet days. Does the thought of marriage fill you with so much dread? To look at you, one would think you were to be executed on St Lawrence's day, not wedded.'

'My feelings are unchanged,' Aylwin said, pausing in the act of putting on his tunic to look squarely at the canon. 'I fear that Lady Elys may be regretting her decision.'

'Has she said anything to give you that impression?'

'Said – no, but her every look and gesture conveys doubt and increasing reluctance.' Aylwin felt the pricking of tears

264

at hearing his fears spoken aloud, and he pulled the tunic over his head, surreptitiously wiping his eyes on it as he did so.

'Father Crispin thinks *both* of you betray doubt and reluctance in your looks and gestures,' Radulf said, after a waiting for the mason's head to emerge through the neck of the garment. 'Have you talked to her about your fears?'

Aylwin shook his head. 'I've not been alone with her for near two weeks. She seems to avoid . . .'

'You used to take a stroll together by the stream in the evenings. Does she refuse to go with you now?'

'I haven't asked her. I don't want to make her be alone with me if she doesn't want it, nor put her to the embarrassment of refusing . . .'

'Hm.' Radulf was silent for a moment, thinking, and eventually said, 'If a third person – namely, Father Crispin – sees doubt and reluctance in *both* of you, maybe Lady Elys sees in you what you see in her . . . Yet you say your feelings are unchanged . . . If you want my opinion – which you probably don't – I would advise you to talk to her, and, more important, *listen* to her.'

'Yes.' Aylwin suddenly came to a decision. 'I'm torturing myself, and it may be all for nothing. Better to know, one way or the other. Thank you, Father!'

Father Radulf made a deprecating gesture, then tucked his hands into the sleeves of his habit, ready to depart, pausing in the doorway to say, 'Take care of that shoulder for a few weeks longer. Peace be with you.'

'And also with you,' Aylwin replied automatically, but with real gratitude, for peace was something he sorely needed in his present troubled state of mind.

The pony's head was beginning to emerge clearly from the stone, and Aylwin was working on the ears and the forelock between them as he thought over Father Radulf's words. He had just resolved to ask Elys to take a walk with him after supper when Father Brian arrived, tapping lightly on the open door before putting his head in and saying, 'I don't wish to interrupt you, but I'm a little worried . . . I wonder if I might talk to you for a few moments? Oh, my word! That's the miller's pony! I'd know those ears anywhere. How delightful. I marvel how you can chip away at a block of stone and be left with the likeness of a living creature. You are truly a great artist, Master Aylwin.'

'I would only claim to be a competent craftsman,' Aylwin replied, comparing the odd ears with his drawing and feeling moderately pleased with his work so far. 'How may I help you, Father?'

He made a long leg and hitched his spare stool out from under the bencher with his toe, and made a gesture of invitation to the canon, who sat down with a gusty sigh, as if he found the summer heat and the weight of responsibility on his shoulders a little too much.

'The problem is money, as usual,' he said. 'We decided in Chapter to use some of the money Bishop Henry sent for the building, and what we'd collected ourselves from our pilgrims for it, to help with the rebuilding of the houses that were burnt, fully expecting to be recompensed by the Earl of Essex for the damage he did to our property – indeed, he virtually promised he would do so, before he started firing d'Aubigny's property! Now, however, he refuses to give us a clipped penny. We've sent him a warning that his offence against Holy Church amounts to heresy and sacrilege, but he's already excommunicate for his other deviltry, so I doubt he'll be much worried by our little threat.'

'So the money's running short for the church building,' Aylwin prompted. 'How bad is the situation?'

'Oh, we've enough to continue the work until the frosts, when building will stop for the winter, and just about enough to pay the masons who will stay to cut stone and tend the new work during the cold months. It's the resumption in the spring which is in jeopardy. I wondered if . . . Well, you know the Bishop very well, and he obviously trusts you . . . If I just write and ask him for more money, he may be angry, or not understand that we had to divert what he had given us . . . We thought that if you would go and explain to him, in person . . . Not now, of course, with your wedding only a month away, but in the autumn, before most of the masons go home for the winter . . .'

'I'm sure he understands that you had no choice but to

use the money to help the poor townsfolk, particularly as d'Aubigny did nothing for them,' Aylwin replied. 'Of course I'll go and talk to him. It's some time since I had a chance to visit Winchester to see my mother, and I expect Lady Elys will be happy to come with me.'

'Of course, de Mandeville may have decided to pay up by then. He can't plead poverty, with all the plunder he's taken,' Father Brian said grimly. 'I've just been with Father Warmand to look at Lady Elys's work. It's very beautiful, and most exquisitely stitched. I think it will be superior to the cope which Rufus – er – took from us, from what I can remember, although I was only a child at the time. That one was heavily worked in gold, but the stitchery was comparatively crude. More glitter than craftsmanship, you understand. Ah well, I mustn't keep you from the miller's pony. The Lord bless you and your work, my son.'

Aylwin thanked him absently, his mind already back on his work. He pushed the spare stool back under the bencher, picked up maul and chisel, and considered his next stroke.

'Can you spare me a minute?' asked a voice, and Master William came in, wiping his brow on his sleeve, for he was sweating heavily, as if he had been doing something particularly energetic.

Aylwin stifled a sigh, put down his tools, and pulled the spare stool out again. 'Trouble?' he asked.

'I dunno. Did you know that Bishop Henry wants the aisles vaulted?'

'Vaulted!' Aylwin exclaimed. 'No, I didn't know that. The whole length?'

'Aye. Nave, chancel and ambulatory. It was intended in the beginnin', he says. Certainly, the springers are there, on the capitals and in the side walls. You'll have seen them, I don't doubt?'

'Yes, I had noticed them, but I assumed the idea had been abandoned. Surely, the masons who built the old work would have put up the vaults as they went along otherwise? It would have been easier to do each bay while they had the putlogs in position than to leave them, and have to go back after the holes had been filled.'

267

'It can be done without too much trouble, I reckon, although it means cuttin' into the old work, and I wouldn't need to pay off so many men for the winter with all that extra stone to be cut. Given there's enough money left, of course. Father Brian's talked to you about that?'

'Yes. I think we can assume that the money will come, especially if the Bishop wants the extra work done.' Aylwin pulled the lobe of his ear, and looked as doubtful as he felt.

'You don't like the idea of vaultin . . ." Master William half-asked, half-stated, interpreting his expression as not relating to his words.

'Do you?'

'No. To my mind, the walls won't take the thrust.'

'You could increase the size of the buttresses. They're no more than flat pilasters.'

'I suppose so, but I reckon that'd spoil the look of the building. I was wonderin' . . . Do you know aught about these new arches?'

'You mean the pointed arch? I've seen them in Italy, and at Cluny and St Denis. But surely – you've worked at Durham?'

'Aye, but they're not truly pointed, and I was but a journeyman then. Would they lessen the thrust?'

'They'd direct it more downwards than outwards, but you don't have enough height to put them across the aisles, without you raise the base of the triforium and alter the roof. I think you'd only ruin the appearance of the building if you tried, and I think you'd still have too much thrust for the walls.'

'Ah well, it were just a thought. I've not seen a true pointed arch myself. I must get myself beyond seas and see some of these newfangled ideas. If I tell Bishop Henry it's my professional opinion that the walls won't take the thrust, will you back me?'

'Of course. It's my opinion too.'

William grinned and gave him a clout on the shoulder – the uninjured one, fortunately – which nearly knocked him off his stool. 'You're a good fellow,' he said. 'I've never met with another master I could work with like I can with you.

By Our Lady! That's the miller's pony, or I'm a mud-builder.'

'Everyone seems to recognize him by his ears,' said Aylwin. 'He must have one from his dam and one from his sire.'

'Likely one or t'other were a donkey, then,' William said jovially, his main worry relieved, if not removed. 'Though that'd make him a mule. By St Barbara! I don't know another man in England can carve like you. Every other carvin' I've seen is stiff and don't look like any real animal or man or plant in the world, but your things all look real and near-alive.'

'I try to carve what I see, so far as the stone will let me,' Aylwin replied. 'Sometimes I'm almost satisfied, but I can never quite persuade the stone to yield what I can draw, let alone what I see. Maybe my grandson will manage it . . .' He broke off, remembering what he had once said to Elys along the same lines, and wondered if he would ever have a grandson if Elys had indeed changed her mind. Could he ever bring himself to marry another woman if he lost her?

You haven't lost her yet, he told himself, and resolved to deal with the problem, settle his doubts and fears, at the earliest opportunity – that very evening, in fact. To that end, he left his work early and prayed before the Holy Cross for some time before going home for supper.

He had fallen into the habit of returning to his work after the meal for as long as the daylight lasted, as did Elys, but that evening, when supper was finished and she moved across to her embroidery frame, he followed her and said urgently, 'I must talk with you. Will you walk out for a while?'

She gave him a startled, frightened look, and said nervously, 'If you wish. Now?'

'Yes.'

As they left the house together, it seemed natural to turn to the left down Church Street and follow the course they had taken, so few weeks ago, when they went to watch the haymaking. As usual, the miller's cat sat by the bridge, watching the fish, and Aylwin bent to stroke it in passing.

The swifts which nested under the eaves of the minster

were wheeling and screaming over their heads, and Elys looked up at them, saying vaguely, 'I wonder where they go in the winter. They always seem to vanish before summer's quite over.'

'I've been told that they bury themselves in the mud at the bottom of ponds and rivers, but that seems unlikely,' Aylwin replied equally vaguely, thinking of what he wanted to say to her, and neither of them spoke again until they were entering the first meadow, where the stream bent to the right, for some unknown reason, for a hundred yards or so, before resuming its former direction.

'It looks quite different with the hay all cut,' Elys said. 'Oh – there are cows – is it safe?'

'They're too busy eating the new grass to worry about us,' Aylwin assured her. 'If they do come near, it'll be out of curiosity, that's all, and I'll endeavour to protect you!'

'Yes,' said Elys, sounding a little doubtful, and she moved over to walk on his right, so that he was between her and the cows as they followed the bank of the stream.

'I think it's time we talked,' Aylwin began after a few minutes of silent strolling. 'Do you still want to marry me?'

'Why? Aylwin, have you changed your mind?'

He stopped and turned to face her, trying to interpret the tone of her voice. Did she sound relieved, or upset?

She took a few more steps, then stopped and turned back to him.

'No,' he said. 'I thought you had.'

The expression of surprise on her face was unmistakeable. 'Why – how could you think that?' she asked.

'You seem to have grown – uneasy – in my company, these past few weeks. I feel that you avoid meeting my eyes, you don't want me to touch you . . .'

Her lower lip trembled for a moment, until she bit it to keep it still, and her wide brown eyes filled with tears, but they did not spill over. Overwhelmed by tenderness, Aylwin lifted a hand, intending to caress her, but then let it drop to his side.

'I'm a foolish, ignorant girl,' she said, her face troubled. 'At first, when it was agreed we might marry, I was so happy that I didn't think of anything else, but then, gradually, I began to realize how little I knew about – about marriage. I can't cook, and – you remember – I didn't even recognize a love-token when I was given one. My mother always talked about marriage as if it was something to be endured in order to have children. I don't think she and my father even liked one another. I can't remember either of them ever showing any affection for the other – indeed, they hardly spoke most of the time.'

'I see.' Aylwin was beginning to understand. 'But surely you realized that it need not be like that? You seemed to enjoy being touched and kissed at first.'

'I did – I do! I didn't know what happened next, though. I know my father used to – to go to bed with my mother sometimes, but they always seemed to be angry about it. I supposed they did something together like animals do – dogs and horses – I've seen those mating, but they don't seem to enjoy it. I supposed babies were born like puppies and kittens, but I didn't really know how.'

'And were you afraid?'

'In a way. It was more that I somehow couldn't imagine you and me like animals. Mother and Maud used to refer to what happened as an unpleasant duty, and I couldn't bear to think that what I feel for you would turn to that sort of dislike . . .'

'You speak of all this – your fears and ignorance – as if they are in the past, though,' Aylwin exclaimed, suddenly realizing that she had used the past tense.

'Mistress Mayngod started talking about it to me one night as we were going to bed. She made it all seem so natural and right. She explained that it's an unpleasant duty without love, but loving the other makes all the difference, and I can understand that. If any other man touched me and kissed me as you do, I'd hate it, but if it's you, I like it. I can talk about it to her, and ask questions, and she explains it all so well. She loved her husband, you know, for all she says that men are more trouble than babies. She helps birth babies, and knows all about it, and how to look after them and their mothers. It's not frightening any more now I know what to expect, although she says that some of it hurts – the first few times with a man – you know – and

271

when the baby comes . . . The trouble is, by the time I'd talked to her and had most of my doubts and fears put to rest, it seemed too late.'

'Too late?' he asked sharply.

'You'd stopped caressing me, and you didn't seem to want to kiss me, or even talk to me any more. I thought perhaps you'd changed your mind. You've been free to do as you please for so long, and a wife and children must seem burdensome to you, and I wondered if perhaps you'd realized that what you felt for me was just a – a passing attraction . . . I didn't know what to do. Mistress Mayngod said it would all come right, and I should ask you straight out, but I daren't . . .'

'Oh, my dear girl!' Aylwin exclaimed, taking both her hands in his. 'I started thinking of all the difficulties – all of them but the ones which were causing the trouble. I should have realized that you might never have seen a truly loving marriage. I forgot something you told me yourself – that you Normans seldom marry for love. I'm a fool! I was worrying about the differences between us, and thought you were finding them too great.'

'What differences?' she asked, beginning to smile a little.

'That you're Norman and I'm English. That your people don't respect craftsmen as we do, so that your people would think you were marrying very much below your rank. That you're convent-bred, and I'm a rough-handed fellow who's knocked about the world and seen the worst as well as the best . . . Do any of those things matter to you?'

Elys considered. 'Not really. Now I'm a craftswoman, I can respect skill in others more than I used to, and now I realize that we craftsfolk are really more important than knights and barons. I love your hands – they make such beautiful things, and every scar on them got there while you were making something lovely. Can I ask you something very private?'

'Of course. I've no secrets from you.'

'Have you ever bedded a woman?' She looked into his face as she asked, her eyes huge and anxious.

'Yes,' he answered without hesitation. 'For pleasure, though not for love, and more than one.'

272

She nodded. 'Mistress Mayngod said it's different for a man, and it's always pleasant for him, unless he really dislikes the woman, but it only means a great deal if he loves her. She says it's better when the man knows how to do it properly, because it has to be learned. Do you think she's right?'

'Yes. Skill increases with practice in anything, even that.' Aylwin was amazed, and greatly relieved, to find it so easy to discuss intimate matters with her, and thanked God in his heart for Mistress Mayngod.

'Did you really think the differences were so important?' she asked curiously.

'Yes. Not to me so much, but because I thought you were realizing them, and beginning to doubt if you really wanted to marry an English mason.'

'Not just *any* English mason,' she said gravely. 'Only one!' Her face suddenly broke into a mischievous smile. 'I think we're a rare pair of fools. If I'd come to you as soon as I began to fear you'd changed your mind, I'd have saved myself weeks of misery.'

'Or I to you,' Aylwin replied, his face still grave. 'It was for me to make the first move, I think, but I was afraid.'

'Afraid?'

'That if I asked you if you'd changed your mind, you might say that you had, and you didn't want to marry me after all.'

'And I feared the same thing. Oh, Aylwin!' She dropped his hands, but only to move forward into his arms, and clung to him as they closed about her.

'Kiss me, my dearest love,' she said, and he lost no time in obeying.

For some time, they clung together in the summer twilight, oblivious of the midges rising from the stream, the birds flying home to roost, and Father Antony, who passed them with a basket of carp from the fishponds in the next meadow, but refrained from looking or commenting.

When they did eventually cease kissing and murmuring disjointed endearments, they found themselves surrounded by a dozen curious cows, which gazed at them with vacant faces, their jaws moving rhythmically, as if nothing like this

273

had ever before disturbed their placid lives. They were obviously mortally offended when the objects of their curiosity burst out laughing, and they moved away with much flourishing of tails and twitching of ears to resume the more familiar business of eating grass.

CHAPTER FIFTEEN

The rest of the time until their wedding day passed in a whirlwind of activity. Elys had made herself a new gown out of a length of blue silk which she had found among the cloth which her mother had left with her, and embroidered the neck and skirt with wide borders of all the flowers symbolic of love and marriage which she could remember, and was frantic that it might not be finished in time. Mistress Mayngod indulged in such an orgy of baking and roasting, of pounding and beating, basting and kneading that she seemed to have turned crimson all over with exertion, and the poor scullions were so confused with flying in all directions to fetch that, borrow this, beg a pinch of such and such, beat this, stir that (not like that, you fool!), that their exhausted sleep was haunted by visions of giant capons, vast mountains of dough, unending piles of roots, and oceans of marchpane, all presided over by a red-faced she-devil with hands like bludgeons and a voice like the last trump.

Father Antony decided that the college could spare a barrel of wine for the wedding-feast, and enlisted Lukin's aid in deciding which was the best vintage of the last few years' produce from the college's vineyard. As a result, they both became disgracefully lightheaded. Father Antony went out in a solemn procession of one, and served the miller's cat with a whole large carp, seethed in butter, on one of his best dishes. Lukin, singing happily, danced into Mistress Mayngod's kitchen and gave her a hearty kiss full on her lips. She boxed his ears for it, and he finished up sitting down in an open flour-crock, laughing uncontrollably and declaring that he loved her to distraction, for which she slapped him with a wet dishcloth, and told him to come back and repeat his words when he was sober, if he dared.

Edwin had spent the whole of the previous night out with his ferrets, which thought this a desirable departure from his normal expectation that they should work during the day, when, as any ferret knows, conies are out of their burrows and harder to catch, and any sensible ferret fast asleep. They had a rare frolic, and Edwin arrived in Mistress Mayngod's kitchen next morning, yawning hugely and so weighed down with conies that he could hardly stagger, and was told brusquely to set to and skin them, as Mistress Mayngod had but one pair of hands, and they were already occupied with pastry-making.

The servants, meanwhile, were cleaning the hall and polishing everything that could be persuaded to shine by means of beeswax and elbow grease, and talked of giving the minster the same treatment as soon as the hall was finished. Matthew and Crispin, faintly bewildered by the turmoil in their normally peaceful home, invited themselves to dinner with Father Brian, whose wife was an excellent cook, but got only cold meat, bread and cheese, for she had gone to offer assistance to Mistress Mayngod.

'Such a great occasion for the womenfolk,' said Father Brian ruefully. 'We poor men hardly count for anything, and I sometimes wonder if the women don't think more of the feast and the finery than the sacrament. Now, which of you will give the bride away? Have you decided?'

As this was the first time either of Elys's brothers had been involved in a wedding, they had not thought about it, let alone decided anything, but Matthew pointed out that it would be difficult for him to walk to the church porch with Elys with proper dignity on his crutches, so Crispin should perform the office for their sister, and he would be one of the witnesses.

In the event, Crispin did not have the chance either, for Sir Richard arrived in the evening, unannounced and unexpected, entering the gleaming hall just before supper and stating, after a brief greeting, that he was come to do his duty as senior male member of the family and hand over his niece to her earthly bridegroom. His choice of words sounded disapproving, but the fact that he had come at all, and was prepared to take an active part in the ceremony, conveyed to Elys that he did, in fact, approve her choice and wish them both well, and she thanked him with proper and sincere expressions of appreciation.

The weather, despite it being well within forty days after St Swithun's, had been fine and sunny all the week, and there were hopes that the wedding-day would be the same, but it dawned overcast and unpleasantly humid. Lukin, arriving early with a fine posy for the bride, said the crawling in his scalp foretold thunder in the offing, and Mistress Mayngod was in a rare taking, a whole pitcher of cream having turned sour between the cow and her kitchen, and set her plans awry.

Aylwin had been banished the night before, after an hour with Elys on the bench in the churchyard during which they had held hands without saying a word, and had spent the night at Lukin's cottage, sleeping peacefully and dreamlessly, much to his own surprise. He woke early, however, and spent the morning in his shed, finishing off the pony's head, to while away the time until dinner, which he took with Father Antony.

The canon had a headache, and seemed disinclined to talk, which suited Aylwin very well as he was wrestling with a bad attack of nerves, the full implications of the step he was about to take having suddenly swept over him, and his mind was full of fears and imaginings. What if he were injured and could no longer work – what would become of his wife and children? What if Elys and his mother took a misliking to one another? What if . . .

'Your mother wasn't able to come for the wedding, then?' Father Antony said eventually, making an effort at conversation, having taken a private vow never to drink more than one cup of wine in a day in future.

'No. She has a shop in Winchester, and didn't wish to be away from it for so long, as it's such a distance away. She sent me a letter, though, with her blessing and good wishes, and a gift for Lady Elys.'

'A gift?'

'An ivory carving of Our Lady with the Christchild. I shall give it her – after the wedding.' He had meant to say 'tonight', but the word had too much meaning, under the circumstances, to pass his lips.

'Ivory carving . . . Oh, yes, I've heard of the ivory carvings of Winchester! There's a group of workers there who are making quite a name for themselves for that work,' Father Antony said thoughtfully. 'Perhaps we might be able to acquire one for the minster one day. Oh, my goodness, shouldn't you be getting ready for the ceremony? I hadn't realized how late . . . That was the noon bell.'

Time had, in fact, slipped by more quickly than Aylwin had realized, and he went back to Lukin's house in a great rush, to wash himself thoroughly, indulging in the luxury of a tub of warm water in Lukin's kitchen, and dressed himself carefully in his best blue tunic and braies and a pair of soft leather boots, clasping a pair of ancient gold armrings over his sleeves above his elbows. He rarely wore them, but family tradition said that they had been given to one of his ancestors by King Alfred, and it could have been true, for they were very beautifully formed in the shape of the elongated bodies of winged dragons with garnet eyes and claws. He had just finished smoothing his hair, and was standing anxiously while Lukin inspected him from all angles to see if he would 'do', when there was the sound of voices and shuffling feet outside, and a thump on the door, which opened to admit Master William.

'We'm come as a lodge to take you to your weddin', he announced formally. 'Here's your nosegay. Have you got the ring-money?'

'Ring-money.' Aylwin promptly fell into a panic, like any bridegroom, and looked frantically around the small hall of Lukin's cottage.

'You put that in your purse not a quarter-hour agone,' said Lukin solemnly. 'You can't have lost that already.'

With coins safely back in his purse, Aylwin emerged from the cottage, and a procession formed up, headed by the youngest apprentice with the flower-crowned pole and trowel which was the lodge's standard. The journeymen followed, two by two, each carrying a pair of callipers, a square or a trowel, with Aylwin next, Master William and Lukin walking on either side of him, the mason's bulky figure plodding along in contrast to Lukin's curious gait.

278

The apprentices followed behind, with a deal of merriment and much less dignity than their seniors.

The minster had as yet no west porch, as the work had not progressed that far, but the men had put up a temporary one of timber and decorated it with flowers and branches, and there Father Brian, in cope and Mass vestments, waited with several of the other canons. The whole area outside was filled with as many townsfolk as could leave their work, as well as some who should have been busy elsewhere. Aylwin, numb with nervousness, passed through the narrow lane they had left for him, his groomsmen following, and went to wait in the porch for his bride.

She came only a few minutes later, heralded by an out-rider in the form of Mistress Mayngod, resplendent in crimson wool, with a massive enamelled brooch on her bosom, which Lukin likened, *sotto voce*, to a breastplate. Next came the cook's two small nieces, scattering the petals of sweet briar roses, which they had spent all morning gathering from the hedgerows, and then Elys, conducted at arm's length by her uncle, stiffly upright in his white cloak, which completely covered everything else he was wearing, excepting his boots. He was frowning severely, but his lips twitched occasionally, and there was a certain buoyancy in his stride, which an interested observer might have seen as a sign that he was really quite happy.

There was, however, no interested observer, for all eyes were on the bride. She had finished her gown only that morning, and loosely stitched many knots of ribbon on it as favours, and, as she came round the corner of the church, they fluttered like butterflies in the breeze. The sun suddenly broke through and shone on her, turning the gown into a shimmering blue haze, the embroidered flowers glowing as if they were enamelled. Her head and face were covered by a fine pale blue silk veil, which was held in place by her best gold coronet, and under it her long hair fell loose to below her waist, in the traditional manner of a bride. She was carrying Lukin's posy in her free hand.

Aylwin took a few steps out of the makeshift porch to meet her, and gazed enraptured, thinking he had never seen anything so lovely in all his life, and wishing that he was a painter, so that he might try to capture that beauty for ever. He did not even notice how the waiting crowd parted and drew back to give her broad passage, or that her brothers followed her, with all their servants coming two by two behind them.

The principal actors in the ceremony entered the porch, Sir Richard, Crispin and Matthew, with Mistress Mayngod for female support, to be Elys's witnesses, and Lukin and Master William as Aylwin's. The sacrament was administered by Father Brian in his most sonorous tones, and both bride and groom made their vows in clear and confident voices. Aylwin managed to retrieve the ring-money from his purse at the right moment without dropping it, and put it safely into Elys's hands. The actual ring had been given to her soon after their betrothal, and she had been wearing it ever since.

To Aylwin, every word and gesture seemed to be happening at a distance, yet with a clarity of sound and vision which impressed every detail indelibly on his memory, so that, even years later, he could close his eyes and see again Father Brian's gnarled hands joining his own and Elys's, and Sir Richard's face breaking into a rare smile, despite his efforts to look severe. Above all, he could remember the glory in Elys's face when he lifted the veil and turned it back over her head, and the soft pressure of her lips on his as they sealed their vows with a kiss.

Once they were married in the presence of everyone who could manage to see into the shallow porch, Father Brian turned and took their hands, one on either side of him, to lead them into the church, the other canons falling in behind them. Immediately within the nave, the crucifer, thurifers and choristers waited, and the latter burst into a joyful psalm as they precessed before the priests up the long nave to the parish altar of St Lawrence, set just before the western arch of the crossing. Everyone else who had come to the wedding crowded in after the procession, and took their places in the nave.

The Mass was celebrated with much joyous singing, and Lukin produced his trumpet from behind a pillar, where he had left it earlier in the charge of a small but determined chorister, and accompanied the *Te Deum* with a clear, ringing descant. The notes seemed to rise round the great pillars and resound in the triforium and clerestory, awakening echoes which sounded as if heavenly trumpets were answering in the far distance.

After the Mass, the bride and groom walked slowly back down the nave, smiling in a dazed fashion and nodding greetings to their many acquaintances in the body of the church, and their supporters followed, the rest of the congregation falling in behind in an orderly fashion.

Outside, Aylwin, who had been to many other weddings, expected that an obstacle of some sort would be waiting for his bride to jump over to symbolize her leap into a new life in the old English fashion, but he was surprised to find two such obstacles. The townswomen had made a garland of flowers, which some of them held stretched across just outside the porch, about a foot above the ground, but beyond that, a couple of the mason's apprentices had built a low wall during the service. It was made of cut blocks of ashlar intended for use in the building, so it was not mortared, but carefully laid in two courses, standing almost two feet high.

Bride and groom came to a halt, and Elys whispered, a note of panic sounding faintly in her voice, 'What must we do?'

'Jump over them,' Aylwin whispered back. 'We'll do it together. Ready – one, two, three, jump! And again – one, two, three, jump!' and Elys, hitching up her long skirts with both hands, jumped as he put an arm about her waist to give her a slight lift and steady her as she landed. There was great laughter and applause, and showers of grains of wheat and barley were thrown over them, and then everyone who knew the bride well enough to presume crowded round to claim a kiss and snatch one of the favours which were stitched to her gown. The women did particularly well, as they all kissed Aylwin as well, and there was an uproar of good wishes, exclamations, and admiration for Elys's beautiful gown.

The seventh thurifer wriggled eel-like through the press of bodies and appeared suddenly close before Elys, gazing up at her with wide-eyed admiration. 'That's the crown I found in the daffydillies! You look like a real queen!' he said. 'Master Aylwin did ought to carve you just like that for a statue of Our Lady!' Elys, smiling, bent to kiss him, and gave him one of the few favours left as a keepsake, which he carried off triumphantly, while she anxiously looked at her skirt to see if the delicate fabric had been injured when the other favours were snatched off. She was relieved to find that they had been stitched loosely enough to do no hurt.

Aylwin, with a sudden lunge, managed to get through to her in time to claim the last favour, which was stitched just below the centre of the neck of the gown, where most people hesitated to take it while others remained. He stowed it away in his purse with considerable satisfaction, for he had several from other weddings, and felt he must have one from his own to add to them.

Eventually, Father Brian, who had been watching benignly from the porch, moved forward with dignity and no suggestion of haste or lack of confidence that a way would open before him, which it did, and he arrived between bride and groom in a suddenly cleared space, to take a hand of each and say, smilingly, 'It gives me – nay, it gives all the college – great joy to see two fine craftsmen united in wedlock, particularly as your work, both of you, adorns and beautifies our minster!'

Aylwin made a suitable reply, although he had no idea afterwards what he had said, and then Elys asked, 'May I give my flowers to you to lay on the tomb of the founder?'

For a moment, Aylwin was stunned, hardly able to believe his ears, and a great wave of tenderness flowed over him to think that his Elys, his darling, a Norman, should think of such a gesture. Father Brian, also moved by it, replied, 'Better still – will you lay them there yourself?'

'I should like that.'

'Come, then.' Father Brian swung round, his cope flaring out round him, and taking each of them by the arm, went with bride and groom back into the church. This time, no one followed as they went back up the nave, round the parish altar, each making a reverence to the Holy Cross as they passed through the crossing and into the chancel.

The founder's tomb, unusually, was placed behind the high altar, and so, being within the sanctuary, was not usually accessible to the laity. Having taken them to it, Father Brian stepped back and watched, smiling, as the young couple stood side by side, looking down on the low table-tomb, which was adorned only with a grotesque lion's mask at each corner, and bore no inscription.

'You know who lies here?' Aylwin asked in a low, anxious voice, suddenly afraid that he might have misunderstood Elys's gesture.

'Yes. King Harold Godwinsson, our last English king,' she replied softly, and then bent gracefully to place Lukin's tight posy of flowers neatly in the middle of that plain slab of grey stone. 'God rest his soul, for he was a great and brave man.'

'Amen, and God bless you for the thought,' Aylwin murmured so that she could just hear him. He had noted and appreciated that she had said 'our' and not 'your'.

She turned her head to smile up at him, and then they turned back to Father Brian, who ushered them back to the crossing, and then let them out of the small door in the south transept, so that they could escape across the churchyard to the house in Church Street without having to pass through the crowd outside the west end.

Once safely back in the house, Elys turned to her husband, and he took her in his arms and kissed her as he had been longing to do since the moment he saw her in her bridal gown, and they were able to enjoy a few minutes of quiet together before the street door banged, and what seemed a crowd of people thronged into the hall.

In fact, it was only Elys's family, Lukin, Edwin, Master William, Mistress Mayngod and the servants, but they made a fine hubbub, embracing bride and groom all over again and chattering excitedly. Mistress Mayngod seized four servants and sent them for wine and the little cakes which she had prepared to stave off the pangs of hunger until the wedding feast.

As they hurried out, Tigrus slipped in through the door

and wove his way through the forest of legs to Elys, where he rubbed himself luxuriously against the soft silk, purring and setting his fur crackling as the silk clung to him in a remarkable fashion.

'There must indeed be thunder in the air for that to happen,' exclaimed Matthew. 'I've had the most peculiar twinges in my foot that isn't there all day, so I thought there must be something brewing.'

'Sit down and rest it, then,' said Crispin, guiding him to a stool. 'Do sit down, everyone. You must all be tired with the long standing and the excitement.'

'Won't the servants be wanting to prepare the hall for the feast?' asked Elys, and wondered why Matthew, Crispin, Lukin and Edwin all exchanged sly grins.

'We're not having it here. This isn't big enough for all the folk who want to come,' Mistress Mayngod said, casting a disparaging eye about what was, in fact, a good-sized hall compared with most in the town.

'Where, then?' asked Aylwin.

'In the church, of course! Where else would be big enough?' Mistress Mayngod replied airily.

Aylwin and Elys looked at one another with surprise and a little consternation, for they had both thought the feast was to be a small affair for family and a few close friends, having the barest idea of the vast preparations which had been going on in this and other kitchens during the past week.

Everyone was glad to sit down, sip their wine and talk quietly for a while, recovering from the excitement of the wedding. Mistress Mayngod, having toasted bride and groom, slipped away, shooing the servants before her, and presently a deal of scurrying could be heard to and fro in the screens passage, and the street door banged several times before someone thought to put a bucket of water against it to hold it open.

Sir Richard, comfortably seated with Tigrus draped across his lap and a goblet of good Rhenish wine in his hand, relaxed into good humour sufficiently to reminisce about the wedding of the Empress to Count Geoffrey of Anjou some sixteen years before, which he had attended and remembered quite well, chiefly for the incongruous difference in age between the bride and groom, she being twenty-five and he not yet turned fifteen. He compared it to today's ceremony, and obviously found the latter much the better affair, which pleased everyone concerned very much.

'I don't reckon anyone ever had a prettier wedding, nor a lovelier bride nor handsomer groom!' Edwin volunteered boldly. He had kept very quiet up to now, having no real business to be present at all.

'Ah. Weddings do make us old bachelormen start to think,' Lukin said gloomily. 'It be all very well, having only yourself to please, but it do be lonely nights, and cooking for one's hardly worth the while.'

'Do you cook your own meals?' asked Elys, who had assumed he had servants.

'That I do. I've a couple-three girls come in to redd out my place, but I boils my own worts and jacks my own roasts, and usually burns 'em, too. That be when I can't cadge something better in somebody else's kitchen, mind,' he added with a sly grin, and pulled his long nose in a knowing fashion.

Aylwin had expected to feel relaxed and happy once the ceremony was over and he was safely married to Elys, who was satisfactorily and obviously glowing with happiness, but instead, he found he was tense and edgy. Instead of joining in the conversation, he sat staring into his goblet of wine, thinking vaguely about the changes he could now expect in his way of life. Not, he assured himself, that he had any regrets. He had won a great prize, one which he had once assumed he had no chance of attaining, and he was happy, but . . . Now, there would be someone else to consider when he wanted to do something. No longer would he be able to go off to see a building or a statue at the other end of the country, or of Christendom, with no more than a formal request for leave from Bishop Henry.

Would it matter? Elys had said she would go with him, wherever he went, but could he expect her to undertake a journey to, say, Dunfermline or Jerusalem, with a small child or two at her skirts . . . ?

285

Mistress Mayngod's messenger arrived to bid them all to the wedding feast before he had pursued his thoughts any further, and he roused himself to join in the fun, remembering that all the effort and goodwill which had gone into the preparation of the feast was in honour of Elys and himself.

He did enjoy it, and cheered as loudly as anyone when the bridecake was broken over Elys's head by Matthew and Crispin, and the more active guests scrambled for the pieces, the choirboys winning the lion's share. Elys was nearly knocked down in the scramble, but he managed to whisk her to safety in time, and stood holding her close with an arm about her waist as they watched the battle.

'Did you notice,' Elys said, obviously reminded by the sight of scattered cake crumbs, 'that all the corn that was showered over us outside the church has disappeared? I wonder where it went.'

'Into the crops of the canons' doves,' he replied. 'There are ravening hordes of them in the columbarium. They'd have come down like the Plagues of Egypt for a fine meal like that.'

'Or an army of choirboys,' Elys said, laughing.

Lukin, who had assisted at many weddings, kept a watch on the consumption of food, and, long before the eating showed any signs of slowing down, he went round and whispered to Matthew, Crispin, Master William, the little bridesmaids and Mistress Mayngod, and they all rose up together, seized the bride and groom, and took them away, to some ribald cheering and shouted good wishes from the revellers which made Aylwin turn crimson, but drew no more than an uncertain smile from Elys, perhaps because she was not sure what some of the words meant.

Mistress Mayngod had removed all her belongings from the upstairs bedchamber back to her kitchen loft, to leave the room free for the newly-weds, and Aylwin's property had been moved in, the chamber had been thoroughly cleaned, and the bed made up with new sheets, with bunches of herbs known to encourage fertility tucked under the bolster. Elys's female attendants conducted her to it, leaving Aylwin downstairs with the men, who contrived to get him out of his clothes and into a nightrobe in a fairly sober manner, any tendency to obscene humour being curbed by the presence of Crispin, and even more of Matthew, who, although not in Orders, had been the beneficiary of a miracle, and was considered especially holy.

After what seemed a long time, Mistress Mayngod called down the stairs, and the men trooped up to see Aylwin safely into bed with his bride. The little girls, full of importance and excitement, sat on Elys's side and flung her two cloth stockings over their heads, succeeding in hitting Lukin with both of them, to everyone's amusement. He grinned and said mysteriously, 'I wonder who the lucky woman will be,' for this was supposed to indicate that he would be the next to marry. Then Crispin blessed them all, particularly the bride and groom, and they all trooped back to the feast, leaving Aylwin and Elys alone together in the dim light of a single candle.

CHAPTER SIXTEEN

The storm broke in the small hours with a vivid flash of lightning which woke Aylwin with a start. He lay still for a moment, bewildered and half-blinded by it, until he recollected where he was, lying in bed in the upstairs chamber, the shutters opened wide to let in some air during the heavy thunder-threatening night. His whole body felt delightfully languid, fulfilled, and lying half across him, her hair wreathing round both of them, lay Elys, relaxed and fast asleep.

He twined a long lock of her hair round his fingers and twisted his neck at an awkward angle to kiss her cheek. She stirred, murmuring his name, then settled again, snuggling against him.

Suddenly, the lightning flashed again, and a massive peal of thunder roared, almost overhead, and she started up with a sharp gasp of shock.

'Whatever was that?' she cried.

'The storm's arrived,' Aylwin replied prosaically, waiting a little apprehensively for her to realize that she was in bed with him.

'It sounded like the crack of Doom!' she exclaimed. 'Did it start without any warning?'

'I don't know. There was a flash of lightning a few moments ago, which woke me, but it might have been coming for some time before that. Are you afraid of thunder?'

'Not really. I don't like it, but mostly because it makes my head feel prickly. Does it worry you?'

'Not personally, but for my beloved buildings,' he replied wryly. 'I'm always afraid one of them will be struck and damaged. In any town or village, the church is usually the highest building, so the one most likely to be . . .'

He failed to finish the sentence, for a blinding streak of lightning lanced down across the window, the thunder cracking simultaneously with a force which shook the house, and there was a smell which he recognized only too well.

'The minster's struck!' he exclaimed, extricating himself from under Elys and tumbling out of bed to run to the window and lean out, staring anxiously across to the church. For a moment he could see nothing amiss, and then, suddenly, there was a glow above the west end of the nave, and he heard shouting. The only word he could distinguish was 'Fire!'

Elys came to his side to peer out, half hiding behind him, for she was as naked as he, and thought someone might see her from the street if they happened to look up. 'Something's burning,' she said.

'The church. Listen, dear love – I shall have to go over there. If the fire spreads to the scaffolds and the centering, it would bring down all the new work, and perhaps burn the whole building.'

'Yes,' said Elys calmly. 'Of course.'

'You understand?'

'Yes, I understand. Be careful, and come back soon.' She stretched on tiptoe to kiss him, and he held her close for a few moments, feeling her body pressed hard against him, as he kissed her, long and thoroughly, then tore himself away to scramble into whatever clothes he could lay hands on in the darkness. Every fibre of his body was remembering the earlier part of the night, his tentative approach, their gentle love-making, the towering delight they had shared, and it was all he could do to make himself leave her and go out to do his duty by the work of his fellow-masons and the house of God in this town.

The rain came as he was running down the churchyard path, descending in a downpour which soaked him to the skin before he reached the west end of the building, where the masons had already formed a bucket-chain to get water from the millstream. He scrambled past them and in through the temporary porch, which some of the apprentices were hastily dismantling by the poor light of half a dozen lanterns.

He found the scaffolding which surrounded the top of the newest-built pillar on the north side was burning briskly,

289

and Master William was up on it, hacking at the smouldering wood to get it down before the centering of the half-built arch and the putlogs supporting the scaffold could burn through and bring down the voussoirs already in place.

It was the custom, because of the difficulties of finding large numbers of straight stout poles, for the scaffolding to consist only of a skeleton supporting a working platform of woven hurdles, and it rose with the building, so that, once it reached any height, the only access was by means of ladders for the men and a hoist for their materials. The rope of the hoist had already burned away, and the hurdles were in flames, so William was balanced on the putlogs, and one of the two ladders was occupied, one above the other, by the last three men in the bucket-chain.

The leather buckets were passing along full with well-drilled precision, for this was far from the first time the men had put out a fire in a half-built church. The top man on the ladder, William's lieutenant, Anlaf, was flinging bucketful after bucketful over the fire and William in rapid succession, dropping the empties to a man waiting on the ground, who passed them back down the line to be refilled.

Aylwin took in the situation in one quick glance, grabbed a sharp knife from the belt of one of the men in the chain, and ran up the other ladder, to begin sawing at the leather straps which held the poles together.

'On your wedding night!' exclaimed Master William, sparing him a glance. 'That one there, as quick as you can, or we'll have the arch down before this night's over.'

Aylwin moved up another couple of rungs and sawed at the strap which William had indicated, glancing to see how near the flames were to wood of the centering, and did not realize that he could see a great deal more than might have been expected in the dark church, even with the flames licking at the putlogs. There seemed a chance that, if either the water put out the flames, or the poles on the side nearest the arch could be brought down, they might be in time. William, having freed and flung down the last of the hurdles, turned his knife on the strapping holding a pole to a putlog, and both men sawed like demons, hardly aware of the water which cascaded over them every few moments.

Aylwin's strap parted first, and William's a second after. Two poles fell away, still smouldering, and crashed to the ground, scattering the bucket chain as they jumped clear, then sprang back into line. Aylwin's ladder lurched and slid towards the other, but Anlaf kicked it until it lodged safely against the carved capital of the pillar.

Within minutes, the remaining two poles which were beginning to burn on that side were cut loose, but one of them, instead of falling, slipped and caught on the centering. Master William, with a great heave of his powerful arms, got himself onto the top of the capital and climbed on the centering to push it free. It stuck, and he flung himself on it, pulling it clear, until it fell to the ground, twenty feet below, taking William with it.

For a moment, everyone was still, struck with horror. It was Aylwin who moved first, bidding Anlaf douse the end of the centering where it rested on the putlogs above the scaffolding which had been burning, for he could not see how it was possible that the scaffold had been on fire without the timbers above it also burning. Then as the bucket-chain jerked into motion again, he slid down the ladder and fell to his knees beside William's still figure, pulling and pushing the smouldering wood away from him before his clothing could catch light.

'Don't try to move him!' exclaimed Father Radulf, appearing on the other side of the unconscious man. 'Bring those lights nearer, boys. Let me see what's happened.'

It was only as half a dozen of the older boys from the school closed in, carrying two horn lanterns apiece with a good candle in each, that Aylwin realized why he had been able to see what was happening so well. It seemed that the candlesticks had been brought from all the chapel altars and ranged across the nave a few yard to the east, and all their candles were alight, and supplemented by more lanterns, some held by canons or boys, and others standing on the floor.

'We brought every light we could find,' said Father Warmand. 'It's Master William. Is he much hurt?'

'God forbid,' replied Radulf, gently moving his hands over the mason's sprawled limbs. 'The left arm is broken

– both bones – but the flesh isn't pierced. That ankle is fractured too. There's a contusion on his head – I should imagine the pole hit him as it bounced. Ah – he's moving.'

Master William groaned and stirred, then opened his eyes and gazed vaguely at the lights around him and the shadowy forms behind them.

'Be this Purgatory or Hell?' he asked anxiously.

'Neither, good friend, and you're not likely to go to either for a long time yet,' Father Radulf replied soothingly. 'You fell, and you've damaged an arm and a foot and hit your head. Now, try carefully – can you move your arms and legs?'

William tentatively moved his limbs, one by one, giving a gasp of pain when his left ankle jerked, and another when he tried to lift the arm on the same side.

'I ache like a load of stone fell on me,' he exclaimed.

'It's more that a load of you fell on the stones,' Radulf said with unexpected humour. 'I hope you've not cracked any of them. Let me help you to sit up . . . Careful, now!'

William sat up, shook his head, winced, took a dozen deep breaths, then said thankfully, 'No ribs stove in, St Barbara be thanked!'

'Good. Now, lie down again, and let me see to that arm, before the bones shift.' Radulf delved in a large basket beside him and brought out two pieces of smooth, flat wood and several rolls of bandage. He gently straightened the broken arm, the lower part of which was out of shape, and felt the area of the break.

'If the broken ends can be brought into alignment, it should mend well, but I'll need help to realign them . . .' he said. 'Master Aylwin – you have strong arms – come round this side of him.'

Aylwin crawled round to William's left side, and, following Radulf's instructions, took hold of the mason's wrist, while the Infirmarian pinned his upper arm to the ground.

'Pull when I say,' said Radulf. 'Don't jerk, and let the pulling be along the proper line of the arm. Ready? Now!'

Aylwin pulled. William gave a strangled gasp and, to everyone's relief, fainted. His forearm grated, then suddenly straightened, and Radulf exclaimed, 'Hold it so.'

292

He swiftly clapped the splints on either side of the arm and wound bandages round it at lightning speed, then sat back on his heels and looked up at the other masons, who had finished their firefighting and gathered round at a distance to watch anxiously. 'Have you one of those useful stone-carriers anywhere to hand?' he asked. 'I must get him to the infirmary to strap that arm properly.'

Anlaf promptly detailed two men to fetch a stretcher from the lodge, and two others to help them carry William on it, then, seeing that the others would be better occupied doing something useful, set them to clearing up the broken and charred remains of the scaffolding. The stretcher quickly arrived, and William was carried off on it, conscious again by now, and directing the men carrying him to remember he was not a block of Caen or ragstone.

Aylwin got to his feet, suddenly aware of his wet clothes and a scorched wrist, but before he could make any move, Father Brian asked, 'How did it happen? Was it the lightning?'

Now he had time to think, Aylwin was puzzled. 'I'm sure it was,' he said, 'for I felt it strike, and smelled the – there's an odd smell when lightning strikes that catches the back of your nose . . . It's odd, though, that it was here, and not the tower, and stranger still that the scaffolding fired, but not the roof-timbers or the centering above it . . . I'll go up and have a look. May I borrow a lantern?'

One of the apprentices stood before him at once, with a larger lantern than the others, and with glass panes instead of horn. 'This is the best one,' he said confidingly. 'Shall I run and tell Lady Elys that the fire's out and you're safe?'

'That would be a kindness. Thank you,' Aylwin replied gravely. As the boy ran off, he climbed the ladder again, put the lantern on the top of the capital and heaved himself up after it, and carefully inspected the upper side of the centering. Its timbers were well-seasoned oak, and had obviously centered many arches in their time, for they were chipped and scarred and daubed with mortar, and the joints were held by pegs which could be removed without difficulty when an arch was completed and set. There was a little scorching visible, but nothing more.

Above his head, a temporary light roofing sloped down from the higher roof of the older part of the building, to shelter work and workers from the weather. It appeared undamaged, apart from a hole with charred edges immediately above the centre of the pillar he was standing on, and, as he lifted the lantern to shed light on it, he realized what had happened, and why.

Three long iron tie-rods protruded from the centre of the capital, sticking straight up through the wattle roof above. The lightning had struck them, burning a hole in the roof, which was of green wattle, and running down to set fire to the hurdles resting on the top of the capital, and the flames had spread from them to the lower hurdles and thence to the poles supporting them.

'Have you solved the mystery?' Father Brian asked from below.

'Yes. The tie-rods project above the roofing. Lightning flies to iron or copper in preference to stone. It was indeed the lightning, and not anyone's carelessness.' He climbed down, using the strength of his arms to lower himself carefully over the overhang of the capital.

'The Lord be thanked for that, and for the masons who were keeping watch in expectation of the storm,' said Father Brian. 'If everyone had been sleeping, the whole church might have been aflame before anyone realized. We were about to start Mattins when they raised the alarm, and we must add a heartfelt thanksgiving to our belated office. Do you go back to your bride, my son, with my blessing and deep thanks.'

Aylwin cast a professional eye over the area affected by the fire, and found that all the wreckage had been cleared and the water swept away, washing the floor in the process. The masons were standing about, waiting, apparently, for his orders, although he had no authority over them, for they all belonged to Master William's lodge.

'There's no more to be done tonight,' he said. 'I suggest we assemble here an hour later than usual in the morning, as we've all had a disturbed night, and then we can see by daylight if there's any damage to be repaired.'

With that, he bade them all goodnight, and left the

church, hearing them all troop out behind him as the canons began to sing their office. Someone made a comment about a 'disturbed night' which made the others laugh, and it was only then that he realized that a double meaning might be read into the phrase as it applied to him.

As he passed through the lower bedchamber, Crispin stirred, sat up, and asked quietly, 'What's wrong? Have you been out?'

Marvelling that the two brothers had apparently slept through the storm, Aylwin replied, 'The minster was struck by lightning, and there was a small fire. All's well now.'

Crispin settled down again, satisfied, and Aylwin ran lightly up the stairs, to find Elys, lovely in the dim candle-light, wrapped in a cloak and sitting on the edge of the bed, waiting for him.

'Oh, thank God!' she exclaimed quietly. 'I was worried.'

'Didn't that young scamp come to tell you everything was all right?'

'Yes. He came and hissed under the window to get my attention. He said Master William was hurt, but you were well and the fire out. Is he hurt badly?'

'A broken arm and ankle, but he's in good hands. I'm soaked to the skin. I'd best get out of these wet clothes.'

He stripped and towelled himself briskly, shivering in the coolness of the night air after the sultry heat which had presaged the storm, then thankfully slid into bed, where Elys took him in her arms to warm him with her own body. He held her close, and began to caress and kiss her.

'You must be tired. Don't you want to sleep?' she whispered.

'In a moment,' he replied, the response of her body banishing any fear that she might be trying to avoid more love-making, and the first birds were tuning up for the dawn chorus when he did eventually fall into a deep sleep.

Elys was still with him when he woke, although it was now full daylight. She kissed him in greeting, and he exclaimed, 'I forgot to give you my mother's gift.'

'A gift? Has she sent me something? How kind of her!'

He slid out of bed, and fetched the carefully-wrapped little parcel from his clothes-chest, watched her face as she unwrapped it, and was satisfied by her expression of pleasure as she looked at the delicate carving.

'It's beautiful!' she said. 'Is it ivory? I once saw a bishop's crozier with a carved head which was like this.'

'In Winchester?'

'Yes.'

'It was made there. It's a local craft, the carving of ivory. I've not seen it done so well anywhere else.'

Holding it carefully, Elys got out of bed and crossed to the opposite wall, where a shelf held her few treasures, and set it in the middle, where she would be able to see it as she lay in bed, then turned back to face him, betraying a little nervous shyness at her own nakedness, but not attempting to cover herself as he looked at her.

'How beautiful you are,' he said, his admiration almost as much that of a sculptor as a lover. 'And here's another gift for you – your morning-gift. Or is that another custom you don't know about?' he added with a half-teasing grin.

'Yes, I've heard of that,' she replied. 'A husband gives it to his bride after their first night together if he's pleased with her.'

'As I am with you,' he said, going to her to slip a heavy gold chain over her head and kiss her. The chain hung down between her breasts, and she looked at it in amazement, for each link was a small animal gripping its own tail in its mouth through the circles formed by its neighbours on either side.

'What a magnificent thing!' she exclaimed. 'Oh, Aylwin, it must be worth a fortune.'

'It's very old, I think. It was given to my grandfather by King Edward. If he was a saint, as most people think, it's almost a relic.'

Elys, speechless, looked up into his face, and her eyes suddenly filled with tears. 'Oh, Aylwin, how good you are to me,' she managed to say after several false starts, and went into his arms again in so natural and spontaneous a way that his heart sang within him, and it was several moments before he realized that his love was crying.

'What is it, sweetheart?'

'Just foolishness,' she sobbed. 'It was so kind of your

mother . . . I did so wish that my own mother might have come to see me wed. We've never been very close, but she was – is – my mother, and I missed her so much.'

'Did she sent you no message?' Aylwin asked, deeply concerned. 'You did let her know we were to be married?'

'Oh yes! I wrote to her, and the Mother Prioress sent a reply, but it only said that Sister Benedict – that's Mother – and Sister Helen would remember me and my husband in their prayers. If only she could have come.'

Aylwin though privately that either Lady Mabilia or the Prioress had been lacking in Christian charity in not arranging for his bride to have the comfort of her mother's presence at her wedding, but he kept his thoughts to himself and soothed her as best he could without voicing any criticism. It took a little while to dry her tears, but she seemed to find comfort in the thought that his mother was ready to accept her as a daughter.

As if echoing his thought, she suddenly said, 'You've never spoken of your family. I know your mother lives in Winchester, but does she live alone? Have you no brothers or sisters?'

'I've two brothers, both masons. Godwin, the next to me, has been working on Chichester cathedral these past six years, and Harold, the youngest, is a journeyman in Durham. He hopes to pass master in a year or so. My sister Maud is married to a master carver in Nottingham. He was a Winchester man, but he decided to go to Nottingham to work alabaster instead of ivory.'

'Will they mind you marrying a Norman?'

'They'll have the sense to judge you by what they find in you, not by your birth.'

A discreet call up the stairs from Crispin set them both scurrying about to get dressed and down to break their fast, and Aylwin managed to arrive in the church not much after the masons, who had brought new scaffold poles, straps and hurdles with them and were setting them up under Anlaf's supervision. He turned as Aylwin joined him, bade him good morning, and said, 'I came back as soon as it were light and looked over the stonework. The top of the pillar and the capital are a bit stained, but a good scrub'll get them clean, I think. The centering's a mite charred on this side, but I tested it with a knife, and it's nowhere above a finger-breadth deep, so there'll be no need to replace it, St Barbara be thanked! I once had to help take down a half-built arch, and it weren't no easy task. We can scrape off the char later, when the arch is finished. Will you be goin' to see Master William?'

'Yes, if Father Radulf permits.'

'Oh, he don't mind. The Master sent for me an hour agone, and we're havin' a lodge-meetin' this evenin' after work. Meanwhile, we'll carry on, if you're agreeable. The others're workin' stone on the bencher, or mixin' mortar.'

'Good. No need to hold up the work – that would only worry Master William,' Aylwin replied. 'I'll go see him now.'

He found the mason propped up on a bed in the infirmary, with a basket-work cradle over his injured ankle and his splinted arm in a sling. He seemed to be in pain, judging by the way he constantly shifted in a cautious manner, but replied to Aylwin's enquiry with a shrug which made him wince, and said, 'I'll do well enough, but Father Radulf says I must keep off the foot for six weeks or so. I've told the men to choose someone meanwhile. Can't let the work fall behind.'

'If there's anything I can do . . .' Aylwin said hesitantly. He would have liked to offer to take over temporarily, but did not wish to appear to be pushing in, for a lodge of masons was a close-knit group which did not welcome outside interference.

'There'll be plenty,' William replied, grinning. 'Anlaf's a good fellow, but only eight years passed master, and he'll need help and guidance. He's got the sense to know it, though, and he won't be shy of askin'.' He gave a grunt of laughter, and added, 'This'll be the first holiday I've had in years. Father Radulf says I can read some of the books in the college library. They've got a treatise on architecture that they've borrowed from Canterbury for copyin'. It's by some old Roman – Vitruvial, or some such name . . . Thank the Lord I learned Latin! I'm lookin' forward to it.'

Aylwin, who had come across a copy of Vitruvius in Italy, said, 'You'll enjoy that.'

The result of the lodge meeting was conveyed to Aylwin after supper that night by a deputation consisting of Anlaf, three other senior masons and the master carpenter, who said that they had unanimously decided to ask him to take charge of the work during Master William's incapacity, as Anlaf felt that he lacked the experience. Aylwin offered a compromise, not wishing Anlaf to feel in any way discouraged, and said that he was willing to advise and help in any way he could, but that Anlaf should give the men their instructions. The look of relief and pleasure which transformed Anlaf's rather anxious and gloomy face told him he had said the right thing, and the two men shook hands on the arrangement.

For a few days, Aylwin divided his working day between his own bencher and the general oversight of the completion of the half-finished arch, and the beginning of its partner in the south arcade, where Anlaf admitted to some uncertainty about the vital erection of the centering. Father Brian found Aylwin overseeing the settlement of the heavy framework as it was carefully lowered by means of a pair of sheerlegs with ropes and tackles. He waited until it was securely in place and the hooks removed before he asked Aylwin if he could spare him a few minutes.

'We've had an answer from de Mandeville,' he said as they moved up the nave, away from the workmen. Aylwin noted that he used the Earl's name, not his title, and was not surprised when he continued, 'He refuses to pay any compensation for all the damage he did to the property of Holy Church. Claims it was an accident.'

'What will you do?'

'What can we do? He's already excommunicate. We held chapter this morning to discuss it, and we've decided that we'll take down the Holy Cross, and tell everyone who comes here – all the pilgrims – that's it's because of his gross injuries against the lives and property of our people. It may shame him when he hears of it.'

Aylwin had been aware, all the time he was in Waltham, that a steady trickle of pilgrims came each day to enter the church by the south door and pray before the Holy Cross, and that many of them had come long distances in search of healing or the granting of some long-held wish, and he thought it would certainly spread word of the Earl's recalcitrance through the length of the land, but whether it would have any effect on that headstrong, violent man was another matter.

'You'll need our help to take it down,' he said, confining himself to practicalities, not opinions. 'It must be done carefully, for fear of damage.'

Father Brian was grateful that help had been offered before he asked, and the work was done the following day, by the same means whereby the centering had been raised and settled on its putlogs. The Cross was fastened to the ropes, then unhooked from the chains which supported it, and lowered with great care on to a bed of blankets spread on the paving below. Everyone who could find an excuse to enter the crossing took the opportunity to look more closely than they had ever been able to do before, and found that the Figure was most beautifully carved in a glossy dark stone, which Aylwin thought was some variety of marble, and the workmanship reminded him of antique statues he had seen in Rome, making him wonder about the age of the Figure, although he said nothing to anyone about his speculations.

The Cross itself was, as tradition held, made of wood, and covered with a thick crusting of silver, which was so heavily tarnished that it was quite black, so the canons had summoned Robert Goldsmith from St Albans to examine the precious metals and jewels which adorned the Figure and the Cross. He proposed to clean the silver with a concoction of his own devising, which he said he habitually used to clean small articles of jewellery with considerable success.

Aylwin happened to be in the church very early on the morning the cleaning began, for he had to carry out a task traditionally reserved for the master-mason in charge of a particular building operation – that of placing the keystone in the crown of an arch. Having a little time in hand while the mortar was being mixed and the stone brought from the lodge, he went to see what was happening in the crossing. He found Robert there, with his two assistants, Father

Warmand and Father Antony, as sacristan and church-keeper, to supervise and assist, Alvin Bisemare the carpenter, who was to see that nothing was done which might harm the wood of the Cross, and Father Edmund, one of the junior canons, who had come either to help or out of curiosity.

Robert had a large collection of pieces of soft cloth and a great stone bottle of his concoction, which he explained must be applied fairly thickly on a small area at a time, left for a few seconds, and then lightly rubbed off, bringing the dirt and tarnish with it.

'Try not to get it on your hands,' he said. 'It may make them itch and be sore.'

'Will it work?' asked Father Warmand dubiously. He had always favoured a good wash in warm soapy water and a gentle rub with old linen for cleaning the altar silver, and distrusted the new invention.

'It's always worked extremely well on small items of silver-work,' Robert replied a shade huffily. 'Even the most intricate pieces. It's a matter of patience, and of being sure to get into all the crevices.'

He rotated his large bottle smartly to shake up the contents, then removed the wooden stopper and poured the liquid into the pottery bowls which had been provided, one for each cleaner. Aylwin, leaning over to see what the liquid looked like, blinked and wrinkled his nose, for it made his eyes water and gave off unpleasant fumes. He went back to his own work, feeling that the proposed cleaning was a doubtful undertaking, and hoping it would not harm the ancient silver.

The raising, lowering and tapping into place of the keystone occupied his full attention for some time, for it was vital that the stone should exert exactly the right amount of pressure on the other voussoirs to hold the arch together. If it was too loose, the arch would collapse under the weight to be placed above it. If it was too tight, the additional stress would buckle the arch, or cause problems with the area of wall between it and its neighbour.

Master William's men were well-trained and prided themselves that their ashlar fitted together so well that the joins could hardly be seen and needed a minimal amount of mortar, so the operation went well. Aylwin tapped the keystone home with a feeling that it was exerting exactly the right amount of stress, and descended from the scaffold above the arch to watch as the other masons began work on the wall above the arch.

'Master Aylwin!' a voice exclaimed from somewhere below his shoulder-level, and an urgent hand tugged his sleeve. It was the small thurifer Elys was so friendly with.

'What is it?'

'There's something amiss – come and see.'

The boy was pointing towards the crossing, where the silver-cleaners were at work out of Aylwin's sight, the parish altar being in the way.

Aylwin, hearing the note of urgency in the boy's voice, strode quickly up the nave, the boy trotting beside him.

'They can't be *drunk*,' he said, 'not in *church*, but they're falling about as if they are.'

In fact, six of the men about the Cross were no longer falling about, but were quite unconscious, and the seventh, Robert himself, collapsed in a heap across the feet of the Figure as Aylwin arrived.

'It's that cleaning mixture!' he exclaimed. 'Fetch Father Radulf, quickly! Anlaf!' In this emergency, he raised his voice well above the customary hushed tones suitable to his surroundings, and shouted, 'Bring buckets of water – a dozen – quickly,' as he pushed the wooden stopper back into the neck of the bottle.

He pulled the skirt of his tunic up and clamped the thick woollen fabric over his nose and mouth with one hand while he dragged the unconscious men well clear of the Cross with the other. The liquid was giving off very heavy fumes, making his eyes smart painfully, and he could feel it, even through the cloth, catching at his throat and nasal passages.

Anlaf and three other men hastened up with filled buckets, and stopped aghast at the sight which met their eyes as they rounded the parish altar. Aylwin grabbed a bucket, prayed briefly that he was not about to make matters worse, and threw its contents over the Cross. Nothing exploded, and the silver looked appreciably cleaner where the water

302

rinsed off the partially dried fluid, so he emptied the other buckets over it in brisk succession.

Father Radulf arrived at a fast sprint, his long robe hitched up to his knees with both hands, the thurifer galloping behind him with his expression a mixture of frightened concern and pleased expectancy, which Aylwin, at any other time, would have been anxious to record in one of his notebooks. Several of the masons' stone-carriers were pressed into service to carry the unconscious men to the infirmary, and more water was brought to douse the Cross and the floor around it, while the little thurifer trotted round opening every door to the exterior which the minster possessed.

The Cross, once well-rinsed, was carefully wiped dry with clean cloths and carried into the south transept, and the floor was scrubbed and mopped dry. The blankets on which the Cross had rested, now soaked and, significantly, dropping into holes, were bundled up and stuffed into an old grainsack. The stone bottle was carted outside by two men with cloth over their noses and mouths, who poured its contents into the bottom of a grave which the sexton had just finished digging, then emptied the bowls after it, dropped in bottle, bowls and the sack of blankets, and finished off with another dozen buckets of water. The sexton complained bitterly that the intended occupant of the grave would sink straight down to Hell in all that mud, and the sack of blankets would be in the way of the body, and stumped off in disgust to dig a fresh grave elsewhere, so the two masons filled in the one they had used, and stamped the earth down with the air of men who had just disposed of something particularly evil.

The unconscious men came round quite soon once they were away from the fumes, but they were all quite blind, their eyelids grossly swollen, with eyes that could not be opened. It was not until Vespers were being sung that the swelling subsided and they began to regain their sight.

The canons and the townsfolk took the whole incident to be a miraculous sign that Our Lord, for some unfathomable reason, did not wish the symbol of His Passion to be cleaned, and the attempt was abandoned, the jewels and gold carefully replaced, once it was certain that the gems were all secure in their settings, and the Cross lay there, gleaming softly in the candlelight and guarded by reliable men, two at a time, for a few days. Then, to everyone's amazement, one of Lord Gilbert's men brought the news that on the very day that the Cross had been taken down, Geoffrey de Mandeville had been struck in the neck by an arrow while he was besieging the castle at Burwell, and it was not expected that he would recover.

The canons were shaken by what appeared to be the result of their action, and charitably prayed for the Earl's soul, although not with any hope of redemption for him, as his excommunication condemned him to hellfire. Under Aylwin's supervision, the Cross was raised again and rehung on new chains, the opportunity having been taken by Henry Plumber, the town blacksmith, to forge them as a thank-offering for his son's recovery from injuries he had sustained during the burning of the town.

De Mandeville died a few weeks later, on St Cyprian's day, a slow and painful death, without any sign of contrition for his many sins. His body was enclosed in lead and taken by his son to the Temple at Holborn, as he had been a member of the lay fraternity of that Order, but even the Templars, as the dead man had not repented and was still excommunicate, refused him interment, and his body was left lying outside their church while his son sought to have the ban lifted.

Meanwhile, Aylwin and Elys were settling down to married life, adjusting to one another with surprisingly little difficulty. They found themselves well-matched as lovers, both seeming to feel the need for the other at the same time, and their love-making never failed to delight and satisfy them both. Aylwin had no doubt that his wife was happy, for she had acquired a new air of serene confidence which pervaded everything she did, and had completely lost the diffident manner which had made her seem younger than her years.

His own work prospered from his happiness and the cessation of his earlier anxieties. The pony's head was finished, and the prominent teeth of the model took on the appearance of a cheerful grin in the stone portrait. Aylwin cut his mark behind the larger ear with a feeling of satisfaction which he had seldom experienced before on finishing a piece of work, and the head, liberally anointed with oil, took its place in the corbel-table between the two lions carved by the apprentices, which snarled protectively on either side of it.

He had selected the block for the next corbel, and was sitting at his bencher, leafing through a notebook and trying to decide what he would carve next – a coney, Apuleius, a ferret or a hind – when Father Brian came in, looking anxious and holding an opened letter in his hand, with an imposing seal dangling from it. 'From Bishop Henry,' he exclaimed. 'Now I don't know what to do!'

CHAPTER SEVENTEEN

'What's amiss, then?' asked Aylwin, concerned to see the normally serene canon looking quite agitated.

'Bishop Henry's going overseas.'

'In the middle of a civil war?' Aylwin exclaimed, startled, for he had always felt that Henry of Blois was the real ruler of England, whether his brother Stephen or the Empress was in the ascendant, and that only he would ever manage to find a solution to the conflicting claims of the two rivals.

'He says all's quiet at present, and likely to remain so for the foreseeable future. He's going to Rome, because his appointment as Papal Legate expired when Pope Innocent died last year, and Pope Celestine refused to renew it – he was a great admirer of Bernard of Clairvaux, and you know his opinion of our Dean. Pope Celestine died in March, and it appears that the Bishop hopes that the new Holy Father, Lucius, will be more sympathetic. Unfortunately, he has a major problem on his hands with the King of Sicily, so Bishop Henry is going to see him, hoping the personal approach will regain him his legateship. I read this between the lines, you understand, but that's easy enough to do.'

'And when does he propose to leave England?'

'At the octave of All Saints, he says. It seems remarkably late in the year to set off on such a journey: how can he hope to cross the mountains in the midst of winter?'

Aylwin smiled. 'Don't forget that he'll not be a solitary traveller, but a bishop, an abbot, a dean and the brother of a king. He'll have a great train of attendants and will move very slowly, making any number of courtesy calls and visits on the way, not least to those who might be persuaded to – er – distract the Empress's husband from sending her assistance. I doubt if he'll reach the mountains until the spring thaw's past. But you said you don't know what to do?'

'About asking for more money. I did ask if you'd be willing to go to him and explain the problem to him, but now that Master William's laid aside, and you're in charge of the work . . .'

'William will be up and about early in October, according to Father Radulf. Allow him a week to work himself in again with me, to make sure all goes smoothly, and I can go to Winchester before the end of the month. It will take me less than a week to get there, given the weather's not too wet, and another week to see him and for him to make arrangements about the extra money before he goes . . . I don't doubt that he'll find you the money, given that he gave his consent to your using what you had to help the poor folk burnt out of their homes.'

'I hardly feel that it's fair to ask you to go away so soon. You'll only have been married a mite over two months . . .' Father Brian said doubtfully.

'Elys will come with me. She's anxious to meet my mother.'

The autumn fair, held on the Feast of the Exaltation of the Holy Cross and the two succeeding days, was in full swing by now, and Aylwin left his work for a while that afternoon to make a few purchases. Elys had already been round the stalls that morning with Mistress Mayngod to lay in stores for the winter, glad to have another opportunity to learn a little more about the goods on sale and the buying skills necessary for a thrifty housewife, and she had remarked at dinner on a fur-lined cloak which had caught her fancy, although she had not suggested that she would think of buying it.

He had no difficulty in finding the cloak. It was displayed with some pride by the merchant who had brought it, and he told Aylwin that the fur, which was very black and glossy, had come from far away to the east, beyond Germany, and he had put it into a good Flemish woollen cloak. It was, naturally, expensive, but Aylwin enjoyed a good haggle, and succeeded in reducing the price by a third before he handed over a full month's wages for it. For himself, he bought a new saddle, his old one being quite worn out with his travels to Italy and back, and half a dozen fine Damascus steel

307

chisels, which had the sharpest edges he had ever felt on such tools.

Elys spent the afternoon wandering round the stalls, unaware that Aylwin was also out buying. She went to the cloak-seller's stall, and was sorry to see that the fur-lined cloak had gone, for she would have liked to stroke the soft fur just once more, and allow herself a brief daydream that one day she would be such a successful broiderer that she would be able to afford such a luxury. The merchant told her that a man had bought it for his wife, and she wondered which husband in the town would buy his wife such a magnificent gift, and felt a little, quickly-stifled, pang of envy.

Her own purchases were made with careful attention to quality and some brisk bargaining, for she wanted a new supertunic for Aylwin to replace the one which had been burned beyond repair when de Mandeville's men fired the houses in market end. He usually wore blue, but she chose a rich dark wine, and found braies to match, thinking the colour would suit him.

He had given her money to buy the supertunic, but she had some of her own with her for other purchases, and went to and fro amid the stalls, looking for more steel needles, which she had found to be well worth their high price, and sewing thread, some fine linen for shifts for herself and shirts and drawers for Aylwin, enjoying the busyness of the fair even more than she had the last one, for this time she had a husband for whom to buy things, and that gave her seeking for bargains more purpose.

It was a great pleasure to her to show Aylwin the clothes she had bought for him and hear his approving comments. She was speechless when he gave her the cloak and could only hug and kiss him in thanks until she had recovered a little from the surprise.

'Oh, my dear love,' she said eventually, 'but it must have cost a fortune. How warm and soft it is. I shall be so comfortable this winter. Thank you, dear Aylwin. I've nothing for you but spices and currants for your eating over the next eight months.'

'There's a reason for buying you a good cloak,' Aylwin

admitted, his expression softened by the reflection of his wife's pleasure. 'I have to go to Winchester for a visit next month, and I'd like you to come with me.'

'To Winchester? Your mother's not ill?' she asked anxiously.

'No, sweetheart. Bishop Henry's going to Rome, and I must go to him before he leaves to ask for more money for the work here, and also for instructions about what I'm to do if his absence lasts longer than my work here. I think he'll be gone for a year, at least, and maybe longer.'

'To Rome,' said Elys thoughtfully. 'I don't suppose he's been elected Pope?'

Aylwin laughed. 'No, nothing like that! They elected another unpronounceable Italian – a Bolognese, I believe!' and he explained the reasons which Father Brian had deduced for the Bishop's projected journey, delighted at her easy understanding, for he gathered from the conversation of various married friends that few women knew, understood, or even cared about the world outside their own little universe of hearth, home, children and neighbours. 'Will you come with me?'

'Of course! I like Winchester, and I'm longing to meet your mother!'

But, in the event, Elys did not go to Winchester with him. In other respects, everything went as planned, starting with the recovery of Master William.

His broken arm had mended well, and he had insisted on using it from the start, constantly clenching his hand on the handle of a chisel all day long, flexing and relaxing his muscles, however much it hurt him to begin with, and gradually extended the range of his exercises until he was lifting small blocks of stone for some time each day, carefully and rather dubiously supervised by Father Radulf.

The ankle was more of a problem. He was forbidden to put any weight on it for six weeks after his accident, but lay on his bed in the infirmary, reading Vitruvius, talking to visitors and other patients, and constantly moving his legs as if he were walking and gripping his chisel. When he was eventually allowed to get up, his legs were in surprisingly good condition. His ankle was misshapen, of course, for it had been impossible to do anything for the fracture but strap it up, keep off it, and hope for the best, but he could stand on it, and presently could walk quite well with a stick. By the second week in October, he was back at work, limping slightly, but growing more sure on his feet every day, and finding his stick very useful for pointing at things and prodding any workman who appeared to be slacking.

'I'm very grateful to you for keepin' things goin',' he told Aylwin. 'We've time now to put in the footin's for the west front afore we need cover all with earth and straw against the frost. I think that, given a good temporary roof and hoardin', we can leave all but the latest pair of arches unswathed. See what you can do to persuade the Bishop against the aisle vaults. I'll have the men work the stone for the west front all winter, tell him, and we'll have the greater part of it up next summer. I'd like some ideas for the west window. I can't quite make up my mind whether to have three equal in size, or a large centre one atween two smaller . . . Wish I dare risk one enormous one, the whole width of the nave. That'd be a sight to see! You've a better eye for a design than I, so see if you can think up a good one, or maybe there's something you've seen somewhere . . .'

Aylwin appreciated that Master William was paying him an immense compliment in virtually asking him to design a west front for what was, after all, William's building, and he promised to give the matter careful thought during the winter, while he was continuing to work on the corbels.

'So you're off to Winchester next week, then?' William said. 'Well, hurry back, won't you? We're all longin' to see what the next corbel'll be, and those two apprentices of mine want to try another one apiece. There's all the north side to be done when you've finished on the south wall, so I expect you'll give 'em a chance?'

'Of course. While I'm gone, let them draw their ideas on a sheet of parchment apiece. Tell them to try to draw from life, not just copy from one of the manuscripts in the scriptorium, though they might find some ideas there.'

That night, he told Elys as he climbed into bed beside her that they could expect to be able to start for Winchester on the next Monday.

310

'Oh,' she said a trifle flatly. 'Well. I'm sorry, dearest, but I can't come with you!'

He was silent for a moment, stunned by her statement, his mind anxiously seeking for possible reasons.

'Don't be angry,' she said pleadingly, misinterpreting his silence. 'I want to come, but, you see, I've missed my courses twice now, and I feel so queasy in the mornings . . . I've not said anything before because I wasn't sure, but dear Mistress Mayngod said today that she's sure now that it's true, for my courses should have started last week, and they didn't, so she says it's important that I don't do anything that might bring on a miscarriage . . . She particularly said I shouldn't ride on horseback . . .'

'Miscarriage?' Aylwin said blankly, hardly making it sound like a question. 'But you could only have a miscarriage if you were . . . Oh, merciful Heavens! The Four Crowned Martyrs protect us! Oh, dear Lord!'

Elys gathered from these disjointed exclamations that he was drawing the correct conclusions and finding them both surprising and extraordinary, so she encouraged him by saying, 'He or she won't be born until next spring, of course, so you'll have time to get used to the idea of being a father, but you do understand that I can't go to Winchester with you just now, don't you?'

'Father!' Aylwin exclaimed. 'Good Heavens!'

'Well, you can hardly claim to be surprised,' she pointed out, finding his stunned voice amusing and endearing. 'My dear, dearest love, we're going to have a baby.'

'Yes. I see,' Aylwin said calmly. 'A baby. Yes. You can't come to Winchester with me. Never mind. You must stay here and look after it – him – her – whatever . . . Yes. I'll tell my mother, and she'll understand, of course. She's had babies – four or five . . . Oh, Elys, perhaps I'd better not go to Winchester either . . . !'

'Of course you must!' she exclaimed. 'It's important. I'll never be the silly sort of a woman who can't let her husband get on with his work just because she's having a baby. Oh, Aylwin,' and she snuggled against him, half-laughing, half-crying out of sheer happiness and tenderness, 'you sounded so amazed.'

'I've never started a baby before, to the best of my knowledge,' he replied gravely, putting his arms round her and shifting her to a more comfortable position. 'It's a grave responsibility, my girl, and not to be laughed at. Do you want a girl or a boy?'

'Whatever God sends us. And you?'

'I don't mind. I'll be grateful for either, once it's safely here. A baby! Fancy that.' And he smiled in the darkness, savouring the joy and anticipation.

'Only the first of many, please God.'

'I don't know about "many". Three or four, perhaps, but I don't want you to be for ever breeding or feeding a horde of brats. Moderation in all things. When I come home, I must find us a house of our own. It wouldn't be fair to Matthew and Crispin to fill their house with crying babies. They don't know yet?'

'Nobody knows but Mistress Mayngod and you. I'd not tell anyone before you.'

So, in the morning, a flushed and unusually diffident Aylwin broke the news to the coming child's two celibate uncles, who were thrown into a state of amazement at their sister's cleverness and some awe at the responsibility thrust upon them by her condition, for neither knew the first thing about the requirements of a pregnant woman, and they felt that they owed it to everyone involved to take good care of their sister during Aylwin's absence. Once Elys had convinced them that this was not a crisis, but a natural process, their nervousness abated a little, and they began to be very pleased about it, and even to bask in reflected glory.

Aylwin left, albeit reluctantly, on Monday, as he had planned, and travelled as far as London with a party of home-going pilgrims, although the death of Geoffrey de Mandeville and the disbandment of his private army by his son had removed the main threat to travellers in this part of England. He left the pilgrims at Bishopsgate, and went to Holborn to call on Sir Richard in the hope of being offered a night's lodging.

The Seneschal seemed not displeased to see him, expressed restrained pleasure at his news, offered him a bed in the lay-brothers' dormitory, then picked his brains for an hour or so on such matters as the necessary depth of foundations on marshy ground, the best type of stone to use for decorative interior effects and the comparative merits of thatch or wooden shingles for roofing. Aylwin gave his expert advice good-humouredly, and enquired with real interest about the progress of the new Temple down by the river, which reminded Sir Richard of another batch of questions and problems.

Once they had all been dealt with, he asked belatedly about his nephews and niece, and said sagely that he supposed Elys's condition barred her from accompanying him to Winchester, conveying that he knew something about the matter, which he did not. He added, 'I suppose you'll bring the boy up in your mystery, but if he shows signs of interest in soldiering, particularly if he would like to join the Order, I'll sponsor him, if I'm spared. I'll stand godfather, of course. It'll be of use to him in the future to have a godfather with some standing in the world.'

Aylwin now knew the Templar well enough to realize that no insult was intended to himself or his mystery, and thanked him in as plain and blunt a manner as that in which the offer had been made, and was then dismissed to his bed by Sir Richard, who had no further questions or remarks to offer.

The road from London to Winchester was well-travelled, and Aylwin was able to join a party of merchants on their way down to the old capital, making the journey in good time and with no problems, the weather remaining dry and warm for the time of year. He went first to his mother's shop and house, which was one of the buildings which had survived the fires and ruin of the siege three years before. It was just inside the north wall, near the Hyde gate and the road to the Newminster. He was warmly welcomed by his mother, in the intervals of her attendance on would-be purchasers of the small wood and ivory carvings which she sold.

When the shop was shut and she could give him all her attention, she hugged him tightly, exclaiming, 'How good it is to see you so well, my dear. And a married man now!

Where's my new daughter? Haven't you brought her with you?'

'She's expecting a baby, and the midwife thought it safer for her not to risk the journey in the early weeks.'

'A baby! But of course she must take care. You should never have thought of bringing her in that condition. Jolting on horseback all those miles with the child not yet properly settled in her. You should have more sense, Aylwin.'

'I did,' he replied mildly. 'As soon as she told me, I said she must stay in Waltham. I'm not a complete fool, Mother.'

'I never thought you were,' she replied, kissing him again. 'Tell me all about her.'

Aylwin was only too pleased to do so, showing her a whole notebook of drawings of her daughter-in-law so that she might at least have some idea of her beauty and perfection.

'She's quite pretty, don't you think?' he asked anxiously.

'Pretty – no, she's not pretty, you great booby, she's beautiful! Oh, but a Norman . . . I never thought a son of mine would wed a Norman, but it's all for the best . . . If more Normans and English wed, one day we'll be one people again, instead of divided . . . We managed it with the Danes, so why not with the Normans?'

Aylwin picked her up in order to kiss her more comfortably, for the top of her head-rail barely reached his shoulder.

It was more than four years since he had last seen her, but she seemed unchanged. A little greyer, perhaps, but still slim and spry and in possession of all her own teeth, despite being past her half-century. She was sorry that Elys had been unable to come, for she longed to meet her daughter-in-law, but she praised her good sense in deciding not to travel at this time, and was delighted with the beautifully embroidered bands which Elys had sent as a gift, saying that she had a length of cloth which was just the right colour for a gown on which to stitch them.

'How are you, Mother?' Aylwin asked. 'You didn't answer when I asked you before.'

'I'm very well, so there seemed to be more important things to say,' she replied. 'Trade has improved amazingly this last year, with the rebuilding bringing people back into the city. What of you? You said you'd broken your collarbone when you wrote to me. Is it healed? Does it hamper your work?'

'It did for a few weeks, but it's quite better now. Have you heard anything lately from the rest of the family?'

'Yes, they all send word from time to time. Maud had another boy at Easter. That's three boys and only one girl so far. Her husband is doing well. He says alabaster is easier to carve than ivory, but also easily broken, so sending his carvings long distances presents problems, with the roads so bad. He sends by water whenever he can. Godwin's wife is pregnant again, and Godwin has his own lodge now.'

'And Harold?'

'Hopes to pass master at the end of the year. I think he has marriage in mind, with his landlady's daughter.'

'He's young to be settling down.' Aylwin sounded disapproving.

'Perhaps he's making up for your dilatoriness! Twenty-six, are you now, and only just wed? Tell me more about your broiderer. She must have spirit, to have stood against her family like that. You're sure she won't turn into a shrew when she's older?'

Aylwin laughed. 'She's a quiet, gentle girl, not a shrewish bone in her whole body! She'll fight for what she believes, but not for the sake of fighting. You'll like her very much, I'm sure, for she has some of your own good qualities.'

On the morning after his arrival, Aylwin walked across the city to the Bishop's residence at Wolverstone Castle to wait on his lord and patron, passing through streets of newly-rebuilt or building shops and houses, and marvelling at the recovery from the devastation and plague which the Empress's attack had brought on St Swithun's city.

The cathedral, he was relieved to see, appeared undamaged, and he entered to pray at the saint's shrine, traversing the immensely long nave and making a respectful reverence as he passed along the choir aisle to the tomb chests of some of the kings of his own people, wondering fancifully if their bones resented the presence among them of the godless William Rufus. There was the usual crowd of petitioners crowded into and around the inadequate space about St Swithun's shrine, but he wormed his way through to light a candle and give thanks for his safe journey and to pray for his wife, his son or daughter, and his work, then slipped out through the north transept to continue on his way.

Henry of Blois knew the value of ceremony, of fine robes and an imposing manner, but he received his trusted servants without these worldly trappings. He was sitting in a simple wooden chair by a charcoal brazier in a chilly stone-walled chamber, wearing the plain robe of a Cluniac monk, when Aylwin was admitted to his presence. He greeted him with a smile and a simple blessing, extending his hand for the mason to kiss his ring, a fine amethyst in a beautiful setting. He was a tall, straight-backed man with thick dark hair and a dense black beard, which he had grown when the late King Henry first appointed him Bishop of Winchester and Abbot of Glaston – rumour said, in order to make himself appear older than his mere twenty-eight years – and as yet there were no grey or white hairs visible, although he was now forty-three. He was striking rather than handsome, with large, sharp dark eyes and a strong hooked nose.

'You're welcome, Master Aylwin Cedricson,' he said gravely, indicating a stool, sufficiently large and elaborately carved to be considered a seat of honour, on the other side of the brazier, and Aylwin sat down, meeting his searching look with calm self-possession.

'How is the work at Waltham progressing? Is Master William recovered from his accident?'

'He's a little lame as yet, but Father Radulf thinks he may dispense with his walking-stick by Christmas. Two bays of the intended three are completed to the roof on both sides, and the outer walls to the junction with the west front,' Aylwin replied succinctly.

'And I suppose you are come to beg for more money, de Mandeville having refused payment for his men's wanton destruction of church property?'

'To request,' Aylwin corrected courteously but firmly.

'Request.' The Bishop acknowledged the difference with a nod. 'Was all the money used for repairing the houses?'

'Not all. About a third remained, but that's spent now, and more stone is needed for the men to work during the winter. They've enough to occupy them until Christmas, but none for the following four months, when they could shape and dress the ashlar for the towers, if they had it.'

'It shall be arranged,' said the Bishop, to Aylwin's surprise, for it would cost him a great deal more money than had been estimated when the work began. 'Tell me about the work.'

Aylwin outlined what had been done in the months since he had first gone to Waltham, producing one of his notebooks, which contained drawings of the elevations and of the corbels and the font to save a deal of explanation, and told the Bishop what had happened to it.

'You'll start work again?' asked the Bishop, after a few words of commiseration.

'Yes. I've ordered the stone from Purbeck. I'll pay for it myself.'

'You will not!' Bishop Henry exclaimed. 'The destruction was not your fault.'

There followed a detailed discussion of both what had already been done, and of what remained to do, in which the Bishop showed a good grasp of the details, for he had been the moving force behind a great deal of church building during his years in office, and took a deep interest in it.

When the topic was exhausted, he requested Aylwin to go to a table under the chamber's small and only window and pour wine for them both from the flagon waiting there into the two goblets flanking it. Aylwin carried the two cups back to the brazier, appreciatively inspecting the fine workmanship of the jewelled gold as he did so.

For a few moments, both men savoured their wine in silence, and then the Bishop said, 'You know, I assume, that I leave for Rome in a few days?'

'I had heard so,' Aylwin acknowledged, noting to himself that he had not once uttered a formal 'my lord' or 'your grace', and that the Bishop seemed neither to have expected nor required that he should. Their conversation might almost have been between two equals, despite their respective ranks and ages.

'I don't know when I shall return. If all goes well in Rome, and the situation here remains at stalemate, I shall visit Cluny. It's a long time since I was in my old *alma mater*, and a brief retreat in the peace of the cloister is much to be desired. When I do return, I hope you will have finished at Waltham. I mean to resign my office of dean there – the king my brother will appoint another worthy of the place, no doubt to Father Brian's relief, for he grows old, I fear, and I cannot give enough time to the office. I shall continue to support the building work, of course, until it's finished. My hospital of St Cross here is building now, and there will be a great deal of work for you there, and elsewhere in the diocese, as soon as you've finished at Waltham. I shall leave full instructions for you with my Chancellor, of course, in case I've not returned when you come back here. I believe you're recently married?'

'On St Lawrence's day,' Aylwin acknowledged, an involuntary smile lighting his face. 'My wife is the niece of Sir Richard de Hastings, the Seneschal of the English Templars.'

'I know him well.' From the expressionless quality of the Bishop's voice, Aylwin deduced that he had no great liking for the Templar, and that impression was confirmed when he added, 'A rigid man, more likely to break than to bend, but infinitely well-meaning.' There was the faintest sardonic edge to the last couple of words. 'No doubt you're anxious to return to your wife, but I have one small favour to ask of you before you gallop off hotfoot.'

'My lord,' Aylwin replied, acknowledging that the Bishop was 'asking' a favour as a courtesy, where he had the right to command.

'My Order has a priory at a little place in Somerset, and they say that the central tower of their church has shown signs of collapsing. Their master mason has taken it down successfully, but he's young and inexperienced. He's built small churches before, but never one with a central tower,

318

and he's requested the advice of a more experienced man before he embarks on rebuilding.'

'I'm a sculptor,' Aylwin stated as a point of fact rather than a protest.

'But experienced beyond your years in mason's work in general, and well-known among the members of your mystery. I hear many tales of your comments and opinions, which are respected for their sound judgment. I'm told that you understand stone better than any man in England.'

Aylwin's expression of astonishment was genuine. He was aware himself that he had a deep affinity with that natural, God-made substance with which he worked, but he had not realized that anyone else knew of it.

'Where is it?' he asked.

The Bishop laughed – a rare occurrence – and replied, 'Somewhere which will interest you, I think! Do you know the story of the Holy Cross of Waltham?'

Aylwin's mind went back to a convivial supper in the house in Church Street, when Lukin had told the story of how the Holy Cross was found and brought to Waltham from Somerset. He recalled that Crispin had expressed doubts about the miraculous aspects of the tale, and Edwin had vehemently insisted that they were true, for his own four-times-great-grandfather had been involved in the discovery, and had made the long journey to Waltham with the precious object.

'The place where the Cross was found?' he hazarded.

The Bishop nodded. 'It was called Lutgarsbury then, I'm told. The name was changed to Bishopston at some time in the last century, but now it's known as Montacute, for the steep hill, like Glaston Tor, which stands above the village. The very hill on which the Cross was unearthed! It was held by the Conqueror's brother, Robert of Mortain, in Domesday Book times, and he built a castle on the top of the hill. A pity, for it destroyed any traces which might have remained of the great pit that must have been there after the finding, for the Cross, I believe, was buried deep. It's very close to Ham Hill, which no doubt means something to you?'

'Ham stone!' Aylwin breathed. 'Is that what they're using?

I've seen some of it – a fine golden stone. It must be a beautiful church they're building. I shall be glad to see it.'

'As no doubt young Master Eustace will be to see you come to advise him.' Bishop Henry looked just the merest trifle smug at having turned Aylwin's reluctance to travel further from Waltham into enthusiasm to see the new priory.

'There's just one thing,' Aylwin said thoughtfully. 'Somerset . . . Is that not well within the territory controlled by the Empress?'

'Yes, but that should cause you no trouble. Ordinary folk are seldom at risk unless they stray too near to Bristol, where Earl Robert's mercenaries patrol and are said to prey on merchants and other men of apparent wealth. Pilgrims still go to Glastonbury and Wells without difficulty, and I shall give you a *laissez-passer* under my own seal. Who would dare to interfere with the Abbot of Glastonbury's own master mason, travelling on his master's business? There's been no fighting in the area for a long time, and, given you keep well clear of Bristol, you'll be perfectly safe. Your horse must be tired after your long journey, so you may leave it here, in my stables, to be cared for, and I've ordered one of my own to be put at your disposal. If it suits you, you may keep it as a small recompense for the additional travelling, besides your usual reward, of course.'

It was a handsome offer, for Bishop Henry was a good judge of horseflesh, as he was of most things. Having attained his goal, he offered Aylwin a further reward by inviting him to see the latest additions to his collection of carved gemstones, many of them antique Roman cameos. Aylwin was delighted, for he appreciated the great skill of the ancient lapidaries who had made these miniature sculptures, and they spent a happy half-hour together looking at them and discussing the fine workmanship. Then Aylwin was dismissed by means of an invitation to take his dinner in the Bishop's hall with the senior members of his household.

For a few more days, Aylwin stayed with his mother, helping her to sort out the stock of her shop, and making a couple of small wooden carvings for her to sell. He visited his old friends, and walked about the city, looking at the new buildings, and the repairs to the churches which had suffered from the ballista missiles of both sides during the siege, but he spent his evenings at home, telling his mother about his travels, his work at Waltham, and giving her a detailed account of his wedding.

He was restless, however, longing to return to Elys, worrying about her and the coming child, and anxious to make his visit to Montacute so that he could hurry home, and his mother, who understood him very well, told him before the end of the week that he should be on his way.

'It's not that I want to be rid of you,' she said, 'but I know how much you want to be with your wife, and so you should. You'll be back in Winchester for good before long, judging by what Bishop Henry told you, so be off with you in the morning, and make that time come all the quicker.'

There was time that afternoon for him to go to Wolverstone again, to see the Bishop's Chancellor, who gave him a neatly-drawn map of the route to Montacute. It showed the road as a straight line, which was far from a true picture of it, and there were little schematic drawings of a church or a monastery where such landmarks and possible lodgings were to be found, small triangles to indicate notable hills, and wriggly lines to show where the road crossed the larger rivers. There was also a slip of parchment with instructions to the Bishop's Master of Horse concerning Aylwin's own beast and the one he was to be given, a *laissez-passer*, and a purse of money for his expenses and wages. Aylwin asked that most of the latter be sent to Elys when the extra money for the minster was despatched to Waltham, together with a brief letter which he had written to her to tell her of his errand to Montacute, and assuring her that he would be home as soon as possible. He had added a final sentence in which he had tried to tell her how much he loved and missed her. It had cost him an hour's careful thought, and was still totally unsatisfactory, but he could do no better.

He also discussed with the Chancellor, who was learned in both secular and canon law, the details of the settlement he had made on Elys, and the Chancellor assured him that it was perfectly sound and within the bounds of legality.

He set out next morning in dismal grey November weather. A chill, irritating wind whiffled in his face, carrying a light but cold drizzle, and the horse, a fine black gelding, disliked it as much as its rider did, and spent the first two or three miles making determined efforts to go back to its comfortable stable, but it eventually accepted that the stranger on its back knew how to ride, and would not stand for any nonsense. After another four miles of good behaviour, it was rewarded with a brief rest and a small crunchy apple, and thereafter took a great liking to Aylwin.

What with the horse and the weather, he travelled only eleven miles that day, and spent the night at Romsey in the nuns' guesthouse, chiefly in order to see the stone crucifix which was carved on one of the walls of their church. The next night was spent at Sarum, where he wished to see the great cathedral, set on its hill, dominating the surrounding plain. A longer ride on the third day ended at Shaftesbury, where the lay-sisters made him welcome in the guesthouse, and stood round him beaming with pleasure as he did justice to their good cooking.

He stopped for dinner on the fourth day at Sherborne, and by pressing on, he reached Montacute by nightfall.

It was a small village, but many of the houses were substantial and stone-built, as was the inn at which he found a good lodging, the priory having only a small guesthouse, which was occupied by Master Eustace and his workmen. Once Aylwin had seen his horse comfortably settled and inspected the bed he had been allocated in the dormitory, he went across to the priory church, for he could see lights shining through the window-spaces, and knew that the masons must be working late.

Sure enough, a dozen men were at work in the crossing, which was shored up on all four sides, the four arches which formed it and had supported the failed tower having been taken down completely. In fact, the men were even now digging up the foundations of the pillars which had supported them. A slight, shortish man was supervising them, and, when Aylwin approached him, he admitted cautiously to being Master Eustace.

'Are you the man from the Bishop of Winchester?' he asked hopefully.

'Yes. Aylwin Cedricson, called of Winchester. How's the work going?'

The young master's eyes widened when he heard his visitor's name. He made no comment on it, however, but held up the lantern he was carrying, and pointed with his other hand as he spoke. The light fell on his face, and Aylwin saw that he was, indeed, young – not much above twenty, with a long, thin face, large dark eyes, and a permanent frown which gave him the look of an anxious greyhound.

'As you see – or, at least, as you'll be able to see by daylight – the piers all began to sink within four or five years of the tower being finished, so we've taken it down. As far as I can judge, the foundations were sufficient, but there must be some fault in the ground beneath them. I've not had charge of a tower-building before, and I'm not sure how to overcome the problem. I want the tower to stand, obviously, but, at the same time, I don't want to put the good brothers to unnecessary expense . . .'

'I'll be able to advise you better when I've seen the foundations by daylight,' Aylwin said, peering down the nearest hole. 'What have you got at the bottom there?'

'Sand.'

Aylwin grimaced. He disliked sandy subsoil as a foundation for anything more than a small pig-sty. 'There's nothing I can do tonight,' he said. 'Come and have supper with me, and I'll take a proper look in the morning.'

Master Eustace accepted the invitation with a look of surprised gratitude – presumably the food supplied by the Cluniac brothers was – monastic, and he instructed his men to stop work for the night. Aylwin noted that he watched to see that their tools were properly cleaned and stacked, and inspected the shoring of the hole in which they had been working before he let them go, and also checked that the timbers supporting the four arms of the church were not under undue strain by putting his ear to them, showing a proper attention to important details, without making a fuss. He concluded that the young man must have good reason to be anxious about rebuilding the tower, for he did not seem to be one for making much out of nothing.

Nevertheless, over supper, he asked, 'Surely there are others of Bishop Henry's masons working hereabouts? I recall hearing that he's finishing the work of his predecessor at Glaston. That can't be very far away?'

'I rode over there when I first came, having seen how the original pillars here had sunk, but the master there told me to deal with my own problems, and not trouble him with them,' Eustace replied, looking embarrassed. 'He said that, if I didn't know what to do, I shouldn't call myself a master-mason.'

'Unfriendly,' Aylwin commented, 'and wrong. Any sensible master welcomes a second opinion on a difficult problem.'

The morning dawned dry, mild and sunny, and Aylwin was up, dressed, breakfasted and out of the inn as soon as the sun rose, looking about him with pleasure at the way the Ham stone glowed in the golden light. The inn, he discovered, was overshadowed by a great conical hill, which rose up only a few yards from the back of the building, and he guessed that this must be St Michael's Hill, on which the Holy Cross had been unearthed. It was crowned now by a small castle, its stark outline given an unexpected beauty by the stone of which it was built, for the sun made it look like a golden tower in some old legend.

Master Eustace was already in the church when he entered, setting his men to work. He greeted Aylwin in a friendly but respectful manner, for he was clearly a little in awe of the Bishop's famous master sculptor.

Aylwin bade him good morning, then climbed down into the hole from which all the old foundations had already been removed, Eustace following him with a lantern. The hole was about four feet deep, and perhaps six feet square, but Eustace stood well back against the side, out of Aylwin's way, as he knelt down and picked up a handful of the sandy soil and let it trickle through his fingers.

'Have you an auger?' he asked. 'This subsoil won't take the weight of a tower – I don't wonder the piers sank.

There should be something better a little lower, with that great solid stone hill so near.'

One of the watching masons passed down an auger, and Aylwin drilled down with it for about five feet, then felt it jar against something hard. He pulled the auger out and tried again on the other side of the hole, with the same result.

'It feels solid below here,' he said. 'If it is, and the other pits give the same result, you've no worries. Take out the soil down to solid rock, and you can build the Tower of Babel here, if you can stand the noise.'

'Pray God it is the same in the other pits,' Master Eustace exclaimed, and hurried to find out by drilling down beside the foundations which were not yet removed.

The hard limestone proved to be there, and solid. In his relief, Master Eustace invited Aylwin and all his workmen to take supper at the inn with him that night, and set them to work to take out the rest of the old stonework and dig the pits down another five feet to the solid rock.

To pass the time, Aylwin spent the morning looking at the finished work, which had some good carving in its decorations, and the afternoon climbing up St Michael's Hill. He had no difficulty in gaining admission to the castle, for he showed his *laissez-passer* at the gate, and a guard was detailed to show him whatever he wanted to see. From the top of the keep, he looked out over an extensive view.

Ham Hill was there, just to the west, the quarries visible on its slopes, and northward lay a range of lower hills, with a range of higher ground on the horizon.

'Glastonbury's just over there – a day's ride,' said his guide, following the direction of his gaze. 'You can see the top of the Tor on a clear day.' Aylwin felt a stirring in his heart at the thought that the oldest, the greatest of all England's shrines was so near. A day's ride – he could not go back out of Somerset without making his pilgrimage there.

Supper that evening was a lively meal, for all the masons were greatly relieved to find that the problem which had seemed so great was, in fact, no problem at all, and they would be able to complete their work satisfactorily. Aylwin drank moderately, and had no difficulty in setting off early in the morning, towards the beckoning wonders of Glastonbury across the Polden Hills and the marshes beyond.

CHAPTER EIGHTEEN

He thought, as he rode along the meandering road, that his journey had really been a waste of time, for Master Eustace would probably have realized himself, in time, that there must be rock not too far below the surface. However, an expert opinion had set the young man's mind at ease, and he would build all the better for that.

In many ways, Aylwin almost dreaded reaching Glastonbury, for fear that he might be disappointed, but the holy place proved to be all that he had hoped. The main church had been rebuilt in what now seemed the over-heavy and old-fashioned style of a half-century before, but little of that now remained, for a new, much bigger church had almost been completed on the same site by Bishop Henry's men, finishing the work begun by his predecessor as abbot. The ancient church of St Mary to the west of it remained, an incredibly antique wattle church, now encased in strong timbers. The monks believed it to have been the first Christian church ever built in Britain, and it moved Aylwin deeply, when he knelt to pray in it, to think how many others before him must have worshipped here in the unimaginably long course of the years.

The place was hallowed by its antiquity, but even more by the last earthly resting-places of so many saints – Patrick lay here, and Bridget, Gildas, Dunstan, and many others of whom he had never heard before. There were two tall pyramids, tapering stone columns, to commemorate them, each rising to nearly five times the height of a man, with the names of all those saints carved on them in lettering so old that it was almost weathered away.

He studied the new church with interest, for Herlewin, its founder, had ordered that it be richly decorated with the stiff, unnaturalistic sculpture of the previous generation, and he could see how much his mystery had progressed in the past twenty years. He watched the masons at work in the new cloisters and on the bell-tower, but did not make himself known to them, for he was resolved to spend only one day here before hurrying home to Elys and his own work. Besides, he recollected their master's uncooperative attitude towards Master Eustace, and had no wish to meet him.

At the end of that magical day, as the early dusk was falling, he climbed the Tor and prayed for a while in the tiny chapel on its summit, then stood outside, looking across the holy site spread out below, overhung by a canopy of velvet sky and winter-bright stars, for the night was frosty. Perhaps, one day, he might be permitted to work here, to add something, even if it were only one figure, one carved capital, to this place which seemed to breathe sanctity.

In the morning, he heard Mass, and then asked the Abbey Guestmaster the best route towards London.

'Take the ridge there,' the monk said, pointing. 'Most of our pilgrims come and go by that route. It will take you to Reading, and no doubt you can find your way from there.'

'Is it safe?' Aylwin asked, wondering if he would be wiser to return by the way he had come.

'From Earl Robert's men, you mean? I've not heard of any of them stopping travellers on that road. They confine their patrols after hostages to the busier roads north of the Mendips, between Bristol and Gloucester. You'll be safe enough.'

'Should I perhaps wait for a company of pilgrims and travel with them?'

'If you wish, but I'm sure there's no need. You'll be safe alone, as you're obviously a working man, not some rich merchant or great lord. Besides, you have our Abbot's pass. Even Earl Robert will respect that.'

Convinced by the Guestmaster's certainty, Aylwin set out homewards along the ridge which ran east, between the marshes, following the instructions which the Abbey Guestmaster had given him, which would eventually take him to Reading, and so on to London. His horse stepped out willingly after its day's rest, and by noon he was well on his way in the brisk autumn weather, when he saw a small wood ahead, towards which the track seemed to lead.

It was a quiet little wood, peaceful, its birch and oak trees still carrying most of their leaves, and those already fallen carpeting the ground with a thick copper and yellow blanket. It reminded him of the Forest at Waltham, and, half-lost in a daydream of home and Elys, he emerged from it straight into the midst of a group of a dozen men-at-arms, riding in the opposite direction.

'And what have we here?' exclaimed their leader, reining in his horse. He spoke in French, but with a thick Flemish accent.

Aylwin felt an uncomfortable sensation in his stomach, guessing that these must be some of those mercenaries of Earl Robert who were said to take hostage any man they came across who looked as if he might have money, and torture him until he sent to his family for a ransom large enough to satisfy their greed, and to kill him, slowly and painfully, if it proved insufficient. He wished most devoutly that he had followed his own instinct and travelled home by way of Montacute. He could only hope that the Guest-master had been less wrong about the power of his Abbot's *laissez-passer*.

'A pilgrim returning from Glaston,' Aylwin replied equably, drawing his horse aside to the edge of the track, out of their way.

'An exceptionally well-mounted one, but travelling alone in these troublous times? A man of some quality, to judge by his dress and horse, yet unescorted? I want to know more about you, Master Pilgrim.'

'My name is Aylwin Cedricson, called of Winchester,' Aylwin replied, frowning a little, for he resented the man's mocking tone, yet had more sense than to invite trouble. 'I'm a master mason in the service of the Bishop of Winchester, travelling on my master's business, and taking the opportunity to make my pilgrimage to Glaston at the same time. And whom may you be?'

The eyes regarding him from either side of the nasal of the man's helm were shrewd and suspicious, and narrowed slightly at the reply, but their owner replied pleasantly enough, 'Jehan of Bruges, at present in the service of Earl

329

Robert of Gloucester. This road doesn't lead to Winchester.'

'I know. I'm heading for Reading, on my way to London.'

'Why?'

'About my master's business.'

'A spy, I'd say,' muttered a burly sergeant who had come up beside Jehan. 'That gelding bears Bishop Henry's brand, right enough, but I doubt the Bishop lends his horses to artisans.'

'I'm a master mason and master sculptor,' Aylwin said, drawing himself up proudly, 'no mere artisan.'

'Hmm. Touchy on the point,' Jehan observed sardonically. 'What proof do you have?'

'Leave him to me,' said the sergeant, a predatory gleam in his eye. 'I'll soon have the truth out of him.'

'Quiet!' ordered Jehan. 'I've a feeling that this one could be important, and not a victim for your iron gag and red-hot knife-blade. Come, your proof, master mason.'

Aylwin pulled his *laissez-passer* out of his purse and held it out. Jehan took it, examined the seal, but made no attempt to read it, for he was apparently illiterate. 'Bishop Henry's seal,' he said. 'Well, *Master* Aylwin of Winchester, you'll have to come with us and explain yourself to my master and the Queen. If you're a spy, they'll hang you, and if not – well – maybe you're worth a mark or two.'

'If I'm a spy, I'm a remarkably incompetent one,' Aylwin said drily, recovering his *laissez-passer* by twitching it out of Jehan's fingers, and putting safely away in his purse. 'Riding about on a horse bearing my master's brand, with a pass bearing his seal, and no attempt at concealment. I suppose you realize that you risk excommunication by ignoring a pass given under his seal?'

Jehan shrugged. 'I'm bound for Hell in any case. You'd be surprised how incompetent most spies are,' he replied, smiling like one of Edwin's ferrets. 'Pretending to be a mason, yet with no toolbag. Riding for Reading and London when the Bishop's in Winchester.' He clicked his tongue reprovingly and shook his head. 'Will you come with us in an amicable fashion, or do we have to truss you like a chicken?'

330

'I prefer to ride in comfort,' Aylwin replied in a similar, half-mocking tone. 'Where are we going?'

Jehan smiled again and shook his head, and Aylwin was left to guess their destination from the direction of their route, which was back the way he had come to the last cross-track, where they turned northwards to a small city, walled and dominated by a fine cathedral, which he thought must be Wells. From there, they pressed on, and made camp in a valley on the far side of a range of hills, which he supposed were the Mendips.

He was given food and sour ale, and his horse was hobbled and turned out to graze with the others, but no one spoke to him. When they settled for the night, Jehan, smiling again, tied one end of a length of cord round Aylwin's right wrist, and the other end round his own left wrist. 'I'll wake at once if you attempt to untie it,' he said. Aylwin felt that he would have preferred an outright threat to that smile, which made him feel like a coney being inspected by a ferret. Jehan then searched his bundle of belongings and removed his razor, having already plucked his knife from his belt. Aylwin recalled that he had another, very small knife concealed inside his belt, but, naturally, made no mention of it. The knowledge of its presence was a slight comfort to him, as was the fact that Jehan did not take anything else from his bundle, or even his purse from his belt.

He had only his cloak to wrap about him, and his saddle for a pillow, and the night was cold. For a long time, he lay awake, wondering where Earl Robert's men were taking him. All this part of the country was still under the Empress's control, or, rather, that of her half-brother, the Earl. Their headquarters was rumoured to be in Bristol, but might equally well be in Gloucester, which must be at least another four days' travel from here. He hoped devoutly that they were going to Bristol, and even more that the Bishop's *laissez-passer* would have its intended effect when someone literate and in authority read it. What if they – whoever 'they' might be – also took him for a spy? Aylwin turned his mind resolutely away from that thought, and busied himself with prayer instead – for protection, for

331

courage, for Elys, who might never know what had become of him.

'Wait and see what happens before you let yourself despair,' he told himself, and concentrated on counting the stones in an imaginary and interminable wall until he eventually fell asleep.

He was roused a little before dawn by a not entirely unfriendly boot in his ribs, and given an unpalatable but sustaining breakfast of sourdough cakes, cooked in the ashes of the campfire, and a piece of dried meat which looked and tasted like old leather, and then the party, with him in its midst, mounted and rode on, still northwards.

They reached Bristol after nightfall, but were admitted by the guard on the bridge gate after a brisk, low-voiced exchange in a mixture of Flemish and English, and clattered over a river that was black and streaked with reflected starlight. After another colloquy at the town gate, they passed under the arch and along a series of narrow cobbled streets, the shuttered windows of the houses on either side dark in obedience to the curfew, and arrived at a third guarded gate, where there was another exchange in Flemish.

Looking up, Aylwin saw a high wall silhouetted against the sky, and higher walls rising behind it, and realized that they must be entering Bristol castle, but his bridle was jerked before he could make out any more. Within the curtain wall, it was much like any other castle, with a bailey overshadowed by a keep, and various impermanent buildings ranged along the inside of the wall, visible in the light of the torches by which some of the garrison were still carrying out their duties, apparently exempt from the curfew. He was brusquely ordered to dismount.

He was hustled and elbowed, rather than pushed, up the wooden stairway to the first floor entrance to the keep, and eventually arrived, blinking in the light of the smoky torches and the deafening noise of a large part of the garrison eating supper, in the great hall. He was found a place at one of the tables between Jehan and the burly sergeant, and served with pottage, burnt roast meat, bread and ale, but no knife or spoon. He managed well enough by drinking the pottage from the bowl and using his fingers for the rest, gripping his precious bundle between his knees for fear of losing it.

Almost as soon as he had finished eating and was licking his fingers clean for lack of a napkin, he was tapped on the arm by Jehan, who, with the sergeant following behind, led him out of the hall, up a narrow spiral stair in the wall, and into a small chamber on the floor above, which was lit by good wax candles and warmed by four charcoal braziers. The stone floor was partly covered by fur rugs, one of which, of a curiously lumpy appearance, raised its head to look at him, and proved to be a sleepy deerhound.

The room was sparsely furnished with a table, at which were set two chairs with arms and backs, and a couple of stools. The chairs were occupied, one by a squarely-built, dark-haired man with a tired, careworn face, and the other by a similarly-built lady, whose face resembled that of the man, but was sullen and frowning in expression.

'Is this your supposed spy?' asked the man in French, looking at Aylwin with weary interest.

Jehan bowed and replied in rather more careful French than usual, 'We found him riding eastward from Glaston, on a horse bearing the Bishop of Winchester's brand, and carrying a letter with the Bishop's seal. He *says* he's a mason.'

'A master mason,' Aylwin corrected, sounding a great deal more calm and confident than he felt.

'A likely story,' the lady exclaimed, her voice as disagreeable as her expression; 'as if the proud Bishop would entrust one of his precious horses to an artisan.'

'With respect, my lady and sister, a master mason is rather more than a mere artisan,' the man said with a trace of irritation. 'Where is the letter?'

Aylwin produced his *laissez-passer* and took a few steps forward to hand it to Earl Robert, for he had guessed who these two were with little difficulty.

Robert of Gloucester read it – apparently, like his father, he had received some education in other matters than warfare, and then re-read it aloud for the benefit of the Empress before tossing it down on the table. As it slid more or less in Aylwin's direction, he retrieved it and put it back in his purse. Jehan started forward, as if to prevent him, but subsided again when neither of the seated figures said anything.

'What business has the Bishop in this part of the country?' asked the Empress, after frowning at Aylwin for a few moments.

'He is Abbot of Glastonbury,' Aylwin pointed out, raising his eyebrows. He had unconsciously assumed his most educated accent, without a trace of his Wessex burr, and this made Earl Robert frown and eye him more carefully. 'In fact, the business was concerned with another of his titles; that of a monk of Cluny. I was sent to advise the mason in charge of repairs to the Cluniac cell at Montacute.'

'About what?' snapped Earl Robert.

'The rebuilding of the tower of their church. Their master mason is young and inexperienced, and asked for another opinion on the foundations, the former tower having proved unstable.'

'And what did you advise?'

'That he dig down another five or six feet, and set his footings on solid rock.'

The Earl nodded, then remarked, 'But the road east out of Glaston is not the road from Montacute to Winchester.'

'As I was so near, I took the opportunity to visit Glaston.'

'Glastonbury? For what reason?' demanded the Empress. Aylwin thought he had never heard a harsher, more unpleasant voice issuing from a woman's lips.

'To make my pilgrimage, and to see the new building there, and particularly the carving. I'm a sculptor,' he replied.

Earl Robert said musingly, 'The Bishop calls you his "valued servant". For what does he value you?'

'For my mystery, for my knowledge of all to do with building in stone, for my skill as a sculptor,' Aylwin replied, dismissing modesty as inappropriate in his present situation.

'Hm.' The Earl seemed to find this a little baffling, and his half-sister, to judge by her expression, completely inexplicable. 'I believe the Bishop does amuse himself by a pretence to interest in – er – aesthetic matters,' the Earl commented. 'We must see how much he really values his

334

servant! Do you think, Master Aylwin, that he values you enough to pay your ransom?'

'That would depend on how much you are asking,' Aylwin replied warily. 'I must point out, however, that I'm a craftsman, not a fighting man. Surely it's – er – unusual to hold a man who is not a knight to ransom?'

Earl Robert grinned, and replied, not unkindly, 'Unusual it may be, but it seems likely that you're worth money, and mercenaries like Jehan here are expensive. I believe a master mason ranks as an esquire, but a particularly *valued* one – shall we say the price of two knights?'

Aylwin pretended to consider the matter, concealing a surge of relief. If the Bishop valued him enough to grant him four knights' fees as an estate, a ransom equivalent to only two knights was a bargain – if the Bishop felt inclined to ransom him at all.

'My lord,' he said after a brief pause, knowing that what he was about to say would be unlikely to have any effect on his hearers, but determined not to let himself be locked up indefinitely without voicing a protest. 'I dare say my master would be prepared to pay for my freedom, but, with the greatest respect, I must point out that I'm a craftsman, not a knight. I have work to finish – God's work – in a church in Essex, and more awaiting me in a church in Winchester. Other masons, also building for God, will be held up in their work if you keep me here. Because of this work, my master probably will ransom me, but he's abroad at present and it may take some time to arrange. Presumably I may give my parole meanwhile?'

Earl Robert gave a bark of laughter which brought the deerhound to its feet in alarm, until it realized that it was only its master barking, and subsided, grumbling to itself. 'Parole is for true knights, for fighting men, not for master masons. You surely don't expect me to take the word of a man who's not been trained in the ways and morals of knighthood? No, Master Aylwin, you'll await your ransom here, well-guarded. Jehan – lodge him in the prison tower. We won't risk the health of the Bishop's *valued servant* in a cellar. He's to be treated as of knightly rank in all respects, save that of parole, as he's quite a valuable asset.'

With that, the Earl made a dismissive gesture with one hand, and lost interest in the prisoner as he turned to lean closer to his half-sister and make some low-voiced comment to her. Jehan gave Aylwin a dig in the ribs, and jerked his head towards the door, then took his arm and propelled him, fairly gently, out of the chamber.

'You're in luck,' he said. 'Stephen of Blois, who calls himself King of England, was chained and kept in a cellar. At least you'll see daylight, and he didn't mention chains, so I shan't either. This way – I'll see you to your lodging.'

'Does Earl Robert make a habit of taking noncombatant prisoners for ransom?' Aylwin asked, allowing his resentment to appear in his voice.

'He'll hold anyone if there's money in it,' Jehan replied cheerfully. 'I knew as soon as I saw the Bishop's brand on your mount's rump that you'd help to provide my wages for a bit. We have to be sure of our pay, you know, or we'll not fight. Why should we? It's not our quarrel.' And to that, Aylwin could find no answer.

The prison tower was on the far side of the keep, as far as Aylwin could judge from the route they took to reach it, but he was unsure how high above ground level they were by the time they had collected the warder on duty from the guard room and climbed another tight spiral stair, passing two heavy, iron-barred doors on the way.

At the third door, the warder stopped, and said, with a touch of humour which seemed to lack malice, 'This is your lodging, good master – almost the best our inn has to offer,' as he pushed the door open and stood back to let Aylwin enter, propelled sharply from behind by Jehan.

He managed, with a stagger, to keep his balance, and the warder kindly stepped inside the door and held up his lantern to give him a brief view of his prison. It did not fill the round of a tower, as he had expected, but was a square with one corner, opposite the door, occupied by an angle of wall with a dark opening in it. A small window showed a patch of lighter grey, and the lantern's dim light revealed a plank bed against one wall, with a folded blanket on it, a table and a stool under the window, and nothing else.

'He's been no trouble at all,' Jehan told the warder. 'He's

no fighting man, but a master mason in the service of the Bishop of Winchester, and it's likely his master values him enough to pay his ransom, so you can treat him well.'

'Has he supped?' asked the warder.

'Yes.'

'You'll get bread and ale in the morning,' the warder told Aylwin. 'Sleep well.'

With that, he slammed the door, and turned the key in the lock with a scrape and a clunk which filled Aylwin with depression. He had been anxious all day, wondering what would happen to him, and had been stifling a persistent fear that he might be hanged for a spy, but the relief he might have felt at being treated as a prisoner of possible value was lost for the moment in a black cloud of gloom. He had always hated small cramped places, and now he was locked into one, in the dark, for an indefinite period of time. Bishop Henry would have left on his long journey to Rome by now, and the demand for his ransom would be received by the Bishop's Chancellor. Would he respond to it, or ignore it, reply with a refusal, or refer it to his master? There was no way of telling, but Aylwin could not imagine that the Chancellor would pay out two knights' ransoms for a man whom he probably considered a mere artisan, and English at that. Most likely he would refuse, but he might, remembering the wording of the *laissez-passer* and the Bishop's gift of a horse, at least send after his master for instructions.

Groping in the darkness, Aylwin sought the plank bed, which found him first, with a shrewd blow across his shins. He wrapped himself in his cloak, put his bundle down for a pillow, and stretched out, pulling the blanket over himself with some hesitation, but it smelled of wool, and nothing else, so he thought it might be reasonably clean.

The planks were very hard, and he was wondering if he would ever manage to sleep on them, when the lock gave its creak and clunk, the door squeaked open, something which rustled was thrown in, and the warder's voice said 'palliasse' before he shut and relocked the door.

Aylwin had to crawl across the floor to find it, but it was, indeed, a lumpy sack of straw, which, once he had pounded and pulled it about, made a reasonably comfortable bed on the planks, and he fell asleep in the midst of a long and confused prayer to every relevant saint he could think of, from the Four Crowned Martyrs and St Barbara, the patrons of masons, to St Patrick, St Gildas and St Dunstan, whose shrines he had so recently visited.

When he woke, the small barred window of his cell was red with dawn, from which he deduced that it faced south-east, and, from some stamping and banging over his head, he also deduced that he was in the lower part of a tower, where it formed part of the keep wall, and the roof and battlements of the keep must be just above him, presumably with the guard changing at dawn.

In the grey half-light, he sat on the edge of the bed and looked about him despondently, wondering how he would pass the time, perhaps for weeks, in this bare, small room. It dawned on him that something of which he now had urgent need was not visible – no bucket! Surely there should be a bucket in a cell? Then he suddenly realized what that projecting corner of wall signified, and darted across to investigate. To his relief, in more ways than one, it was a garderobe. In fact, it was quite luxurious, having its own small barred window, and a stone bench with the necessary hole cut in it, instead of the more usual hole in the floor. He looked down the shaft, and saw that it sloped for a short distance, then opened into the vertical main shaft, so it must serve other cells, both below, and above, in the part of the tower which projected above the keep.

By standing on the bench, he could just manage to peer out of the little window, but could see only the sky and the top of a distant line of hills, so he returned to the cell and tried the window there, which was larger and lower. Standing on the table brought the lower edge of the opening level with his chest, so that he could look down as well as at the distant view. Below him, he could see the garderobe shaft projecting a little, and sloping out at the bottom, where it opened on to a margin of ground, perhaps twenty feet across, which sloped down to the river, the bank of which was partly obscured by bushes and even a couple of small trees, which he thought was careless of the garrison, who should have kept it clear of cover for possible attackers.

The river was only close to the castle immediately below him, and it turned away both above and below this point. To his left, it turned nearly a right angle, but to his right, it was only a slight turn, enough for him to see the bridge, which he thought must be the one he had crossed during the night. There were ships in the river, riding at anchor, and more of them tied up against quays on the opposite bank. Several small boats and larger barges were passing up and down the channel. From the fact that the men rowing the boats were pulling hard one way, but going with the current the other way, he worked out that the river flowed from his left to his right. After a little thought, he recalled its name – the Avon.

The now familiar creak and clunk of the lock made him jump down from the table as the door opened, and a lugubrious-looking man with lank dark hair, bushy eyebrows and a bulbous red nose elbowed his way round it, carrying a wooden tray. He kicked the door shut, put the tray on the floor, and nudged it towards Aylwin with his foot.

'No use thinking you can saw through them bars and climb down to the ground,' he said mournfully in English. 'To start with, them bars is solid iron and set a good hand's breadth into the stonework. When you've gnawed through them wi' your teeth, you got a hundred foot drop, wi' no handholds, down to the ground, and men dropping things on your 'ead whiles you're climbing down. You just stay 'ere, calm and quiet, and wait for your ransom, there's a good fellow, eh? I 'ears you're a master mason. That right?'

'Yes,' Aylwin replied briefly. He estimated that his window was, in fact, about eighty feet from the ground, but, under the circumstances, twenty feet more or less made little difference.

'I'm called Alfred,' said the man. 'After King Alfred, you know. You're English.'

'Yes. Aylwin Cedricson of Winchester,' Aylwin replied, thinking that, as the man seemed friendly, it would be sensible to encourage him. He might be helpful.

'Got a brother who's a mason,' Alfred went on, sounding

extremely mournful about it. 'Could've been one myself, only soldiering seemed more exciting. Got a broken leg at Lincoln, and now I'm too lame to do ought but trail up and down these stairs, carrying food to prisoners. Take your dishes, will you? I need the tray.'

Aylwin knelt to move the platter of bread, the small jug of ale, a larger pitcher of water, and a bowl of greyish-looking mush and a wooden spoon and cup off the tray on to the floor, and handed the tray to Alfred.

'Dinner's at noon, when everyone else has eaten,' he said, and went out, banging and locking the door behind him.

Aylwin took his food and drink to the table and sat down to eat slowly, to pass the time. The bread was stale, but edible, and the grey mush was thick porridge sweetened with honey, and tasted much better than it looked. He assumed that the water was intended to supplement the ale for drinking, but he sacrificed some of it in order to wash himself, using one of the two spare shirts in his bundle as a towel. The water was icy, but the cell was so cold anyway that it made little difference.

The day was incredibly long. He had only two sketch-books with him, and one of those was almost full, so he used some of the odd spaces between drawings to make tiny sketches of ideas for the west end of Waltham minster, and then made a series of even tinier drawings of anything which came into his head. His dinner eventually arrived, brought by Alfred again, who observed that it was mortal cold and raining, which Aylwin had noticed, for the wind blew a scurry of raindrops in through the window every now and again.

'Better keep your spoon. You'll not get another,' Alfred said as Aylwin put his breakfast dishes on the tray after removing his dinner. 'Can't let you 'ave a knife – you might cut me throat with it and escape, and then I'd be in real trouble with the warder. Married man, are you?'

'Yes. I was married in August, and my wife's expecting our first child,' Aylwin replied. 'Are you married?'

'I was. She ran off with a sea-captain four or five year ago. Good riddance – she were a proper nagger. Reckon 'e's probably pushed 'er over the side by now, if 'e's got any sense. Women is queer cattle, don't you think?'

Aylwin managed a rueful smile, and replied, 'I suppose they are, but I'd give a great deal to be at home with mine at this moment!'

Alfred nodded, took his tray, and departed, leaving Aylwin to eat his tough meat with his fingers, and spoon his pottage, which was thick and palatable. The bread was fresher this time, and there was another jug of ale to wash it down. It occurred to him that he was being treated very well, for a prisoner – as well-fed, probably, as most of the garrison, and given a clean, dry cell, with the luxury of its own garderobe. Presumably he had Bishop Henry's description of him as his 'valued servant' to thank for it.

Supper arrived at dusk, when there was barely enough light left for him to see what he was eating, and then there was nothing to do but go to bed and try to keep warm in the unheated stone chamber, which would probably have been cold at the height of summer.

In the morning, he thought he should try to keep track of the days as they passed, and made two marks inside the cover of one of his notebooks for yesterday and today. There were three rows of seven of the marks before there was any variation in the routine of his imprisonment. Every day crept by on leaden feet. He drew very small pictures for a while each morning between Alfred's visits with breakfast and dinner, and walked to and fro between window and door, the longest stretch the cell allowed, to a count of two thousand paces every afternoon, for exercise, and thought he would go mad after a few more days of this isolation and boredom.

He prayed often, and thought about Elys, wishing he could send his thoughts to her in some way. He asked Alfred if it would be possible to send a letter to her, but Alfred, after sucking a hollow tooth for a few moments, said, 'No. Can't see any way to that. More that my job's worth. Sorry. I'll get you another of them books what you draws in, for a penny.'

As the book cost nearly a penny to buy, being made of vellum between wooden boards, Aylwin accepted the offer

341

with gratitude, and could at least draw more pictures to help pass the time, when Alfred brought it to him, concealed inside his grubby tunic and a little stained about the cover, apparently with gravy.

The break in routine, when it arrived, brought no good news. It consisted of a brief visit from Jehan, who unlocked the door, put his head in, and said, 'I thought you'd like to know – the Bishop of Winchester's gone abroad, as you said. His Chancellor replied to the message Earl Robert sent him. He said to take good care of you, as his master values your skills, and he's sent after him to ask for instructions. He hopes to have a reply after Christmas.'

Before Aylwin could say anything, he withdrew his head, shut the door, and locked it, and Aylwin was left to sit with his head in his hands, a prey to despair and misery, until Alfred arrived with his supper.

''Eard the news,' he said. 'Shame. Brought you some apple pie to cheer you up. Saved it from me own supper. You'll 'ave a long wait now, couple of months at least.'

'I suppose so,' Aylwin said gloomily, and then, more to keep the man talking a while longer than for any real wish to know, 'You said your brother's a mason? Does he find much work hereabouts? I suppose this castle . . .'

'Oh, the castle's finished but for the moat – they're still digging that! No, Wulfstan – that's my brother – he's working on Earl Robert's priory, in the fields north of the town.'

'You mean it's outside the town walls? That's unusual.'

'I wouldn't know. The Earl took a bit of land from the open fields, without so much as by-your-leave, and that's where it is, across the river – not the one you see out there, that's the Avon. I mean across the Frome, the little river. There's not much doing there now, a'course, with frost at night, but Wulfstan's still working, shaping stone and doing a bit of carving. He sleeps out there most nights, in the lodge. He says it's cosy enough, and with eight childer at home, who can blame him.'

'Yes – the frost. Any chance of a couple more blankets?' Aylwin asked hopefully.

'Cost yer.'

'How much?'

'Penny apiece.'

Aylwin fished out two pence and held them out to Alfred, who took them, bit them, and put them in his own purse.

'Gi's yer tray, then. I'll bring 'em presently.'

Aylwin wondered if he would, but he was, it seemed, an honest man, for the familiar creak and clunk signalled his return an hour or so later. He said nothing, but when the door had been shut and locked, Aylwin groped his way across to it in the dark, and tripped on a large soft bundle, which proved to be two good large blankets in a sack.

Jehan returned in the morning, and said briskly, 'Tidy yourself up, now. Earl Robert wants to see you.'

Aylwin smoothed his tunic with one hand and brushed that stubborn forelock back with the other, and said mildly, 'I haven't been able to shave, as you took my razor.'

'The beard suits you,' Jehan assured him, ferret grin in evidence. 'Come along, now. And don't try to run away, because you'll only get as far as the cellars, and they're dark, cold and wet.'

Earl Robert was in the chamber where Aylwin had seen him before, but alone this time. He was again sitting at the table, but appeared to be reading a number of documents, which were arranged in two neat piles. He continued reading for a few moments after Jehan entered with Aylwin, but then he put down the parchment he had been studying and said, 'I trust my man informed you of the situation concerning your ransom? Unfortunate for you, of course, but at least the Bishop's Chancellor seems to consider it likely that the Bishop will pay your ransom – eventually. Why has he gone overseas?'

'Did the Chancellor not tell you?' Aylwin countered warily. It occurred to him that there were several reasons why Bishop Henry might have gone abroad which could be worrying for Earl Robert. To seek help from the French king for Stephen, for example.

'You claim to be his valued servant – does he not confide in you?' the Earl asked. 'You must be much about his court at Winchester – surely someone in your hearing there mentioned where and why he had gone, even if he didn't tell you himself.'

'I've been working for some months in Essex,' Aylwin answered carefully. 'I went to Winchester to report to the Bishop on the progress of the work, there having been an accident to the master in charge of the building. I was only with the Bishop for half an hour or so, and we talked about the work, and then he explained about the problem at Montacute, and asked me to go there before I returned to my own work in Essex.'

'But did he not tell you where he was going, or when he expected to return?'

Aylwin's mind ran swiftly over the conversation with the Bishop, and then answered, quite truthfully, 'No.'

Earl Robert stared at him for a while, then gave a sigh of either irritation or regret, and said, 'Very well. You may return to your cell.'

Aylwin could not resist a slight, ironic bow, but the Earl had returned to his documents, and did not appear to see it. Jehan jerked his arm, and they left the chamber together.

'You wasted a chance there,' said Jehan reprovingly. 'If you'd told him what he wanted to know, he might have let you go.'

Aylwin shrugged. 'I can't tell him what I don't know,' he said, misleadingly but truthfully.

Back in his cell, he thought grimly that he had not given his master's enemy any information of use or comfort, but it did not relieve the bleak outlook for himself, or for poor Elys, who must be worried by now at his failure to return or send her any message. He had confidence in her quiet determination and courage, but it hurt him to be the cause of anxiety to her.

There seemed to be only two courses of action open to him. One was to stay here and wait until his ransom arrived – assuming that Bishop Henry agreed to it being paid. The alternative was even less certain, and involved considerable risk, but seemed the more desirable, for Aylwin was not idle by nature, nor given to inconveniencing his friends.

CHAPTER NINETEEN

Elys had stood outside the house in Church Street, waving goodbye to Aylwin when he set out for Winchester with a cheerful smile, which grew more and more strained as he rode down the street and across the ford, and vanished altogether as he disappeared from sight down West Street. Then she went indoors and resumed work on the cope, blinking back the tears which would fill her eyes, and telling herself that every mason's wife must get used to seeing her husband go away for months at a time, wherever his work took him, and at least her own man would be back in three or four weeks.

Master William called to see her later that day, limping up the churchyard path, his stick tapping at every other step, and said sympathetically, 'It's hard to be parted from your other half when you've not been wed long. I had to go up to Durham two months after I wed my Aldith, and I remember how it felt. It's not so bad for a man, for he has his work to do, but it's powerful hard on a wife.'

'I didn't realize you were married,' Elys said, touched by his concern.

'Oh, that were years agone, when I were a young journeyman. She came up to join me for a while that job, but later, when the childer came, she stayed in Norwich, and I went home to her in the winter, when the work stopped.'

'But doesn't she travel with you now, when the children are grown?'

'She died. It were one summer, when I were workin' up in Scotland, at Dunfermline. She were dead and buried before I even got to hear of it. That were a bad year for sickness in Norwich.'

'I'm sorry,' Elys said. 'I didn't know.'

'There's always the work,' he replied obliquely. 'Work's a great comfort. You've got your craft to be busy with, and that's better nor sittin' and mopin' whiles you spin the wool and pod the peas. I always thought a wife'd be the better for havin' a craft of her own to work at, and not be tied to cookin' and cleanin' and tendin' childer.'

Elys did, indeed, find her work a comfort. She had finished the main part of the cope now, and was embroidering the golden lettering on the orphrey, the border which ran round the front edges of the cope. Like the cope which William Rufus had taken, with other treasures, from Waltham, to endow his father's foundation in Caen, it bore the words *Dominus dixit ad me*, and it was a challenge to her ingenuity to place the lettering so that the first word, on the right-hand side of the wearer, would balance the other three words on the left side. She managed it by putting a cross before the *dominus*, and overlapping the two letters of the *ad* so that they occupied only one space.

After that, she had only the hood, with its descending dove, and the morse, or clasp, to do, and the whole cope to assemble and line, and she thought that she might have it finished by Christmas, or, at least, by Epiphany, after which, being green, it would be suitable for wear on ferial Sundays.

Father Warmand gave her a bundle of good wax candles, for the hours of daylight were growing short now, and told her that she must not hesitate to ask for more when she needed them.

'You'll hurt your eyes if you try to work without a good light,' he said. 'There's many a good broiderer had to give up the craft because of overstrained eyesight, and even gone blind, and that's a wicked waste of God's gift for the sake of a few pennyworth of candles! We'd rather wait longer for the cope than have you suffering headaches and worse, child!'

Elys promised not to try to work with inadequate light, and always had at least four candles burning when she worked after dark, and, as Matthew and Crispin often brought their copying home to do in the warmth of their own hall rather than in the chilly scriptorium, and the orphrey could be worked on a tambour frame, being comparatively small, they put all their candles together on the table, and sat round in a group to do their work in a really good light.

Privately, she counted the days until Aylwin would come home again, reckoning that it would take him a week to get to Winchester, a week to see the Bishop and visit his mother, and another week to come home. She knew that, being a strong and active man, he would probably manage the journeying in less time, but she refused to think of his absence lasting for less that three weeks. Only twenty-one days, she told herself, only twenty, only nineteen . . .

The tally was down to three, and she was trying not to feel disappointed that he had still not come home, when a messenger arrived with a party of men-at-arms and a small wagon, bringing the extra money for the building work. He had first to report to Father Brian and Father Antony and help them to count the money, but as soon as he was free, he hurried across to the house in Church Street with Aylwin's note.

Elys greeted him pleasantly, having heard from Lukin that he had come from Bishop Henry with the money and a new block of Purbeck stone for Aylwin. He introduced himself as Richard of Romsey, one of the Bishop's knights.

'He would have sent Sir Fulk, but he's gone home to his family on leave, to be married. I've brought you a letter from Master Aylwin – you are his wife?'

'Yes, I am. Thank you for bringing it,' she said, taking the letter eagerly, with a fleeting thought that Fulk must have given in to his family, but with no feeling of regret, and she remembered to send for refreshment for Sir Robert before excusing herself to read the precious letter.

Aylwin had written to her in English, but she knew enough of the language now to be able to read and understand it, and the loving message at the end of it helped to lessen her disappointment that the waiting was not yet over. Another two weeks at the most, and he would be home.

'Where is it that he's gone?' she asked. 'He says it's a place called Montacute in Somerset. Is it near Wells? We went there on pilgrimage, for Matthew, my brother, you know.'

'I believe it's the other side of Glastonbury from Wells,'

Sir Robert replied. 'Aylwin said he'd be interested to go there, because it's where the Holy Cross of Waltham was found in Cnut's time. I don't understand that. Why did they bring it here, if it was found all that way away?'

'I believe there was a miracle – I was told about it once – the cart on which the Cross was to travel wouldn't start to move until the lord of the manor told them to bring it here, and then it started of its own accord.'

Lukin, of course, knew that the Bishop's messenger had come, and he followed his long nose to Church Street after supper to see if the knight had any interesting news to impart. He was delighted to hear that Aylwin had gone to Montacute.

'Oh, that be a wonder!' he exclaimed. 'I'd give a mortal lot to go there and see the very place! When he comes back, it'll be a great thing to hear about it. Wait 'til I tell Edwin. That's always had a hankering to go there and see where that's forebears did come from. Talking to someone what's been there'll be next thing to going thatself. Oh, Lady Elys, I be sorry you'll have longer to wait for him, but what a chance. That'd never bear to miss that.'

'No, I suppose not,' Elys said wryly. 'I expect he'll manage to get to Glastonbury as well, as it's nearby. Really, nobody ought to pass over a chance to go there, least of all a mason.'

'You went there with mother, didn't you?' asked Matthew. 'Poor Elys. All those weary miles the two of you travelled on my account, and all the time the answer was here, in the same county where we were living.'

'I don't grudge the time or the travelling,' Elys replied, smiling. 'I've seen so many interesting places and great churches because of it, while other women see nothing but their own village all their lives. I've some wonderful memories and, after all, if we hadn't gone to Rome, I might never have met Aylwin.'

Lukin opened his mouth to point out that she would have met Aylwin, for had he not been sent here, to Waltham, so soon after she arrived herself? Then he shut his mouth again, thinking it wrong to spoil her little speech when it had obviously been a comfort to Matthew that she had not considered her pilgrimages a waste of time.

For two more weeks, Elys tried not to count the days, keeping herself as busy as possible. She felt very well, now that the morning sickness had passed, and there was plenty to do, with her stitchery, and helping Mistress Mayngod in the kitchen, for she was learning to cook, and was proud to be able to say that the pie served up for supper, or the bread at dinner, was her own unaided work, but the time dragged. When the two weeks had passed, she was disappointed, then, as another week went by in leaden minutes, she began to be anxious, and she could see that others were worried too.

'Of course,' said Crispin unconvincingly, 'something may have happened to delay him. Perhaps the problem at Montacute was a particularly difficult one, and he'd have to stay until it was solved, wouldn't he?'

'The roads are bad now, with winter coming on,' Matthew pointed out. 'There's been a deal of rain these last few weeks, and mud can slow a horse and tire it, so that the rider can only manage a few miles a day, where he can go much faster in summer.'

'Yes,' said Elys blankly, and could think of nothing to add. It was no comfort that one of the women with whom she had struck up an acquaintance during the summer stopped her in the street one day and said, 'So your man's not back yet? I expect he's enjoying a bit of freedom. Most men find marrying and settling down burdensome, after a lifetime of doing as they please. After all, Master Aylwin's been used to travelling all over the place, and it'd be no wonder if he missed being free to come and go as he pleases. He'll come back to you when he's had his fill of gadding about and his conscience starts to prick, never fear. My man was much the same, being a carpenter, you know. He went off for near a year after we'd been wed six months, and came back happy enough after that, saying that being tied to a wife and home had come to be more than he could bear, but he settled down pretty well after that, having got the restlessness out of him. A man gets to feel trapped by marriage, like a wild creature in a cage, 'til he's old enough to think more of comfort and good cooking than of roaming the world.'

At the time, Elys laughed and said she was probably right, but afterwards, in the loneliness of the upstairs bedchamber, she wondered if the woman was right. Had Aylwin found the ties of marriage and the coming child too much to bear? Had he taken the opportunity to leave her, to be free again? She wept and prayed and tried to remember that he had shown clearly enough that he loved her, but the seed of doubt had been sown, and, as the days passed and he did not return, the doubt grew and tormented her.

Early in December, the Bishop's Chancellor had the consideration to send a messenger to Waltham for no other purpose than to let her know that Aylwin had been taken by the Empress's men, and was a prisoner in Bristol Castle. 'The Empress is demanding an exorbitant ransom for him,' he wrote. 'It is quite unjustified, as he is but a craftsman, and not a noble, or even a knight, and it is beyond my power to pay it without my master's permission. I have sent Sir Fulk Fitzmichel to my lord Bishop to tell him of the matter, but I have no knowledge of his exact whereabouts at present, as he intended to make many visits on his journey across France. However, you may be comforted by the knowledge that my lord thinks highly of Master Aylwin, and that, as the Empress has set so high a ransom on him, she will make sure that he is kept in good health, as otherwise she will get nothing for him.'

Everyone in Waltham was horrified by the news. Aylwin was popular with the townsfolk, the canons and the masons, and many folk went out of their way to tell Elys that they were praying for his safety and early release. 'Bishop Henry will pay,' she was assured a score of times. 'He'll never let such an artist rot in prison, you may be sure.'

'The Empress had King Stephen kept in chains in a dark cellar,' she said bitterly to her brothers, one evening when they both repeated the same assurances to her.

'But she wanted him dead,' Crispin replied. 'Aylwin's only of use to her alive and well. She must be desperate for money, with only the West Country to draw taxes from, and all those mercenaries to be paid. If she lets their wages fall into arrears, they'll not just refuse to fight for her, you know – they'll be ready to sell her to the King, or take themselves off to serve him against her. They go where the money is, and they've no interest in right or honour, only in regular pay.'

Elys tried to take comfort from what they all said, but, as the weather turned colder, she was haunted by the thought of Aylwin locked in an unheated cell, cold and wretched, perhaps taking a chill or an ague. She wrapped her wonderful furlined cloak round her when she went out, but would have been only too glad to send it to him, if there had been any means of doing so.

Christmas drew near, and she busied herself in making New Year gifts for her brothers and friends, working fewer hours in the day on the cope for a while, although it was almost finished. She made a shirt for Aylwin in the finest linen she could obtain, determined not to lose hope that he would be home to receive it before the twelve days of Christmas were over.

Despite her anxiety and unhappiness, something happened on Christmas Eve at which she could not help laughing. Edwin Warrener, on behalf of the canons, who employed him, went round the homes of the canons' tenants, delivering a coney for every member of each family, and was given so many cups of spiced ale or homemade wine that, inspired, no doubt by a drink-clouded memory of his friend Lukin's earlier exploit, he finished up by staggering into Mistress Mayngod's kitchen and proposing marriage to her in a flowery speech in which most of the words became inextricably garbled, but the meaning emerged clearly enough.

Mistress Mayngod was stuffing the goose for the next day's dinner at the time, but she paused to listen with amused attention, and, when Edwin reached the conclusion of his speech and sat down abruptly on the floor, she put a dab of stuffing carefully on the end of his nose, and said, 'You're drunk, Master Edwin! No, I won't marry you, and you know very well that you don't really want me to. Think how miserable you'd be, living in the town, away from your conies and your deer and wild boar, and how miserable I'd be in that hut of yours, with fur and ferrets all over everywhere and wild creatures snuffling under the door o' nights.

You're welcome in my kitchen for a warm and a bite to eat any time, but only as long as there's no more talk of marrying.'

Edwin was so relieved that he staggered off to the hall, where the family had just finished supper, and told them all about it with such dramatic gestures and such a good imitation of Mistress Mayngod that even Elys was laughing helplessly by the end of it.

'You've a lump of stuffing on your nose!' Crispin exclaimed between hiccoughs of laughter.

Lukin arrived as Edwin was finishing his tale and the two young men were trying to suppress their laughter and express proper sympathy with the rejected suitor. Of course, Edwin had to tell his tale all over again for his friend's benefit, setting off fresh gales of laughter as his imitation of the lady grew more extravagant and his report of his proposal speech more elaborate.

'You don't sound like that broke your heart,' Lukin commented, having listened with amazing gravity to the performance.

'I'm that relieved you wouldn't believe,' Edwin admitted seriously, having sobered up considerably in telling his story. 'I just felt I ought to offer for she, like she expected it, but so long as I'm free of her kitchen and her good pies, I'd rather live wi' my ferrets and the wild creatures in whatever sort of mess I choose.'

Lukin nodded solemnly, and said, 'Quite right for you, Edwin,' and then sat unusually silent and thoughtful.

Mistress Mayngod herself entered the hall presently, carrying a tray of platters and spoons, a jug of ale, and cups for all the company.

'It being Christmas Eve and you all off to church soon, you'd best have some ale inside you to keep out the cold,' she said.

Lukin went to mix spices and sugar to flavour the hot ale. When it was ready, he handed the cups round, and when he came to Mistress Mayngod with hers, said seriously, 'Matilda, will you make a wretched bachelor happy?'

'I thought I'd already done that,' the cook replied, her eyes twinkling above her rosy cheeks, casting a sly glance at Edwin, who grinned back, then bent his head to dip a finger in his ale and offer it to the ferrets to lick.

'A second wretched bachelor,' Lukin amended.

'And how may I do that?' Matilda asked, suddenly serious.

'Marry me.'

She looked at him consideringly. 'You seem to be sober and in your right mind,' she said, pursing her lips. 'Very well. I'll marry you, but not 'til Lady Elys and Master Aylwin leave here, and I'd still want to do the cooking here until I get a girl properly trained to take over from me.'

'Agreed!' said Lukin promptly.

'That's settled, then,' said the prospective bride in a brisk and businesslike fashion. She hugged the little man to her bolster-like bosom and gave him a hearty kiss, and his long, mournful face broke into a huge smile.

Elys felt her eyes fill with tears at the transparent happiness in his expression, and she realized that she had always felt sorry for him before. She was glad that he had found himself a wife who would care for him properly.

The Christmas night service was very long, and the minster was cold, despite the crowded congregation, the charcoal braziers and the myriad candles. Elys huddled her warm cloak closer about her, and wondered if Aylwin was being permitted to attend Mass this night, and if he would be given any good food for the festival. She supposed that he would have been reasonably well-fed during his imprisonment, to keep him healthy, but the idea of him alone, cold, perhaps with only rough, unpalatable food to eat on Christmas Day, was heart-breaking. She clasped her hands before her face as she prayed, to hide the tears which were running down her cheeks, and Mistress Mayngod, who was a deal more sensitive than she appeared, put a comforting arm round her shoulders and patted her arm in sympathetic understanding.

Presently, some of the peace of Christmas crept into Elys's mind and heart, and she raised her head to look up at the Holy Cross, gleaming in the candlelight. Robert of St Albans' deadly concoction had, in fact, removed much of the dirt and tarnish when it was washed off, and the

Cross shone much more than before. Elys prayed whole-heartedly that the Christchild who grew to be the Man depicted on the Cross would send his angels to watch over Aylwin and bring him safe home, and felt a new confidence and a strange comfort well up inside her, so that she left the church that night feeling much better and happier than when she entered it.

Outside, she looked up at the stars in the velvety, frost-clear sky, and thought that perhaps Aylwin was looking at those same stars, if his cell had a window. She clasped her hands over the bulge of the growing child, and said to him – her – inside her head 'He'll be home long before you're born. If you're a girl, we'll name you Mary, for you'll be born in the Virgin's month, and your father shall carve a lovely Christchild for a thank-offering.'

Despite the lateness of the hour – or the earliness of it, for it was past midnight – when everyone went to bed, they were up early in the morning, while it was still dark, for there was much to do. Lukin was to spend the day with them, and he helped Crispen and the menservants drag in the yule log and set it across the hearth, with Matthew lending the hand which was not occupied with his crutch. It was he, as head of the household, who scraped the flint and steel to fire the tinder and set it beneath the log, a great piece of an old oak which Edwin had found fallen in the Forest.

While they were doing this heavy work, the women decor-ated the hall with bunches of holly and other evergreens, and Mistress Mayngod, at Elys's invitation, climbed on the table to hang a kissing-bunch of mistletoe and gilded apples from one of the beams, as Elys, in her condition, thought it better not to do it herself.

Edwin arrived in time to go to morning Mass with them, and Elys, glancing across to where her brothers were stand-ing with him during the service, saw, with a mixture of amusement and shock, that he had brought his companions with him, for a dozen sinuous pale bodies were clinging to his shoulders or poking their heads out of his cloak, behav-ing as decorously as if they understood where they were and why. They had their share of the Christmas goose as

354

well, and the plum-porridge, for Mistress Mayngod brought in a big platter for them, and they crouched round it in a ring by the warm hearth, eating amicably and daintily together. Tigrus had his platter too, but on the opposite side of the hearth.

After the meal, the humans slackened their belts, then the servants went home to their families for the rest of the day, leaving Elys, her brothers, Mistress Mayngod and their two guests sitting round the hearth, somnolent after the heavy meal, to tell stories and sing carols for a while.

Before it grew dark, they all wrapped themselves up warmly and went for a gentle amble along by the millstream, Lukin remarking as they crossed the footbridge that even the miller's cat was too full of goose to be out fishing today, and Mistress Mayngod threw handfuls of stale bread to the ducks which were cruising and diving there.

They went to Vespers before supper, and sat long over the meal, with more stories and songs, and Lukin's mulled ale to lubricate their throats and voices. It was very late when they went to bed, and Elys could hardly keep her eyes open as she undressed, shivering in the cold, despite the brazier's warm glow. Despite her tiredness, she took down two of her treasures from the shelf, and held one – the little bird which Aylwin had given her last Christmas – while she prayed with her eyes on the other – the ivory Virgin and Child which had been her mother-in-law's wedding-gift to her, and she included the giver in her prayers, for she, too, must be gnawed with anxiety for Aylwin's well-being.

CHAPTER TWENTY

Aylwin spent some time during the next few days and nights at his cell window, and ascertained by observation that the guards on the walls took little notice of anything which happened on the river bank below, for twice he saw men fishing there among the bushes which grew just above the tide-line. He noted that they came from somewhere to his left, so presumably there must be access to the river bank in that direction. As far as he could tell by watching and listening, no patrols ever passed along the bank, despite the fact that there was a broad strip of land between walls and water, even at high tide. Apparently Bristol castle was considered to be safe from possible attack, which was not, he supposed, an unreasonable belief, as Earl Robert's mercenaries patrolled the roads for several miles around the town.

When it grew too dark to see anything from the window, he sat on his bed cutting and tearing his blankets by feel into strips about six inches wide, using the little knife which he had carried hidden inside his belt while he was in Italy, for fear of being captured by brigands. It struck him when he retrieved it that it was ironic that he had not had need of it until now, in his own country. He knotted the strips of blanket end to end, pulling hard on the knots, and hid the growing rope in the garderobe, where Alfred never bothered to look, and covered the bed with his cloak, so that the absence of the blankets would not be noticeable to a casual glance. He sometimes thought longingly of Elys's fur-lined cloak as he shivered while waiting to fall asleep.

After the blankets, he tore up the sack in which the extra ones had arrived, as it was made of a strong, closely-woven fabric. He then considered sacrificing his cloak at the last minute, but Alfred brought him two more blankets – a gift, he said, from his brother to a fellow-mason. Aylwin received them with heart-felt expressions of gratitude, and tore them

356

into more strips during the next night, adding them to his rope, which was now nearly long enough. He was thankful that his training had included measuring heights by eye to a fair degree of accuracy, so that at least he could be sure that he would not run out of rope at a dangerous distance from the ground.

During all this time, he waited for Alfred to notice the thinness of the covering on the plank bed, but Alfred never so much as glanced in its direction during his brief visits. The next night, the last blanket joined the end of the rope, as did the sack of his palliasse, leaving nothing but a pile of straw on the bed.

There was moonlight that night, enough creeping through the garderobe window for Aylwin to see what he was doing as he tested his rope and tied one end of it securely round the strong upright bar across the window. Then he let the other end down the shaft, and, recollecting what would be at the bottom, he collected the straw from his bed and dropped that down the shaft too, hoping it would cover some of the filth. He waited a while, shivering with a mixture of anticipation and apprehension, for the clatter and crash of the portcullis falling in the bridge gate-house, which would tell him that nobody would be crossing the bridge before morning. He began to pray.

The crash and thuds from the bridge came unexpectedly, startling him, and the shout of 'Gate barred!' which followed jerked him into action. He hesitated, suddenly afraid of what was before him. He had to think of Elys and steel himself to make the attempt for her sake, and then to make his final plans quickly, before his courage failed.

The walls of the shaft would be slimy – unpleasant . . . He had no wish to go out into the world with his clothes soiled with ordure, so he stripped off everything but his boots and wrapped his clothes and bundle of belongings in his cloak, tied it securely, and pushed it down the shaft.

With one last, desperate prayer, he spat on his hands, seized the makeshift rope, squeezed himself through the opening in the garderobe seat and, crouching in the narrow shaft, let his feet slide down the slope, controlling his speed by holding tight to the rope. Once he reached the main shaft, which was wider, he could brace his feet against the side and go down hand over hand. The smell was unpleasant, but no worse than he had encountered in other places, and the rough stone scraped his back from time to time, but the shaft had been built unnecessarily wide, to his relief, for he feared he might become stuck in it. Nevertheless, he thought that, had he built it, he would have made it narrower in both directions, to prevent prisoners escaping down it, to reduce the projection from the castle wall, and to save stone, and he grinned to himself in the darkness for considering the matter professionally at such a time.

His remaining great fear was that he would be heard by whoever was in the cells below his own. He knew there were at least two of them, and presumably other chambers below them, and he could only hope that nobody in any of them would be seized with a desire to use the garderobe while he was climbing down, for they could hardly avoid hearing his boots scraping against the wall.

He could not see the openings he passed, for he was facing the outer wall of the shaft, and he had lost track of how far he had descended, so he was caught unawares when he looked down and found that he could just make out his own feet, which were now below the top of the opening at ground level.

His rope was just long enough, leaving him only a couple of feet to drop on to the straw at the bottom. He almost tripped over his bundle, and quickly opened it and dressed himself in the angle between the tower and the wall, on the lookout all the time for any sign of anyone who might see him. If he kept close to the wall, he thought that no guard on the top of it would see him, save by leaning out at a perilous angle between the battlements.

There were patchy clouds in the sky, and the moon disappeared behind them at frequent intervals. He used the periods of light to plan his movements, and the darkness to make them, slipping along, close to the wall, until he came to a turn in its direction, and there he found the dry ditch which would become the moat when it was finished and flooded. In its shelter, he passed under the road which ran out eastwards from the main gateway, thus solving a problem which had been worrying him, and continued in it to about halfway along the north side of the castle, trusting that the guards on the gatehouse would have their minds more on possible attackers trying to break into the castle than on one prisoner trying to break out of it.

There was a narrow street running along the ditch here, with a row of dark houses on the side opposite the castle wall, and a quick look along the street showed him that it passed through a gate in another wall – that of the town, presumably – where it joined the castle wall. A narrow street led off northwards just before the gate.

During the next spell of darkness, he was out of the ditch, across the first street and hastening up the turning in seconds, but then came to a barrier, gleaming in the moonlight as the clouds moved on. It must be that smaller river which Alfred had mentioned.

There was a bridge, and he could see open country on the other side, but the bridge was in full view of the town walls. With a sudden flash of inspiration, he pulled the hood of his cloak over his head, which he bowed in a suitably monkish manner, and strode over the bridge as if he were a brother returning to the new priory from a visit to the outer town. Who else might be expected to be going this way at night?

Beyond were the town's open fields, and the lane ran on northwards between them, so he walked on, occasionally glancing behind him, but he was apparently the only man abroad on this cold night. He wondered how he would find the turning to Earl Robert's priory, then called himself a fool for forgetting that such a building required stone. Sure enough, the moonlight revealed deep ruts in the lane, and presently some of the deepest of them turned off to his left towards an oddly shaped building perhaps half a mile away.

As he neared it, he found, as he expected, that its odd shape was due to its being a half-built church. The mason's lodge was at the west end, and a brazier was burning inside, the cheerful glow visible through the chinks in the wooden walls.

He prayed to St Barbara and the Crowned Martyrs before he knocked on the door, hoping he had not made a mistake in coming here. The door opened abruptly, and a jovial voice with a strong Somerset accent bade him enter, but exclaimed in surprise when he stepped into the firelight and pushed back his hood.

'This be'nt young Edward,' one of the half-dozen men sitting round the fire cried. 'Who be you, stranger? What be you adoing 'ere?'

Before Aylwin could reply, a quiet, rather nasal voice exclaimed, 'Aylwin of Winchester! It *was* you they had prisoner in the castle, then! We heard that it was Bishop Henry's own master mason, and we were just planning how to rescue you.'

'Galien!' Aylwin exclaimed. 'What are you doing here?'

'Working,' Galien replied with an eloquent shrug. 'I'm master carpenter of Earl Robert's works. I don't care who pays me, given the work's for God, as you know. Come to the fire and meet these good fellows.'

The man who had opened the door proved to be Wulfstan, Alfred's brother, and he and his fellows had indeed been planning how they might rescue Aylwin, for they were seething with indignation that a master craftsman should be held to ransom.

'They got no right imprisoning you,' Wulfstan said earnestly. 'You be a freeborn Englishman, a master mason, let alone being a great artist in the carving. This stupid war of theirs is nowt to do with us craftsmen, and they got no right for to drag us into it. Still, what can you expect? A woman as'll keep a crowned and anointed king in chains in a cellar's got no respect for anybody, for all she's half-English hersen, the shrew. Earl Robert's only Norman, and maybe knows no better. He pays our wages, but knows nowt of any craft save warfare, if you can call that a craft.'

'Well, this craftsman's saved us the trouble of rescuing him, so now we must work out how to get him safely away,' said Galien, who had reached out and clasped Aylwin's hand for a moment by way of greeting, and needed to make no more demonstration of his feelings than that, for Aylwin knew him to be a very reserved man.

'Yes. Some'ow we has to get him down to my cousin's ship,' said Wulfstan. 'Trouble is, they'll be searching tomorrow, soon as they find out he's gone. Best get him away tonight, I reckon, fellows?'

There was a general murmur of agreement, and then one man asked simply, 'How?'

After a pause for thought, Wulfstan said slowly, 'Thorsten's ship's below where the Frome joins the Avon, but on the far side of the river. Who do we know what keeps a boat along the Frome?'

'Me,' said one of the others, a thin slip of a man with a shock of carroty hair. 'I keeps it under the west bridge.'

'And you'd lend it, Jan?' asked Wulfstan.

'Aye. I'll come with you, if you like, to see you bring it back safe.'

'Can you row?' Wulfstan asked Aylwin, who admitted apologetically that he could not. 'No matter. Jan and I'll do the rowing, and you can steer us. The Frome goes three-quarters round the town, almost under the wall, and joins the Avon just below the east bridge, by the castle.' He drew a rough map on the earthen floor with a pointed stick. 'We'll cut across the fields to Jan's boat here, and row down to the quay where the ship is.'

At that moment young Edward, an elderly greybeard, arrived at last with a barrow loaded with a basket of bread and cheese, a pot of stew in a box of hay to keep it hot, and a small barrel of ale. The planning was suspended for a while as everyone gathered round the fire to eat, some of them toasting their bread at the fire on the ends of their knives. A spare platter and cup were found for Aylwin, who, despite having had his supper some hours ago, was glad to accept a share of the good food.

'What are you doing in these parts?' asked Galien, who was sitting next to him. 'I thought you were settled in Waltham for another year, at least.'

Aylwin explained his journey into the West Country, and asked, 'How have you been faring, friend?'

'Well enough. I like it here,' Galien replied. 'The men are friendly, and don't care what a man is, so long as he's agreeable and does his work well. It suits me very well. What happened to your Norman lady? Did they pack her off to the nunnery in the end?'

'No. She refused to go, and now she's my wife,' Aylwin replied. 'That's why I'm so impatient to get back to her – there's a baby due in a few months!'

Galien congratulated him a little absently, and Aylwin, guessing what he was trying not to ask, said, 'Her brother made an excellent recovery.'

'Ahhh!' Galien breathed softly. 'Was there any – any difficulty about it?'

'No. The whole town celebrated another miracle, and the few who wondered had the sense to keep quiet. I thought of trying to send you word, but I didn't know where you'd gone.'

'If you be ready, Master Aylwin,' Wulfstan interrupted, 'we'd best be moving.'

Aylwin quickly embraced Galien and clasped hands with the masons who were not coming with him, then followed Jan out of the lodge, Wulfstan close at his heels. It took a few minutes for their eyes to become accustomed to the darkness, but then they hastened south-eastwards along a track which presently joined a road.

'We can walk openly,' Jan said. 'I sometimes bring a couple of the lads fishing at night. That's where we be to if any stops us and asks,' and he started to discuss fishing prospects in a normal voice, explaining how the fish lay deep on cold nights, and would need a long line put out to catch them.

'We've no lines,' Wulfstan exclaimed.

'In the boat,' Jan replied tersely. 'They do talk of digging a new channel for the Frome, and taking it straight down to Avon instead of curling round the town like it do. 'Twould improve the 'arbour and give deeper water, they reckons. I say 'twould ruin the fishing.'

He rambled on as they walked, keeping up a steady flow of conversation which always seemed to come back to fishing, until they reached the west bridge, which was just outside the west gate. The heads of two guards could be seen over the battlements of the gatehouse, outlined against the sky, and Aylwin shivered, not entirely with cold, and wondered if, after all his efforts, he would find himself chained in some noisome cellar in the morning.

'Who's there?' called one of the guards.

'It's me, Henry Brandon: Jan Fisher,' Jan called back. 'I'm taking these two out in the boat. Want to come?' His accent was broader now than it had been earlier.

'Too chilly for me!' the guard exclaimed. 'Bad enough up here, but on the water . . . ! Mind the cold don't . . .' and he added a remarkably coarse suggestion of what it might do, at which Jan and Wulfstan laughed heartily, Aylwin joining in a breath behind them.

The boat was moored to an iron ring in the bridge abutment, and they were soon aboard and afloat, the two local men rowing, and Aylwin doing his best to steer by telling them whether to pull to left or right or straight ahead, the boat having no steering-paddle. They nearly rammed the bank to start with, until Jan explained that what they needed was the boat's right or left, not their own.

The river curved round the sleeping town, which towered blackly above them within its strong wall, the moonlight gleaming softly on the weathercock on the top of the one church tower visible above the wall from this angle. The water ran dark and smooth as glass, with an occasional cluster of stars drowned in the depths.

Presently, they came out into the much wider Avon, and were caught by the ebbing tide, which swept them along more rapidly than they could row, so Wulfstan shipped his oars and Jan used his only to steer.

'Look over to your left,' whispered Wulfstan. 'Can you make out the quays along the bank? One of the ships should have two lanterns at the masthead.'

'One above the other?' Aylwin asked quietly, knowing that sound travels far over water. 'Yes, I see it.'

'Steer us towards it, then.'

All three kept silence as Jan rowed, save that Aylwin occasionally whispered, 'Right a bit – steady,' or 'A shade more left,' and presently the boat pulled in against the quay to which the ship was moored.

Wulfstan stood up, holding on to a wooden ladder fastened to the quay, and Aylwin, realizing that Jan would not be coming ashore, said quickly, 'I don't know how to thank you for your help. I came looking for you, hoping you might give a fellow mason advice on how best to get clear, but I didn't expect you to take risks for me . . .'

'No trouble, and no thanks needed,' Jan replied. 'We couldn't leave a man like you to freeze all winter in the castle, losing the skill of your hands with the rheumatics. All I did was bring you fishing.'

'Aye, and no thanks to me, neither,' Wulfstan growled. 'We meant to get you out of there some'ow, but you got yerself out, and all we did was bring you down here. You'll work your passage with Thorsten, that's all.'

'Nevertheless, I'm grateful,' Aylwin said.

'You've said your thanks – now let it be.' Wulfstan sounded embarrassed. 'Jan, mind the boat. Come on now. My cousin's aboard.'

He climbed nimbly up to the quay, Aylwin following, and led the way up a short gangplank on to the ship, where a burly man with a thick beard sat on a bale of goods with a lantern between his feet, guarding ship and cargo.

'Wulfstan? Have you brought him already?' he exclaimed in a remarkably sepulchral tone. 'That's good. I'd have been sore pressed for an answer if anyone asked why we didn't sail in the morning, as we're fully loaded.'

'Name of Aylwin. Got hisself out and found us, without waiting for us to get in to him. I'll be off now,' Wulfstan said hurriedly, and disappeared back the way he had come before Aylwin could say anything.

'Thorsten,' the bearded man introduced himself briefly, and he hurried Aylwin, clutching his bundle, down into the hold, where a small lantern cast a dim light over the cargo. Most of it appeared to be pigs of some dark metal, which Aylwin assumed to be lead from the mines in the Mendips, but the spaces at either end were packed with bales. Thorsten pulled one of these out of its place and pushed Aylwin into the space which it had concealed.

'Crawl through. It opens out a bit further in,' he said. 'I'll come for you when we're at sea and it's safe.'

Aylwin crawled through the narrow tunnel, the strong, rancid smell telling him that the bales around him contained wool. There was a bigger space at the back, just large enough for him to turn round and sit with his knees drawn up and his back against the hard-stuffed bales behind him.

He must have fallen asleep soon after, but he woke suddenly, alarmed at the total darkness and not sure at first where he was, when the ship gave a lurch, and then began to pitch and roll, creaking and protesting in every timber, and he guessed that they must be out of the river and on the open sea.

A short while later, a little light filtered along the tunnel between the bales, and Thorsten's deep voice bade him come out, which he did with relief, for his hiding place had grown claustrophobic, and he had been fighting down panic for the last ten minutes or so, wondering what would happen to him if the ship sank.

'You smell like an old sheep,' Thorsten commented. 'Come up to my cabin, and we'll break our fast.'

As they emerged on the deck in the ship's waist, Aylwin saw that it was well on into the morning, but the sky was so grey that he could not judge the time. They were well out at sea, with land visible on both sides – a coastline to larboard and a flat-looking island to steerboard. The sea was greyer than the sky, with steep waves, their crests breaking and streaming spume down a brisk wind. He shivered with cold.

'Steepholm,' Thorsten said, pointing to the island. 'A good following wind,' and he turned to indicate the great square sail, its wadmal cloth straining at its seams and sheets as they ran before the wind. There were six men about on the deck, watching the sail or keeping lookout, and the steersman on the steerboard side of the aftercastle raised a hand to Thorsten to signal all was well as he and Aylwin climbed the ladder to the higher deck.

'We'll make Porlock afore dark,' he called.

'This is your ship?' Aylwin asked Thorsten, looking about him with interest. 'She's large.'

Thorsten grinned approvingly. 'She's called *Wavecrest*,' he said proudly. 'One of the best craft along this coast. We're bound for Southampton. That suit you?'

'Very well!' Aylwin exclaimed. 'I can easily reach Winchester from there, and get help on my way home.'

'The lead's for Winchester, so you can go with it. It's wanted urgently, or we'd not be sailing with it so late in the year. It's not a cargo to be sent overland on winter roads, being so heavy. Come and eat.'

They went down from the aftercastle again, and into a small cabin sandwiched between it and the main deck, where they shared a meal of dried meat and hard biscuit, washed down with ale.

'We don't light a fire at sea,' Thorsten said by way of an apology, 'but we tie up at night and have hot food then. Poor tack this, but it'll keep you going. I hope you weren't too uncomfortable down below, but I thought the Empress's men might stop the ship in the narrows and search if they'd missed you. Wulfstan thought this'd be the best way to bring you away, for they'll search the roads out of Bristol for miles. That damned woman hates to let anyone best her, and Earl Robert's too short of money to let a likely ransom escape him. Now we must find you some warmer clothing. It's rough at sea, this time of year.'

It was, indeed, very rough, and Aylwin was glad that *Wavecrest* entered a little harbour each night of the voyage, or anchored in a sheltered bay. He lent a willing, if unskilled, hand with hauling on ropes when the sail had to be swung round to make the most of the wind when the ship changed direction in relation to it. The coastline seemed to change its direction constantly, and he had only the haziest idea of the shape of this extreme westerly part of England, and was not sure where they were.

He lost count of the days as well, for they all seemed the same – cold, wet, grey and extremely uncomfortable. His stomach revolted frequently against the constant pitching and rolling, but, if he ate sparingly in the morning and at midday, he managed to avoid vomiting, and by working with the seamen, he even managed to keep fairly warm in the clothing they had lent him.

One morning, they pulled out a long way from the coast until it was barely visible as a line of formidable cliffs on the horizon, and Thorsten, hauling on the sheet beside him as the ship turned fairly sharply to larboard, apparently to head back towards those cliffs, bellowed 'Land's End!' in his ear.

'What?' Aylwin bellowed back, puzzled.

'Land's End. The end of England. That's as far west as England goes. We turn east here, and sail along the south coast!'

A fitful sun appeared later, and Aylwin found that they were now sailing north-east, as if they were going back on their tracks. In fact, they proved to be entering Mount's Bay, and they tied up in a tiny harbour within sight of the strange peaked island which Thorsten said was called St Michael's Mount.

'This part of the world seems to have more that its share of conical hills named for St Michael,' Aylwin commented. 'I've seen one at Montacute, and another at Glaston, and now this.'

'I've never been as far inland as Glaston,' Thorsten said wistfully. 'I'd like to go there, but it's too far from the sea. I don't feel right if I can't smell or hear the sea.'

The wind changed during the night, and they had some difficulty in creeping out of Mount's Bay in the morning, but it swung round enough later to let them clear the Lizard and get into Coverack that night. To help Aylwin work out where they were, Thorsten drew a picture of the coastline for him on one of the few remaining pages in his last notebook, and he referred to it frequently while the grey, cold days crept past as slowly as the ship crawled from headland to headland, scuttling into shelter as night closed in and the wind fell away, often leaving them hardly enough to make harbour, but always rising again before they had cooked and eaten supper.

They kept Christmas in Lyme Bay, staying ashore for a whole day, to go to church and eat a good roast dinner at an inn. Aylwin did his best to be as cheerful as his companions, but he longed to be with Elys on this festival, which, of all festivals, turned a man's thoughts to family and home. He prayed long and deeply for Elys and the unborn child during the Mass, and was grateful when the seamen, apparently sensing that his heart was not in the merriment, let him sit quietly at the end of the table, without attempting to rally him from his silence, or even to get him drunk.

They sailed at dawn next day and made good progress in the next three days, but they left Poole on the fourth morning in worsening weather, and Thorsten shook his head two or three times as they clawed out of the great harbour.

'We'll run for the shelter of Hengistbury,' he said, 'and shelter in Twineham haven. I'll not try to enter the Solent until this abates.'

They scraped round Hengistbury with the sail reefed up to a mere few inches of cloth, just enough to give them steerage, and crept into the sheltered haven of Twineham behind the Head with visible relief on every face, and there, it seemed, they must stay until the winter gale blew itself out.

'You could try to go overland from here, I suppose,' Thorsten told Aylwin doubtfully. 'There'll be a heavy sea after this blow, and I'd be glad of the extra pair of hands, but as you're in a hurry . . .'

Aylwin longed to be on his way, he had enough money in his purse to buy a horse, and he could be in Winchester in two days, but Thorsten seem reluctant to let him go, and he was under a great obligation to him. After all, without the shipmaster's help, he'd still be freezing in Bristol Castle, waiting to hear when his ransom would be paid.

'I'll stay with you to Southampton,' he said. 'Er – while we're on the subject – you've not mentioned how much I owe you for taking me as a passenger . . .'

'Passenger?' Thorsten snorted. 'I take no passengers. You've worked your passage, hauling and drawing with the men, and made quite a good seaman, for all you're a mason. I want none of your money, man!'

'And what of Wulfstan and Alfred? Neither gave me a chance to offer . . .'

'With good reason, that being they didn't want you to offer,' Thorsten retorted. 'Alfred did it for the enjoyment of outwitting the Empress, and Wulfstan on principle, him being furious that a craftsman was being kept from his rightful work! You could send him word that you'll give him work if he ever comes asking for it, if you like, but keep your money for your wife and childer, and don't go offering it where it's not wanted.'

Aylwin apologized, and Thorsten said magnanimously, 'No offence given nor taken, lad. There's a fine new church abuilding here. Why don't you go and see it while you've got the chance?'

It was not in Aylwin's nature to miss an opportunity to see a fine building, and Christchurch minster was easy enough to find, for it dominated the little town. Like Waltham, it was a collegiate church of secular canons, so he had no difficulty in entering it, for the doors stood open to all comers.

He soon discovered that there had formerly been a much smaller church here, as at Waltham, and the rebuilding had already been going on for nearly half a century. The nave was now nearing completion, but, as the rebuilding had been started, unusually, at the west end, the chancel was still the old work, which looked incongruously small and heavy against the lighter, higher new building.

It was a disappointment to a sculptor, however. The stonework was well-laid, with almost invisible joints, but there was no carved work save a little axe-cut chevron decoration on the arches, so he spent only a short time looking at the building, prayed for Elys and himself, and for a safe final leg of his voyage to Southampton, and then went to the inn nearest the minster.

His intention was to find out if he was now far enough east to risk sending a message to the Bishop's Chancellor in Winchester, so, after being served with a cup of good ale, he casually asked the innkeeper who was the lord of the town.

'Baldwin de Redvers, Earl of Devon,' the man replied. 'In case you're wondering, he's for Queen Matilda and the Earl of Gloucester.'

'Your trading and travelling lies westward, then?' Aylwin felt cautiously towards the information he wanted. 'You don't have any trade or contact with Winchester, I suppose?'

'Never did have much,' the man said, refilling Aylwin's cup without waiting to be asked. 'The Forest lies atwixt here and there, and folk don't like to go through the Forest much, since the Red King were killed there. There's other risks, too. The Forest Law's still enforced there, in spite of the troubles, and there's a deal of things the verderers can take a man prisoner for. Even so much as look at a deer, and they'll likely maim you or hang you, it seems nowadays. No, nobody from here goes to Winchester that I knows of, and I knows most things! You got friends there?'

'My mother lives there. I thought I might send to tell her I'm on my way home,' Aylwin answered truthfully enough, if a little inaccurately, for he would have asked the Chancellor to let his mother know he was safe.

The landlord shook his head. 'Better not try. The Earl's men have enquiring ways, if you get my meaning. They'd arrest you and your messenger as spies, and you'd find yourself in Exeter Castle, like as not.'

Having tried the hospitality of Bristol Castle, Aylwin was not anxious to compare it with that of any other such establishment, so he shrugged and said, 'It's no matter. I'll send from Southampton when we get there.'

'You do that,' the landlord said sagely, 'and don't go telling too many folk you're bound for Southampton, neither.'

The wind began to slacken during the night, and by next morning, Thorsten decided to set sail, saying that he would rather be out of the Empress's territory – even this outlying part of it – as soon as possible. The seamen raised no objections, and Aylwin did not feel qualified to offer an opinion, although he thought the sea looked exceedingly rough.

He soon found out that it was even rougher than it looked from the safety of Twineham haven. The waves tossed *Wavecrest* about as if she were a child's toy boat, and at times rose so high that she was left wallowing in a trough, her heavy wadmal sail flapping idly and the great yard slatting about in all directions until the sea heaved her up on to the next crest, where she could feel the wind again.

Their progress was oddly crab-like, for the sea was trying to push them closer to the land, while the wind was just westerly enough to let her be steered against the thrust, and they were moving steadily eastwards, albeit in a diagonal fashion. Unfortunately, before they had been at sea two hours, the wind began to rise in sporadic gusts, and to swing to the south.

'Now St Nicholas aid us,' Thorsten exclaimed. 'If the wind swings any further south, we'll not get into the Solent! Another few points more to the east, and we'll be on Hurst Spit! We'd best stand out past Wight, and come into the Solent the other side of the Isle, I reckon.'

He stood on the aftercastle, his eyes darting about as he watched the fluttering ribbons on the rigging which showed the direction of the wind relative to the ship, the set of the sail, the waves coming up behind the sternpost, and the dark, menacing line of the shore, which seemed to be creeping closer.

'Steer a few more points to steerboard,' he growled at the steersman. 'Brace the yard round harder, lads,' in a bellow to the seamen.

Aylwin hauled with the rest on the sheets until the yard lay diagonally across the ship, and the steersman anxiously watched the leading edge of the sail for the first warning flutter that would tell him he was sailing too close to the wind. *Wavecrest* crept on, taking the heavy seas on her quarter, and going no closer to the land.

It was at that point that the rope broke.

Aylwin had no idea what it was called, or what its function was. He only knew that he saw it snap suddenly, and the next moment he was one of a pile of bodies flung down on the sloping deck and hard up against the bulwarks as the yard swung further round, lying almost fore and aft, and the ship gave a violent lurch. The larboard side dipped far enough to ship a mass of water; then, as the seamen picked themselves up and ran to remedy matters, knowing what to do without waiting for orders, the mast swung back to steerboard, penduluming across the sky above Aylwin's upturned face as he still lay where he had fallen on the deck. There was a peculiar grinding noise, the mast swung back to larboard, and, as he scrambled to his feet, the ship seemed to settle down, rising and falling on the waves as before, but with one curious difference. The deck was now canted down to larboard, and remained so, even in the troughs.

Thorsten, who had also been thrown off his feet, came down the ladder and grabbed his arm. 'The cargo's shifted!' he exclaimed. 'Damned lead: too heavy to move when you want it to, but ready enough when you want it to stay still. Come and give me a hand.'

Aylwin followed him down the ladder into the hold, and found out quickly enough what Thorsten was talking about. The pigs of lead, which he had last seen lying neatly, row by row and layer by layer across the bottom of the hold, had all shifted sideways, and bales of wool were lying about as if someone had been throwing them at random down the length of the ship.

Thorsten surveyed the confusion by the light of the lantern which hung from a deckbeam and was kept burning at all times, and said, 'There's nothing we can do but pray it'll not shift further, and get ourselves ashore as fast as we can.'

'Couldn't we move some from this side across to the other side?' Aylwin asked, trying the weight of a pig. With his strong arm and back muscles, he could lift it, with an effort, but he realized that it would take two men to a pig to move it any distance.

'No time,' Thorsten replied, shaking his head. 'If the sea catches us on the beam just once more, we'll be sailing on our side for the few minutes left before we capsize. We'll have to beach.'

He ran back on deck, and began to issue a stream of orders. The men looked apprehensive, and most of them glanced frequently towards the shore as they carried them out. The ship turned before the wind and headed for the shore, her heavy list now very apparent, and the timbers of her larboard side groaning ominously at the unaccustomed strain the shifted cargo was putting on them. The steerboard side was now so high that the steering oar barely reached the water.

'What happens when we beach?' he asked a seamen as, their orders carried out, they all stood watching the cliffs and the beach, occasionally visible above the waves, rushing towards them. 'Will the ship be wrecked?'

372

'Looks like sand and shingle, not rock,' the man replied, considering his answer carefully. 'Like as not, we'll run sweetly up on shore, and there'll be no more than a bit of scraping. Then all we have to do is reload the cargo, and wait for the next spring tide to float us off.'

'Next spring!' Aylwin exclaimed. 'But that's months away.'

'Not spring – spring *tide*,' the man said. 'Don't you know about tides? They change according to the phases of the moon, from neaps, which are little tides, not much out, not much in, to springs, which go right out and come right in. It's neaps now, so come the next springs, in a couple weeks' time, the tide'll come much higher and float us off.'

During the conversation, they had both, like everyone else, been watching the shore come closer and closer. It was a fine beach, Aylwin could see, of pale yellow sand, which looked soft enough for a ship to run quietly up out of the water, but he saw that the seamen had all found a rope to hold on to, so he did the same, pressing himself close the steerboard bulwark and holding tightly to a part of the rigging.

The steersman gave a shout and swung the loom of his great oar forward, so that the blade rose up behind the ship, and *Wavecrest* struck with a great scrunching sound and a tremendous shock. The mast snapped a foot or so above the deck, the yard crashed down, swinging as it did so, and the rope to which Aylwin was clinging gave a violent jerk, throwing him sideways across the bulwark. He looked up, and saw the end of the yard coming down like a giant bludgeon, straight for his head, and flung himself frantically further out over the waist-high bulwark. The yard caught him a sweeping blow on the shoulder, and brushed him aside like a fly, so that he was thrown completely over the side of the ship. For a long, long second, he saw a grey, foam-streaked wave reaching up to snatch at him, and had time to regret that he had never learned to swim, and then he gave one despairing cry of 'Elys', and the sea took him, the undertow dragging him downwards and outwards, away from the ship and the shore. There was a roaring in his ears like all the waters on earth, and he knew he was drowning.

It was not a comfortable business, to his surprise, for he had heard somewhere or other that drowning was a fairly easy death. The sea smashed him down on to rocks and pebbles, which bruised his ribs and knees, and something which felt like an iron bar twisted tightly about from wrist to shoulder, was dragging painfully at his left arm, and he grabbed at it with his other hand, meaning to pull it off before it wrenched his arm from its socket, but something deep in the darkness which was flooding into his mind told him to hold on to it, and he did, although it cut into his flesh and pulled him this way and that, like a living thing trying to get away. His body was dragging along the shingle bottom now, as if he were being towed along by a runaway horse. It was painful, for most of the pebbles seemed to have sharp edges, and he was being dragged across them faster and faster, with the hungry sea still crashing down on him and trying to pull him deeper into its depths.

Suddenly, his head broke the surface, his eyes filled with blurred light, and his starved lungs took in a great gulp of air. Blinking, he saw to his amazement that half a dozen men had hold of the other end of that iron bar, which was a rope, and they were hauling him up the beach as if he were a great flounder.

'Never seed a whale with yaller hair before, have you?' asked Thorsten's voice in an unusually jovial tone. The pulling stopped, and Aylwin lay high and very wet on the beach, shivering, gasping and retching as the rope was unwound from his arm and rough, kindly hands thumped him on the back.

The dark winter days passed slowly on after Christmas, and Elys had all her small gifts finished in time for New Year's Day. She had made embroidered pencases for her brothers, a length of braid for Mistress Mayngod with fruit and leaves embroidered on it, a cap for Lukin, and a dozen little soft collars, each embroidered with flowers and conies, for Edwin. They were all delighted with their gifts, and Edwin put collars on the two ferrets which he happened to have with him, and, as they made no objection, but sniffed at each other's and then ignored them, he announced that they were very pleased and grateful for them.

The servants were given money and lengths of cloth as their gifts, but Mistress Mayngod, who was more a member of the family than a servant, received a fine copper pot 'to cook Lukin's dinner in'. She gave Elys some embroidered baby-clothes, saying ruefully that they were nowhere near as good as Elys's work, but they would do for everyday, and also produced an enormous plum and spice-filled cake to be shared by the men, and there followed another long, pleasant evening spent in eating, drinking and telling stories, of which Lukin seemed to have an unending store.

All Elys's other gifts were needles, apart from a wooden case from Edwin to keep them in, and she was prompted by this wealth to work hard at finishing off the cope, which she was now assembling, hoping to have it ready by Epiphany. The two pieces had been joined and the embroidery carried across the seam, and she had now to put in the interlining and catch it in place, then the lining, and the orphreys had then to go along the straight edge, sandwiching the three layers. To make sure it was all done smoothly and would hang right, she cleared a part of the hall floor of rushes, spread out clean sheets, and laid the cope out flat, so that she could crawl round it, smoothing and pinning the layers in place. Her body was thickening now, and she was thankful she was no bigger, or it would have been difficult to crouch over the spread-out fabrics. As it was, she had to stretch upright from time to time, or she got cramps and pains in her back.

On the eve of Epiphany, she stitched on the hood and the morse, wrapped the cope in a clean cloth, and carried it over to the minster through the first tentative flakes of snow which were fluttering down from a leaden sky. Some of the masons were at work in the church, plastering an area of the stonework which had been completed back in the early summer and was now thoroughly dry. They greeted her with a mixture of respect and friendliness, and she asked if they had managed to go home for Christmas.

'Bless you, lady, we're here because us've no homes to

375

go to,' one of them replied. 'Master William always lets the married men go home for the winter, and keeps on us single fellows, the lodge bein' all the family us has. There's plenty to do, cuttin' and shapin' stone on the benchers, and seein' the frost don't get in the new work. We has us own feastin' and merrymakin' in the lodge, and the townsfolk's been good to us, and made us welcome at their tables, too. Is that your fine cope, then? Be it finished at last?'

'Yes,' Elys replied. 'I'm just taking it to Father Warmand,' and she went on up the nave and across to the sacristy in the north transept, where Father Warmand was waiting, impatient to see the new cope. It was only when it was unwrapped and spread out on the wooden copechest that she realized that the masons had trooped after her, and were crowded in the doorway, craning to see her work.

'Come in, come in,' Warmand exclaimed. 'That is the finest cope I ever did see, and you've fulfilled every hope I had of it.'

It did, indeed, look very fine, spread out before them all, and the masons all murmured appreciation, for, being good craftsmen, they recognized fine work when they saw it. The tree burned with unconsuming fire in the candlelight, the birds and animals glowed like jewels, the dove seemed to be truly about to alight on the topmost branch, the words on the orphrey gleamed and seemed to stand out from the dark red silk behind them, but it was the morse, which showed the Cross supported by two angels, which pleased Father Warmand the most.

'You've put the very image from our seal on the morse!' he exclaimed. 'It marks the cope as the property of this minster for all the world to see! If any man, king, bishop or whoever, takes this cope away from us, as Rufus did the other one, it will stand a continual reproach to him. I must say, though, that it was worth losing the other one to have this in its place. I can just remember seeing the old one, and it was nowhere near as beautiful as this.'

Elys blushed and smiled, happy that her work was pleasing. 'It shall be dedicated at High Mass tomorrow,' said Warmand, 'and worn on ferial Sundays from now on.'

With her cope finished and paid for, Elys did not immediately begin on the festival cope which the canons now asked her to make, but planned to give herself a short holiday to make small garments for her baby, and to spend more time praying in the church. A day or two after Epiphany, she spent a couple of hours there in the afternoon, and rose, stiff and cold, from her knees as the early dusk crept in upon the candlelit area beneath the Cross, and turned to leave the minster.

As she neared the south door, the wicket suddenly opened and a man in a dark hooded cloak entered. The hood shadowed his face, so that only a fair, curly beard showed, and she did not recognize him, but something – perhaps only hope – told her that this might be the longed-for messenger from the Bishop's Chancellor. The child in her womb stirred, and she stopped, one hand going to her breast in a gesture of apprehension of good or ill, as the man walked towards her, pushing back the hood as he came.

She did not recognize him in the darkening church until he was very close, and then she swayed, almost falling, and he caught her in his arms, saying apologetically, 'My dearest girl, I wasn't able to send a message until it was quicker to come myself. Oh, my love, I've missed you so much!'

'You're safe, and that's all that matters,' she replied, clinging to him, hardly able to believe that he was here at last.

They stopped to pray together in thanksgiving for a while, and then went home, where Matthew and Crispin were so pleased to see Aylwin safely back that they were almost incoherent, laughing and crying, wringing his hands and patting his back between exclamations and fervent words of thanks to Our Lord and all the saints for bringing him home.

Lukin, naturally, arrived soon after, bringing Edwin and an assortment of ferrets, and they were invited to stay for supper so that they could hear Aylwin's account of his adventures. For Elys's sake, he underplayed the dangers, making the descent of the garderobe shaft seem an easy matter, but he had to tell the truth about the grounding of *Wavecrest*.

'And then the mast broke, the yard fell down, and it

377

knocked me overboard,' he said. 'I thought that was the end of me, for the sea was crashing on the shore, and it dragged me away and down until I thought my lungs would burst. I didn't realize that I was still clinging to the rope, which had broken away at one end, but was still fastened to the mast at the other. They say a drowning man will clutch at a straw, but the rope was certainly more use to me than any straw, and I certainly clung to it. The steersman saw me go over the side, and dived in after me. What with the rope and his help, some of the seamen were able to haul me back and get me on shore, and there I was tipped up and emptied out on the beach. It was bitter cold and I was half-frozen, but they wrapped most of the sail round me, lit a fire, and rubbed me until I began to feel alive again.'

'Was the ship totally wrecked?' asked Lukin, agog with excitement.

'No. She ran up on the beach, and when the shipmaster examined her, he found very little damage. Some men from the fishing-village nearby came to help, and I was taken off to one of their houses, where I was put to bed for a day. They helped to set the cargo to rights and rig up the remains of the mast enough to carry a sail. When the wind dropped and the sea calmed down, they helped to get her afloat again. She'd grounded at low tide, and the high tide made it possible to get her afloat with a deal of pushing, and some of the fishing boats towing. We sailed round to Southampton – I was recovered enough to go with the others – and two of the fishing boats came with us, to see us safely to port. I left my good seafaring friends there and went to Winchester, where I found Fulk just returned from France, where he'd found Bishop Henry, who had sent him straight back with instructions to his Chancellor to pay my ransom at once. It was a great satisfaction to me to be able to tell the Chancellor that he could spare the Bishop the expense, although I was grateful to know that he had been willing to pay so much for me. I called to see my mother, and set off from there next day, and – well – here I am.'

Elys had said nothing while he was telling his story, but he watched her face throughout, and her expressions told him how she felt about every part of it. When it ended, she took a firm grip on his hand, and held on to it with both her own, as if to tell him that she would never let him go away without her again, but would accompany him, no matter what.

After supper, many of Aylwin's friends and acquaintances called to see him and express their pleasure and relief at his safe return. A great deal of ale was drunk, and Edwin became extremely elevated and had to be put to bed on a spare truckle in the lower bedchamber with his inseparable companions.

Matthew observed soon after that Aylwin, the first excitement of his homecoming having worn off, was looking very tired, and firmly sent away the last of the visitors so that he could go to bed, for which he was very grateful.

When they were alone together upstairs, he and Elys clung together in silence for a long time, occasionally kissing, but mostly content just to be in one another's arms again, until at last Aylwin said, yawning, 'I'm sorry, sweetheart, but I'm in no fit state to love you as I would wish tonight. After all my adventuring, and travelling from Winchester as fast as a good horse would bring me – and I gave the poor beast scant rest – I'm exhausted. Will you forgive me?'

She smiled, and pushed him gently towards the bed. 'It's enough to have you home and in my arms tonight,' she said. 'Time enough for lovemaking when you're rested.'

When they were in bed, he took her in his arms again and kissed her, then, with a sigh of relief and pleasure, stretched out full length and closed his eyes, saying, 'It's so good to be with you again.'

Almost at once, his eyes flew open and he sat up with a jerk and a gasp, then doubled over sideways under the covers, reaching down towards the bottom of the bed.

'What is it?' asked Elys, alarmed.

There was an upheaval under the covers, and then he emerged again, and held up a small, somnolent bundle of creamy fur.

'It's one of Edwin's damned ferrets!' he exclaimed, and they both collapsed in helpless laughter, while the small animal's red eyes glared at them in sleepy indignation for rousing it from a snug and comfortable sleep.

POSTSCRIPTUM

It took King Stephen a year to find time to appoint a new Dean of Waltham, and it was typical of him that he managed to lay the foundations of later confusion by appointing another Henry, a mild-seeming but capable priest with considerable experience as sub-Dean of another minster.

The Waltham canons, knowing their king's renowned lack of judgement, assumed that it was luck, or, more probably, the Will of God, that Dean Henry was, in every way, suited to his new position, and their immediate liking for him was strengthened by the interest and enthusiasm he evinced when Father Brian and Father Warmand showed him round the schools and the minster. To crown the excellent impression he had made, he paused before the altar of Our Lady in the transept with an exclamation of delight.

The old wooden figure of the Virgin had been clothed in a beautifully embroidered robe and moved to a new niche to one side of the chapel, and her old place above the altar was now occupied by a fine stone carving of the Madonna and Child, and it was this which had caught Dean Henry's attention.

'What a wonderful statue!' he exclaimed. 'Whose work is it?'

'It was carved by Master Aylwin of Winchester,' Father Brian told him. 'He also carved our font, and many of the corbels under the church roof. He was working here until a few weeks ago, and he gave us this just before he left, as a thank-offering for the safe delivery of his first child, a fine boy. The face bears – er – some resemblance to his wife, who made the robe which our old statue is wearing and gave it for the same reason.'

'Very fitting,' the Dean commented placidly. 'I've heard of the craftsman, of course. Is he not in the service of my predecessor? Does the child thrive?'

'He's a fine strong boy,' Father Brian replied with vicarious pride. 'I had the pleasure of baptizing him in the name of Lawrence, and he shouted most lustily when the blessed water touched him, and struck me, unintentionally of course, in the face with his fist. Father Warmand was one of his sponsors, with our reeve and his wife for the other two. The family has returned to Winchester now, and we miss them very much.'

'May the Lord bless them and their lovely child,' said Dean Henry, beaming benevolently, to which the canons added a fervent *Amen*, and exchanged pleased smiles behind the Dean's back.